Praise for *THE SECRET OF THE GLASS*

"Celebrates the eternal charms of Venice, Murano glass, and Galileo, with the story of a courageous 17th-century woman glassmaker."
—*Publishers Weekly*

"One of the best written novels of Venice I have ever read."
—*Historical Novel Review*

"Five stars. Outstanding Pick for 2010. Absolutely superb!"
—*Book Illuminations*

"A beautiful story by [a] master storyteller." —*CataNetwork Reviews*

"Elegant prose, alluring style." —*Historical-fiction.com*

"This is 5-star historical fiction." —Alex McGilvery, *Armchair Interviews*

"History comes to life as Morin re-creates the lush and dangerous world of the Murano glassmakers. Like the brilliant glass, her story swirls together colors of political and religious intrigue, murder, and romance." —*RT Book Reviews*

Praise for *THE COURTIER'S SECRET*

Finalist: National Readers' Choice Award 2010

"Morin debuts with a novel as opulent and sparkling as Louis XIV's court and as filled with intrigue, passion and excitement as a novel by Dumas. [A] feast for the senses." —*RT Book Reviews*

"Morin fills her tale with maidens, mistresses and musketeers mired in intrigue." —*Publishers Weekly*

"Absolutely enchanting. Obviously a very talented writer, Donna Russo Morin has created magnificent characters that you cannot help but fall in love with; they are so vibrant and full of life."
—*Front Street Reviews*

"A wonderfully spun gem of a story."
—Je

"I couldn't put it down." —*Historical-*

BOOKS BY DONNA RUSSO MORIN

The Courtier's Secret

The Secret of the Glass

To Serve a King

TO SERVE A KING

DONNA RUSSO MORIN

KENSINGTON BOOKS
www.kensingtonbooks.com

To my sons, Devon and Dylan.
If the only steps to take would be the same—
to hear your voice,
and speak your name—
Then I would take them again and again,
. . . and again.

DRAMATIS PERSONAE

*denotes historical character

*François I (1494–1547): King of France 1515–1547.

*Anne de Montmorency (Monty) (1493–1567): Lifelong companion of François I. Soldier, statesman, diplomat; marshal of France 1522; Constable of France 1538.

*Philippe de Chabot, seigneur de Brion (1492–1543): Lifelong companion of François I. Soldier; Admiral of France 1526.

*Henry VIII (1491–1547): King of England 1509–1547.

*Charles Brandon, Duke of Suffolk (1484–1545): Lifelong companion and brother-in-law to Henry VIII; lord president of the council.

Geneviève de Hainaut Gravois (b. 1518): Niece of Madame de Montlhéry; Maid of Honor to the duchesse d'Étampes.

*Anne de Pisseleu d'Heilly, duchesse d'Étampes (1508–1580): Maid of Honor to Louise de Savoy, mother of François I; titular mistress to François I 1526–1547; married to Jean IV de Brosse; created duchesse d'Étampes 1533.

Arabelle d'Aiguillon (b. 1520), Béatrice d'Azelleures (b. 1512), Sybille de Laval (b. 1514), Jecelyn du Fabiole (b. 1519): Maids of Honor to the duchesse d'Étampes.

Sebastien du Lac (b. 1512): Soldier, Scottish Guard to the court of France.

*Henri (1519–1559): Oldest surviving son of François I; Dauphin of France.

*Diane de Poitiers (1499–1566): Daughter of the seigneur de Saint Vallier; widow of the duc de Brézé (1531); assumed title of *grand sénéschal* of Normandy upon his death; lifelong mistress to Henri.

*Charles V (1500–1558): King of Spain 1516; Holy Roman Emperor 1519.

Readers, friends, if you turn these pages
Put your prejudice aside,
For, really, there's nothing here that's outrageous,
Nothing sick, or bad—or contagious.

—François Rabelais (c. 1494–1553)

TO SERVE A KING

❦ 1 ❦

It is the little victories,
That bring us the big ones.

—Ignatius de Loyola (1491–1556)

1520

Beneath an unmerciful sun, the squire dropped the flag with a flourish. Riders kicked at glistening flanks; horses charged forward with little between them save the narrow wooden poles of the lists. Hooves thundered upon the jousting field; the pounding boomed in the ears. Dirt clumps flew up into the air as if tossed in celebration. Weighted and encased in full armor, plumes on helmets bobbing with every gallop, the combatants raised their lances with steely determination, eyes locked upon the impending opponent as they cradled their weapons in the crook between bicep and chest.

Nobleman, courtier, commoner, and peasant jumped to their feet in the overflowing, banner-festooned stands, holding their breath as the two kings bore down upon each other. The impact, when it came, burst out like two worlds colliding. Lance met armor, snapping with a riotous crash and a splintering of wood, and the air ruptured with gasps and cheers. Each competitor had broken his lance upon the other; yet both had kept their saddle. The match was a draw, again.

François quit his black steed with deft agility, tugging off the cumbersome helmet with agitation. Beneath it, his thick chestnut hair lay matted with sweat to his face and jawbone.

"Well done, Your Majesty," Montmorency called out as he approached, raising his voice above the unabated cheering. Beside him, a slight man brandished a satisfied sneer as he scissored his short legs, hurrying to keep up.

With a sidelong look of annoyance, the young king of France scoffed, struggling to remove his gauntlets.

"Do not patronize me, Monty." Finally relieved of them, François threw the thick, padded leather gloves to the ground, words slithering out between grinding teeth. "Damn it all, I cannot best the man."

"That is true," Philippe de Chabot said as he picked up the gloves and slapped them together to dislodge the fresh mud. "But neither can he best you. There are worse ways to spend a day of sport."

In the bright sunlight, François squinted slanted eyes at his companions, his valued friends since childhood, his closest advisers since becoming king five years ago, and felt the heat of his ire cool. Perhaps there *were* other ways to triumph over this adversary yet.

In Henry VIII, François found everything he detested in a king—a hedonist obsessed with the quest for power and pleasure—and yet a part of him strove to imitate this nemesis whom he would never admit respecting, though respect Henry he did. The faults François railed against in his archrival were ones others attributed to François himself. How disgusted he would be to know it.

"Besides," Chabot continued with a shrug of his small shoulders, "you are much better looking."

Monty barked a laugh as François snickered, cuffing Chabot in the arm.

"You must pay your respects to your opponent." The gruff, aged voice doused the conviviality of the young men. Chancellor Duprat approached, skinny legs waddling under a rotund body. "King Henry awaits your hand, Sire."

"Of course." François accepted the intrusion and instruction without argument. Accompanied by his triumvirate of men, he stalked across the rutted tourney field.

"Well ridden, Your Majesty," he called as he approached his challenger, outstretched hand in the lead.

With a devilish smile upon his plump, freckled face, Henry accepted the hand thus offered. "And you, Your Highness."

Cardinal Wolsey, rotund form looming in red cassock and mozzetta, hovered by Henry's side as always, as did the dukes of Suffolk and Norfolk.

These two rivals politely embraced, between them a pull of genuine affection, more potent after the last few days together, yet sharp with the edge of competition, like two loving brothers forever bent on besting the other.

"A worthy match indeed," François conceded. "One deserving of a hearty toast."

"More than one, I should think," Henry agreed. "I will see you at table?"

"It will be my honor." François accepted the invitation with a sweeping bow.

As the men separated and made to quit the field, the crowd erupted into another burst of applause, colorful banners flourishing. With magnanimity, each sovereign acknowledged the accolades with a wave, a nod, and a smile as they quit the field.

A young man standing along the front rail took his pretty wife by the arm, hoisting his daughter higher in his grasp, and began to lead them through the departing congested throng. "Come, *mes amours*, I must prepare to attend the king at table."

"Of course, my dear," replied the delicate woman at his side, skin flushed from a day in the sun.

The toddler in her father's arms put her head down onto his strong shoulder, blond curls falling on her face as her eyes grew heavy, then closed. Exhausted from the excitement of the long day, she would sleep peacefully tonight.

The royal combatants retired from the tourney field, entourages in tow, each to his own opulent encampment. These men of power and privilege endured no discomforts; though ensconced in make-shift, temporary lodgings, each camp contrived astounding accommodations for this auspicious meeting.

Months in the making, the summit was unlike any conducted before. Leaders who had been overlooked waited with equal amounts of wonder and fear, because any accord between France and England could only spell trouble. The possibility of orchestrating a great peace enticed the English king. The opportunity to bring another to his cause against his rivalry with Charles V of Spain, newly appointed Holy Roman Emperor—chosen by the new pope over François himself—had inveigled the French king forth. A grand meeting, an opportunity to talk; diplomacy and deal making decorated by a grand festival. And yet the undercurrent of competition between the two young and brash *chevaliers*, the constant quibbling for any modicum of superiority over the other, no matter how miniscule, permeated every facet of this audacious assembly.

In the shallow Val d'Or at the very edge of English-occupied France, near Calais, halfway between the castle ruins of Guînes and Ardres, they had met on an early June afternoon.

Henry would have a castle no matter where he laid his head. In the shadow of the Château de Guînes, the Palace of Illusions had been erected with sections brought from England already assembled. Covering an area of more than two acres, it was a convoluted construction of wood and earth covered with a painted canvas to resemble stone and formed with turrets, parapets, and windows. Within its vast rectangular interior lay a courtyard boasting two magnificent fountains fed by three pipes—one for water, one for hippocras, and one for wine.

In a meadow on the outskirts of Ardres, the French had pitched their tents, almost four hundred of them, some as large as any castle's great hall. Many of the nobles in attendance had forfeited all property, selling their fields, their mills, their forests to attend the event with appropriate honor. Surmounted by pennants of golden apples and emblazoned with their owners' coats of arms, the tents of velvet and cloth of gold spread out across the countryside like wild flowers. The field shimmered as if the gold grew from its earth. But no pavilion rivaled the splendor of François's tent.

Taller than any other and sixty feet on a side, two ship masts lashed together supported the mammoth cloth of gold. Blue velvet lined the interior, decorated with fleurs-de-lis and gold embroideries from Cyprus.

Beyond splendid, yet the kings' accommodations paled in comparison to the events conducted over the course of the summit.

Banquets, dances, and mummings filled the nights; a feat of arms—jousting at the tilt, an open field tournament, a foot combat at the barriers with puncheon spears, swords, and two-handed swords—filled the days. The kings were the most rowdy and jubilant attendants of all. In their company were their nobles, their friends, and their women. François had brought his mother; his wife, Queen Claude; and his mistress, the Comtesse de Chateaubriant. Regal and silent by Henry VIII's side, stood Catherine of Aragon, with countless fair maidens waiting to warm his bed. As the kings made merry, their ambassadors and delegates made diplomacy, Wolsey speaking foremost for England, while the Queen Mother, Louise de Savoy, spoke for France. Many words passed between these two equally keen minds, but little of lasting consequence was said.

Henry rubbed at his midsection, a replete, resounding belch coaxed forth from the embroidered brocade–covered protuberance. Attendants scurried around him, cleaning the remnants of the evening's festivities like ants upon an abandoned picnic ground.

He watched them from his elevated perch on the velvet chair in the corner of the vast room; watched, but cared little about their performance. The last of the guests had retreated in the early hours of the morning, leaving the king in the company of his most reliant confidants.

"Have we found out who the young women are?" Henry spoke to his men, but his unfocused, bloodshot eyes never strayed from the buzzing workers before him, mesmerized, in his hazy stupor, by their tedious, repetitive movements.

The bearded Charles Brandon, Duke of Suffolk, stepped forward, if a bit unsteadily, wine sloshing in a tightly gripped chalice. "They are Thomas Boleyn's daughters, my lord, Mary and . . . and Anne."

Henry pulled himself up from his slump and whipped round, all at once full of eager attention. "Certainly not?"

" 'Tis true, Your Highness, they have been in the French queen's company for some years and are quite soon preparing to return to our homeland."

With sensual, languid movements at odds with his rugged physique, the king reclined once more. "Be sure to send them a personal invitation to court."

"Of course, Your Highness. As you wish," Suffolk assured him, but not without a roll of his eyes and a salacious smile at the small group of men gathered in duty and imbibing.

"Are we done here, Wolsey? I tire of these games." Sounding like nothing so much as a spoiled, petulant child, Henry's bulbous bottom lip stuck out in a pout.

"I believe we have done all we can here, Your Majesty," the cardinal said with neither enthusiasm nor disappointment. "You have done well to sign the treaty."

Henry snarled at him. To make peace with the posturing François rankled; the hand that wielded the quill itched.

"You will see great results from this, I assure you," Wolsey pacified.

It was the slightest of changes, but the king's pout reformed, a devilish grin blossoming in its stead. In that moment, Henry found the joy of the situation in which he found himself: As the lesser of the three world powers, both France and Spain courted him. A master manipulator, he intended to exploit the state of affairs for all it was worth.

"Send a message then, would you, Wolsey? Tell the emperor I would like to talk. He should know of the ostentatious display we have witnessed here. A man with so much to prove as our François, putting on such a show, must have something to hide."

"Of course, Majesty, but per—"

When the hand of his king flicked in his face, the cardinal's thoughts froze on his tongue. Henry leaned forward, resting his free hand upon one knee, eyes fixed upon the young man rushing toward him. The pale, snaggletoothed youth approached his sovereign, lips forming words aching to launch from his mouth. Henry's quieting hand flicked from Wolsey to the approaching squire, who clamped his mouth shut, eyes bulging in fear at the abrupt command.

"Cease and desist." The king's booming voice pummeled the air. "You are all relieved. Make for your beds."

Every manservant and chambermaid dropped whatever lay in their hands, and took themselves off without thought or question. The small gathering of courtiers drew closer to the king, put on guard at once by the abrupt change in his tone and demeanor.

"Speak," Henry barked the instant the last servant had quit the chamber.

With a twitch and an Adam's apple–bobbing swallow, the young man made his report.

"Your fears have been confirmed, Your Highness. The man in question has indeed been seen in clandestine conversations with members of the French contingent."

"Bastard!" spat the king, pounding a fist on the arm of the chair and spewing upon the floor, as if the word and gesture were not enough to rid him of his venomous rage.

The messenger quaked in his worn leather boots, bulging insect eyes once more protruding from his long face. Only Suffolk remembered him.

"You may leave us, good sir. You have done well. Have no fear." With a calming hand upon the youngster's shoulder, the duke turned him toward the door, helping him away with a firm yet gentle nudge. Turning back, Suffolk met with the king's blazing stare.

"You know what to do?" Henry moved not a bit, his voice low and quiet, yet his rage was there for any to see did they know what to look for.

Suffolk's full lips thinned in a grimace, but he bowed, spun on his heel with determination, and left; not a one questioned his compliance with whatever the king demanded of him.

The screams of human and animal mixed in a grotesque chorus, filling the predawn hours with their horror and revulsion. The monstrous flames rose into the black sky, roaring like cannon blasts in the day's most hushed hours. Men, women, and children fled from the orangey blaze in fright while soldier and guard ran toward it. But it was too powerful, too repulsive, and it was impossible to break through to its heart, to penetrate the barrier and save those trapped within. They stood at the aperture of the tent now fully ablaze in the apex of the English camp, waiting to catch those fortunate enough to escape from the fiery cataclysm.

The pandemonium swirled about the inferno like the oxygen that fed it so splendidly. For within every neighboring tent, the brilliance of the flame appeared alive upon the walls, the nexus of its glow indistinguishable through the pale canvas. In terror they ran out of their tents, into the fray; haphazard, undirected commotion. No matter how removed from danger, they ran and screamed, the sickening scent of burning flesh fueling their fear.

"Help us, please," one foot soldier yelled to a passing nobleman, a young man of strong arm and back, capable of hoisting a bucket of water as well as any. But the pampered gent continued his furious retreat, sparing not a glance at the soldier begging his aid.

Coughing and sputtering, survivors staggered from within, but the child emerged without a sound—without a scratch—as if oblivious to the danger she escaped, her long, curly blond hair wafting upward in the rushing air of the blaze at her back. From behind the soldiers, a woman clad in a silk nightgown flung herself forward, as if waiting for this very moment. Snatching the child in her arms she ran, a silent angel intent on her mission.

"How many billeted here, do you know?" one guard called to another as they stood together before the blaze. Few of them remained, so many of them had already rushed toward the physician's tent, the wounded leaning on their shoulders or cradled in their arms.

"No idea," his companion struggled to answer, the flames devouring all the air in and around the tent. "Can't be many. So many . . . already out."

The first soldier acknowledged him with a squinty-eyed nod, holding up a hand in a vain attempt to block the heat from his face, feeling his eyebrows singeing upon his skin. With a hue and cry, both jumped back. The tent, devoured by fire, pitched toward them, collapsing forward with nothing but ash left at its base. Within the crumbling of the remaining wood frame and disintegrating canvas, a whoosh of flames rose higher as one wrenching, agonizing scream roared above the din.

For one suspended moment, the men stood motionless. In the next instant, they moved. Without word or gesture, each bent his head down and charged.

"Could we not have devised a less overt manner in which to deal with this matter?" Henry hissed into Suffolk's ear.

Outside, the smell of burning rubble clung to the air like the desperate grasp of a scorned lover. Dawn's pale gray light tickled at the edge of the earth. In this broken place, physicians and surgeons attended to the wounded while soldiers and servants tread warily through the charred ruins in hopes of finding other survivors. Inside the king's pavilion, the tension clung to every tendril of smoke that slithered in.

"Be gone." Henry dismissed his attendants and guards with an angry flick of his hand, those who had rushed in at the first burst of flames, and threw himself into the embroidered crimson and wood chair in the corner. Head bent, shoulders curled, Henry pierced Suffolk with a potent stare.

"I do not believe it was intentional, Sire—the fire, I mean." Suffolk shook his head, unsure at this moment of the debacle's details. He rubbed roughly at his forehead, as if to clear the jumble of thoughts in his mind. "He was wounded as well. Certainly it is not in an assassin's plans to be injured while carrying out his duties."

"Not a proficient one, at any rate." Henry bit off the snide words. "Was he at least successful? Did any others perish in this debacle?"

"The initial reports confirm the target has been eliminated. His wife and daughter as well. One other died—no one of consequence—but many are grievously wounded."

Henry shook his head of red and gold curls. "Well, there is something in that, I suppose."

"I will find out more."

"Yes, you will." With agitated impatience, Henry tapped his foot on the wood below his feet as Suffolk hovered by his side. "Now."

"I . . . of course, Your Majesty." With a quick bow, the duke took his leave, fairly running as his sovereign's ire pushed at his back. He stopped short at the door, halted by the apparitions standing in the aperture.

Wrapped in a silk shift and dressing gown, the woman looked no less haughty; her soot-stained chin rose from her chest and she walked toward them with shoulders squared. The child at her feet was nothing less than a saintly specter, dressed in white, blond curls forming a halo about her small face.

"I must speak with the king, *s'il vous plâit*," the woman decreed, the English words lyrical in her heavy French accent.

"I'm sorry, my lady," Suffolk began, "but I'm afraid . . ."

"Let her pass," Henry barked.

Stepping around a bowing Suffolk—perplexity emblazoned on his handsome face—the woman brought the child with her.

Henry rose from his chair, walking forward to greet her, and the confusion crinkling Suffolk's ruddy face fell to slack-jawed shock.

"Madame de Montlhéry." Henry leaned over her hand as she made her obeisance. "Are you all right?"

"I am well, Your Majesty, *merci*."

"I am most grateful for all your efforts on our behalf this night," Henry said with a small shake of his head. "I am only sorry it has been botched so atrociously. But I am confident no aspersions will be thrown your way."

The woman's pale eyes strayed not a whit from his face. "I owe you my life. There is nothing you could not ask of me."

Henry smiled benevolently, looking down at the child at their feet.

"And who is this adorable creature you have brought to visit me?" he asked, and began to lower his large frame.

"She is my cousin's daughter."

The king straightened as though struck, head snapping toward Suffolk, accusation sharp in his blue eyes. "His daughter? Are you sure?"

"Yes, Your Majesty," Madame de Montlhéry murmured, shuddering at the blast of her sovereign's fury.

"I thought you said they had all perished?" the king snapped at the man hovering by the door.

"It is what I was guaranteed, Your Majesty," Suffolk defended.

"Well, your assurances are meaningless, as is your control of this situation."

"His wife lives, as well," the woman put forth. "She is . . . her face has been . . . no one will recognize her, I assure you. Nor do I believe, with the extent of her injuries, she will last much longer."

Henry clasped his hands across his muscular chest, his knuckles turning white, the skin straining across the bone, clamping down upon his irritation, though sorely tested.

"Suffolk," the king hissed through bared teeth. "Take thee off and see for yourself that the man is dead. I trust nothing this day."

"Your Majesty." The duke bowed, rushing off, no doubt, with thanks to be gone from his incensed ruler's presence, no longer certain his lifelong friendship could protect him further.

"Mum? See mum?" The tiny voice was no more than a squeak, the tug upon Madame de Montlhéry's gown timid yet insistent.

They looked down upon the child as if seeing her for the first time, her presence all but forgotten in the turmoil of the past few moments.

Madame de Montlhéry looked at Henry expectantly, lips parting with elusive words.

Henry lowered himself on bended knees, making himself as small and unmenacing as possible. His smile spread wide, and it chased away any vestiges of annoyance left upon his features. The little girl shrank back, clutching the woman's legs, taking refuge behind the folds of her gown.

"Would you like a treat, my dear? Are you hungry?"

"She loves plum tarts, Your Highness," Montlhéry informed him.

"Is that true? Would you like a sugary plum tart?" Henry asked the wide-eyed urchin.

Though she offered a halfhearted nod, the child remained in the wake of the woman's skirts, her large eyes growing moist and full with tears.

"Goodness, she is a sweet poppet, isn't she?" Henry's voice eased with tenderness.

"She is that, Sire," Montlhéry responded.

"How old is she?"

"A bit more than two."

Henry stared at the child, the pixie nose that spoke of her English heritage, the exquisitely shaped mouth of her French blood, the rosy cheeks, and the pale yellow ringlets.

Henry squinted. "Her eyes. Are her eyes . . . violet?"

The woman smiled with pride, a smile edged sharply with bitterness. "They are, Sire, like those of her *grand-mère*."

"Do you know what I have learned in my few years as king, madame?" Henry straightened, his gaze anchored on the child at their feet.

"No, Your Majesty, but I long for you to tell me."

"I have learned that weapons take on all forms. I have learned that beauty can be such a weapon."

The woman stared down at the child, a different light glinting in her eye. Where she had looked at the girl as a burden, she now gazed upon her as a blessing.

Henry began to pace, his slipper-shod feet plucking out a soft rhythm as he trod a circle around the woman and the child in the otherwise silent chamber, his hands once more clasped together, the steepled index fingers tapping lightly upon pursed lips.

"With your help, madame, I will make her my most powerful weapon."

Madame de Montlhéry lowered her head of fading blond curls, and made her pledge. "I am yours to command, Your Highness, as always."

Henry stopped before her, smiling with satisfaction. "Take her to your home, madame. Raise her as a proper French woman and as your niece, but teach her to honor me above all, above God. Teach her not only to read and write, but languages as well, especially Italian." Henry grew more and more inspired, moving again, spurred by dawning insights, striding to his chair and back again. The light behind his eyes glowed as his thoughts coalesced. "Teach her to cipher, and to shoot."

Montlhéry's head tilted. "To cipher and . . . and shoot?"

"Yes, my dear, to cipher and shoot." Henry jumped to stand before her, grabbing the woman by her shoulders and leaning in, bringing his face within inches of her own. "We will make her the greatest spy there ever was, madame—not a person who became one in adulthood, but one *reared* as a spy. Is it not brilliant?"

"B . . . brilliant, *oui*," Madame de Montlhéry responded, but with little confidence. She stared at the king with ill-disguised confusion.

"And most important of all, madame"—he lowered his voice to a scheming whisper, conspirators bent over their cauldron of plans— "we must teach her to kill."

The heavy, dreadful words hung in the air between them; the silence hummed with their evil intent.

The child stared up at them, comprehending little of what passed between them, mesmerized by it all nonetheless.

"Can you do this for me, Elaine? Can you?"

She swayed at the sound of her name upon his lips. How well she remembered him speaking it as he saved her from the marauding French soldiers who violated her beside the lifeless body of her dead English husband; and months later, as he took her in the night with tenderness and passion.

"*Certes, oui*, Henry. For you I can do anything."

He pulled her hard against him for a quick moment, only to thrust her back. Eager, he lowered himself again to the child. The small girl stared at the man before her, stepping out of the shadow of the woman, as if longing to bask in the magnetic man's light.

"What is her name?"

Elaine drew in a long draught of air, desperate to gain control, to breathe normally once more. "Geneviève, Geneviève de Hainaut."

"No, she cannot carry her father's name." He spoke with a soothing tone of comfort and kindness, knowing the child would understand this better than any words. With care he reached out a hand to Geneviève, watching for any sign that she might pull away from him.

"Come to me, child," he cajoled, his voice as seductive as if he coaxed a lover to his bed. Their eyes met and he felt the thrill of capture. "You are mine now, and always will be."

The tiny bud-shaped mouth twitched with the slightest of smiles and Geneviève took a step forward, and then another. Henry reached out both hands to take her in his arms, and she surrendered as though capitulating to a beloved parent.

Looking up at the woman he had once known as a lover, Henry beamed, victorious. "Let her be known as Gravois, Geneviève Gravois, for it is indeed from out of the grave I have pulled her."

Elaine curtsied low, knowing she had secured the protection and loyalty of this king forever, yet feeling a tear of heartbreak and jealousy, as if she had lost him as well, lost him eternally to this child.

"As you wish, Your Majesty."

As Henry rose, child firmly in his embrace, curled around his powerful form with head resting upon his shoulder, a squire rushed in, stopping short at the sight before him.

"Yes, what is it?" Henry demanded of the silent page.

"The French king, Your Highness. He is here and wishes to see you."

"Of course. Give me but a moment and send him in." Henry nodded with complete composure and turned to Elaine. "Quickly, madame, behind the screen."

Elaine needed no further prodding; fear had gripped her at the thought of François I finding her in the chamber of Henry VIII. She scampered to the screen and its hidden chamber pot, her heels clicking out a frightened percussion. No sooner had the clacking faded away, than it was replaced by the clanging of armor and swords. Into the room François swept, contingent of fellows, as always, in his shadow.

"*Majesté.*" He rushed to Henry's side, no smile of greeting in his eyes or upon his lips, purposeful with sincere concern. "*Comment allez-vous?* Are you all right? We could see the blaze from our camp. I came as soon as I could."

"Have no fear, I am quite well. Many thanks."

François shrugged off his gratitude. "What has happened here? Do you know?"

"I am looking into it, but already I have been assured it was nothing more than an accident—an overturned andiron, it would seem."

"How dreadful. Have many perished?"

Henry chose his words with great care. "Four are dead, and many more injured."

Henry hefted the child, slipping in his arms, a little higher. Though she grew heavier, she appeared wide awake, watching and listening to the two men with great intent. Henry smiled at her and her attentiveness.

"I have brought my physician and my surgeons." François gestured toward the group behind him. "They are at your disposal."

"Quite generous of you, but there is no need. My people have everything under control, I assure you."

The penetrating eyes of the French king scanned his rival's face with blatant suspicion. In the moment of any catastrophe, a helping hand should be accepted with grace.

Henry recognized the mask of displeasure but cared little. His goal was to keep François from learning much, not to acknowledge his magnanimity.

"But I am deeply grateful, nonetheless," Henry placated. "And I will alert you at once should the need for aid arise. You have my solemn promise."

"*Très bien.* As you wish, of course. You will keep me apprised of the situation, I am sure." François gave a small bow of acquiescence. For the first time, he noticed the child cleaving comfortably to the king's shoulder. "And who is this beauty?"

"This? This is my cousin's child. She seems to have wandered from her family in the ruckus," Henry said.

As if she knew they spoke of her, the little girl plucked her head off her pillow and looked the French king in the eye. François laughed at her charm.

"You will take good care of her, yes?" François gently patted the little girl's slipper-clad foot.

"Rest assured, Your Majesty. It is my greatest mission."

"*Bon, bon,*" François nodded. "We will talk soon, Henry."

"Of course, François."

With another bow, the Frenchman turned, and with a gesture to his compatriots, began to exit the makeshift castle.

As the king and the child watched the group quit the chamber, Henry pulled Geneviève closer; the little girl squirmed at the intensity of his grasp.

Leaning down, his mustache prickling her soft, tender skin, Henry whispered in her ear.

"That is the man who killed your parents."

The creature writhed on the cot, her whimpers accompanied by the shushing sound of ragged skin rubbing against rough muslin sheets. The physician and his assistant worked upon her wounds, but there was little effort in their ministrations. The burns covered more than half her body and most of her face, the flesh raging red, raw, and moist.

"Has no one come looking for her?" the physician asked.

"Not a one." The woman beside him shook her wimple-clad head.

"Perhaps there is no one," he clucked pitifully. "Perhaps she had made her way to the tent for the night. Such carousing as took place, who knows who ended up where."

"A paramour?" the woman suggested.

"Perhaps. In any case, she won't last long now. Continue the acanthus and thorn apple until her time comes, which, God willing, should be soon. The least we can do for the poor wretch is keep the worst of her pain at bay."

The physician stepped away, off to administer to someone with a chance of survival, and the woman reached for the crushed herbs and warm water on the small table by the bedside. In the dim light of the tent, she mixed the minced dried leaves with the liquid, stirring as she crooned to her patient.

"This will help you, my dear. I swear it will, you'll see." With the tip of the small wooden spoon, she drizzled the concoction into the wounded woman's mouth whenever she opened it to moan and croon.

"I wish I knew what you were trying to say," the caretaker told her patient, gaze pitiful upon the festering flesh. "I wish I could hold you, but it would only bring you more pain."

She stayed with her patient for a bit longer, stroking the small spot upon the woman's head that remained unscathed, until the dying creature began to drift off to sleep.

"Gen . . . gen . . . viève . . ." Gnarled lips mouthed the words. In her haze-filled mind, the wounded woman reached out her hand to the handsome man and the beautiful, golden-haired child, but neither heard her cry, neither took her hand.

❧ 2 ❧

My alliance is well begun,
But I do not know how it goes.

—Clément Marot (1496–1544)

1539

The quiet of the small château grew more oppressive than ever, as if the old woman's illness chased all noise from its walls, all life from its grounds. Though the cook prepared a meal few would eat and the kitchen-hand plucked the egg from beneath the chicken, the muffled sound was no more than that heard by a babe in the womb.

Geneviève stood on the precipice of rebirth; she knew the moment had come, and her aunt's dying would neither hinder nor hasten it. She sat on the floor in the middle of the chaos that had become her chamber; worn brown leather trunks—both packed and unpacked—formed a parapet around her. Little consideration went into what she would take, for she would bring everything, leaving nothing behind. She would never come back to this place.

Pushing back the tangle of pale yellow curls falling in her eyes, she gazed at the sage walls and satin bedclothes of the same hue. She had lived all her life within these walls and she would miss them not at all. She would spare neither an ounce of sentiment at the separation nor an iota of remorse at its lack.

Geneviève's violet gaze fell upon the new gowns that would accompany her; the brocade was sumptuous, the velvet rich and plush. The tight-fitting bodices emphasized her long, narrow torso, and the low, square necklines revealed more of her creamy skin. Yet she found little joy in them, thrilled more by the short bow that fit so perfectly—felt so natural—in her hands and the dagger with its sparkling, jeweled hilt.

Crumbling the flounce of her simple traveling gown in her hands, she rose to her knees and waddled over to the bed. There she picked up the miniature portraits, holding one in each palm of her long, thin hands, and stared at them as she had for so many hours, so many days before this. She did not know their names, for it was hammered into her that such knowledge could kill her, but she knew them by the swell in her heart as she looked upon them.

The hint of a smile brushed her lips—one corner of her mouth rising as if with a gentle tug of an invisible string—at the sight of her mother's rosy cheeks, and the amber of her eyes. At the sight of her dashing father—his proud bearing, his long but pleasant face—a yearning for something she could neither describe nor name churned in her depths.

She lay the pictures back down on the quilt with great care, as if she would injure her parents were she not cautious with their likenesses. She picked up another, that of the king—her king—King Henry VIII. His unswerving gaze held hers, spoke to her, and the curved lips reminded her of her own. Countless were the times she had gazed at her mouth in the looking glass, pretending she had inherited the distinctive feature from him.

Yes, she would pack it all—the miniatures of her parents, the weapons, the gowns and ribbons and jewels. All of it would come with her. Everything save his picture and his letters. Those she must surrender, leaving no tangible connection between them.

The bundle of parchment sat in her lap, wrapped in a robin's-egg blue ribbon. Some of the sheets had begun to darken and brown, for they were close to twenty years old. So many had worn spots; creases folded and unfolded time and again were wearing thin. How many times had she sat in this very spot, poring over the words of encouragement from King Henry VIII? How many times she had cried over them, laughed over them, she could not recall. She knew only that she heard the sound of their words in her head more often than that of her own voice.

She gathered them to her, the missives and the miniature, and made her way to sit before the low fire smoldering in the grate. For a moment her hand hesitated, forward motion halted but with the slightest of quivers. Reaching for inner fortitude, she quelled the fear, dampened and extinguished the emotion, as taught.

She untied the satin ribbon and began to place each piece of parchment on the burning embers, one by one. With each wad of material, the flames rose higher and she felt the heat caress her skin. As the blaze devoured them, Geneviève recalled their words, knowing every phrase, every sentiment, as well as she knew her name. She had clung to his words of encouragement and devotion through the long, lonely years. She had dedicated herself to her lessons as he urged her to do. And she had basked in his approval when the next letter came.

"What are you doing, mam'selle?"

Geneviève turned in surprise to the apron-clad girl standing in her chamber. So immersed in her task was she, she had not heard the servant enter nor approach.

"You startled me, Carine," she reproached her maid.

"I knocked on the door, mam'selle, twice, but received no reply. I thought the chamber empty." The petite brunette zigzagged through the cluttered room and squatted beside her mistress. "What are you doing?" she asked again.

Geneviève held the last letter in her hand and placed it with great gentleness upon the waning fire. "Just cleaning up."

"Why did you not call for me?" Carine's pert nose scrunched with concern; she was anxious to please her new mistress. She had heard the stories of ladies' maids come and gone, year after year, leaving the château and the town itself. No one could tell her if

Geneviève's own contrariness sent them packing, one after the other, or if they had been dismissed. It seemed the young beauty was an enigma, though she herself had found a youthful lady of no ill temper. In reality, Carine had not yet interpreted the true nature of her mistress's temperament at all.

Geneviève turned back to her task. "This I had to do for myself."

All that remained in her lap was the small miniature of the red-headed king. She kept it covered, cupped in the palm of her hand. Her eyes fluttered closed; she heaved a deep breath, and tossed it in.

It fell upon the flames, sparks flying as the combustible paint caught fire. The two women watched in silence as the corners of the small canvas curled up, blackened, and turned to ash.

Her befuddled gaze volleying between the fire and her mistress, Carine squirmed in the silence. "Your aunt asks for you."

Geneviève nodded without turning from the grate. "Yes. Yes, of course."

She jumped to her feet, reverie broken, and studied the cluttered room. "Could you finish this, Carine?"

"Of course, mam'selle." The maid began gathering and folding the few items remaining, thankful to be put to work.

"Are your own things ready?" Geneviève asked.

"Oh yes, I've been ready for hours." There was no mistaking the eagerness in the young girl's voice.

Geneviève's rosebud mouth twitched in a slight gesture of a smile. "Then I will pay my last visit and join you in the foyer. Is an hour long enough to finish the packing and have everything into the carriage?"

"Leave it to me," Carine replied with conviction. "All will be ready."

With a curt nod, so like that of the aunt who had raised her, Geneviève left her maid to her chores. At the door she faltered, throwing back one last look at the fire and its glowing ashes.

Picture and letters may be gone, but the bond—the allegiance bordering on fanatical—remained. It was time.

Knocking with one knuckle, Geneviève entered the dark, cavernous room. Diffused light from gaps in the curtain were too feeble to reach the high vaulted ceiling or the far corners of the large and stately room. The cherrywood panels and deep maroon wall and bed coverings brought more gloom upon the somber chamber. The silence hummed and Geneviève tiptoed into it, having no care to disturb it.

As she neared the bed, she spied the small mound of her aunt beneath the heavy covers and the large form of the black-gowned physician propped in the chair beside her. The bitter scent of illness mingled with the aroma of herbs in the stifling room in dire need of an airing out. Surely, a tiny bit of fresh spring air would do the dying woman no harm, Geneviève thought as she neared her aunt, but she kept such thoughts to herself. She gave the doctor a nod and he returned her solemn greeting with a silent, seated bow.

Geneviève approached the bedside and leaned forward, thighs brushing against the hard mattress upon which her aunt lay. The woman's sharp features were hidden in the dimness, but as Geneviève's eyes adjusted to the gloom, the familiar pointy nose and jutting chin became visible. Though death marched near, there was little softness to the bony face, as if the woman greeted it with the same stony demeanor in which she had spent her life. Thin gray strands of hair lay on the pillow and thin, papery lids lay closed over her eyes.

Lengthy minutes ticked by but the woman remained motionless. Believing her asleep, Geneviève began to creep backward to the door.

"Leave us, monsieur." The warbled voice both startled and commanded.

The large man rose from his chair and left the room without a word, passing Geneviève, rooted to her place. It had been a test, yet another; she should have known. Her whole life had been a test, one administered by this woman with a cold, stern hand.

"Are you ready? Has everything been taken care of?"

"*Oui, ma tante.* It is all prepared as instructed."

"*Bon, bon.* As it should be."

With tremendous effort, the feeble woman lifted her head off her pillow, thin arms pushing at the mattress as she tried to raise herself up. Geneviève rushed over, taking her aunt by the shoulders and boosting the frail woman up, pulling the pillows into a heap to support her. With a sideward glance that was neither grateful nor pleased, Elaine acknowledged her niece's assistance.

Geneviève felt her teeth grind, then released the reaction. All her life, she had tried so hard to please this woman. From her earliest memories, she had done everything asked of her. No matter how difficult, no matter how heinous, she had done it all in the hopes of eliciting some affection, any sign of tenderness, from the only mother she had ever known. But even now, as they were about to part for what may well be the last time, there was no offer of affection, not a morsel of sentiment extended from the woman who had raised her.

"In the table, there." Elaine pointed one bony finger at the credenza along the mullioned windows. "Open the top drawer and bring me what you find."

Geneviève did as instructed, retrieving a large velvet pouch, and placed it upon her aunt's lap.

Untying the satin cord, Elaine reached in. "These are for you."

The first item drawn from the bag was a book, bound in Moroccan leather with gold embossed letters on its spine: *Pantagruel*, François Rabelais. Geneviève accepted the book and opened it, turning the whisper-thin pages tipped in gold.

"He is the man's favorite author, and this the most popular work of the moment. No one will question that you carry it with you always, and you must never let it out of your possession. This book holds the key. *Comprenez-vous, oui?*"

"I understand, *ma tante*, of course I understand."

Through the long hours of lessons, of learning the languages and the ciphers, Madame Elaine had been a hard taskmaster, never once responding to the child's exhaustion, or revulsion. She had watched with implacable neutrality as the woodsman held the small furry animals, as the young girl sobbed while exterminating them. Nor had she praised Geneviève as the young woman endured hours of lectures and mind-altering persuasion, completing each new assignment with ease, as she translated the most complex of ciphers, as she slaughtered and butchered animals without a second thought.

Elaine reached into the pouch once more. The locket hung on a long golden chain of delicate links that tinkled together as her aunt dropped it into her palm.

"Open it," the elderly woman commanded.

On each side of the open oval locket were the pictures of two faces, at once familiar, undeniably related.

"Your *grand-mère* and the woman who raised you. If any should question your lineage and your allegiance, we are the patent of your heritage."

Geneviève stared at the small painted faces; the physical likeness was undeniable. She wondered if their temperaments were the same as well, if her father was the same type of person as her aunt.

It had not taken Geneviève long to understand that the coldness of this woman's heart ran to her very core; it was not an assumed state adopted in order to coax more work from the child. It was who she was. This woman had found little chore in teaching the child to have an emotionless demeanor, for she owned it completely. As a curious adolescent, Geneviève had tried to find out how Madame Elaine came to be who she was, but no matter how tentatively she broached the questions, no response was ever forthcoming. Geneviève would leave knowing as little about her aunt as when she came.

"Take the last one out yourself." Her aunt held the black bag out and Geneviève took it, squaring her shoulders against the shiver. She clasped the small square shape her fingers found and brought it forth.

She knew the face at once.

"Who is it, Geneviève?"

"It is the king, François I." Geneviève heard it herself, the slightest tinge of distaste in her voice.

"You cannot react like this, girl." Old and dying though she may be, the noblewoman could still bark a forceful command.

Geneviève assessed herself, finding her shoulders and shapely top lip curling upward. With an inward breath, she relaxed both.

"Who is in the picture, Geneviève?"

"He is the king," she repeated, her voice ringing with respect. "François I."

"*Whose* king is he?"

Thrusting her chin up, Geneviève looked her aunt square in the eye. "He is *my* king. My one and true king."

For a moment the women's gazes locked, the teacher's scouring the student's. All of a sudden, the old woman broke the connection and her body slithered down the pillows. All strength had left her. Her job done, her life's work complete, there was nothing remaining to hold her to this world. She would wallow in her illness until death came calling.

Geneviève waited, hating herself for the expectancy she felt in her heart, for one word of fondness to mark this leave-taking. Her aunt closed her eyes and turned her head toward the windows. Chiding herself for her foolishness, Geneviève turned toward the door.

"You will tell him, won't you?" The voice faltered and its vulnerability stopped her, drawing her back.

"Madame?"

"Tell Henry, make sure. Tell him I have done my duty well."

That the parting words between them would be of King Henry came as no surprise to Geneviève.

"He will know, *ma tante*. As do I."

On the seat across from her, Carine bubbled with excitement, leaning out of the open window to stare at the pale green meadows of spring as they rushed past.

"It is all like a dream, is it not, mam'selle? I cannot believe I am leaving. I have never left town in the whole of my life."

Geneviève gave her a silent, indulgent look in reply, but her hands, clad in lambskin leather, clenched tighter on her lap. She wouldn't tell her maid that she had never left this place, either, not in all of the years gone by. There had been many times she had longed to run, when she had learned what lay in her past, when she was told what was planned for her future. No, she couldn't share her own excitement and fear. But to herself she admitted her misgivings. She feared the future—yes, it was true. And yet there was a need, like an insistent itch, to do what she must, to fulfill her destiny, regardless of its brutality.

❧ 3 ❧

May the height of these great mountains
Not affright or rebuff us.

—François Rabelais (c. 1494–1553)

The journey from Montlhéry to Saint-Germain-en-Laye, where the king currently stood in residence, spanned the course of four days as it skirted the grand city of Paris on its northward track. But one day of rain plagued them, a stroke of luck in early spring.

Try as she might, Carine had failed to coax conversation from her mistress and in the end surrendered to the silence, seeing to her embroidery when the road was smooth, dozing when it was not.

Five years separated her from her companion, and yet Geneviève looked upon Carine like a child. Perhaps the girl's unfettered exuberance distinguished them, divided them so distinctly as youth and adult. Thankfully, the girl learned fast how best to serve her mistress. Relieved when Carine's attempts at discourse had subsided, Geneviève's head was far too full of words to trust her mouth to keep them imprisoned. So many times on the long journey it had pulled at her, the raging desire, the explosive need to quit the carriage and run back to her room, slamming and bolting the door behind her. Words of fear and failure sniped at her, chanting—as they had before—again and again in her mind.

I cannot do this. I won't. I cannot do this. I won't.

With a forceful clamp, she silenced them, allowing others to take their place. Insistent, prodding commands plagued her, the tenacious voice of her aunt telling her what she could, what she must do. She stifled the loquacious nagging as she always did. Under her breath, she recited the names of the royal family and those of the courtiers, a litany of lessons learned, until the monotonous repetition lulled her to sleep.

"Wake up, mademoiselle, wake up!"

Geneviève's eyes snapped open; her hand flinched toward the dagger strapped to her ankle by the lacy garter. But she discovered no threat through her sleepy gaze and with descending clarity, recognized the interior of the carriage, felt its bumpy gait beneath her, and saw the bright-eyed face of her maid sitting across from her.

"Carine, *mon Dieu*, whatever is the matter?"

The excited girl bobbed up and down in her seat, a determined digit pointing out the window. "Look."

Sitting up, Geneviève rubbed the sleep off her face with the back of one hand and peered out the open window. Bright afternoon sunlight assailed her, sparkling off the vast river running parallel to the tree-lined road, and she squinted against the glare, nostrils quivering at the robust scent of fresh water rising up to greet her. Craning her neck, she looked to the front of the vehicle and the panorama stretching out before them, any remaining lethargy chased decisively away.

The château rose up grandly on the rise ahead. Beyond the imposing ironwork gate, the exterior details of the yellow brick palace came into view. Exemplifying the medieval style in which it was built, square with towers at each corner, this fortress palace now bore the distinctive mark of its current monarch. In close collaboration, François and the architect Pierre Chambiges had added two stories upon the foundation laid by King Charles, augmenting it with distinctive touches, transforming it into the current age. With the addition of a terraced roof constructed of large stone monoliths conjugated by buttresses of long, iron tie bars, there became a delicacy to the edifice, as if the mighty castle now bore an intricately crafted and bejeweled crown upon its head. Here the king had married his first wife, and here his second son, now the Dauphin, had been born.

"You are excited now, mademoiselle, are you not?" Carine twittered, her face close to Geneviève's, their heads framed together in the open carriage window. The delight had skimmed across her mistress's restrained features like the wind across a calm pond, and she had seen the ripples. The young maid smiled with satisfaction; she began to recognize the small changes, the tiny glimpses that revealed the woman's true emotions. It was as if she had discovered some secret treasure and vowed to keep its knowledge all to herself.

Geneviève straightened and the curtain fell once more across her face. "It is an imposing structure, worthy of the king."

Carine sat back as well, but not without a smirk, one Geneviève refused to acknowledge.

As the carriage rumbled to the gate, the driver handed Geneviève's papers to the renowned Swiss Guards who stood at the aperture every hour of every day. Carine blushed at the handsome men in their white and gold tabards. Within seconds, they opened the iron bars and the carriage rumbled through, turning right onto the main approach. Before the crunch of wheel upon gravel ceased, *valets de chambre* flocked around them, extracting the trunks, reaching in to help the ladies disembark.

"Welcome to Saint Germain, mademoiselles." Dressed in blue and gold livery, a tall fellow, well but not resplendently dressed, bowed to Geneviève. "How may I be of service?"

"I am Geneviève Gravois, niece to the Baroness de Montlhéry, who sends her best regards to the king. I am here for my post as lady to the duchesse d'Étampes."

"Of course, mademoiselle. This way, *s'il vous plait*." The man bowed, one arm crossing his waist, the other directing Geneviève into the château.

On legs weak from long days of travel and more than a touch of apprehension, Geneviève moved toward the door.

"Mam'selle?" The timid squeak poked at her from behind. Carine stared after her mistress and the man escorting her, eyes large and frightened like a captured church mouse.

"I—" Geneviève began.

"They will show you the way, young lady." The valet jutted his chin toward the two squires who continued to off-load the luggage from the carriage. "They will bring you to your mistress's rooms."

Carine dipped a quick curtsy and Geneviève continued on, grateful for the man's efficient response, as she had none of her own. Her life's lessons had attempted to prepare her for its purpose, but now, in the moment of beginning, she realized how much she still needed to learn. There was little to prepare one for the life of the courtier. Most lived it from the moment of their birth, and its particulars came as naturally as learning how to walk. But Geneviève had lived a simple life for twenty-two years, almost twenty of them in nearly total seclusion; what she needed now most of all was the time she had lost. Courtiers had had their whole lives to learn what she must in a matter of days.

The *maître d'hôtel* took his place a few steps ahead, leading her through the enormous front door, passing beneath the triple Roman gothic arches.

"Your own room is located on this floor along with the other ladies who serve the duchesse and the queen."

Eleanor of Habsburg and her attendants lived side by side with the king's *maitresse en titre* and her attendants; it was the way of life for French nobility. Indeed, strict rules of precedence dictated the entire structure of the king's household. Prince and princesses of the blood and their families inhabited the château proper, as did most cardinals. Depending on their closeness to the king, the royal family's attendants resided on either the ground or the first floor. The king, the queen, and the king's mistress inhabited the entire second floor, as did Anne de Montmorency, François's constable and grand master of France. No one but the king's children, *les enfants du roi*, were allowed to live on the third floor, above the king. Members of the royal staff—secretaries and the like—were housed in outbuildings along with unmarried noblemen of lower standing. Anyone whose title began with *premier* took precedence over persons of higher social standing, their close proximity deemed necessary to the service of the king.

The pompous servant brought her through the marble foyer and across to one of the many spiral staircases, one of the distinctive architectural touches in the palace. Idiosyncratic in construction, with intricate carvings and ornamentations, the staircases provided the sole means of movement and access through the château, as all the *appartements* were constructed independent of one another. Few corridors existed, and those that did spanned no more than a small portion of each wing.

"The king is in residence, is he not?" she asked as they reached the third floor and entered a short hallway.

Geneviève had followed her guide, taken with the breadth of the château and its relative quiet. They had encountered no more than a smattering of people along the way, men dressed somberly—of serious mien, intent on reaching their destination—and a modicum of servants. There was little evidence of the thousands of courtiers who made their home with the king and with whom she would make her life.

"*Oui*, mademoiselle," her guide replied. "The weather is very fine today. Most are at the hunt, while others take the opportunity for an afternoon's rest."

Geneviève grimaced. She had studied the ways of the king for years and knew he preferred to dedicate his afternoons to some sort of physical activity. In springtime the forests of Saint Germain were bountiful; the court would take every opportunity to avail itself of the abundance.

"Is the duchesse with him?" she asked.

"Of course, mademoiselle. She is always with the king."

Geneviève thought she detected a tinge of emotion in the

man's reply but could not fathom it, nor elicit any explanation. For the moment, her primary goal was to secure her place in the hierarchy that was life with the king. There would be plenty of time for more in the coming days.

At the first door along the short passageway, the man stopped before the posted guard, who tipped his head in obeisance and opened the entryway. Geneviève stepped into a warm and inviting salon, welcomed by the delicate and tasteful opulence. The sun shone brightly through light and airy silk curtains of primrose and pine that matched the embroidery-covered walls and the upholstery of the scroll-worked furniture. Satin pillows tossed about haphazardly gave contrast to the rich tapestries and exquisite paintings adorning the walls. The room spoke of taste and refinement, and yet of a playful femininity.

"May I have something sent to you while you wait? Any refreshment?" Poised at the door, the valet stood with one foot stepping into the corridor.

Geneviève hesitated to respond, as if to keep him from leaving her alone. "No, *merci*. I will be . . . I am fine."

"Very well," he said, and with a bow was gone, the door swinging closed behind him.

Geneviève stood in the center of the room, not knowing what to do with herself, at odds with her unfamiliar surroundings. Growing bold, she looked around, peering through the door into the duchesse's private chamber. The same blissful beauty reigned here, dominated by the enormous bed sitting upon a dais. Piles of pillows sat atop the finest fluffy coverings. It was a bed fit for a king.

Returning to the spacious sitting room, Geneviève perched herself on the end of a winged armchair and waited. Streams of sunlight chased sprightly dust motes across the room as she festered in the silence, solitude that gave birth to mixed emotions of dread and anticipation.

The laughter reached her first, a merry herald, the door bursting open before she lurched to her feet.

The women streamed in amidst their chatter and laughter, like a rush of air bursting through an unlatched window. Cheeks rosy, hair windblown, they wore the effects of an afternoon outdoors as elegantly as they wore their red hunting costumes.

In the center of the whirlpool, Anne de Pisseleu d'Heilly walked with the conviction of her position. Though she wore the same attire as her ladies, the air of distinction was her accessory alone. Doffing her riding gloves and dapper chapeau, she brushed past Geneviève, as though the sight of a stranger in her sanctum was no cause for surprise. Accoutrements cast aside, Anne smoothed her shining chestnut hair, turning her gaze decisively upon her visitor.

Geneviève felt the penetration of the emerald green eyes. In their depths, she glimpsed intelligence and cunning balanced with a tincture of kindness and welcome. She dropped into a deep curtsy, fanning out her skirts in the greatest of respectful gestures.

"I have come to serve, if it pleases you, madame," she said reverentially, keeping her head lowered. "I am Geneviève Gravois."

"Ah yes, of course." With graceful release, Anne plunked herself into the largest, fluffiest chair before the cold fireplace and motioned for Geneviève to rise. Her maids of honor eddied around her, one taking a brush to her hair, another pulling boots from her feet, while two others stood ready by her side.

"Ladies, our newest companion has arrived. Let us welcome her."

As if within a well-choreographed dance, the four women turned together and curtsied to the newcomer. Anne reached up her hands in a wide gesture, and the two women at her shoulders clasped them affectionately.

"Geneviève, these are the Mesdames de Laval and d'Azelleures, Sybille and Béatrice, sisters to each other, and cousins to me."

Geneviève bowed in her turn, struck by the resemblance between the three women. The lovely pair shared the same heart-shaped face and high, prominent, freckle-flecked cheekbones with their relation, if not her mantle of preeminence.

The daughter of Guillaume, seigneur de Pisseleu, the duchesse d'Étampes's family tree included many sisters and brothers, all of whom had Anne to thank for their elevated status. The Pisseleus now boasted bishops, abbesses, governors, and a cardinal, as well. Many a courtier complained of Anne's use of her position to better those of her family, and yet they would do the same without a moment's thought.

"This lovely one here is Arabelle d'Aiguillon. She is the daughter of the comte de Vandreuil." Anne put one hand on the shoulder of the pert, golden-haired girl at her feet. "And behind me is Jecelyn du Fabiole, a distant cousin to the king himself."

The raven-haired woman behind Anne continued brushing her mistress's hair with no more than a black-eyed glance of acknowledgment spared for Geneviève.

"*Enchanté*, mademoiselle." Arabelle released Anne's second boot, rose, and curtsied once more, warmth of welcome in her shining blue eyes.

"Monique and Lisette are not among us today, but you will meet them in due time," the duchesse remarked. "So tell us, Geneviève, how come you to court?"

Jecelyn continued to brush the long auburn curls. Anne closed her eyes now and again, luxuriating in the ministrations. The sisters fluttered about the room, straightening things needing no straightening, and finally sat, birds resting in their well-fashioned nest. Arabelle rang a small bell found upon the claw-foot table before the windows, and within seconds, an apron-clad girl rushed through the door.

Arabelle handed her Anne's muddy boots. "Some wine, if you please, Clothilde. Come, Geneviève, sit with me here."

Taking her by the hand as if they were old friends, Arabelle brought Geneviève to the settee situated across from their mistress.

"It is my aging aunt's greatest wish for me to be here," Geneviève answered Anne's query.

The pampered duchesse laughed, but not unkindly. "She must have indeed desired it greatly, for she paid a dear price. Why have you never married? You are what—twenty years old, *oui?*"

"Two and twenty, madame, as of last month." Geneviève faltered not at all. "I have lived my entire life in the country, with no one but my aunt and our servants for company. There was little opportunity to meet anyone appropriate."

"Well, that explains it. No doubt you've been sent here to find a husband."

With a wave of her small-boned hand, Anne dismissed Jecelyn from her chore and sat up straight and tall. Arms draped casually over the arms of her chair, there was nonetheless undeniable intent in her posture and expression.

"You will find a loving home here, *ma chérie.* I am good and kind to those who are good and kind to me. But be warned—if you think you have come to seduce the king, you will feel my wrath." There was no rancor in her tone; its cold conviction carried a far more believable and frightening threat.

Geneviève felt a surge of repulsion at the thought of a dalliance with the man responsible for the death of her parents, the man whom she'd been sent to destroy, but it was angst that must remain buried deep within.

She rose and crossed the few paces between her and Anne in a trice. Once more, she fanned out her skirts, lowering herself to within inches of the floor.

"My allegiance, madame, is to you and no other."

She heard Anne's satisfied sniff and looked up, accepting the well-pleased smile offered her.

"I believe our sister could do with a wash and a rest, Arabelle.

Bring her to her chamber and make yourselves ready for the evening's festivities."

With a swish of skirts Anne rose, and Geneviève was surprised to find the duchesse stood a few inches shorter than she; such regal demeanor as was Anne's that she gave the impression of tall dominance.

"I look forward to our first evening together."

Geneviève dipped once more. "As do I, madame."

"Come *chérie*." Arabelle took Geneviève's hand again, leading her from the room and their mistress's company.

"That was very well done of you," Arabelle said as the women descended the staircase and entered the fray that was now the first-floor hallways of the palace.

The once quiet foyer and its small tributaries were now riotous with people and noise, color and cacophony. Though she felt like an intruder, an obvious imposter, Geneviève found they passed through the horde with the stealth of ghosts, two among the thousands who made their home with the king.

"What was?" Geneviève asked, raising her soft voice over the din.

"Your first audience with the duchesse." Arabelle smiled brightly. "I scarcely spoke a word the first time I met her."

"She is an imposing woman," Geneviève agreed.

"Imposing, yes, but she is gracious and loving to those who are loyal."

Geneviève caught a hint of a frown smudging the face of her new acquaintance.

"You mustn't believe some of the things you will hear, Geneviève, but allow your own experiences to dictate your impressions of our mistress."

Geneviève studied Arabelle. Glowing peach skin and a button nose above a sweet, smiling mouth; a true classic beauty—young and innocent—beneath the mass of luxurious curls, yet in her words, Geneviève heard aged wisdom. She would keep close to this surprisingly bright woman.

Down the two stairs and along the winding corridors, the women trudged through the crowds.

"Do not worry about finding your way at first. Learning each palace can be a daunting task," Arabelle told her as they came to a halt before a door along the outside of the ground floor corridor. "It will be my pleasure to escort you until you are comfortable on your own."

Geneviève gave her the ghost of a smile that felt the most comfortable upon her lips.

"Oh, mademoiselle, there you are!" The excited squeal found them the instant they set foot into Geneviève's chamber. Carine rushed forward, bobbing her curtsy midflight, and pulled her mistress farther into the room. "Is this not the loveliest chamber?"

Geneviève staggered forward on her maid's arm, indeed pleased by what she found. All cherrywoods and maroon upholstery, her accommodations flaunted a serious sophistication suited to her. Her chirping maid preened at her accomplishments, for everywhere Geneviève looked, the room spoke of cozy familiarity. One trunk remained at the foot of her bed, the keeper of undergarments and special possessions. All others were gone, their contents—her gowns—no doubt hung tidily in the large garderobe standing sentinel in the corner. Upon the dainty vanity before the single wall-length window, her cosmetics had taken their place beside her brushes and trinket boxes, and upon her bedside table stood her miniatures of her parents and King François, and her book—*the* book—as well. Geneviève felt a profound sense of relief at seeing it there.

"You would not believe what a wonderful time I have been having. There are *so* many people here, so many servants, and they are all quite friendly and helpful. There is a handsome young scullion who was here, and he brought me the tiniest but sweetest of tarts and a mug of ale, without my having to ask at all." Carine stopped her twittering tirade when she ran out of breath, but her delighted smile continued unabated.

"Hush, Carine, hush yourself," Geneviève chided gently, flicking an embarrassed glance between her servant and her guest. But Arabelle laughed a lovely giggle.

"Have not a worry, Geneviève. She has the right of it. It is most exciting to come to court. I cannot imagine how much more it would be for having lived forever in the country."

"*Merci*, Arabelle, you are most understanding."

"I have chosen your wardrobe for the evening, mademoiselle." Carine had found her breath once again. "I hope you find them pleasing."

Geneviève stepped over to the raised bed and found her lavender gown trimmed with ribbon and encrusted with bits of amethyst, and the matching headdress, laid out upon the covers; beneath them, the matching shoes, their thick ribbons tied in large, beautiful bows.

"It is perfect, Carine. Well done." Geneviève offered the excited girl a deserved morsel of encouragement.

Behind them Arabelle poked through Geneviève's things—curious, not intrusive—as if through the touch she might learn more about her new companion.

"It is a shame you did not arrive a few hours earlier. It was a rousing hunt today to be sure. Do you hunt?" she asked.

Geneviève almost laughed. If this woman knew her truth, how confounded would her delicate sensibilities have been. "Oh, I do. I enjoy it very much."

"Then I cannot wait to partake of it with you by my side. What fun it shall be. Hopefully it will not be as long or as tiring as today's. I swear we had to chase that stag for hours, but the king was most determined to bag this particular one, having spotted him weeks ago when we arrived." Arabelle covered an indecorous yawn with the back of her hand. "Pray forgive me. I fear I am more tired than I thought. As you both must be after your long journey."

With a nod and a glance to Carine, whose own eyelids looked heavy despite her zest, Geneviève agreed. "It has been a long day."

"And it is far from over," Arabelle said as she stepped toward the door. "Let us all take a few minutes' rest. I shall return in an hour to escort you back to Madame's chamber where we will make her ready for tonight's banquet."

"*Merci*, Arabelle, you are most kind." Geneviève dipped as the young woman retreated, and flopped upon the bed once the door closed behind her. Already she felt exhausted by the stress of her charade, though in truth she had spoken not a single falsehood.

Allowing Carine to strip her down to her chemise and to draw the heavy velvet curtains closed, Geneviève lay upon her bed as the maid tiptoed from the chamber. Staring at the maroon and gold canopy hanging overhead, she rubbed her flat stomach as if to quell the fluttering beneath her young skin. *So far, so good*, she thought, and closed her eyes.

❧ 4 ❧

The king of gentlemen,
and the gentleman King.

—Frederic V. Grunfeld, *The French Kings*

The flock of ladies stepped back and gazed upon their handi-work, each with a critical eye for the smallest detail.

"I think she needs another strand of pearls," Sybille clucked as she walked a circle around her cousin, squinting with a critical eye.

Béatrice sucked her teeth with impatience. "No, dear, it will be too much. Her beauty is more than any adornment could add."

Geneviève followed Arabelle's lead, fetching whatever acces-sory Madame de Laval requested, returning them as Madame d'Azelleures instructed. Jecelyn primped the duchesse's hair, showing no response to the menial requests, her haughty de-meanor denouncing them as beneath her. Monique and Lisette now among them—one tall and thin, one short and plump, both plain but pleasant—tidied up the chaos such bustle left behind.

Anne stood as impassively under the scrutiny as she had during the long tedium of the dressing, as the layers of clothing—shift, underskirt, hose, gown—encased her body. Certain in her splen-dor, she trusted her maids of honor had done their due diligence. Upon her resplendent gown, alternating stripes of emerald satin sat beside those of cream velvet on the full, heavy skirt. The huge, puffed upper sleeves of the emerald satin and the more fitted cream velvet of the lower arms flanked the jewel-encrusted green bodice. The same pearls and emeralds adorning her neck and ears sparkled from her matching crescent-shaped headdress. Below the few exposed inches of her rich chestnut hair, her exquisite eyes— huge within the small, delicate face—shone with the same brilliance as the jewels gilding her gown.

"Is she not the loveliest you have ever seen?" Arabelle whispered to Geneviève.

There was no denying the beauty of the woman's features—the sensual mouth and the creamy skin. If her foothold as one of the land's most beautiful women was not set in stone by the splendor of her face, her figure was equal evidence. With a tiny waist— smaller for the tightly laced stays she wore—and her full, firm breasts, her king and lover often boasted that her body was no less perfect than that of Venus herself. She was a knight's daughter, and the lofty bloodline revealed itself in every bit of her aspect.

"She is a beauty to behold," Geneviève responded with no need for subterfuge, but unlike Arabelle, she found no fulfillment in decorating her enemy's lover.

Arabelle's reply never left her lips as the door burst open and a bear of a man filled the space, arms thrown as wide as his full-lipped smile.

"I have come to take you to dine." His booming voice thundered with conviviality.

This man required no heraldic announcement; so noble and majestic did he appear, he would be known as king had he worn rags and worked in the fields. Geneviève recognized him in an instant. Though his trim beard boasted more gray than brown hairs and his long nose hung lower than in her miniature, she knew him unequivocally. This was King François in the flesh.

No matter how she had steeled herself for this moment, she was not prepared. All at once, the fuming anger bred into her blood every day of her life assaulted her like the blow of a sword. Upon its heels, fear tread, but it was not as strong by half. The wave of emotion was like a tidal force; she quivered with it and the urge to wrap her hands around his thick neck and squeeze—until all life ran from his body—overwhelmed her. She spun from it and him, pretending to busy herself with discarded gewgaws. A light touch upon her arm broke through the haze of murderous fury. Geneviève looked up from the delicate hand and into Arabelle's kind face.

"Be not afraid," she whispered with a small, generous smile. "Our benevolent king is not to be feared. And it is most likely he may not notice you, though not unkindly meant. When he sees her, he sees little else."

Bracing herself with a grind of her teeth, Geneviève turned to face the man who haunted her dreams and gave birth to her nightmares.

He was one of the tallest men she had ever seen, standing a head taller than the average Frenchman. Named for the Italian hermit who had prophesized his royal destiny, the king's stature and bearing proclaimed forthrightly the fulfillment of that divination.

The dark, smooth cap of chin-length hair fell across his face as he lowered his lips to Anne's cheek, his watery-milk complexion flushing like a schoolboy, his almond-shaped amber eyes filling with an undeniable tenderness.

"Are you ready, *chérie* Hely? Are you as excited as I?" François stepped out of the embrace and raised his arm parallel to the floor, calling Anne by the most informal of nicknames as only her intimates dare.

Resting her hand upon his, Anne smiled up at him. "Very excited, my liege. I have been thinking of nothing else for hours."

Their words sent a twittering among the other ladies in the chamber.

"The Italian musicians have arrived," Arabelle explained.

"Tonight will be their first night. It is sure to be a magnificent evening. You have come just in time."

Behind the grandiose couple, the ladies followed, joined outside the door by some of the king's *gentilshommes de la chambre;* some were friends, some advisers, a few were both. The Cardinal de Tournon wore his red cassock and four-cornered cap as dashingly as the Admirals Philippe de Chabot and Claude d'Annebault wore their bejeweled and embroidered doublets and trunk hose, decorative swords clanging at their hips.

For all the courtiers' splendor, the king commanded the stage. His velvet navy blue doublet, encrusted with rubies and sapphires, was perfectly tailored to his large physique; though his abdomen had grown thick with the passing years, the muscular, powerful athlete he remained was very much in evidence. The slashed balloon sleeves revealed the rich red silk shirt beneath and added to the vast width of his broad shoulders. The velvet navy toque, ostrich plumed and jeweled, he wore tilted to one side. Below the navy trunk hose, thick, tree-trunk-like thighs tapered to oddly thin calves covered in the finest red silk stockings.

"Most of the stories aren't true, you know." Geneviève's scrutiny did not go unnoticed, and Arabelle refused to let it continue without remark. "The scabrous tales of his wicked behavior—they are no more than deliberate inventions of the writers from the House of Bourbon, all of whom had served the treacherous duc."

Geneviève would not tell this devoted subject that her opinion arose from knowledge of the king's true brutal nature, that she had felt the sting of it herself. What concerned her most was that a glimmer of it had shown in her expression. She must gather herself, at once and for good.

"You misread me, I think, Arabelle," she said in her most gracious voice. "I look upon our king with great deference. All my life I have heard of him. It is so very awe inspiring to see him in the flesh."

Arabelle glowed with reverent fidelity, and perhaps more than a bit of feminine infatuation. "Once you come to know him, not only as king, but as a man, you will see how truly magnificent he is."

The king chortled with delight at a courtier's comment, the sound expanding as it echoed off the palace's stone walls. Everywhere the signs and symptoms of François's all-encompassing renovation work spewed into their path, but he stepped unmindful around piles of stone and wood.

As they neared the great hall, enticing aromas of roasted meats and freshly baked breads assaulted their senses, reaching out to them, as did rousing conversation punctuated by bursts of provocative laughter.

At the end of the corridor, the queen and her cortege awaited. Releasing Anne's hand with noticeable reluctance, the king approached the queen and took hers.

Indistinguishable as the queen consort of the land, the small, pale redhead curtsied, no more than a shadow of a smile on her pouty, prim lips. Her simple gown of mauve silk, modestly sprinkled with encrusted jewels along the neckline and matching headdress, did little to foster a majestic mien. Not a word or gesture passed between them that spoke of the synergy of a husband and his wife; indeed, there was little of a marital relationship binding them. Eleanor, the king's second wife, was the sister of the Holy Roman Emperor, Charles V, one of François's greatest rivals.

Twenty years ago, as each young man came into his ruling maturity, Charles had won the bid for Holy Roman Emperor, a seat both had clamored for with the same fanaticism. His deeper purse and beneficial family connections had snatched the prize from François's eager grasp. The bitter emptiness in the Frenchman's hand had never stopped burning his skin and he scratched at it like a perpetual itch.

Later, as Charles's prisoner for over a year, his country falling apart in his absence, François had little choice but to offer his young sons in exchange for his own freedom, compelled as well as a widower, to marry the emperor's widowed sister. Charles had been the master, could have shown mercy and asked for other tokens, ones not so dear. But he had not, and what François now felt for him would forever be tainted by lingering resentment.

Such umbrage had stained the union of Eleanor and François from the onset, as surely as ink stained the scribe's hand. Eleanor had known it with great surety, as if it had been written long before the day she met him, his mistress standing by his side. From the first, François could not forsake Hely for his wife, could not sleep with Eleanor, and she had soon given up any attempt to compete with the woman touted as the loveliest of the learned, the most learned of the lovely. François needed no children from his second wife, having many already from his first, though few survived. Eleanor was a needless necessity and she acquiesced to the role without rebellion.

With the king and queen leading the way, the duchesse close behind, the procession turned a corner and the soldiers posted at the archway snapped to attention, their halberds pounding upon the stone floor with one sharp, cohesive crack. Before the sound died away, heralds took up their horns, blasting the arrival of the king.

Geneviève shrank into her haven of anonymity. Ready to don her persona, prepared to take on all that it entailed; tonight she would do her best to watch and witness, intending for this night to be one of study and speculation.

Try as she might to foster a mien of dispassion, she felt reduced by the grandeur she witnessed. Encompassing nearly the entire wing of the palace, the great hall of the Château Vieux overflowed with courtiers, and the cries of "Votre Majesté" rang up and filled the air of the massive vaulted ceiling, the wind rattling the three-story panes of glass separating the chamber from the courtyard beyond. Rich fabric rustled as every attendant bowed or dipped in obeisance, but the king brought them upright with a free and generous swing of his arm and a call of *"Mes amis, bonsoir!"*

Astounded by the breadth of the assemblage and the opulence of the scene, Geneviève leaned toward Arabelle. "It is remarkable that I should be lucky enough to time my arrival with such a lavish event."

"Oh, this happens at least once or twice a week." Arabelle smiled. "The king insists upon it. He believes it is the best way to keep his people happy, to keep them busy and making merry."

The king escorted the queen through the maze of furniture and courtiers to the long head table and placed her in one of the two vacant chairs in the center of the banquet, with a shallow bow over her hand. He sat beside her, turning to his companions who filled the table to his right. Chabot and d'Annebault sat in the row, as did the king's youngest children, his son Charles—the duc d'Orléans—and daughter Marguerite, both blossoms of young adulthood. On the queen's side of the table, Constable Montmorency sat after the Dauphin and his wife.

Two main tables abutted that of the king, perpendicular to his and equally spaced. At one, the duchesse d'Étampes perched herself at the end, nearest to the king, and Arabelle led Geneviève to sit with their mistress, finding a place amidst other courtiers, many of whom looked upon Geneviève with undisguised curiosity.

At the opposite table sat the Dauphin's mistress and her own entourage of ladies and gents.

The king seated and each player to their place, servants flocked through the room, huge silver platters piled with every possible delectable held aloft, the first placed upon the perfumed linens of the king's table.

With a hearty laugh encouraging everyone to imbibe, the king dug in to the meat course, crowned by a slab of venison from the very stag caught this day. With the venison came partridge, wild boar, and rabbit, succulent and juicy, exquisitely prepared. Sumptuously gowned and groomed courtiers tore into their food, one hand upon their knives while the other picked the food off their plates and popped each tender morsel into their mouths.

Geneviève began her meal, so very aware of how different this one was from every other meal in her life. Never before had she eaten in the company of so many others, having taken most of her meals alone or with her aunt. Her life of solitude was finding balance in this greatest of opposite extremes.

"Monsieur the duc de Nevers," Arabelle announced to Geneviève with a nod of indication to the man beside her. "Next to him is the duc de Ventadour, and the marquis de Limoges is on his right."

Arabelle introduced her to the many of Anne's noble league . . . their names jumbling together. To all and sundry, Geneviève responded in kind, "*Enchanté*. It is my great pleasure to meet you."

Her lessons echoed in her ears—the repetitive drilling and recitations, the sting of her aunt's fan had she failed to respond correctly. As her guide offered more names, Geneviève knew their positions . . . the prince and princesses of the blood, the courtiers and the men of the king's chamber, and the others who were nothing more than *filles de joie suivant la cour*, those grasping, always hopeful court-followers. With half an ear intent upon the goings-on at the king's table, the ladies and minor gentlemen of the king's chamber shared the scrumptious victuals set before them.

"What a magnificent addition to our table," announced the marquis de Limoges, turning his attention from Jecelyn seated beside him. Geneviève felt the prick of the woman's black gaze from beyond his shoulder.

"You are most kind, monsieur," Geneviève assured him.

"Please, mademoiselle, call me Albret." Picking up his plate, the russet-haired man stood and strode the few steps to where Geneviève sat, and squeezed his thick warrior's body between Geneviève and Anne's cousin, leaving behind an agitated Jecelyn. "Why have you not come to court sooner?" His wide smile and laughing brown eyes dimmed. "Tell me you are not married?"

"Not married, no." Geneviève shook her head, taking another small bite of the meat pie upon her plate. "I have been caring for an ailing aunt who insisted I come. She has many nurses about her now who can give her much better care than I."

Albret's parodied sadness became sincere. "I am sorry for her illness, though thankful it has brought you to our door."

Geneviève tipped her head to the side, turning her striking eyes upon her new acquaintance, and smiled a small, benevolent smile. The man's solace seemed sincere and his attention flattering. The marquis smiled back, ill-disguised enchantment upon his ruggedly handsome countenance.

"Who is this marvelous creature?" The deep male voice was a purr, charming and seductive. "I know I am new to court, but beauty such as this I would have remembered."

As food came and went, so did the visitors to the main tables. With each such visit, Geneviève witnessed the divisiveness of the court splayed out before her; more than one fracture split jagged gaps through the room and those in it. Though years had passed, the *noblesse d'épée*—the nobles of the sword—had not come to terms with the new nobility, those considered the *noblesse de robe* and *noblesse de lettres*, who had been given their nobility—or worse, purchased it. And so the very manner of their nobility divided them. The old nobility in France—the evolution of the chivalric knights—mingled with the new, and tolerated them as they were forced to do by their king, who recruited so many of his friends and advisers from among the newer ranks. But their own superiority they wore as ostentatiously as they did their velvets and jewels.

Within these two groups were another two. Though all showed their allegiance to their king above all others, their private commitments—political and social—lay divided into two camps: one for the king and Anne, and the other for the Dauphin and his mistress. The distinction of cliques was as apparent to the newly arrived as it was to the seasoned courtier, splitting the swirling throng like a butcher cleaves meat from the bone.

Geneviève watched the machinations with beguiled interest. Here already she had found a small gift to send to her master.

What would Henry do if he knew of the breach running through the middle of the French court, running so deep it separated the king from his heir?

"Ah, Raymond, this is Mademoiselle Geneviève Gravois. Geneviève, please make the acquaintance of Baron Pitou, another new friend to the court, if I may be so bold as to call you friend already."

"I would not have it any other way."

Geneviève bestowed her small grin toward both men, taken aback for a moment by the beauty of her newest acquaintance. His rippling waves of golden hair and eyes the blue of a breathtaking summer sky dared to triumph over the opulence of his indigo doublet and hose and the finely sculpted body beneath. Her heart thudded before such male beauty, such unfamiliarly pretty masculinity.

"Be not overwhelmed by the attention of these scamps." The nasal twang of Jecelyn du Fabiole caught them all unawares as it screeched above the table's conversation. "You are the newest bauble at court, Geneviève. Once your novelty and sparkle wear off, they will soon forget about you."

The smiled faded from Geneviève's lips and she turned to look at the ungracious woman, a grim stare assuring Jecelyn she would not accept such cruel trifling. "Indeed, I see by the lack of companions by your side how it must be."

Jecelyn countered with a sneer, as if bitterly pleased by Geneviève's brashness.

Raymond was the first to break the uncomfortable silence. "Such a beautiful, intelligent addition will never be taken for granted, I assure you."

"*Merci, mon seigneur,*" Geneviève said quietly, breaking the combative gaze.

As Jecelyn rose, a shallow curtsy of leave-taking offered to the table, Arabelle leaned over to whisper in Geneviève's ear. "Watch her, *mon amie*. She will not leave it there."

Geneviève gave her a nod of understanding as she watched Jecelyn flounce away, watched as men clamored to walk by her side. Why such a striking beauty would begrudge a newcomer to court some friendships, she could not imagine, but she would, as warned, be wary of this wily woman.

"Your plate seems so empty, mademoiselle," Albret chastised. "Look at these beautiful salads and fruits. You do a disservice to the king not to partake of his generosity."

"I am quite full, I assure you." Geneviève allowed the knot of tension to release her. This was her first night at a magnificent royal court; she had worked all her life to be here. She could allow herself one night to relish its stately offerings with gusto.

"Then you had better loosen your stays, mam'selle"—Raymond laughed as he added more delicacies to Geneviève's now overflowing plate—"for there are another three courses to go."

Geneviève's brows rose precipitously. "Surely not?"

"Ah, *oui*," Raymond assured her. "But have not a care, it will take hours for it all to be served and there will be much entertainment in between."

"Your chalice is empty, as is yours, Arabelle." Albret filled their goblets, drawn by the others at the table whose own cups needed refreshing, and together the group drank a toast.

"*Bonsoir*, monsieur. I hope you are having a pleasant evening."

Geneviève's ears pricked as the sound of the duchesse d'Étampes's voice, so tight with vexation, reached her from the end of the table. Though the woman's words were full of amiability, there was little in the tone to match the sentiments. Slowly, so as not to draw any undue attention, Geneviève turned to see with whom Anne spoke. Anne de Montmorency bowed over the hand of the king's mistress, his thin lips brushing the air.

Second to the king, as constable and grand master, Montmorency was the most powerful man in the realm, overseeing operations both military and domestic. He controlled the staff and the running of the king's household and held the nation's purse strings. Most crucial of all, he ensured the safety of the king. Through these protector's eyes, Montmorency searched for threats to his ruler, no matter if they came from the arms of his mistress.

"Madame Duchesse, you look exquisite tonight." The kindness of his greeting lived in his words alone, never reaching to put a smile on his lips nor any warmth in his somber eyes.

"And you are dashing, as always, Constable," Anne replied in a like manner.

The lack of geniality between these two vibrated with every oversweetened sentiment spoken, pleasant tones off-key with terse, discordant notes, like the hollow peal of a cracked bell. Whether it was their constant struggle to be the king's greatest confidant and adviser, their opposing views on the new religion sweeping their country, or Montmorency's allegiance to the queen, there were simply too many rifts for their relationship to bridge, and neither cared to try.

"Monty, my good fellow, would you tell them we will soon be ready for our entertainments?" the king called kindly to his constable, using the nickname so long ago adopted to save Montmorency any embarrassment caused by his feminine, given name. The irony that the king's mistress and his constable shared a name was not lost on many.

With grace, Montmorency tipped his head, though not without a degree of relief to be done with his duty toward the king's mistress. "Of course, Your Highness. I will send a page to fetch the musicians at once."

"*Merci*, Monty." François rose, forsaking the head table to draw near his mistress.

Geneviève saw no acknowledgment by the king of the tension between his two dearest intimates, but whether he was blind to it or refused to see it, she could not fathom.

"Ah, finally, huzzah!" Albret's rousing cheer sent the entire table to squirming. "The Italians are on their way."

From the side door, a long line of instrument-wielding musicians filed out and took their place in the corner of the room, sitting with their lutes and hautbois, their violas and a spinet; to their right gathered a choir in velvet robes. Poised dictatorially before them stood two men, one in the robes of the choir, one in doublet and pansied slops, tambour sticks in his hand—similar faces, relatives of some sort, distinguished by the short curly hair of one and the shoulder-length waves of the other. These were newest members of the *chapelle de musique*, the musicians of the royal household.

"They are quite handsome, are they not?" Arabelle giggled to Geneviève behind a cupped hand.

"Which ones?" Geneviève asked.

"All of them," Sybille and Béatrice answered with harmonious twitters of their own.

"They are Italian," Béatrice confirmed as if that were explanation enough. Pointing to the two leaders, she educated the table with a smug whisper. "The taller man is Giuseppe, and the other his brother, Eliodoro."

Under the reign of François, so many Italians had become permanent fixtures at court. Italian blood pumped through his own veins, bequeathed by his maternal great-grandmother, Valentina Visconti. Yet François wished it were more; but it was not an oddity, a Frenchman who longed to be an Italian. So many of the French had adopted the more formal, polite manners of the Italians. Diplomats and ambassadors had always abounded, but the king had chosen to fill his household and chamber with the Mediterraneans as well: doctors, a steward or two, musicians, and a few *écuyers du roi*, the simple men of the household. Nor was the infusion limited to men. Frenchmen returning from Rome and Venice brought with them the day's most popular and coveted adornment, the Italian woman, and their influence infested the court with a greater sophistication and a tendency to extravagance. Such profligacy required dependency on the king and his munificence, and such reliance on a ruler who demanded such extravagance found the nobles incurring the ridicule of the satirists.

As the discordant noise of tuning instruments halted and the rapturous sound of a chanson began, all hushed to bask in the melodious music. As the first few measures rang out, instruments blending with voice in a joyful sound, applause greeted the performers. Clément Janequin's "La Guerre" was the king's favorite composition, written in honor of François's magnificent triumph in the Battle of Marignano. Light, fast, and rhythmic, it had distinct short sections, oft repeated, rousing the crowd to heights of stimulated enjoyment.

Before the last notes slipped away, François leaped to his feet, rushing forward to pay his respects to the musicians. The brothers rushed to accept the accolades, one jostling the other to be the first to greet the king.

"Bravo, bravo," François bellowed with sincere appreciation, Anne applauding by his side.

"Grazie, mille grazie, Vostre Maestà." The beaming pair bowed low before their patron and benefactor.

"We are so very happy you are pleased," said Giuseppe.

"And we are so very grateful for the magnificence of our new home," intoned Eliodoro, in proficient if oddly accented French.

As musicians of the chapel, they would receive not only the benefit of a room in whatever palace the king resided, but all their meals, their clothing, and a small stipend as well.

"It is I who thanks you," François assured them magnanimously. "You are a marvelous addition to our court."

Indeed their presence was a coup for the French king, having stolen them from the emperor's Spanish court. Such competition for artists was an important component of the cultural rivalry existing between the great kings and their courts. François had won a small battle with their acquisition.

"La volte, la volte," the king cried. "Such is our pleasure."

The musicians ran back to their places as the dance floor filled with courtiers, all eager to do their king's bidding.

"Dance with my son, Anne, would you? Dance with Charles," François implored her, as he took his seat once more.

"Of course, Your Majesty," she readily agreed with a flash of a beatific smile. Though he enjoyed the vigorous dance, there were often times, more often of late, when the king preferred to watch than to strain his aging body. The memories were pleasing in and of themselves.

Young, vigorous, and full of life, the exuberant Charles jumped to do his father's bidding. The youngest son, he possessed neither the seriousness of his now deceased oldest brother nor the sullenness of the current Dauphin. Having been born third in line to the throne, Charles had never entertained any thoughts of possessing the crown and this nonchalance permeated both personality and purpose. The death of his brother had thrown such dalliance into disarray, and he now donned the itchy cloak of second-in-line without much grace, indeed scratching at it whenever possible.

"We must dance," Raymond cried, grabbing Geneviève's hand, hauling her to her feet and onto the floor before Albret could make a counteroffer. With grace, he partnered Arabelle and the couples stood side by side waiting for the notes to begin.

Anne glanced down the row at Geneviève. Her cheeks rosy with excitement, she offered her new maid a smile of encouragement. At the last minute, as the musicians struck the first notes of the stirring song, another couple joined the throng, taking their place beside Anne and Charles. Anne's smile faded like the glow of the sun behind rushing storm clouds. Alongside his brother, the Dauphin Henri now stood, his partner, the inimitable Diane de Poitiers.

Twenty years his elder, Diane had been Henri's mistress for the last nine years, since he was no more than fourteen years of age. The rivalry between the mistresses had begun as soon as their acquaintance. And yet this woman, though older, clad as always in black and white, challenged both the beauty and grace of the duchesse d'Étampes. The entire court looked on in vicious delight as the two feminine powers vied for attention, as they threw their bodies into the dance to outdo the other in agility and mastery of the difficult dance.

The athleticism required for the leaping movements and *entrechats* suited the baron and his young, powerful physique. Geneviève entrusted herself to the strong arms of the nobleman as she had the series of dance teachers Tante Elaine had hired for her. The loss of honor he would suffer at any faltering would hurt him far worse than any physical bruise she might endure. As they swirled about the dance floor, Geneviève watched the duel between Anne and Diane, and the baron watched Geneviève, a dance within a dance until the music reached its climax and the dancers applauded, a glistening sheen of sweat on their faces, the air thick with their body warmth and odor.

"You are a magnificent dancer," Raymond murmured in Geneviève's ear as he led her back to their table, one hand poised with propriety upon the small of her back. The warmth of his palm lingered upon her flesh, as if the moist silk of her gown evaporated beneath his touch.

"I am only as proficient as he who leads me," Geneviève replied, jumping into the fray that is courtly volleying, with the acumen of a veteran. But in truth, she was inordinately pleased and flustered by the man's compliments and attention, happy to have him as company as they returned to sit once more with Arabelle and Albret.

The meal resumed and continued for hours, exactly as the men warned: course after course accompanied by intermissions of entertainment. Acrobats and jugglers punctuated the fowl and game course. A solo performance by Il Divino himself, Francesco Canova da Milano, introduced the fish. And more dancing preceded the dessert course.

Once more Geneviève partnered Raymond, having taken a turn with Albret and other young courtiers eager to meet the newest of the duchesse's ladies. She had lost track of time and her feet ached, yet her lips spread demurely as the *gaillarde* brought them together and sent them pirouetting down the length of the hall, allowing her to place her hands upon his hard, strong shoulders. Only one blemish spoiled the perfection of the evening; or rather, one person.

As she had all evening, Jecelyn did her utmost to remain in Geneviève's notice, to prove her dominance as she preened. Surrounded by men at all times, laughing loudly, dancing recklessly, she strove to be the center of attention. As the ostentatious woman disrupted the loveliness of the dance's cohesion, as her disharmonious movements wreaked havoc upon the uniformity of the choreography, Geneviève could not pull her gaze away from the black-haired beauty. Jecelyn du Fabiole was a virtuoso of coquetry and Geneviève hated that she watched her, that she felt what she did—a curious concoction of admiration and jealousy—as if she betrayed herself.

With a thunderous note and a final swirl, the song rushed to a close and the dancers fell upon each other, an exhausted assemblage, panting for breath.

"Would you care . . . for more . . . wine?" Raymond offered between heavy gulps of air.

Geneviève had no breath to speak, but nodded and smiled as Raymond laughed, took her hand, and led her toward the courtyard entry and the door left partially open. She closed her eyes in ecstasy as the chilly breeze of the spring night twirled around her body, cooling her with its soft caress, tingling upon her moist skin.

"Wait here, *ma chérie*. I will fetch and fill your goblet." Raymond left her with a soft kiss on her cheek and Geneviève skittered at the unfamiliar sensation. Raymond laughed, mistaking her innocence for coquetry, and rushed away, no doubt in a hurry to return.

"Again, Eliodoro, you were too loud."

Geneviève turned to the annoyed whisper at her back and found she stood but a few feet away from the musical brothers, who, like her, had made their debut this night.

"You know not of what you speak, Giuseppe." A hair's breadth shorter and darker of skin, the wavy-haired brother turned away with a look of annoyance.

"Look, see it there, the *mezzo piano*." Giuseppe pointed to the note-covered parchment, shaking the sheaves in his brother's face with a crisp rattle. "It is the mark for softness."

They bickered as siblings were wont to do throughout time, throwing each other into an unbecoming light, and yet Geneviève would have given anything for a sibling, for a bothersome younger sister with whom to bicker. Her aloneness had been so complete, sibling arguments would have been much preferred to the encompassing silence from which she never found escape.

Eliodoro gave Giuseppe a scathing look. "I may be younger than you, but I am not a child. Of course I know what it means. I read this language better than you could ever hope to."

"Blasphemy," the older brother roared, pale face turning red. "I am . . . you are . . ." He sputtered with anger, spittle flying from his mouth. "I . . . you . . ." His eyes bulged. "Mother always loved me best!"

Geneviève threw a hand upon her mouth before the bubbling burst of laughter escaped, her shoulders bobbing in silent mirth.

"Come, you two, desist with your bickering. They are serving us now, and it is a glorious meal indeed." The raven-haired, dapperly dressed hautbois player rushed by them, a nod and devilish smile for Geneviève as he sashayed past her as well.

Though not an expert on courtly love, she was quite sure from his gait and demeanor that neither she, nor any other lady at court, would be his type of lover. Geneviève cared little of such preferences and smiled back, further entertained by his adroit and effective handling of the brothers and their sibling squabble.

"Did he mention food?" Eliodoro spun round to follow the way of the passing musician.

"I believe he did." Giuseppe dropped the sheets of music onto the top of the spinet, they and the argument forgotten at the mention of victuals, tossed aside like gnawed bones.

The brothers sauntered away, a cohesive unit bound by their appetites. As they passed from her sight, Geneviève at last allowed voice to her soft laughter, enchanted by the small vignette performed as if for her amusement alone.

"I have gone to heaven and glimpsed my first angel."

Geneviève twirled round. Raymond stood frozen, a goblet in each hand, a worshipful expression upon his handsome countenance.

"You are magnificent when you smile." He approached and handed her the cool chalice full of burgundy wine. "You should endeavor to wear one more often."

Geneviève accepted the refreshment, feeling the moist condensation forming upon it, smelling the ripeness of the fruity beverage within. She lowered her head bashfully to sip at the full-flavored liquid.

"If tonight is any indication," she said, summoning the courage to look at him over the rim, "I am quite sure there will be plenty of occasions to smile."

"My only hope, then, is to share them with you." Raymond clinked his goblet upon hers, and gestured to the door. "Come, let us take a stroll. I'm in need of fresh air."

Geneviève followed, grateful as well to escape the warm, stuffy atmosphere of the great hall. Stepping through the glass and iron framework of the door, the coolness rushed to greet them, the brash sound of riotous reveling dying away, replaced with the season's first cricket songs, the low hoot of an owl as accompaniment. He led her to the stone railing of the small patio abutting the building and overlooking the vast courtyard a few steps below.

"Tell me, Geneviève, what do you think of king and court?" Raymond leaned over the balustrade, resting his forearms upon its hard surface. "It must be quite a change from the quiet life you've always known?"

Geneviève rested her back against the railing, looking up at the palace looming into the star-studded night sky, stone behemoth pale in the twilight. "Indeed it is. It is everything I had ever imagined, and so much more than my aunt had told me," she said, her excitement undeniable. It may have been François's court, the man upon whom all her animosity fell, but it was a resplendent and glorious court, and her eagerness to be a part of it was genuine.

"And the king, what think you of him?" Raymond rose, turned, and took a step closer. He stood no more than a few inches from her now, and she felt his thigh brush against the skirt of her gown, felt his intense scrutiny on her face, and smelled the wine-dipped sweetness of his breath.

She stole a glimpse of him, strikingly beautiful in the diffused light of the torches scattered about the courtyard. Titillated by his nearness, a quiver stirring in her belly, she guarded her words and their meaning with utmost care. "Why, he is the very picture of generosity and munificence. Truly the greatest king the world has ever known."

Resting her hip against the railing, she dared to face him, a test of her resolve in her quest as well as in her womanhood. She smiled her small grin, tempered as it was with a morsel of courage.

Raymond threw back his head and laughed, a spring breeze picking up his golden waves and sending them out behind him. With one hand, he grabbed his goblet and tossed it back, draining it of the remaining wine. The other he placed upon her waist and gently rubbed at the curve he found there.

"You are a true courtier, Geneviève. You have been taught well."

His face lowered, filling her vision, blocking out all other sights. A sudden humming filled her ears. Her lips parted, surprised at his forward gesture, incited by more than a speck of desire. Geneviève wanted his kiss, had thought about one such as this through many a lonely night. It was her due; was not the mercenary allowed the spoils of war? Enveloped in the cool air, she felt the warmth rise up her body and blaze upon her cheeks.

Raymond's lips grew closer, full and moist, creeping toward her with agonizing slowness, until at last, mercifully, touching hers with the softness of the wafting breeze. Closing her eyes, Geneviève languished in the feeling, allowing the tip of his tongue to explore the edges of her mouth. Daringly she leaned closer, feeling the tips of her breasts brush against his hard chest. Her head swam with the pleasure of it.

Geneviève heard the low, feral groan from the back of his throat.

With swaggering abruptness, he flung the goblet from his hand; it clanked upon the stones of the courtyard with a harsh clang. With both arms he pulled her roughly to him, smashing their bodies together. His lips became demanding, crushing hers. With little grace, he shoved his tongue into her mouth, forcing it farther and farther open, as if to gag her.

Geneviève brought her hands up to his chest, no more thoughts for the pleasure of its hardness, and tried to push him away, but the effort was futile. She opened her eyes, cringing at the evil, mocking intent so clear on his features, the handsome swain now a gargoyle. With ill-disguised brutality, he grabbed at her breasts, pulling upon her neckline, tugging it farther and farther down until the air scathed her skin.

The arm swung round as if released by a catapult. Her hand, fisted and tight, connected with his face. The sound of crashing bone and flesh rang out, eerie in the stillness of the night.

"*Salope!*" he roared, thrusting her away, bending at the waist as he held his throbbing face in his hand. "You bitch! What are you doing?"

It had been no gentle rebuff, no lady's slap of propriety. She had struck him as a soldier would strike down his enemy, weaponless combatants facing each other with bare fists upon the battlefield.

Geneviève looked down at the end of her arm, at the balled fist and the knuckles white with rage, a fury threatening to overwhelm her. Geneviève was frightened, not of him, but of herself.

"I . . . you . . ." she sputtered, releasing the clench with a shake of her hand, feeling the pain upon her skin and knuckles for the first time. "You had no right—"

"*Tais toi!*" he barked. "Leave me be. There is not enough money in the world for such abuse."

Mouth agape in horror, chest heaving with ragged breath, Geneviève watched him stalk away, unsure if she should follow, if she should try once more to make amends. But, in truth, she could not imagine what she might say. True, he had no right to abuse her, to take such liberties so soon in their acquaintance. She had accepted his kiss, but that was not . . .

Her thoughts trailed away, brushed aside like an annoying insect as his words came back to her.

There is not enough money in the world for such abuse.

A puzzle lay in the midst of this moment; it hovered on the hazy edges of her thoughts, but the truth eluded her. Her head screamed with the fullness of the night . . . the food, the drink, the king, the dancing, and now this. A tidal wave of crushing emotion surged against her. She had but one thought—to return to her room and the sanctuary she would find there.

໑ 5 ໑

Such sickly plant may bloom awhile,
Beneath the sun of royal smile.

—John Thomas Mott, *The Last Days of
Francis the First, and Other Poems*

Geneviève thought herself lost—the faces she passed, the winding corridors she tread—none looked familiar. She rushed and hurried through the dark and deceitful path of an impenetrable forest, stone walls looming over her like colossal trees, and she feared she would flounder forever through the blackness. She turned yet another dimly lit corner, one she was certain she had trod before, and there, standing with a group of other white-capped girls, stood Carine. Never had Geneviève been so thankful for the sight of anyone.

Catching herself, she bit down hard on her relief, rubbing her face as if to wash it clean of emotional residue. She raised her chin, slowing her pace to one befitting a lady of her stature. As the bevy of maids bobbed, she gave them a curt nod and grabbed with veiled desperation for the door Carine held open for her.

Before the portal closed behind her, before the ease of escape found her, Carine rode in on her wake.

"*Ça va*, mademoiselle? How are you?" she asked, a lilting, singsong greeting. "Have you had the most splendid night? We all heard of the incredible entertainments. We peeked in at one . . .

mon Dieu, what have you done to your hand?" Carine hurried across the last few inches separating them, taking Geneviève's right hand in hers.

Perched on the far side of her bed, bracing herself against its softness, Geneviève looked down at the hand she had used upon the baron's face. With unearthly stillness, she studied the raw knuckles, the drops of drying blood where the pale skin had split.

"Silly me," she said, not one iota of silliness in her voice. "I scraped them upon the wall as I danced. It was all in great fun, I assure you."

Carine graced her with a glance of ill-disguised confusion, fetching a cloth from beneath the ewer and basin. With a tender touch, she patted the offensive gashes. Geneviève closed her eyes at the coolness upon her abraded skin.

"I will fetch some camphor from the infirmary. I will return in a trice." Carine made to rush from the room, intent on her mission, but Geneviève called her back.

"Not tonight, Carine, but many thanks. I will keep it wrapped in this cloth. What I need most is some rest."

Her appeal so genuine, Carine at once capitulated.

"Of course, mademoiselle. Let me help you."

The woman began the process of removing her mistress's gown. Detaching the sleeves from the stomacher, Carine took extra care as she guided the heavy material over the chafed hand. Untying the laces came next, Carine at Geneviève's back; the slipping of satin ribbons through eyelets broke the silence. The laces removed, Geneviève turned round to allow Carine to remove the bodice.

The paper fluttered out from between bodice and shift, swirling to the ground like a leaf falling from a tree.

"What is this, mademoiselle?" Carine bent down and retrieved a small, folded square of parchment. "Did it fall from your gown?"

"Give me that." Geneviève snatched it from her maid's hand, cupping it protectively in her palm. A million fabrications came to mind, but all sounded hollow. She chose the silence of a lady, one exempt from explanations.

Carine said nothing more of it, but the smile on her face spoke volumes. Her own romantic fantasies supplied an explanation in the place of hidden truth.

Stepping out of the heavy skirt, Geneviève dismissed her curious attendant.

"*Merci*, Carine. You may leave me now."

"But . . . but, mam'selle," Carine began to argue. "I have n—"

"Have no fear, I can finish myself." Geneviève donned a congenial mask. "I believe I can hear your new friends outside. Go on, enjoy yourself a little more."

Turning the girl away gently but insistently by the shoulders, Geneviève rushed her from the room. "But not too late, mind you. I expect you to attend me bright and early to start our first day."

"Of course, mademoiselle." Carine allowed herself to be hurried along, confusion scrunching her youthful face. She peered at her mistress, brow furrowed beneath her cap, as the door closed in her face.

Geneviève threw her back against the door, latching it securely. Raising two balled, quivering fists, she pushed them against her lips until their quavering—and her panic—receded, waiting with the patience of the fisherman who longs for the outgoing tide. She allowed the steely control to descend upon her, never forgetting the piece of parchment clenched tight in her hand.

On steadier legs, Geneviève removed to the bedside table and the small chair beside it. Leaning toward the flames of the triple-branched candelabrum, she unfolded the paper with the tips of her fingers, revealing its message beneath the pale light cast by the long tapers.

With a gasp of startled discovery, she gaped at the jumble of letters covering the small square. Geneviève jumped up, all action and purpose, snatching her book from the tabletop and the quill and ink pot from the drawer beneath, and rushed to her vanity, thrusting aside the perfume bottles and cosmetics, caring little when a few fell to the floor with a tinkling collision upon the rushes. The sweet, woodsy scent of labdanum burst into the air, released as stopper separated from bottle top. Geneviève noticed its redolence not at all.

The years of puzzles pranced in her mind as she studied the incoherent text before her. Letters, not numbers; this was a substitution cipher, a polyalphabetic substitution, to be exact. She had solved so many of them, revealing the location of each small treat. But where was the key? She could not solve it without the text pair key.

Geneviève picked up *Pantagruel*, the book she had kept by her side through the long journey to the palace. What had her aunt said—what were her exact words? Geneviève rummaged through her memory, tossing aside needless knowledge as though she searched an old trunk.

The book holds the key.

That was it; she remembered it now. Geneviève had known then the book would be part of her ciphering, but she believed she would use it with an alphanumeric code. She rubbed the embossed leather as if coaxing the answer from it with her caress. Opening the cover, she turned page after page, searching for a hidden cipher disk or a pairing table, the crinkle of the paper like the tick of a clock in the silent room, but she found nothing helpful. She turned the last page, her vexation and frustration burning in her throat, ready to slam the book closed and throw it against the wall, when she saw the inscription on the inside back cover: *All is not seen that may be gleaned.*

It was her aunt's handwriting, Geneviève recognized it, but the meaning of the encrypted message was as much a mystery as the woman herself. Geneviève reached out a hand to rub the words, as if to conjure their meaning like a sorceress.

It was the slightest of bumps, no more than a slight ridge beneath the scrawl and the parchment, barely perceptible by the tips of her fingers. Her hand stilled, as did her breath, yet she quivered with the thrill of discovery. Geneviève extracted the small jeweled dagger from beneath her skirt, and bent close over the book. With the delicacy of a surgeon, her bottom lip between her teeth in a trap of concentration, she inserted the knife tip beneath the edging and worked her way around the rectangle of the cover, until she had pried the flap away.

Revealing the small piece of parchment, no more than a three-inch square, she sat back, smiling with relieved satisfaction. Across the top edge of the small square was the full alphabet in its proper order; beneath it another complete alphabet, but in an altogether different configuration.

Geneviève snatched up the message that had tumbled from her bodice, and—

"*Mon Dieu*." She blasphemed aloud, chastising herself with sudden insight. Baron Pitou and his abrasive groping; it was purposeful, yet she had responded like a naïve, sullen child. What must he think of her? Geneviève thumped her elbow on the table and hung her head upon her hand, ruminating bitterly upon her actions.

All she had been taught had changed; her sensibilities, her self-awareness were not as blind as her rage had been. They had taught her to be a soldier, but one of cold calculation. There had been nothing cold about the outrage she had felt, and yet his offense had not been of so great a magnitude. Her response had been as white-hot as a branding iron, nothing of the dispassionate mien she had been taught. She searched deep inside herself; where did such ire come from? Did it fester within her, seething in her secret places? The possession of it had overwhelmed her; she saw it now in hindsight, its ferociousness blinding her like a mask.

The knuckles that had crashed into Raymond's face throbbed; she could only guess at the pain he must be feeling. Geneviève could think no more of this now. She would find the baron tomorrow and make amends. They shared allegiance and she must keep herself in his good graces.

Geneviève turned her attention back to her message; it was but a few lines and she had it decoded in a matter of minutes. She read it once, and yet again.

> *My dear Geneviève,*
> *You are fulfilling your destiny. You have our love and God's blessing. Bring your first message to the monastery. Ask Father Bernard to hear your confession. Remember, you are never alone.*
> *Henry R*

With the page clasped firmly against her chest, the beat of Geneviève's heart thumped through the thin parchment. Time passed unnoticed as she vacillated between reading the missive and holding it dear. It was as if he knew what lay in the depths of her heart, how alone she had felt in the den of the enemy. But his words were a succor lifting her up, setting her on her feet, and placing her back upon her course once more.

Only when she had indelibly etched each word on the pages of her mind, did she bring the two pieces of parchment—the message and the key—and a long, lit taper to the alcove of the cold fireplace. Crouching down, she held the paper over the flame, index finger and thumb holding the tip of a corner as the lick of fire ate it away, as the ashes fell onto the empty grate.

The words had vanished with the paper upon which they were written, but the spirit of the sender held her fast.

But disdain is vice and should be refused,
Yet nevertheless it is too much used.

—Henry VIII (1491–1547)

He stomped about in a pattern of perturbation in the small room behind the great hall, from the windows to the fire and back again. One hand thrust upon one hip, King Henry's round, puffed cheeks held the high color of his agitation, his leather heels pounding out a rhythm upon the hard stone floor as decidedly as the drums of war called soldiers to battle. He did nothing to contain his anxiety, expecting instead for those around him to give him the assurance he needed.

"This does not look promising to me, not at all." Henry stared squinty-eyed at the miniature in his hand, as if willing the countenance upon it to come to life, to see the woman with more clarity. He skidded to a stop before Thomas Cromwell, who met the gaze of his king without a speck of aversion, his thin, stern mouth closed firm.

Cromwell stood one step ahead of the others, a row of lords behind his back, the points of their venom no more sharp than if they held daggers against his flesh. Charles Brandon, Audley, Dudley, and more, all loathed him as a grasping parvenu, as disliked as Wolsey, if not more. Only Cranmer, the archbishop of Canterbury, called Cromwell friend, and yet the elder statesman did little to defend him or his position.

"I assure you, Sire, she is a beauty to behold, though the likeness does her little justice," Cromwell said, holding out his hands in supplication. "Now is the perfect time to ally ourselves with the German princes. Every day they grow more and more suspicious of François and his vascillating. The pope asks him to act against them and they ask him for allegiance, but he is as irresolute on the subject as ever."

"No doubt the pope will see such an alliance as an act against him." Brandon's voice cut with a sharp edge of derision. "Can we afford to further distance ourselves from the Vatican?"

Mumbles of agreement echoed through the chamber, but whether they were in agreement with Brandon's contention or desired to speak against Cromwell, it was difficult to tell.

"Have we had any more word on communications between France and Spain?" Henry asked the room.

"Nothing decisive, Sire," Audley mumbled. "We are sure they are communicating, but the nature of the negotiations remains elusive."

"We know the Italian princess is magnificent to behold," Brandon said bawdily, rousing a low but lewd chorus of agreement.

Henry sniffed with a smirk and a nod. "Yes, of that I am sure. But we have not heard from them, either, have we? You can give me no assurances there?"

The councilors and ministers all shook their heads with obvious disappointment.

"My lord, I can assure you—" Cromwell began, anxious to defend his choice for the king's next bride.

"No one can seem to assure me of anything!" Spittle flew from Henry's mouth as the full import of his anger fell upon the men in the room like a heavy rain.

Cromwell shook his head, jowls waggling. "Your Highness, listen, I beg you. I am certain both France and Spain are courting the

Lutheran princes. We must align ourselves before they can turn them against us."

The king's curved upper lip curled inward, like an angered feral dog. "This is maddening. How can we purport ourselves to be the greatest nation in the world when we have no idea what is happening in it? If you are certain, you will bring me proof."

"Uh . . . yes, yes of course, Your Majesty." Cromwell lowered his shifting gaze.

"Dudley?" Henry called, without removing his scathing perusal from the minister's blotched countenance.

"My lord?" The young, pointy-chinned Earl of Warwick stepped before his king with a dashing bow.

"How goes our project in France? Is she in place?"

"She is, Your Majesty," Dudley assured him with a smile. "And first contact has been sent, by you, of course."

For the first time that day, a genuine grin played upon the agitated king's lips, and the collective sigh of relief was as loud as any alleluia chorus. Cromwell alone quaked with turbulent emotions.

"And she is with the duchesse d'Étampes?" Henry dropped his hands to the sides of his rotund belly as he climbed the steps of the dais and threw himself onto his throne.

"Yes, Your Majesty," Dudley said.

Henry nodded with a cynical but satisfied grunt. "Wonderful. François tells her more than he would ever tell Eleanor. It is our weakness, these mistresses of ours."

A friendship that can be ended,
Didn't ever start.

—Mellin de Saint-Gelais (1491–1558)

The morning sun did not rise as eagerly as did Geneviève, bounding out of bed, calling for Carine and her gown, rushing from her chamber to that of the duchesse with little time wasted on her grooming. Her plan for the day was full, and she refused to tolerate delay or to be waylaid.

She was not the first to arrive at the room of her mistress; already ensconced by Anne's side, Anne's cousins shared in the woman's morning meal and a conversation unaccompanied by any smile. Four other ladies sat about the room, seeing to their books or their stitching.

"Ah, Mademoiselle Gravois, how nice to see you looking so chipper this morning," Anne greeted her with a raised goblet. "Have you broken your fast yet?"

Geneviève dipped a curtsy and rushed forward to the small table in front of the windows, bright with the low sun. Fresh, hot bread crusted with cheese, cold partridge, and apple tarts upon silver plates covered the sage linen, and at the table's center stood a pitcher of hot spiced cider and waiting goblets.

"My apologies, madame. I did not intend to be late for my duties." Geneviève stood contrite by Anne's chair.

"Have not a care," Anne assured her with a dismissive wave. "My troubles found me up before the sun. My cousins and my maids have served me well. Sit down and have something to eat. You look a little green about the gills."

Geneviève did as bid, Sybille handing her a plate and Béatrice a goblet, without request, resuming their conversation as if there had been no lapse at all.

"By the end of the night the bags beneath her eyes were as low as her chin," Sybille intoned, popping a morsel of apple tart into her mouth.

"They were not as low as her breasts," Béatrice tutted snidely. "She really ought to wear a gown more befitting her age."

"Diane is beautiful, no matter that she is ten years my senior, and we all know it, but I care not one whit for her beauty." Anne stared past the women seated opposite her, out the window and into the distance beyond, as if her rival stood upon the lawn alongside the row of dark green yew trees. "I care that the number of her adherents, including the Dauphin's, grows larger every day, and that many in their midst hold the king's ear."

Anne had little fear of other women, women whose beauty boasted naught more than feminine flirtations and feminine wiles. Beside her, they would pale in comparison; a second sun never shone as bright as the first. But this woman, this Diane de Poitiers, was different and it was her novelty Anne feared most, as the sun fears each day to fall to the moon.

Diane's paternity—the daughter of the seigneur de Saint Vallier, who had colluded with Bourbon in the greatest act of betrayal perpetrated against the French crown—fed Anne's revulsion. Her devotion to François would not waver; his enemies were her enemies, as were their enemies' children.

"She is rallying the most devoted to her cause and they are putting more and more pressure on the king with each passing day. Yet I know deep down he is sympathetic to the Lutherans and Calvinists. At the very least he is open to them. His own sister has told me so." Anne pushed her plate away, more than half her food uneaten, rubbing at her head with a moue of pain. "I worry the king is himself unsure of his position on the matter. He is by birth and education a Catholic, and yet he possesses such a liberty of spirit, such a curious intellect, he is like a wondrous child who looks upon all new things with indulgence. How much he is loved for his generous thinking and yet how ridiculed for the same."

Geneviève thought, as did so many of François's critics, that such ambiguousness sounded like the symptom of an irresolute mind.

"Queen Marguerite, the king's sister, is your good and stalwart friend. There you have a potent ally," Sybille placated.

"Yes, and Diane has the constable by her side. It's as if we play a game of chess, each with our own powerful pieces. Who moves them with the most mastery will win."

Geneviève nibbled at her own repast in complete silence, refusing to intrude on the revealing, intimate dialogue, not daring to ask for the jam, out of reach across the table.

"Cousin, you have proven yourself her superior time and again. This latest challenge will be no different."

Anne bestowed a look of gratitude upon Sybille. "How the woman can proclaim she is the most pious while a mistress—and to a man, a child, twenty years her junior—is beyond my understanding. The hypocrisy is so symptomatic of her beliefs."

The door to the chamber opened. Arabelle and Jecelyn curtsied as they entered, the lightness of one in stark relief to the darkness of the other. Geneviève felt her wariness rise with Jecelyn among them, her feelings of unease in this woman's presence, though unexplained, returning with the morn.

"The king comes, madame," Arabelle announced as she approached.

Anne's smile changed her entire face; gone were the wrinkles of worry chasing her beauty away, the gloominess replaced with a glow.

François arrived at the door before Anne stood, but she jumped at the sight of him, crossing the room with a quick, light step. The king wore a simple doublet of brown silk braided in gold, a yellow shirt of linen and lace showing through the slashings. His simple golden chain of office held amber stones that matched his eyes, and in his brown velvet toque he wore a hawk's feather.

He held her small hands in his large ones, leaning down over them, kissing one then the other with the most temperate caress. His eyes held hers fast, bound by unfettered devotion.

"I am off to council but needed a glimpse of you to start my day," he spoke with soft tenderness.

"And my day is brighter for it," Anne replied.

There was little mistaking the affinity between them, one begun well over a decade ago in those festive, heady days following François's release from the Spanish prison. He had chased her then with the same dogged determination as the hound did the fox. How strange it was that they had François's own mother to thank for their meeting.

Louise de Savoy, the powerful woman who had ruled France as regent during her son's captivity, cared little for François's first choice of lover, had indeed made the comtesse de Châteaubriant's existence a misery in her son's absence. Louise had been only too willing to offer him a tantalizing distraction, bringing her new maid of honor with her to greet her son upon his release. Little did Louise realize that she would be introducing her son to the woman who would become—if the heart were the regulator of relationships for royals—the king's true mate. Anne's role at court remained unsurpassed, as did the place she held in François's heart; she lived at the very center of both, the fiery molten core of king and court.

"I will see you soon at chapel?" François asked, brushing her cheek with the back of his hand.

Anne's eyes fluttered at his touch. "Of course." She would be wherever he asked her to be. Unlike the queen, Anne accompanied the king everywhere, his wife in all manner of life, save legal.

* * *

Afternoon rain brought a quiet to the castle. With the king again sequestered with his council, the women were free to amuse themselves in whatever manner they chose. Anne took to her bed, the pain in her head needing the curtains to be drawn and a tincture of valerian root to be ingested. Their mistress attended and on her way to slumber, Arabelle and Geneviève tiptoed from the somber chamber, gently closing the door behind them.

They perched themselves together on one of the vacant settees like birds on a roof, as quiet as the other half dozen of Anne's ladies scattered about the room. Some read, while others, like Arabelle, worked upon their embroidery.

"We haven't had much chance to talk since your arrival, Geneviève," Arabelle said as she threaded her needle with deep turquoise floss. "I believe you said your aunt raised you?"

"*Oui*, she did," Geneviève responded with unintended curtness.

"Were your parents away at court?"

"My parents are dead," Geneviève reported, devoid of emotion. Her foot tapped impatiently upon the floor and her eyes flicked to the door.

"Oh, *mon Dieu*. I am so sorry." Arabelle reached to give Geneviève's hand an affectionate squeeze.

Geneviève shrugged off the sympathy as she retrieved her hand. "It is of little consequence. I was very little when they died. I remember them not at all." She told the lie with ease, pushing down the gurgitation of anger that always rose in her at the thought of her parents' demise, and the man responsible for it.

Arabelle gazed at Geneviève with eyes round with compassion. "I'm sure your aunt was a loving substitute."

Geneviève fought the urge to laugh. "My childhood was all it needed to be."

Arabelle recommenced her work, an expectant silence falling upon them. Geneviève twitched in her seat. It was proper for her to ask after Arabelle's life, to return the interest, but she had no patience for pleasantries.

"Would it be acceptable to return to my rooms?" Geneviève whispered. Her mistress's continued bed rest was a vital part of her plans, and she took extra care not to disturb her. "I would like to write my aunt and tell her I have arrived safely and been welcomed warmly."

"Of course, of course," Arabelle assured her, a furrow of concern forming between her eyes. "There are many of us here to attend our mistress. Have not a care."

"Go along with you," Jecelyn chimed in, her skirts puffing up as she flounced down upon the seat beside Arabelle, in the warmed place Geneviève had vacated. "I will keep her good company. There is nothing you can do for the duchesse that we cannot."

The woman offered a counterfeit smile with her overly sweet sentiment.

With a cynical glance at her, Arabelle urged Geneviève on with a genuine smile. With relief and no pause to examine the reasons for Jecelyn's politeness, Geneviève rushed from the room, rounding down the spiral staircase, skirts flying out behind her, quick steps echoing up into the high stone circle of the stairwell. But once at the bottom, she caught herself up short. Where did she begin to look for a man in a palace she knew nothing about?

It was midafternoon and the court was at its leisure, not at the hunt nor involved in any other sport. Where would a nobleman who was not a member of the king's council be? Where would a gentleman pass his leisure time? The idea burst upon her and she spun left, making a run for the great hall.

Fires burned in the giant stone recesses along the far wall, warding off the chill of a rainy spring day, but the crackle was no more than a simmering undercurrent, the low murmur of a babbling brook behind the cries of the forest animals.

Knights, soldiers, pages, and men of all sorts filled the long wooden tables in the hall, a serving girl or two scattered in the mix.

Their riotous calls ebbed and flowed as cards were slammed down in defeat, as a chess bishop took the life of a queen.

Geneviève stood on the perimeter searching the faces, bearded and clean shaven, common and regal, but she found no familiar features. Granted, her male acquaintanceship at court was limited, but she should be able to find one of the men from her company the previous evening.

A young serving boy passed, a tray heavy with mugs and a pitcher balanced upon splayed hands, frantically serving a court confined indoors.

"Excusez-moi," she said, stopping the young man with an out-stretched hand.

"Mademoiselle?" He tarried but did not halt.

Geneviève skipped beside him. "Have you seen Baron Pitou, or perhaps the marquis de Limoges?"

The young man's face scrunched up with thought. "I know not of a Baron Pitou and the marquis is no longer at court. I saw him leave myself this very morn."

"The baron is new to court," Geneviève explained, hoping to jog the lad's memory with more information, though she had very little to give. "Tall and young, with wavy blond hair and blue eyes."

The boy did stop then, his gaze scanning the vast room. "I'm sorry, mademoiselle. Perhaps you might ask at the stables. The lads there know every man by their horse."

"An excellent suggestion." Geneviève sent him on his way. *"Merci."*

For a few moments more, she searched the sea of faces, but found neither Baron Pitou, the duc de Ventadour, nor any of the men she had met. She left the room as swiftly as she had entered, making for the stables, stopping in her rooms long enough to gather her cloak and throw it about her shoulders. In a determined rush, she found her way through the maze of the palace's first floor and out to the stables.

The smell of wet horse clung to her nostrils and she held her hand against her nose in a vain attempt to hinder its assault.

"Excuse me, young man?" From the door of the vast wooden outbuilding she called to the first squire she glimpsed within, unable to push herself across the boundary and farther into the odorous, airless interior.

"Has Baron Pitou come for his horse today?"

"Who, mam'selle?" The rugged man wiped the dirt and sweat from his face with a ragged cloth.

Geneviève repeated the name and his description as well, but once more she received an unsatisfactory and surprising response.

"I know of no such gentleman. And if he is in residence, he did not come by horse."

With a silent, frustrated curtsy of thanks, Geneviève turned away disappointed.

"Try at the laundry," he called after her. "The maids there might help. They clean all the rooms. Perhaps they would know of your gentleman."

Geneviève waved her thanks, enthusiasm once more ignited by possibility.

Back in the castle, Geneviève begged directions, running the distance of the ground floor to the opposite end. But in the cavernous, steamy chamber, she found no satisfaction. Blazing a crooked path through the rows of women bent over the pools of hot water and scrubbing boards, beneath the tents of drying sheets, she queried them all. But not a one of them had heard of Baron Pitou, cleaned his rooms, nor changed the linens on his bed. It was as if he never existed.

Downtrodden, Geneviève began the trek back to the far wing of the castle and her rooms, refusing to give up the search, peeking into every open door, no matter how intrusive or discourteous her behavior may be.

The colors flashed by—greens, yellows, and blues blurring in her peripheral vision like a fleeting landscape glimpsed from an open carriage window—so vibrant they stopped her in her tracks, and she sidled back, tipping to the right to peek in the open portal.

Wearing a slate-colored smock, the artist caressed the canvas with his brush, the scene he rendered so vivid Geneviève thought to jump in and run across the beckoning meadow.

"Come in, mademoiselle. I would not mind."

His greeting startled Geneviève; she lowered her head, cha-grined like the child caught filching another's toy, but she did not retreat.

"*Bonjour,* monsieur." She stepped across the threshold. Though small, as petite as her own, the room was elegantly appointed with polished mahogany furniture upholstered in auburn velvet, clean rushes upon the stone floor, a warm fire dancing in the small grate, and everywhere paintings lay propped against every available space.

He turned, and his lopsided smile came as warm as any wel-come could be. His long, thin face, topped by a dashing chapeau and punctuated by a prominent, arched nose, was much younger than she expected, unattractive yet affable.

"Good day to you, mademoiselle . . . ?"

"Gravois, Geneviève Gravois." She dipped a fine curtsy.

"Mademoiselle Gravois." He bowed low, his brush waving the air with a graceful flourish. "I am Lodovico Rinaldi Ribbati, *molto lieto.* It is so very nice to make your acquaintance."

"And you, Signor Ribbati."

"Ack, no, no!" The young man turned his twinkling, deep brown gaze back to his work with a shake of his shaggy-haired head. "Call me Lodovico, *per favore.* I hear 'Signor Ribbati' and I think my father is here. It makes me want to run away." He laughed and leaned toward her. "He is not a very nice man."

Geneviève smiled with delight at his candid chicanery. "Per-haps you should paint him unbecomingly then."

Lodovico laughed. "Oh, I have, mademoiselle, many times."

His dexterous movements upon his canvas continued unabated

as they spoke and Geneviève looked on in wonder at such a gift; it was as if he possessed two brains, each able to function on a different task.

"They are very happy to be there," Geneviève said, her eye on the two figures in the background of the resplendent meadow. "I can feel their joy."

He turned with a frown and whined, "You can?"

Geneviève swallowed, floundering at his response, thinking she had complimented him. "Uh, *oui*, but . . . but I like it. It is quite beautiful. But perhaps you endeavor to paint as the other Mannerists do?" she asked, pale brows high upon her crinkled forehead.

It was Lodovico's turn to be surprised, pleasantly so. "Yes, I do. You know of art then." But with a frown, his displeasure returned. "But I'm quite inept at it. It appears I am unable to keep my heart out of my hand."

He waved his brush-brandishing appendage as if angry with it.

"Yes, and those lucky enough to look upon your work feel all that is in your heart. It is a wonderful thing," Geneviève assured him, stepping past the young artist to study the other canvases lined up along the wall, drinking in their colors, wandering to the places they took her.

"*Mille grazie*, Geneviève, but the king has brought me here as a disciple of da Vinci's, and I am afraid I am failing him miserably. He looks for Titian and I give him Brandoni."

Geneviève looked over her shoulder. "Brandoni? I do not think I know of him."

"Precisely." Lodovico stabbed the air with his brush, saffron paint dripping onto the floor. His thin, bony shoulders slumped. "King François is certain to replace me and send me back, back to that father of mine."

Now, more than ever before, the French court studied Italian literature and art. François recruited these artists as tenaciously as a general fills his army. Geneviève bit her lips, stifling her smile, and returned to her new acquaintance's side.

"The king has Rosso and Primaticcio to give him art showing him the true construct of man. He will need you to show him man's soul."

Lodovico's smile brightened his face as if kissed by a ray of sun streaming through a crack in dark and thunderous clouds. "It would take a special talent to paint a man's soul," he whispered with revelation.

"Indeed it would." Geneviève nodded.

He turned back to his work then, and plied his brush with renewed vigor.

"How come you to be at court, Geneviève? I don't believe I have seen you here before."

Geneviève told him her story; it tasted more real on her tongue every time she repeated it.

"Ah, that explains why a beautiful lady with your knowledge of art would not have been at the king's salon. Your aunt has taught you well. And what of literature? Do you know as much there?"

Geneviève gave a one-shoulder shrug. "I love books and have read a great deal. I'm not sure if that makes me knowledgeable, though some may claim it does. I have read the classics, of course—Horace, Ausonis, and the like. And I am very partial to Rabelais's *Pantagruel* of late." She laughed inwardly at her own jest.

"Then you must come when next the king calls us to his chambers. You would enjoy the evening immensely, I am sure."

Geneviève hedged. "I am certain my duties will keep me far too busy for such entertainments."

"Oh no, Madame la Duchesse always attends such evenings, and her ladies with her."

Geneviève remained evasive.

"Rabelais is often there, as are Saint-Gelais and Marot." His voice teased her with such names, like a sleeping mouse taunted a hungry cat.

Try as she might to remain blasé, her eyes widened and her mouth formed a circle of wonder.

Lodovico knew he had her on the hook. "They read from their own works upon occasion. As does the king."

"The king?" Geneviève balked. "The king writes poetry?"

"Prolifically," Lodovico declared. "He would warmly welcome an erudite mind such as yours, especially one accompanied by such a face. You would make a marvelous addition to his merry band of ladies."

Geneviève's expression soured more than a little.

"Oh, do not be misled. I do not mean it in a vulgar manner, though it may sound so."

"My aunt did teach me well, sir, and she taught me to guard myself." She had felt an instant camaraderie with this young artist— an intuitive, though questionable, reaction. "The reputation of François and his court was part of my education. There are so many pitfalls for a young, inexperienced woman in a life such as this."

Lodovico put down his brush and palette, and took Geneviève's hand in his paint-spattered one, though she gave it with great reluctance.

"Like you, I heard the stories of a young, hedonistic king, and I have no doubt they are true." His unwavering gaze pierced her. He would give her his testimony for the sake of François as well as their budding friendship. "But you must understand. For one man he has lived two separate lifetimes. There was the life that came before . . . before Queen Claude died, before the war, and before the loss of his beloved son and daughters. Then, he lived for mindless pleasure, when egotistical conquest was his main pursuit. Grief, captivity, a distasteful marriage—you can concede such tragedies may change a man."

There was no denying the passion of Lodovico's admiration and conviction, or the truth of his recitation. Less than four years ago, the death of the king's daughter Madeleine had come within months of his son's, the Dauphin François, children he cherished like little else in his life. His existence was wrought with disappointment, in denial of its initial promise. As news of François's hardships reached their ears, Geneviève and her aunt had become convinced the man received everything he deserved.

"To be sure, a man of heart would change with such suffering." She had only to look at her own soul to know how disaster altered life. But she believed not at all that François was a man of heart.

"Do not think me naïve nor blind. Much of the court remains bent on the steadfast pursuit of pleasure, but life close to the king is as changed as he. You do believe me, don't you?"

Geneviève found a smile to reassure him. "I think you are a kind man who would not put a new friend in harm's way."

Lodovico heaved a sigh of palpable relief. "Then you will join us one evening?"

"It will be my pleasure." An evening of intellectual conversation with such masters as Marot and Rabelais would be a thrill, as it would to be again in the company of Lodovico, and Geneviève didn't bother to pretend otherwise. She felt nothing of conquest or duplicity from him, nothing more than an offer of true friendship. Wearing heavy layers of deceit, she could see others with startling nakedness.

"I will leave you to your work then, with the promise of another pleasant encounter." Geneviève curtsied.

"I look forward to it with great joy." He bowed, picking up his tools as she retreated from his chamber.

Geneviève pondered the man's obdurate opinion. He was not a stupid man; she was sure he believed wholeheartedly in François's reform, and perhaps he was correct. Yet change though he might, a murderer could never wash the blood off his hands; such a stain would last forever.

❧ 8 ❧

It's good fishing in troubled waters.

—Peter de Blois (1130–1203)

His morning ablutions and dressing done, performed as always in the presence of his many courtiers and distinguished guests, his shirt presented to him by the most honored among them, the king crossed the salon from bedchamber to council chamber, eager at last to begin the day.

Yesterday's rain had evaporated and the warm sun of May set the world to tingling; he avowed he could see the lavender and yellow primrose grow, the splendid aromas bursting into the air like an assault on the senses. An afternoon in such redolence would be sweeter with a morning well spent.

The *conseil étroit* consisted of no more than thirty or forty men at one time; François's inner council, they were privy to all matters of his reign, unlike the *grand conseil*, the large judicial body governing the nation. With these men—these chancellors, marshals, admirals, and the grand master—François decided on matters of state and finance, making the crucial decisions with their guidance and input. The final pronouncement was his alone to make, having established a strong authoritarian rule from the onset of his reign. As his predecessor had begun, a greater centralized nation existed in France than at any time before.

All rose as the king entered the chamber; others followed him, taking their places either at the long table dominating the room, or along the wall if their rank did not allow the privilege to sit. Swords clanked in scabbards hanging jauntily from waists, and the room filled with the noise of armed and medaled men settling down.

François looked with a bright smile upon the rows of men attending him. "The duchesse d'Étampes and I are pleased to announce the continued success of the Collège de France."

As he expected, a rousing cheer followed his pronouncement.

"The curriculum is stupendously diverse and vast." He leaned forward, gaze intense, one long finger pointing out to punctuate the air. "We cannot make informed decisions unless we are completely informed, and it must be information without prejudice."

Not a man among them doubted he referred to the narrow religious views expounded at the Sorbonne. While men like Chabot and Du Bellay reveled in the king's decree, others—most notably Montmorency and the king's son Henri—swallowed back their displeasure.

"The readers are scholars from around the world," François continued with enthusiasm. "Italy, of course, but also Spain. England as well. Politics shall have no place in education."

More than a few men looked sideways at their neighbors, surreptitiously suspicious of such forward thinking, unsure if this was a wise course. But not a one spoke his reluctance aloud.

"We must also continue to strengthen our nation's language. I have spoken to Ronsard and Du Bellay. Their work continues and must be supported." François tapped the table as if plucking out a merry tune, inordinately pleased with himself and the events.

The small group of writers referred to as La Pléiade included Pierre de Ronsard and Joachim du Bellay, a prestigious assemblage committed to enriching the French vernacular and to developing French literature, replacing Latin with the king's language, one derived from the old *langue d'oil* of the Île-de-France and northern provinces.

As the king made his pronouncements, the majority agreed with sycophantic uniformity. These great noblemen searched for their personal power, adrift in a world no longer ordered by the feudal construct. Unable to secure their rank by warring amongst themselves, they were reduced to currying favor and blindly supporting the king for advancement. It made for far less acrimonious council meetings but a weak, disenfranchised aristocracy.

As the discussion of the new college and literature subsided, Montmorency cleared his throat, the braying of a donkey amidst the dulcet bleating of sheep.

"I am afraid we must discuss the events of two nights past."

Any affability in the room evaporated, doused as decidedly as a drenched fire, taking with it François's smile and geniality. Another church had been desecrated, more statues defiled, as Protestants demonstrated their disgust with the Catholics.

François glared at Monty; men close enough noted the twitch of the king's jaw muscles beneath his stubble-covered skin. "The authorities have dealt with the offenders. There is no need to discuss the matter more." He leaned back in his chair, crossing his long legs at the ankles and his arms across his barrel chest.

"I respectfully disagree," Monty replied stubbornly. "Yes, the *gendarmerie* squelched this particular upheaval, but there is certain to be another, and another."

Admiral Chabot harrumphed. "You are quick to predict such dire events."

"It is no prediction," Monty countered querulously. "It's been happening for years and will continue to happen until we enact laws to stop it once and for all. And when the Catholics take it upon themselves to act where we do not, what then?"

"The constable is right," the Dauphin spoke out, shocking many with his contribution. Since the death of his brother, Henri had taken his place at his father's council table, and while it appeared to many that François tried to heal the long-standing fissure between him and his son, Henri seemed unready or unwilling to forgive. A father's contrition could come too late for absolution, and affection could be merely an affectation of political necessity. On every issue they argued, though the Dauphin preferred to keep his opinions to himself in public, while furthering his own agendas behind the scenes. "It is our duty to set boundaries."

"They must learn to co-exist by themselves," François interjected, ignoring his son's annoyed expression. "Do we oversee every minor argument among our children?"

"This is no minor argument, Your Majesty. The Calvinists are bent on violence."

"It is the hedonism and greedy lifestyle of the men of the church which encourages their anger and their loathing." Chabot snapped like a guard dog at the end of his leash.

Monty spared him but a sidelong look and continued his plea to the king.

"The behavior of the heretics cannot be allowed to continue unabated." He slapped his open palm upon the tabletop, more and more of late the voice of dissension among the king's men. Some wondered if his growing allegiance with the Dauphin and his mistress was not fraying his bond with his king and childhood friend. Others surmised Montmorency's animosity toward the duchesse d'Étampes formented his falling from favor.

"There is a fine line between heretic and humanist," François countered, conversation tipped with warning. "For every man who perpetrates an act of violence, there are ten others wanting nothing more than freedom of thought."

"But, Your—"

"No more, Monty—no more on this today." He held up a hand, his face closed and implacable. "I will ask for daily reports on any further acts of aggression and will revisit the topic if need be. Will that suffice?"

"It would seem as if it must." Monty sat back from the table, a withdrawal no less obvious than if he had walked from the room without dismissal.

"*Bon.* Then I would like to ask if there is any further thought on the last communication with Spain."

"There have been no outward signs of friendship, Your Majesty," the cardinal de Lorraine spoke up, but the acrimonious delivery of his report came as no surprise to anyone; his aversion to Spain was widely known.

"It is true, *Majesté.*" The warbled reply came from none other than Galiot de Genouillac, the seventy-five-year-old hero of Marignano. Warrior, *chevalier de l'ordre de Saint-Michel,* and diplomat, François had made Genouillac the *grand écuyer de France,* one of the greatest officers of the crown; his advancing age did nothing to detract from the value of his advice. "The emperor is much less decisive than the king of England, though I trust neither at this point."

"But the Germans are forever asking for your assistance, Your Highness," Monty reminded him. "They soon must be answered."

François's gaze lit once more upon Genouillac, whose long, thick white beard brushed against the elder man's chest as he shook his head.

"I will make no pledge until I hear from Charles. His response will determine my own." François rubbed at his high forehead; the joy with which he had entered the room but a few hours ago had dissipated, his troubles clear in the shadows now clinging so tenaciously to his long face.

The morning's bells began to peal and he could not have lent an ear to their sound with any more relief.

"It is of the hour, messieurs. I have the need to pray on these matters."

"I knew tonight would be a joyous occasion."

But two steps into the salon of King François, Geneviève's new friend Lodovico merrily accosted her. Out of his artist's smock, clad in a maroon velvet doublet and trunk hose, he looked like the scrawny scarecrow of a wealthy farmer. Taking her hand, he tugged her toward the room's far corner, beyond the mass of humanity clogging the center of the room, and the few empty chairs waiting there.

"But . . . my duties." Geneviève leaned away, trying to keep her place beside Arabelle in the entourage of the duchesse.

"Have no fear, Geneviève," Arabelle assured her, with a smile and a bob for the artist. "Here we are free to follow our own pursuits as long as we keep one eye on our mistress should she need us. I can think of no one better with whom to spend your inaugural evening at the salon than our Lodovico."

The artist doffed his toque and smiled at Arabelle. "I have always said you are as sweet as you are fair, mademoiselle."

Arabelle curtsied. "And you are as silly as you are talented."

Her friends laughed and Geneviève found it hard not to breathe the jovial air between them. She capitulated to Lodovico's insistence and followed him on the winding path amidst the courtiers, huddled together in groups of twittering tête-à-têtes and jovial jocularity, or perched upon couches, partaking of the many delicacies served by pages armed with overflowing silver trays.

No other reception room in the palace boasted such splendor as the king's salon. Rich tapestries covered the walls and a tightly woven rush mat cushioned the floor. The finest furniture, the most glittering golden sconces, and the grandest sparkling silver candlesticks enveloped the visitors in its palpable embrace of luxury.

Lodovico plopped Geneviève into a tawny golden armchair, grabbed two full goblets from a passing page, and flopped into the matching seat beside her, his plain face bubbling with amusement in the light of the triple-branched candelabrum set upon the claw-foot table between them. The sweetness of the beeswax melded sensuously with the deep ferment of the burgundy.

"Did I not tell you what a magical place this is to be?" he asked with the unfettered enthusiasm of a child. Leaning toward her, he held a pointing finger discreetly against his chest and aimed it into the heart of the room. "Look there, at the balding man by the king's side. That is Rabelais. And the round-eyed, bearded man who relinquished his chair for the duchesse? That is Marot himself."

The three men held the center focal point in the room, perched on intricately carved wing chairs placed before the hearth. All the room's activity pulsed from this assemblage, the core of its vibrant energy, and though everyone held their own small conversations, they did so with an ear to their king.

Geneviève tried to appear impassive, but her training failed her in the face of such great artists. "Who else?" she urged her guide on. "Who else is here?"

Lodovico gave her a conspirator's smile. "Well, there are Chabot and Montmorency, of course; Charles and Marguerite; and a member or two from the House of Guise, but they are only here to spy."

Geneviève choked on her own spittle.

"To spy?" she managed to croak.

"The Guises belong to the Dauphin and Diane," Lodovico announced matter-of-factly, and once more Geneviève wondered how deeply the chasm ran through the king's court.

"Will they not be here tonight?" Geneviève asked. "The Dauphin and his mistress?"

Lodovico raised one brow with comical skepticism. "It is a rare occasion indeed that they would spend a night of intimate entertainment with the king and the duchesse. Once upon a time, perhaps, but not very often of late."

Geneviève's gaze roamed over the room. "I cannot help but notice that there are far more ladies than gentlemen."

"Oh, sì. It is the way the king is most comfortable," Lodovico agreed. "After all, it is how he spent his childhood."

Raised by a strong, authoritative mother and a doting sister, François grew up surrounded by other women as well, his illegitimate half sisters whom his mother raised as her own. In the garden of the king's life, he was the central stalwart fountain and women the flowers encircling him. If his years as a libertine had abated, his appreciation for feminine beauty and company had not.

"He is finely attuned to the feminine sensibility but not softened by it." Lodovico looked upon François with undeniable admiration. "He acknowledges all of their worth without losing any of his own."

Geneviève kept her beliefs to herself; she thought it imprudent to remark upon François as a master manipulator who mayhap found it easier to prey upon women than men.

"Is it not said that even a stone has a divinity?"

The outlandish statement rose above all others and the appreciative laughter that followed turned all attention in the room to François and his companions.

"Ah, so it is true," Marot chided the king in jest. "You *have* been reading the Cabala."

François chuckled. "I have been reading everything. Scholasticism allows us to study the beautiful words of the Bible, humanism reveals what the ancient civilizations of Greece and Rome have to teach us, and mysticism opens us up to possibilities beyond our world, beyond our very beings."

The room rumbled with a wide array of reaction. Astrology, alchemy, all fell under the purview of a modern day prince's study, including the Cabala. Geneviève longed to ask Lodovico if such words on another's tongue would not be labeled as heresy, but she kept her mouth shut.

"Yes," Rabelais agreed, rubbing his stubble-covered chin. "A stone may have divinity, but only a king can grant nobility."

The king shook a finger at the poet, but not without an accompanying smile. "I can make a noble, but only God makes a great artist."

"But you are an artist yourself." Accomplished as one of the great *rhétoriqueurs à la cour de France*, Marot had a great capacity for flattery, especially for his king. "Why do you not read us something of your latest work?"

"Oh yes," Anne agreed prettily. "Please do, *Majesté.*"

"I would embarrass myself before such talent as we have here tonight," François obfuscated with deftness, a nod for the men beside him, a wide-armed gesture to the room at large. "Here we have the best of poets, painters, and musicians. Mine is not a talent but an unrequited hope."

As if his words were the magic required to call them forth, a small gaggle of musicians rushed in through the door. At once, Geneviève recognized one of the Italian brothers. Eliodoro looked harried as he flung one arm to the back of the room, directing his quartet where to set up their instruments, while the other remained at his waist.

"Ah, here is what we need." François acknowledged them with a spirited call, pleased for the distraction, as if genuinely reluctant to speak of his own work. "Some music."

"Why *were* you so late?" the spinet player hissed as he passed Eliodoro. "We should have been here an hour ago."

Eliodoro sneered. "My damn brother, curse the day he was born. He took all my clothes. These are his. They are all I could find, but they do not fit."

"You jest?" The other musician stifled a snicker behind his hand.

"Why would I joke of such a thing, Massimo? Look."

Here the drummer held up both hands and, without any movement or prodding, his pumpkin-shaped hose began to slip from his slim hips.

Massimo's eyes bulged as he cackled with laughter. Eliodoro looked sheepishly about, forcing Geneviève to turn her attention away.

"I hear Alberto da Ripa will be playing tonight. He is an exceptional lutenist," Lodovico said as the musicians began to play.

But Geneviève heard little of his words or the music; her attention returned to the king and his new discussion.

"I know you are frustrated by the silence of Spain, Your Majesty." Chabot had replaced Marot by the king's side as the poet stepped away to mingle with other guests. "I will ask our ambassador to endeavor to get a reading of the emperor's mood."

François propped an elbow on the arm of his chair and put his chin in his hand as he leaned toward his friend and adviser. "It is indeed preying upon my mind more and more. He does neither of us any good by vacillating."

"There is no kindness waiting for you on that shore." Anne spoke her mind with certitude, her opinion as valued by the king as that of any other minister. In truth, she was one of his most valued advisers, often taking her own chair in council chambers.

Lodovico prattled at Geneviève, music played behind her, laughter rang out around her, yet she focused all her concentration on the king and his conversation. Her aunt had been clear: Any news of France and Spain was of the utmost concern to King Henry. So excited by what she heard, the hand with which she held the goblet trembled, and the liquid within rippled like a pond touched by a strong breeze.

Dipping her lips for a drink, she braved a look at the group before the hearth. Her throat closed with a whispered gasp as her gaze locked with Anne's, as the duchesse raised a finger and crooked it at her.

Geneviève placed her goblet upon the table. "My mistress beckons," she said to Lodovico, and stood.

"Of course, *cara mia*, I will keep your seat." He smiled at her as if nothing were amiss.

On shaky legs, she crossed the room beneath Anne's unwavering stare, her ears pounding with the sound of her own heartbeat as she approached the king and his royal entourage.

"Monsieur le Roi." Anne put a tender hand upon François's forearm and he gave her his immediate attention. "I do not believe you have met my newest attendant, Mademoiselle Geneviève Gravois."

The king turned his gaze upon Geneviève, and though his eyes held a smile, she threw herself into the deepest curtsy, hiding her face with her posture and tilted headdress, as if he might see the truth of her with one glance.

"You honor me, mademoiselle," said the king with a lilt to his deep baritone, believing her deep obeisance equaled her respect. "Arise."

Geneviève thought she would be sick, and the horrific image of her vomiting upon the king of France sobered her. She rose with as much grace as she could muster and looked her enemy in the eye, her hatred lending her the strength she needed so desperately.

"Well, what a beauty you are," François remarked, and more than a few of the men around him tutted their agreement. With elbows propped and hands clasped across his velvet- and jewel-clad abdomen, he leaned forward with squinty-eyed intent. "Your eyes are violet, mademoiselle," he said, as if he told her something she knew not.

"*Oui, Votre Majesté,*" Geneviève replied, refusing to quail under such acute scrutiny.

"I have seen such eyes once before." The king no longer looked at her, but somewhere—some time—else. "I was a young buck, no more than a lad, and she was a magnificent beauty. Montlhéry, the Baroness de Montlhéry. Odette, I believe her first name was."

Geneviève stared at him, slack-jawed. "My grandmother."

The king laughed, but not in the least harshly, a stark antithesis to the piercing stare Anne bestowed upon her.

"Why such a surprise?" the king asked. "Do you think me too feeble to remember my youth?"

"No . . . no, of course not, Your Majesty," Geneviève stammered with a spirited shake of her head. "I am surprised a relation of mine should be remembered at all."

The king's faraway look returned but now with an irrefutable sparkle of pleasure.

"Such a beauty as hers, and yours, is hard to forget. I believe the day I met her was the day violets became my favorite flower."

A thousand emotions coursed through Geneviève's veins—repulsion, fear, hate, trepidation—she fought to respond as a devoted courtier.

She dipped him her deepest curtsy once more. "You honor me and my family, Your Majesty."

It was the perfect rejoinder and the room twittered with talk of the wonderful new courtier arrived at the palace.

"More wine," Anne demanded of her.

"Of course, madame." Geneviève rushed to do her mistress's bidding, fearing the duchesse's wrath; she had never forgotten their first conversation nor the woman's warning, and she had no wish to lose her important position at court because of the king's philandering eye. She returned to Anne's side in a flash, a jeweled goblet full of the sparkling yellow wine the duchesse preferred.

"*Merci*, Geneviève." Anne took the goblet from her hand, but took no sip. "You may leave us."

Geneviève bobbed and turned to leave.

Chabot leaned in closer to the king and whispered something in his ear. François's expression turned sour.

"I have no money for war. If pushed, we cannot afford to respond."

Her instinct was to stop, to plant herself firmly at the royals' feet and hear every word they next spoke. But she had received her dismissal, and, by force, must leave, or else incur Anne's ire. Pulled in two directions, one foot turned one way, and one another. She tumbled with the grace of a crippled ox, toppling into the deft hands of Admiral Chabot himself.

"Are you all right, mademoiselle?"

"Yes, *merci*. My apologies, monsieur." She braced herself against his strong arms and recovered her balance. "*Pardonnez-moi.*"

The aging soldier released her without another moment's thought, and Geneviève rushed away, certain Anne's sinister glare punctured her back. She retreated to the anonymity of the far corner and her chair beside Lodovico.

"You did well, my dear, very well indeed. Right up until the part where you almost fell onto the king," Lodovico teased her, brandishing his lopsided smile and rubbing the back of her hand. Her head hung in her other hand and she peered at him through splayed fingers, embarrassment burning her cheeks.

"Do not be dismayed, Geneviève," Lodovico begged her. "You have been forgotten already. Look."

Steeling herself, Geneviève peeked about the room. Her friend spoke nothing but the truth. The courtiers once more chatted boisterously, straining to hear their chatter above the growing din of people and music and clanging salvers as a wave of servants served a late supper. Not a one looked at her, not in interest or jest. Her gaze stopped at the door and held, captured with perplexed curiosity.

Two men she recognized—the musician Giuseppe and the hautbois player—and a delicate, dark-haired beauty beside them, leaned over the threshold, their bodiless heads peeking around the door's frame. The men laughed with unrestrained glee; the young girl alone had the decency to hide her mouth behind a long, graceful hand. Geneviève felt a moment's ire, thinking they laughed at her, until she followed their gaze and saw the true target of their mirth.

Giuseppe's brother conducted the small group of musicians in the corner, one hand marking the rhythm upon his tambour, the other leading the instruments through the song. With no hand left to keep them in place, his oversized hose slipped farther and farther down his legs. At the moment his genitals were about to be exposed to the room, he missed a beat, bending to retrieve his wayward garment, cheeks burning redder than his brother's blood, which he longed to shed.

Geneviève felt the giggle in her throat and the gratitude in her heart. Her anxiety had tried to get the better of her, but at its passing, she knew she had much cause for celebration.

She offered her companion her brightest smile. "Would you get more wine, Lodovico? I believe my goblet stands empty." The delighted painter clapped his hands together. "That's my girl." He jumped to his feet. "Let us enjoy all the abundance the king is willing to share."

"We would like the windows opened," the king announced, as the air grew thick with the heat and odor of bodies at play. His desire became instant reality with a whoosh of balmy, fragrant air as the pages thrust open the heavy-framed casements.

The ohs and ahs of the refreshed revelers joined the song of the nightingale.

"I believe we are ready to progress." François slapped his large hands on his knees and a thunderous cheer shook the tapestries upon the wall.

Lodovico jumped up with his own shouts and applause, and Geneviève joined in hastily, confusion stiff upon her forced pleasant expression.

"The court is to move, Geneviève. Isn't it wonderful?"

"It is," she agreed, comprehension dawning upon her as the last day of the condemned man sees the first rays of sun. "More wine. We must have more wine to celebrate."

Lodovico laughed as he filled their goblets for a third time.

Many a goblet they shared, as the gathering lasted long into the night. Anne stayed until the latest possible hour, always by the king's side, always his first and most cherished confidant. Arabelle and Geneviève stayed with her, until only the *gentilshommes de la chambre* remained, many of whom would bed down within the same large room as the king, his most intimate companions.

Under Louis XII, such men had been called *valets de chambre*, but the term had become synonymous with servant, and François would have better for his dearest cohorts, elevating them to the same lofty heights he himself inhabited. Commoners now held the posts of valet, but they served him as such, caring for his possessions, fetching for him whenever bid.

The ladies attended the king's *coucher*—the nightly bedding ritual, as convoluted as the morning's *lever*—before bidding Lodovico good night and attending the duchesse at her own preparations.

As the ladies of Anne's chamber watched her servants remove the many layers of her clothing, Geneviève gathered her strength, fortified by the flagon or more of wine she had imbibed through the night.

"I know we are to leave in a day, madame." Her voice croaked like an insulted frog. She cleared it and continued. "And I fear I have been remiss in my obligations."

Anne didn't open her eyes, as if already asleep, having little to do with her own preparations for bed. "You have done nothing untoward, Geneviève, fear not."

"No, madame, I meant my duties to my aunt." Geneviève felt the curious gaze of Arabelle and the probing stare of Jecelyn as they extracted a nightgown of pristine linen and lace from the garderobe and moved about the room, dousing most of the candles in the privy chamber. "I promised her I would visit the monastery and write her all about it, but I did not realize my stay here at the château would be so fleeting."

"Indeed, we are beginning the season's journey earlier than normal," Arabelle offered kindly. "It has been such a fair and warm spring. We've had no more than specks of rain. The roads are passable much sooner this year."

"It is incumbent upon us to do as our king bids." Jecelyn directed her bitter rejoinder to Anne's other attendants as she smiled with charm at her mistress. The two young servants paid little heed to the conversation as they finished their chores.

"Of course, I meant no disrespect." Geneviève forged onward, abrogating any offensive inference. "I wonder if perhaps I could visit the monastery tomorrow."

"There will be much to do in preparation," Anne replied, and Jecelyn smiled as if claiming victory.

"I understand, madame. I need no more than a half hour's time to see enough to describe it to my aunt." Geneviève refused to surrender, more determined than ever. "Little time to spare to fulfill a dying woman's wish."

Anne sighed, dismissing the servants with a flick of her delicate, lace-rimmed wrist. "Very well, but no more."

Geneviève curtsied quickly, a smile for Anne and Jecelyn as well. "*Merci beaucoup*, madame. You have my promise."

They tucked their mistress in bed with the tender attention of a mother to her child and crept from the room, each woman taking the last of the burning candles with her.

In the presence chamber, they bid good night to one another and to the sisters, whose evening it was to sleep with their mistress.

"Do you need me to show you the way to the monastery?" Arabelle yawned behind a hand.

"Or perhaps I may ask the duchesse if she would like me to accompany you," Jecelyn offered, though not as well-intentioned.

"I thank you," Geneviève replied, with a nod for Arabelle. "But I am sure I will find the path. We mustn't let our duties suffer any more than they should."

Arabelle grinned with a circumspect, sidelong look at Jecelyn, who had nothing further to say on the matter.

Geneviève slammed the door behind her, dismissing Carine with few words of explanation. The king's plans had sent her into a panic. She had to get a message to her sovereign, had to let him know all she had gleaned this day, but there was so little time. She had chased away Baron Pitou with her monstrous rage, the one man who could have helped her. She knew of but one outlet for messages and it was here, at this château. Geneviève felt as if the hemp connecting her to England was fraying one thin, ragged strip at a time; if she did not get a message out, the tenuous bond might well be severed.

From her notions box she retrieved her ink pot and quill, gathering her book and a small sheaf of parchment from her bedside table, her mind whirling with her message and how she would transmit it. She would use an alphanumeric code, not willing or able to spend the time on a polyalphabetic substitution and its key. She threw herself onto the rushes before the hearth and added two sturdy logs to the low-burning embers. She would swelter in the added warmth, but she needed the light. She stripped herself down to her shift, discarding the satin saffron gown, and set to work.

Every word of her message would become a set of three numbers, indicating the page in the book, the paragraph on the page, and the word in the paragraph. She had so much to tell—the cracked condition of the French court, François's fiscal inability to make war—she had to fill both sides of the small square of parchment with the squiggle of numbers. And as she painted the paper with her communication, her smile grew. Not the restrained, half gesture she offered to those of the court, but a true smile that dimpled and plumped her cheeks.

In her mind, each set of numbers and the word it represented was a gift she offered her king. She imagined him as he read it, his blue eyes sparkling beneath his red hair. She saw him smile; she felt his approbation—that which she so desperately craved—as if he were in the room with her.

Untold hours passed as she constructed her message with the slow translation into cipher. She rolled her head on her neck, squeezing the taunt shoulder muscles with one ink-stained hand. Her body ached with exhaustion as the candle shrank and the quivering light cast lengthening shadows upon the stone walls, but never had she felt more purposeful.

Rich in hope and poor in earthly gold . . .
Leave me my hope; without it I am cold.

—Alain Chartier (1385–1433)

The cacophony began before the sun flung itself over the horizon. Rugged men barked orders, silver plate clanged against copper pot, females fussed over folded linens. The palace was a beehive of frenetic activity as hundreds of people prepared to move the king and his court.

Geneviève made her way past the stables, where the grooms trained the horses to carry women, watching as they taught the stately beasts to lower themselves on their front legs as though they knelt in prayer. She sprinted through the symmetrical gardens with their well-manicured lawns, the grass turning from light spring bud to deep myrtle, and the blossoming shrubs and hedges with their plump, moist buds. Beauty in hand, soon to be abandoned for that which lay upon the horizon.

She shivered as she stepped into the looming shadow of the monastery. Built hundreds of years before the château proper, there was nothing grand or opulent in its architecture. The slate square spoke of the somber, pious existence lurking behind the cold, anodyne façade.

The shrieking hinges of the two-story wooden door announced

her arrival far better than any bell. She bent forward and then leaned back as she put the weight of her body into the effort to open it and the sound echoed into the empty, vaulted-ceiling foyer, returning back to her—a faded wail—as though in warning.

Her contracted pupils were useless in the dim recess. She jumped back from the ominous beings welcoming her: crouching gargoyles and floating specters with ravaged faces. Geneviève closed her eyes, forcing her breathing to slow. When she opened them again, she distinguished the statues standing guard at the inner door and the saintly tapestries adorning the walls.

She skulked forward through air thick with cloying incense and melting wax. Crossing into the inner sanctum, she stopped, unsure which of the three passageways before her to choose.

"How may I help you?"

The hushed, benevolent greeting struck her with the force of a pummeling ax and Geneviève jumped, hands balling into fists, heart slamming against her chest. The cassock-cloaked man had materialized out of thin air. Her fearful gaze found him in the shadowed corners of the vestibule.

Geneviève swallowed back the rush of fear. Focused observation returned as her panic abated, and she glimpsed the smooth-skinned face of a young man within the gloom of his hood, pale hands clasped together at his hemp-bound waist.

"If I may, I would care to make my confession," Geneviève whispered, afraid to shatter the unearthly silence holding sway over the monastery.

"I can hear your confession, my child," the man replied, though Geneviève thought him younger than she.

She curtsied with great pious humility. "If it would not be too great an imposition, I would choose Father Bernard to hear my sins."

Geneviève bit her tongue as she realized her blunder. For all she knew, this man was Father Bernard; that she did *not* know him could reveal her subterfuge.

The young monk bowed. "I will call him. Please wait in the confessional." His long, pale-skinned hand and scrawny wrist escaped the bell sleeve of his cassock as he gestured through the door before her. With the same stealth with which he had appeared, the man evaporated through a side door, leaving Geneviève to wonder if she had imagined him all along.

Passing through the curved archway, the chapel of the monastery opened before her. On the left side of the transept, beyond the long rows of pews, Geneviève spied the closet of the confessional, a boxlike room within this room, much like the stool closets in the palace, save for the crosses carved into the door. Multicolored rays of light streamed in through the stained glass windows of the clerestory's eastern wall, the ochre and blue like a bloody sky upon the oak pews and granite floors.

Geneviève entered the tiny chamber. In the middle of the room stood one lone chair. In each of the four corners yellow glowed from single-candle torches, the only light in the windowless chamber. There was no screen concealing the chair, there was no *priedieu* before it. Geneviève would face her confessor, knees upon the hard stone floor. She had not practiced the sacrament of confession often in her childhood; perhaps her aunt had known it for the hypocrisy it was in a life meant for such iniquities. Geneviève had found neither succor nor blessing in the act.

She perched herself on her knees, gathering beneath them as much of her lavender gown as she could to cushion them. Thankfully, no more than a few minutes passed before the door opened behind her and the man took his place in the hard, armless chair, the wood squeaking in protest as it accepted his corpulence.

"God is listening, my child." The voice warbled as the words puffed out on thin breath.

Geneviève, head bowed from the moment she had heard the priest enter the room, stared at the floor, brows knit in a wrinkle upon her brow. Was she to give a true confession? She was here to deliver a message, not to bare her soul to this man. But the heavy silence bade her to confess, having interpreted no signal that the priest would receive her covert communication. Geneviève had no choice but to turn the hard vision of truth inward upon herself.

"I have lied, Father." Geneviève spoke the ironic honesty. Up to this day, she had committed few acts that God would call a sin. What she held in her heart—the anger and the hatred—were something different altogether, but she felt sure any deity that did exist would absolve her for just cause. "I have thought ill of others."

"Have you regretted your feelings?" the man asked with little more than a mumble, as if he channeled the voice of God from the far distance of Heaven.

The memory of Baron Pitou, the scourge on his features after her fist collided with his face, the fruitless search for him the next day, came to Geneviève's mind.

"*Oui*, Father, I regret it most sincerely."

"Then God will be merciful and forgiving."

Geneviève lowered her head, scavenging the recesses of her mind for something else to report to this man. One day she may have more to say, may hope to cleanse herself of a bloody stain, but perhaps not. Far more important than the state of her immortal soul, she scavenged her mind for some word that would work magic; some unknown code to turn this priest from confessor to conspirator.

As if knowing she had nothing further to add, the priest leaned over her, chanting the Latin that would absolve her of her sins, forming the cross above her head over and over with a beefy hand.

"Pray tonight, my child," he told her as he sat back. "Pray to our God in the words of His Son and you will feel His benevolence."

Geneviève dared to look up then. The tent of his dirt-colored cassock hid the obese body, not a speck of the chair visible beneath him. The heavy jowls of his ashen face hung far below his chin, and vein-laden lids covered his eyes. The dismissal was clear.

Geneviève staggered to her feet, wanting nothing more than to grab the man by his rounded shoulders and shake him until he told her what she wanted to hear. But his closed expression brooked no argument, welcomed no discourse. On the verge of angry, frustrated tears, she quit the confessional chamber, unable to stop herself from slamming the door behind her.

The clatter echoed through the rafters and she stalked off down the long aisle, balled fists quivering by her sides, feeling the harsh stare of Jesus upon her back from His place on the cross at the head of the nave, but caring little for its denunciation.

"Won't you give alms for the poor?"

Geneviève scuttered to a stop, nearly toppling forward as her feet came to a halt, but her body continued on with momentum. Bracing herself on the curved, carved end of a pew, she turned round.

Standing in the middle of the nave, the mammoth man who was Father Bernard stood, casting a shadow large enough to rival that of any of the chapel's statues. In his age-spotted hand, he held out a small, slotted basket.

Her innards quivered with excitement as she took those few steps back toward him.

"The poor are in greater need than ever. I will personally see your donation put into the proper hands."

Geneviève's eyes fluttered closed in a moment of relief. Here at last was the prayer she had come to hear. She grappled for the small drawstring bag dangling from her wrist, grabbing the small folded square of parchment and a few coins, and dropped them all into the basket.

"Thank you, my child." Father Bernard's cloudy blue eyes, as pale as a winter's sky, caught hers and in them, she glimpsed a smile.

Geneviève took his hand and bowed over it.

"I am most privileged to do my part."

❧ 10 ❧

Distance is nothing;
It is only the first step that is difficult.

—Madame Marie du Deffand (1697–1780)

"You can do this, Geney. Give it another try." Arabelle looked up at her friend, her eyes wide and hopeful yet not without a shadow of doubt. She stood poised by the horse's side as if ready to catch Geneviève should she tumble from the mount, again.

As instructed, Geneviève wrapped her right leg around the front of the curved pommel while her left leg hung down the side of the horse. She held the reins in her gloved hands as if she hung on to the very thread of life. Already the bruises on her derrière ached where it had collided with the gravel of the stable courtyard, and she had no wish to feel its brutal hardness once more.

Never had she ridden a horse upon a sidesaddle. In all the days of her youth, she had ridden astride while hunting, hidden by the forests surrounding her aunt's modest château, or upon a *sambue*, as befitting a lady. Though there was little control while upon one of these chair-shaped platforms, which forced the rider to remain turned outward, body perpendicular to the horse's own, she had long since mastered the art of traveling upon one. To learn a new skill set, here and now, as the entire French court surrounded her, as spiteful courtiers gazed upon her, was proving a frustrating chore.

With mumbled words, Geneviève cursed the name of Catherine de' Medici. Though the Dauphin's wife was a pale presence at court—and only a desperate one to be pitied, at that—she had brought the newfangled means of feminine saddlery to France and therefore was deserving of all of Geneviève's curses.

Three short blasts of the heralds' horns sent her already skittish mount into spasms, and Geneviève reached down and clung to the chestnut mane.

"Hold still, you ungodly beast," she hissed, ignoring the mare's angry neighed response.

"We must hurry," Arabelle urged. With agile deftness, the graceful woman stepped into the stirrup hanging from the lowered horse's back, and launched herself upon the saddle. "It is time to leave. We must take our place with Anne at the front of the line."

"If you cannot ride, then perhaps you should find room in one of the wagons, Geneviève." Jecelyn rode up beside them, her body barely moving with the little effort it took her to stay upon her mount, a formidable stallion as black as her hair.

Geneviève clung tenaciously as her horse sidled haphazardly, jerking her long head up and down as if to pull the reins from Geneviève's hands, nervous at the feel of a diffident rider upon her back. As she found herself about to tumble to the ground once more, Geneviève shifted her hips beneath herself, her teeth grinding with the effort, and found a modicum of balance.

"I am obviously not so experienced as you in riding playful beasts." Geneviève pulled left on the reins, and her horse came alongside Jecelyn. She found herself received in her enemy's world, and with such acceptance came a return of her natural fortitude. "I do believe I have the hang of it now," she said with an innocent batting of her eyes.

Ignoring Arabelle's snicker, Jecelyn's thin red lips cut a swath across her pale face. "Make sure you keep in that saddle, Geneviève. Rest assured, if you fall, you will be left behind. The king waits for no one. Do I not speak the truth, Arabelle?"

With a cluck of her tongue and a snap of her rein, she cantered off, caring not about any response.

Arabelle shrugged one shoulder at Geneviève. "Unfortunately, she is correct. When the king is on progress, he is a determined traveler. The duchesse will not look kindly upon you if you cannot keep up."

Urging her sorrel mare forward, the creature's blond mane flapping with each step, Arabelle led Geneviève's horse, who followed instinctively.

"Why does she dislike me so?" Geneviève asked with a jut of her chin toward Jecelyn's back.

"You are a new beauty at court," Arabelle said as if the few words sufficed.

Geneviève shook her head. "I don't believe it. Beauty comes and goes at court as readily as the wind. You are far more beautiful than either she or I. There must be more to it."

Arabelle's fair face bloomed beneath her jaunty mauve riding hat. "*Merci,* Geneviève, but perhaps your beauty, like hers, is so unique, so . . . exotic. It threatens her more."

Another three horn blasts rent the air and Arabelle spurred the horses on faster, rushing past the long row of wagons, carts, and carriages lining the lane around the palace.

"There is no more time for this now. We leave!"

Geneviève held on as they rushed forward, not slowing their pace until they could see the standard-bearer who would lead the enormous contingent onward, the gold fleurs-de-lis bright upon the blue background of the banner, the gold tasseled ends dancing in the breeze.

A few short lengths behind the herald, the stately form of the king—resplendent in a royal blue velvet riding costume—sat upon his enormous stallion, his *gentilshommes de la chambre* fanning out behind him like the gaggle that followed the lead goose.

In their wake, the queen's carriage marked her place, though she would remain hidden and protected from the harshness of nature for the duration of the journey. Figuring prominently between husband and wife—literally, as she did figuratively—rode the duchesse d'Étampes, surrounded by the colorful petals of her entourage, the dashing cavaliers who forever flocked to her side, and the king's merry band of ladies.

As Arabelle and Geneviève took their place with these chirping ladies, Geneviève turned in her saddle, gaze following the never-ending line of travelers behind them. As far as the dusty brown trail weaved through the yellow-green countryside, so did the line of people, horses, and wagons.

With each progress—the movement of the court through the kingdom during times of good weather—the king brought his entire household with him. His family, his advisers and courtiers, and every attendant and servant required to keep him, and them, happy . . . confessors and carvers, secretaries and surgeons, barbers and bread carriers, sumpters and spit-turners, and everyone in between. All fed, clothed, and housed at the expense of the king and those he taxed.

François brought with him not only the people he held most dear, but his most cherished possessions as well. Carts piled high with trunks and chests filled with every necessity, took their place in line; from the most inexpensive trinket to invaluable artwork, all were packed and guarded with the greatest of care. Behind them were the animals attached to the court. Those required for food—the oxen, sheep, cows, and chickens—and the king's pets—his dogs and birds, and his lynx.

It took more than a hundred men to coordinate the move, to arrange the transport of what was tantamount to a small-sized village, and close to twenty thousand horses to pull or carry. In charge were the *fourrière*—the animal keepers—and the *maréchaux des logis*, who supervised transportation of furniture, allocated lodgings, and issued lodging permits. Under the reign of François I the court had grown to nearly ten thousand, and with each progress, regional courtiers came and went, taking the opportunity to look in on their properties, and any lonely wives left behind.

Geneviève stole a moment to look back at the château as it fell away in the distance. It had been her home for such a short time, less than a fortnight, and yet it had served her well. The kitchen coffers echoed now with emptiness, the castle's latrines overflowed. The skeleton staff remaining would clean and scrub, refresh and replenish, preparing for the court's return, whether it be in two months or two years.

As a youth, François had traveled more extensively, though such nomadism was not a result of feudal survival but a desire to keep more apprised of his realm's condition; it had also afforded the sportsman ample opportunities to hunt in a variety of regions. Times of royal progresses were dictated by the seasons, with little movement taking place during the harshness of winter or in the thaw of early spring, when the roads were little better than quagmires.

The sun was a glowing orb, midway into its day's ascent, and the château was no more than a fading memory on the retreating horizon, and yet Geneviève's legs ached with the effort to maintain her posture upon the sidesaddle.

"We are for Blois, *oui?*" she asked Arabelle, her stalwart companion. Arabelle stayed close to Geneviève's side, though the social occasion of a progress might tempt her to go elsewhere, as if ever ready for her new friend to tumble to the dusty road.

"Blois, yes," Arabelle answered.

"Château de Blois." Geneviève mused on her childhood lessons. "The home of the king's first wife, Claude. That is what, two days hence?"

Arabelle looked upon her friend with pity. Geneviève's discomfort was plain on her face and in the tight set of her jaw. "Four, most likely."

"Four?" Geneviève's eyes bulged.

Arabelle did her best not to smile, nodding silently in sympathy as she watched Geneviève's shoulders slump, reaching out as her friend slipped in the saddle and scrambled to right herself once more.

Hearty male laughter played a duet with husky feminine mirth, and Geneviève tossed a quick look over her shoulder. By the Dauphin's side, rode the regal Diane de Poitiers . . . astride. Geneviève stared with ill-concealed envy at the woman's comfortable position upon her horse—one leg braced on each side of the saddle—not bothering to conceal her jealousy, in spite of Arabelle's laughter.

"There are few women who dare defy convention as does Madame de Poitiers," Arabelle said with a hint of grudging respect.

"After making a thirteen-year-old child her lover, there is little left in her reputation to be defiled." Jecelyn had joined them, though why she chose their company was beyond Geneviève's ken. Beside her rode a fiery redhead, freckles visible beneath her mask.

Many of the women had donned the nondescript masks as the journey began, those once worn by every female courtier and noblewoman as they traveled through the countryside, believing their anonymity brought them a modicum of safety. These days most women offhandedly dismissed the danger, opting instead for comfort.

"Mademoiselle Gravois?" The redhead beckoned with the smoothness of cream and the warmth of the summer sun. "I have been longing to make your acquaintance."

Geneviève did her best to make an obeisance as she jumbled along.

"Geneviève, this is the marquise de Moissons," Arabelle politely interceded.

"*Enchanté,* Marquise," Geneviève said.

"Oh, please, call me Solange. And if I may, Geneviève?"

"It will be my pleasure," Geneviève replied. There was nothing disagreeable about this woman, and yet she had come with Jecelyn. Geneviève felt a tingle of trepidation in her legs, as if she had sat overlong in one position.

"Solange is the king's cousin. They grew up together," Arabelle explained. "She is a longtime member of the king's favorite group of ladies."

Solange laughed. "And now you have revealed my age, though I wear this mask to hide it."

The other women laughed with her.

"Yet you are as youthful as ever," Arabelle assured her.

"Which cannot be said for La Sénéschale, no matter how much gold she drinks," Jecelyn sniggered.

"Gold?" Geneviève and Arabelle chorused dubiously.

"Indeed." Solange leaned toward them. "It is rumored she has gold melted and drinks it regularly to retain her youthful appearance."

Geneviève's eyes snaked sideways to get a better look at the infamous beauty. Diane's thick blond hair swirled in a high pile upon her head, perched upon a long, elegant neck. Her blue eyes shone with intelligence and humor. Though sturdy of build, there was a regal stature about the woman, as if she could joust with a king and bed him with equal proficiency. Again, the flirtatious laughter with which Madame de Poitiers awarded her lover hovered toward them upon a playful breeze.

"She is certainly making up for all those years with that ancient husband of hers," Jecelyn said without looking back at the couple.

Geneviève turned back round, head bobbing ungracefully as her horse ambled along the rutted road. "Was he much older than she?"

"Much?" Jecelyn's black eyes bulged, incredulous. "Forty years! I cannot imagine the fortitude she must have mustered to bear him not one but two daughters."

Geneviève pictured shriveled, age-spotted hands upon her own youthful ivory skin and shuddered.

* * *

"Leave me to my misery," Geneviève groaned as Arabelle pushed her out the low door of the inn and into the brightly lit town square. Much of the village population had come out to see the royal entourage off, but whether it was to bid them a fond farewell or cheer them away, it was difficult to discern. "I cannot go on. I will spend my days here in this small burg. I will wither away like the untended roses of my aunt's garden."

She had never felt so weary. Three days in the blasted contraption of a sidesaddle and her body ached. Three long days of new acquaintances and endless conversations, and she had naught to show for it—not a speck of worthy information—nothing save an ache in her body that ran deep to the bone.

"Come along, Geney." Arabelle urged her as she would a child she must force to do a chore, with a touch of a mother's indulgent impatience, using the insufferable nickname Geneviève had not the strength to reprimand her for.

They approached their horses, and once more Arabelle lofted onto her mount, as if she were the most graceful of dancers and the horse's back was no more than a foot high. Geneviève stood beside her horse with an expression of contempt for both animal and friend. She knew she must lift her leg to begin the climb, but no matter how her brain goaded her limb on, it refused to capitulate.

"Yipe!" The high-pitched squeal escaped her flapping lips without thought as strong hands encircled her waist and tossed her up into the saddle with the ease of a petal on the breeze. Geneviève grabbed the pommel to keep herself from sliding off, but she needn't have bothered—the hands held her firmly in place. She followed the powerful yet graceful fingers, up the thick arms encased in leather, to a face alive with mischief.

"At your service, mam'selle." The gallant smiled, revealing rows of perfect white teeth and a set of dimples the likes of which Geneviève had never seen.

"I . . . um . . . *merci*." Geneviève could not decide if she was thankful for his assistance or insulted by his unsolicited familiarity. She could not deny how grateful she was to be upon her horse without the least bit of exertion, nor could she refute the power of that smile.

Humbly doffing his toque to his waist, he bowed. "Sebastien du Lac."

There was something modest in both posture and tone and Geneviève dismissed her apprehension willingly.

"Geneviève Gravois, monsieur. I *am* grateful for your assistance. It would seem I am not the equestrian I thought myself to be." There was little need to be falsely self-effacing; she had indeed been humbled by the last few days of travel. All those years upon a horse, riding beside men, hunting with equal if not better accuracy, had given her an arrogance that, though not apparent, was no less a part of her.

Sebastien smiled at her honesty. "There is nothing weak about needing some assistance now and again." He bowed once more as Arabelle drew her horse up beside them, her gaze mesmerized by his handsome countenance. "May I ride with you ladies for a while?"

"It would be our greatest pleasure," Arabelle assured him, and Geneviève did not doubt her sincerity for a moment. His beauty was indeed potent—a day would pass more swiftly with such a view—but the fear of falling upon her face in the dust before such an Adonis was an unsettling prospect.

It was not long before other women joined them, more than on any other day. The herald gave his blast and the procession moved. Though the fourth day of a long journey, there was a lightness to the assemblage, and the courtiers' raucous laughter chased the robins from their nests. They would arrive in Blois this afternoon and the promise of arrival brightened all their spirits. The roads soon became a congested clog of courtiers, a cavalcade stretching out a kilometer or more, forcing all other travelers to give way. In their wake lay veritable devastation as they consumed or confiscated any stored food or goods from the villages and towns along their route.

They rode on as the village gave way to flat farmland, fuzzy with feathery green carrot fronds and alive with waving, young wheat. Farmland fell away to forest and the stately trees formed the gothic arch of a cathedral over their heads, the sun sneaking through to dapple them with spots of brightness.

"I am thinking this is your first progress, Mademoiselle Gravois?" Sebastien remained as close as the jostling horses allowed.

"It is, sir," Geneviève replied, ignoring Arabelle's pixie grin from the other side of their escort. "I arrived at court but a short time ago."

"You will find it gets easier each time," he encouraged, one dimple peeking out at her.

Geneviève felt a stitch in her side, the cost of her efforts to stay astride. "It is hard to imagine at this juncture," she said testily but shook off her irritability, wanting nothing more than to be distracted from it. "Have you been at court long, monsieur?"

He nodded and his jet black hair caught the golden morning light. "Two years, mademoiselle, having served in the Garde Écossaise for the duration."

Geneviève's grip tightened upon the pommel, the bones of her knuckles protruding hard against the now bloodless skin. Of all the positions at court, how ironic that he was a member of the Scottish Guard. Formed in the previous century by Scottish noblemen who came to France to protect King Charles II, these prodigious archers had protected the life of the king of France ever since. They were his bodyguards and they would willingly— gladly—sacrifice their lives to save his.

"You are a member of *les gardes du corps du roi?*" she asked, and though she attempted mere curiosity, her voice squeaked with incredulity.

Sebastien's gaze flicked away from her tight grasp on the pommel. "It is my great honor, though I am often called upon to guard his favorite, as well. So it would seem that we shall see much of each other."

Geneviève gave no reply. She stared at him as if she looked through him.

"Does that displease you, mademoiselle? Is it me, or soldiers in general you do not like?"

His candor roused Geneviève from her ruminations. "On the contrary, I have great respect for soldiers—warriors of all kinds. You could say I feel empathy for them." She offered him her half smile innocently. "And I do not know you well enough not to like you. On that score, we shall have to see."

She tossed her words at him playfully—recognizing the foreign tongue of an accomplished courtier in her statement—and he accepted them eagerly, both dimples making an appearance.

Mischief sparkled in his eyes the color of a twilight sky. "You offer a challenge, mademoiselle, and I have yet to meet one I could not conquer."

Geneviève smiled coquettishly back at him, unsure where her façade ended and her truth began, the line between role and self already becoming blurry.

Their party increased in number. The bevy of women attracted by Sebastien's company, in turn attracted more of his fraternity, and they were soon rife with the protection of many a Garde Écossaise. It was a merry party indeed that rode behind the king and his favorite, cresting a small rise under a high sun and scuttling puffs of pristine white clouds.

A young gallant riding at the head of the group, Arabelle by his side, pulled up on his reins, spinning his mount back upon its rear legs.

"Messieurs. Blois is ahead. To your posts."

All eyes scanned the horizon and saw a group of low buildings perched on a distant rise.

Sebastien sidled his horse beside Geneviève's palfrey and

reached for her hand, loosening her fingers' rigid clasp upon the pommel with a throaty laugh. Pressing his lips to the smidgen of flesh revealed between glove edge and lace cuff, he captured her in his gaze.

"I thank you for passing the morning with me, mademoiselle."

Though she found little air, Geneviève replied, "And I thank you for your help. I am pleased it put me upon my saddle and our friendship upon its path."

"Friends, are we?" He waggled his brows preposterously. "Then may I call you Geneviève?"

He spoke her name with the lyrical accent of a Gascon; upon his lips, it became a song, but she knew it for the courtly music it was.

"At your pleasure, Sebastien."

He bent over her hand once more, put heel to horse's flank, and rode off.

"That's all you will ever be to him, you know—a friend. He likes his women thinner."

Geneviève slumped at the sound of Jecelyn's voice. It had become the noise of all things irritating. Geneviève's bottom ached, her arms throbbed, her hands felt swollen in her gloves. Her feelings for Jecelyn were much the same as those for Sebastien; neither friendship nor acrimony could be trusted, for there was little another person could promise her as an absolute. As taught, as ingrained in her, she would rely on no one but herself. Many words came to Geneviève's mind, powerful sentiments sure to wound Jecelyn as proficiently as she could with her dagger or her bow, but she didn't bother. She had no time for romantic intrigues and she had no energy for constant petty skirmishes. Geneviève allowed the woman to pass without argument or response. She had much bigger game in her sights.

Before the city's gateway, decorated with the king's emblem—a crowned, fire-breathing salamander—the most prominent citizens waited to greet him, resplendent in their colorful finery. On either side of the vast portal, musicians announced the king's arrival and a thunderous cheer whooshed through the waiting populace.

A festival of grand proportion awaited the king upon his entry into the fair city of Blois; a celebration in sight and sound. What had been a sedate and simple event for King Louis XII a half century ago had, for François I, become a splendid sacred spectacle, tinctured, of course, with the flavor of political undertones.

With great fanfare, the king climbed up on the dais, smiling as he stood beside the *prévôt des marchands* and exchanged vows long before the tail end of his convoy gathered round. Geneviève lined her horse up beside the duchesse d'Étampes and Arabelle at the very front of the stage. Anne smiled with pride at her lover as he played his part in the ceremony with great drama.

"I swear to maintain the town's privileges. . . ." The king raised his arms in a wide, benevolent gesture.

"We swear to obey our king and no other. . . ." The *prévôt* spoke for his people, bowing before their sovereign.

The gifts offered, the king receiving the keys to the town in exchange for a small casket of gold coin, François took his place upon a litter draped with a rich canopy and was carried off in procession upon a carefully prepared route through town. He waved regally with a jaunty tip of his head to the never-ending line of villagers festooning both sides of the wide main thoroughfare.

People hung from every window, waving and cheering, calling to the king and wishing him long life. Sand and rushes covered the road, hiding the black line of sewage running in a squiggle down its gutters, obliterating its offensive fumes. Instead, the air was redolent with the great feast being prepared—mouthwatering aromas of freshly picked fruits and sweet pastries. Great tapestries hung over the façades of many of the grand homes as if the entire town had become a magnificent mural.

"Madame." Arabelle raised her voice to be heard over the cheering, and pointed a finger toward a particularly large and colorful tapestry. The scene depicted the king at hunt, splendid in his hunting costume, blazing colors of a fall landscape behind him. By his side was a beautiful woman, green eyes sparkling with the thrill of exertion, cheeks blooming like a budding red rose. The artist had captured Anne's beauty—her inner fire and passion, as well.

The duchesse smiled and shared her silent pleasure with the ladies riding beside her. Geneviève craned around in her saddle, squinting at every tapestry they passed. Not a one displayed the image of the queen.

As they neared the cobblestone square, the festivities set forth for the king's entertainment gained momentum. Upon columns of whitewashed wood made to resemble those of the Coliseum, young women dressed in togalike costumes stood, each one holding up a letter of the king's name. Between the columns, the town's principal families enacted *tableaux vivants*, and François was obliged to stop before each and watch the short play in its entirety. In one, the king defended peace against the duke of Milan and the Swiss bear. In another, he appeared as Hercules, gathering fruit in the garden of Hesperides.

The head of the procession pulled out of the wide square, the road leading to Blois winding like a ribbon before them, snaking through the small, lush forest surrounding the palace. It would take hours for the remainder of the king's assemblage to pass through the town, but the citizens would continue to perform for their benefit, until the very last of the royal household passed by.

Of all Geneviève had seen this day—the sumptuous decorations, the human sculptures, the amusing plays—the castle rising up before her took her breath away as nothing else had; it was perhaps one of the most famous castles in all of France. Built in the thirteenth century by the counts of Châtillon, it had become a royal possession through the duc d'Orléans. Most importantly, it was the very spot where Jeanne d'Arc had received her blessing from the archbishop of Reims before successfully engaging the English in Orléans.

Drawing ever nearer to the front of the four-storied palace, the two sets of loggias dominating the façade—one above the other and over them a third floor of square openings—Geneviève was reminded of delicate lace. She prayed her siege, though covert, would be as successful as that of the most holy of female warriors.

❧ 11 ❧

Opportunity makes the thief.

—French proverb

The two women sat in the cool shade of the tall yellow yew trees, their somber, lace-trimmed gowns spread upon the marble bench. The queen and the Dauphine looked more like someone's nursemaids than the ruling feminine royalty of the land, their solitude adding to their inconsequence. Catherine had sent their ladies off to pick flowers, assuring them they would call if need be.

"Do we dare?" Eleanor whimpered at her companion. The queen's hood sat far down upon her small face, sienna hair hidden beneath the bleak, unembellished taupe material.

Though more than a decade the queen's junior, Catherine's fortitude belied her years. The jeweled headdress Catherine wore did little to become her, pushed far back on her head, the frizzy, straw-colored wisps of hair straggled out in all directions, her hard, chiseled features appearing all the more sharp. "What do we do that is so egregious? We do no more than postulate what we have seen."

"But no doubt it was on king's business," Eleanor said sheepishly.

Catherine hopped to her feet, kicking at the ground as if she were a child denied. "Yes, yes, and Diane does the Dauphin's business and we are naught more than the forgotten wives. Well, I am tired of being inconsequential, and I will stand it no more."

The women's gaze held, seeing each other for what they were. One the sister to the king of Spain and the Holy Roman Emperor, the other the niece of a great pope, and yet they were as feckless as lint that blows in whatever direction the breeze sends it.

"I have had enough of this barren life," Catherine sniped, though whether she referred to her inability to birth an heir or her own disenfranchised existence, it was hard to fathom. "I have heard great wisdom from a new acquaintance. Michel de Nostredame is his name. His words tell me to master my destiny. I say we begin to take back what is ours."

Eleanor murmured an unintelligible response; she had not the fire of Catherine. Though she craved her husband's attention, at her age she had grown accustomed to her fate. She could not deny her fear of Anne's growing power; the woman had flaunted it in her face every day since her marriage. Perhaps there was some satisfaction to be found in taking the duchesse down a peg or two.

"Very well, then." Eleanor rose to stand beside her friend, two women so unalike, drawn together by a mutual purpose.

"*C'est magnifique.*" Catherine clasped her hands together in satisfaction. "Tell the tale to your most loquacious lady, as will I. We will let them do the rest."

She took Eleanor's petite, cold hand and wrapped it in the crook of her arm. They strolled together through the garden, unremarkable against the flourishing pink peonies and yellow tulips—no more than shrubbery among the petals.

"That witch!" The duchesse d'Étampes threw open the door between the privy and audience chambers. It crashed against the wall, bounding back and closing itself with a slam. Sybille and

Béatrice rushed through in Anne's wake, missing the rebounding wood by inches. "I will see her dead this time, I swear it."

Her hysteria echoed through the chamber, the heavy tapestries covering the stone doing little to muffle the guttural cry. Arabelle and Geneviève jumped to their feet, their embroidery falling to the ground, forgotten.

"What is wrong, madame? Are you harmed?" Arabelle implored with a tremulous voice before the warning gaze of the sisters could stop her.

"What is wrong?" Anne raged with dripping sarcasm, as if Arabelle offended with the query. "Poitiers. She is all that is wrong with the world."

The duchesse stomped from cold hearth to sunlit windows and back again, kicking pillows across the room, toppling furniture with one-armed thrusts, possessed by her anger.

"Another rumor is feeding the court," Sybille whispered to Arabelle and Geneviève, as if she had not already told her cousin the nasty tale and wished to keep it from her. "This time they are saying she is bedding the baron de Beauville."

Another screech filled the air, brutal and harsh, like a banshee's wail. "Beauville, of all people. He is a disgusting old man, more than thirty years my elder. I would rather suffer the plague than allow his spotted hands and crusty lips to touch me."

"Please, madame, you m—" Béatrice began, but it was no use.

Anne dug in her heels, throwing up a hand toward the door as if Diane de Poitiers stood in its frame. "She may like the feel of thin, cold skin upon her, but I do not." She turned her finger upon the women who stared at her, speechless, as if for a moment they believed the blasphemous gossip. "I am faithful to my lord and master. I am the king's greatest love, and he mine. It shall always be thus . . . it shall . . ."

Her last words trailed off, breaking to pieces like thin glass against stone; threatening tears diluted the sting from her angst. She threw herself into a chair.

"My mystic, Geneviève. Bring me my mystic."

Geneviève's jaw came unhinged; her violet eyes darkened as they bulged from her pale face. "I . . . uh, madame, I—" She took two hesitant steps forward, ready to confess her ignorance.

"Come, Geneviève, come."

It was a command, given by Arabelle as she grabbed Geneviève's hand and yanked. Geneviève's body jerked along without recourse.

"Where are we going?" Geneviève hissed at her once on the other side of the outer door.

Hushing her with a finger to her lips, Arabelle led her farther down the corridor, tiptoeing upon the small square tiles as if in escape.

"We are going to bring Madame Arceneau to the duchesse. Perhaps she will see something to appease our mistress."

Geneviève looked askance. "A mystic?"

"Ah, *oui*. She is one of the best. They say that when Madame found her, the woman produced a sealed document from a locked chest, which described every detail of the gown the duchesse wore at that very instant."

The women rushed onward, heels heavy upon stone, no longer worrying that they would disturb their already agitated mistress. The presence of a mystic at court did not surprise Geneviève; for centuries, royalty sought the advice of seers and, like the wretched sidesaddle, Catherine de' Medici had brought with her the Italians' profound belief in a soothsayer's powers. Now many members of the high court retained their own spiritual guides. Geneviève's aunt had consulted a mystic on rare occasion. Now, as then, Geneviève held little faith in any genuine gift a clairvoyant may claim to possess.

"Well, if she does not 'see' something to cheer the duchesse, perhaps she can pretend," Geneviève quipped as they rushed through the palace.

Unlike the château at Saint-Germain-en-Laye, corridors connected every room and floor of this palace perched on the bank of the river Loire. With the coming of court and the best of late spring weather, the corridors teemed with courtiers.

Geneviève searched every face they passed, desperate to see some kind of sign, any glimmer of recognition that would reveal her next accomplice. In the week since their arrival at Blois, she had learned nothing of use to the English king, but the lack of an umbilical cord frightened her. In her communiqué, she had told King Henry of her travel to the Loire Valley with the court. The progresses of the European kings were well-known, no doubt he would have heard of it even had she not advised him of the move. And yet she had received no dispatch, nothing to inform her on how next to send a message if she had one . . . no Baron Pitou. Geneviève had vowed not to make the same mistake, and she opened herself to new people and new friendships, her persona behaving as her true self never would.

Arabelle led her on a winding circuit to the very lowest floor of the imposing château. With each level they descended, the population thinned, the air thick with deep silence. Staggered snippets of light dotted the long hallway and a few haphazard wall sconces created diminishing yellow circles, like signposts vanishing in the distance. No tapestries adorned the walls; no rushes warmed the floor of stone.

"Are you sure we are in the right place?" Geneviève whispered, afraid to disturb the ominous foreboding of the subterranean passageway, certain she had heard the scurrying of rodents beneath their feet.

Arabelle nodded with confident urgency. "*Mais, oui.*" She knocked on the third door on the left. Geneviève hesitated, pulling up beside the portal and flattening her back against the cold wall.

"*Entrez-vous.*"

The high-pitched command slithered through the cracks of the door. Geneviève felt the greatest urge to pull Arabelle's hand back as her companion reached for the latch.

"Madame Arceneau," Arabelle greeted as she passed through the portal with a quick curtsy.

But as Geneviève made to follow, she screeched to a halt, her feet refusing to move a step more; a sudden twisting in her gut made it impossible to cross into the umbra-filled room.

From the threshold she waited, squinting into the room lit only by candlelight, unable to deduce if there were any windows or if all the windows were covered. She could discern a pale smudge of a face in the distance, perched in a chair at a small round table covered with maroon velvet.

"My mistress bids you to come immediately," Arabelle said resolutely, half hidden from Geneviève by the shadows claiming the room as their own.

"But she was to come to me to—"

"No, not today." Arabelle squelched her reply. "Today you must come to her."

"If it is what she wishes."

Geneviève bubbled with barely contained laughter at the sound of the voice; a piercing, juvenile falsetto, it seemed more appropriate to a whiny five-year-old child than a grown woman.

From the dim recesses of the room came the sound of glass tinkling against glass, shuffling feet crossing to and fro. All of a sudden, Arabelle turned and left the room, the woman right behind.

As the mystic stepped into the meager light of the hall, Geneviève pursed her lips in confusion. Madame Arceneau was a petite woman, her slight form overwhelmed by a hooded black cloak trimmed with purple braiding. The face within was not of a craggy crone, as Geneviève expected, but of a very plain woman with nary a wrinkle in sight. The woman's skin was translucent, every bluish vein distinguishable beneath the opaque membrane. Shifting a heavy black leather satchel from one hand to the other, the soothsayer raised her eyes.

Geneviève gasped and jumped back, colliding with the wall behind her. The woman's eyes were as white as her skin, the pupils imperceptible from the sclera. Madame Arceneau's gaze drifted across Geneviève, moving on as if she didn't exist.

Arabelle placed a stilling hand on Geneviève's arm. "I'm sorry. I should have told you."

Geneviève jogged her head with closed, tight lips. "Is she blind?" she managed to ask.

Arabelle shook her head. "She can see perfectly. It is her second sight which has turned her eyes so."

Geneviève did not believe it, but she had no wish to have such a gaze fall on her again. She hung back, following Arabelle as she followed Madame Arceneau. It took them twice as long to return to the king's wing of the palace and Anne's chambers; Madame Arceneau shuffled along, not from age as Geneviève had expected, but from an apparent weakness, as if she possessed neither the energy nor the fortitude to impel her body. Her belabored breathing became ragged as they turned from one staircase and onto the next.

"Madame, at last you have come." Anne rushed toward the mystic as soon as she entered the room. Geneviève had never seen the commanding duchesse display such vulnerability, tempered though it was with her seething anger.

"You must show me how to overcome my enemy. Tell me she will be gone soon."

"I will tell you all I can see, Duchesse, as always." Madame Arceneau made her way unguided to Anne's privy chamber; she had been here before. "But you must allow me to prepare."

"Of course, of course," Anne rushed on, waving her hands at her cousins impatiently. Sybille and Béatrice hurried into the bedchamber, pulling the table away from the window, pulling the heavy curtains across the leaded glass.

From the doorway, Geneviève watched Anne fidget as Madame Arceneau brought out her bottles and her potions, her herbs and her tools. With excruciating slowness, she placed the bottles on the table and unstoppered them, sprinkled a circle of chalky powder around the table, and brought out a heavy pewter talisman, which she placed upon the chair before sitting on it.

With a pointy-fingered hand, she gestured at the chair opposite her and Anne flung herself into it.

The woman took both of the duchesse's hands in hers, and for a few minutes everyone in the room held their breath, save the seer herself. Her eyes closed, her head rolled in small circles on her shoulders. When her lids fluttered open, the expression of perplexity shone in their hesitant gaze.

"What is it?" Anne hissed at her, but the woman gave no reply.

She reached down into her bag and withdrew a deck of tarot cards, dealing them out in a cross pattern upon the table. Silence reigned save for a strange tap, tap, tapping. The curls piled atop Anne's head quivered as her foot twitched against the floor, drubbing out the strange, tense rhythm.

Three times the mystic dealt the cards and three times she pushed them together in a pile.

"There is a new threat, but, for now, I can see no more." Her tinny squeal offered no apology but her gaze scurried away.

"There is nothing new about the threat of La Sénéchale, or her hatred of me." Anne rose slowly from her chair, once more a regal and controlled mistress. She leaned forward, fisted knuckles braced upon the table for balance. "I had hope. I expected you to tell me the method of my triumph over her or at the least that she would soon expire on her own. She is ancient."

Madame Arceneau gathered her possessions, and with great care returned them to their place in the weathered valise. "I can only tell you what I see in this moment, Duchesse. There is no telling what I may yet see. You know this to be true."

"I know you have failed me, seer." Anne straightened, spun to the windows, and thrust the curtains open. A glimmer of a sickening smile appeared on her lips as she watched the grimace of pain flash across the mystic's face, as she turned her delicate eyes from the brilliance of the streaming sun. "Take thee to your potions and prestidigitations and find me an answer. Reveal how I am to triumph over this *salope* or you will discover yourself back in the hovel where I found you."

The ethereal woman, her eyes closed, gave an imperceptible nod at the threat, hearing no truth in its warning. She rose from her chair, took up her satchel, and made for the door, passing close to Geneviève as she did.

Though she had no conscious intention, Geneviève took a quick step away, as if she feared the mere possibility of physical contact with the mystic. Like lightning through a storm-ravaged sky, the possibility that the soothsayer knew Geneviève's true purpose at court flashed in her mind, but she dismissed it as no more than a passing shower.

❧ 12 ❧

With time all things are revealed.

—François Rabelais (c. 1494–1553)

"Come, Geneviève, we are to play lansquenet." As they entered the king's audience chamber, the small group veered to the left, heading toward the expanse of gaming tables spread out before one of the room's mammoth fireplaces; within its gaping maw, a small fire smoldered, chasing away a late-season chill with its modest flames.

"Yes, join us, Geneviève," the petite Lisette echoed Arabelle's invitation, scampering quickly ahead on tiny slippered feet with obvious relish. She who looked the most sedate, in truth was the most precocious. But Geneviève stopped with unexpected abruptness, forcing Arabelle to skip spryly aside to avoid collision.

"No, thank you. Cards are not a favored pastime of mine."

Perhaps her dismissal was far too brusque; the hurt of it gazed at her from Arabelle's downcast eyes. Geneviève had grown reliant on and comfortable with the other woman's company and her kindness; Arabelle had been Geneviève's first true acquaintance when she had first arrived at court. Finding such comfort in another's companionship disturbed her. She needed to withdraw, to raise her inner defenses, as much as was possible when cohabiting with thousands of people.

"I am content to enjoy the music," Geneviève explained, heading toward the opposite end of the room and the small gathering of musicians.

She circled about the large expanse of the king's audience chamber, unsure what to do with herself, stewing in the juices of her own discontent. Lodovico had not yet arrived to amuse her, a message had not yet come to appease her, and tonight the feuding brothers worked together without conflict, the strains of instruments and voices working in perfect concert. She felt Arabelle's concerned gaze dogging her every step, refused to see the confusion and concern within it, and busied herself with a study of the room. Rich, bright tapestries and gloomy, pious paintings covered walls of gilded navy and maroon. Wood and leather heels clicked upon square and diamond patterns of inlaid tile of blue and white, yellow and black.

"Vergikios arrived this morning. I have asked him to join us this evening." The king trilled like a schoolboy who chattered of his first crush.

"Have all the crates been constructed?" Anne asked with little more than dutiful interest. The couple strolled about the room as if ambling about a garden, each with a jeweled goblet in hand, a long trail of courtiers following close behind like the wake of a slow-moving boat. Geneviève joined their ranks as the parade passed by. She caught sight of the cavalcade as it crossed in front of a gilt-framed looking glass. In the cloudy reflection, she looked into her own eyes, but saw no one familiar.

François failed to notice his mistress's lukewarm demeanor. "There are only a hundred so far. I'm sure we will need another hundred before the deed is done. Vergikios will oversee the actual packing."

Angelos Vergikios, a Cretan scribe, had come on the recommendation of Georges de Selve, the French ambassador to Venice. François had talked of little else but Vergikios and books for the past few days. Anne was grateful for the king's obsession; it had diverted his attention from the nasty rumor of her infidelity and the smoldering choler it had caused between them. But after hours of sermons on the topic, all began to show signs of weariness. Now that the man had arrived, now that the work on the reorganization of the king's library and its proposed move to Fontainebleau had begun, all were sure there were many more hours of nothing more than the talk of books.

Little remained at the Château de Blois to entice the king to live within its majestic walls; it had been the home of his first wife, Claude, and here she had given birth. The ghosts lurking in the halls kept him at bay for more and more months at a time. Yet one thing remained that the king held dear . . . the magnificent library. He could not bear to be parted from it any longer, and he had brought his court with him as he supervised the packing and relocation of the thousands of tomes to Fontainebleau.

"So many, Father?" the pale Marguerite twittered from behind the couple. She shared François's passion for books. After the loss of so many children, the king kept this, his youngest child, close and protected, and she had absorbed his great love of the written word with little other activity to occupy her.

"Indeed, *ma petite*." François smiled back at his daughter.

Anne uh-hummed a response, but it was enough to encourage the king to further discourse.

"They are all to be wrapped in the purest linen to prevent any damage and absorption of moisture. We have instructed that covers be erected on all the carts to be sure."

"You've certainly thought of everything, *Majesté*. Very impressive."

François smiled at his lover's praise. "These are the world's greatest words, *ma chérie*. They are the keys to humanity's enlightenment. They must be protected."

Anne caressed the arm she held close. "They will—"

"Stop!"

The roar reverberated through the cavernous room. Clanking

armor beat time with furious footsteps. Bodies scattered. Women screeched in fright. Men called out in warning. Geneviève spun round as did those nearby.

A raggedly dressed man tore through the room. Sharp halberds chased him down, wielded by soldiers intent on pursuit.

"Your Majesty, please, Your Majesty!" The man's ravaged cry cut a swath through the crowd surrounding François. Men rushed to the king's side, Montmorency and Chabot among them.

The king pulled upon Anne's arm and yanked her behind him. Throwing wide his long, thick arms, he shielded three other women, Geneviève included.

"Hear me, Your Highness, please."

A distance yet away, the man threw himself to the floor, sliding across the smooth, glossy tile.

One massive soldier, legs longer than the fleeing miscreant was tall, overtook his target. With a propelling grunt, he jumped over the man as he fell to the ground. With dancer-like grace, the warrior jolted to his feet before his king, spun on his heel, and raised his lance. The crowd gasped as the deadly point stopped inches from the prostrate man's heart. In a fractured second, three more spears rose, ready to skewer the man's back.

"I know you." The king's enraged whisper broke the stunned silence; his brow furrowed with a devious squint of his long, slanted eyes.

Geneviève rose on tiptoes to peer over François's shoulder. The man's fear-ravaged face broke apart; his sobs shook his slight body.

"You do, Your Highness, you do know me." His voice cracked. "I served in your son's chambers for a time. Your son François."

A cloud besmirched the king's already blotched face. If the man hoped to appeal to a father's sentimental grief, he had touched the wrong chord.

With one large stride, the king stood before the man, crouched over him like a vulture upon a cliff top. The man scurried to his knees, looking up at François with pleading in his bloodshot eyes.

"Yes, you served him well, if I remember correctly," the king said bitterly. "And yet you have betrayed me, betrayed him."

The man put his hands to his ears as if to stave off François's enraged words, shaking his head in abject denial. Geneviève had never seen a man so pitiable.

"No, Your Majesty, I have not. I d—"

"You allowed an unlawful gathering to take place in your establishment!" François roared.

"I was lied to, I swear. It was said to be a meeting of craftsmen. They—"

The king turned in disgust. "Take him away." He jerked his head at the soldiers.

"Please, Your Majesty, you cannot take my home. I have six children," the man begged, reaching out for the king, grabbing a fistful of François's doublet.

François spun back, yanking his clothing out of the man's clutch with a fisted hand and kicking out, landing a powerful blow against the man's chest, sending him flying backward with one ferocious gesture.

"You dare!" the king yelled as the soldiers grabbed the man, forcing him flat against the hard, cold ground, spears and booted feet pinning him to the floor. "For your betrayal I have taken your home." Spittle flew from François's thick lips; his body trembled with fury. "Your insolence has now cost you your freedom. Your children can spend the rest of their lives visiting you in prison."

Face crimson with rage, the king raised one hand, a long finger pointing at the door in silent command.

"No, I beg you!" the man screamed as the halberdiers yanked him away by the scruff of his clothes. His feet pinwheeled as they tried to find footing, but it did him no good. They tossed him out of the room like a rag doll, his cries fading away as they dragged him through the palace.

Silence hung suspended in the wake of the violence.

"Continue," the king of France ordered, an edge to his voice as he shook off his fury, straightening his velvet and jeweled doublet, brushing his fine clothing as though to rid himself of the man's taint.

In an instant, music filled the chamber, voices chattered and laughed, cards were dealt, and the courtiers mingled once more, the party resuming as if never interrupted, as if by the magic of the king's hand nothing untoward had taken place.

Geneviève stood rooted in the abyss of the horrifying events. *Here,* she thought as she stared at the king, as she watched him smile at Anne and his men, and drink of his wine. *Here is the man who killed my parents.*

No more than gray dawn light caressed the sky, but she trudged out of the castle, her longbow and arrow-filled quiver upon her back. She cared little that dew stained the hem of her vermillion moiré silk gown as she swept a path in the moist green lawn behind her. Geneviève needed to be away from the castle and all who slept in it. She needed to find release.

The archery butts were abandoned, as she knew they would be; it was far too early in the morning for most courtiers, nor did the sport enjoy as much popularity in France as it did in other countries. Birds twittered and cawed, gathering their breakfast, indifferent to the lone intruder. She felt confident in her solitude.

Geneviève's step quickened as she strode onto the field and the fresh scent of the earth anointed her nostrils. It had been so long since she felt the bow in her hand, the power of the shot; she trembled with anticipation like the lover an inch away from the juicy lips of her beloved. From beside the mounds of turf, she gathered as many plaster targets as she could hold, and threw them haphazardly over the grassy knoll, returning to the edge of the field, at least two hundred meters away.

Taking the bow stick from her back, she pulled on the strap of the quiver until it sat perfectly placed at her shoulder. Gripping the center of the varnished stave with her right hand, she drew an arrow with her left, coupling its nock to the bow string. She raised her arms to slightly above shoulder height, her string hand brushing her cheek with a feathery touch. Pulling back on the cord with a two-fingered draw, she felt the stave bend, felt the animal-gut string stretch to its limit with a drawn-out creak. In this moment, she and the instrument became one, a lethal weapon.

Closing one eye, Geneviève aligned the arrow a hair's breadth above a target. Upon the blank ceramic sphere, she imagined his face, the face of king François. With all the pressure of the taut string and compressed bow, with all the ferocity of her hate, she released.

The arrow flew from her grasp with a strident twang, stave vibrating as it sprang back into shape. Her practiced eye followed the projectile as it arched through the air. Her heart leaped in ecstasy as it struck dead center, shattering the target—and the king's face—into fragments. Her stomach churned at her delight in hate satisfied.

Arrow after arrow she loaded into her weapon, eyes squinting with steely, deathly determination. With each shot, she fed the beast within, replacing her powerlessness with brutal control. Her body shook with adrenal surges, and yet her aim exhibited inhuman precision. The images of the previous night haunted her: François's brutality coming upon the heels of his words on enlightenment. Geneviève laughed bitterly at his hypocrisy, frightening the robins hopping in the grass as they scavenged for the day's first worms. With each shattered disc, she felt an appeasement of her hate, and yet she recognized the hate for the poison it was. She trampled on the part of her that longed for the antidote. Time became meaningless as she emptied her quiver, covered the butt with more targets, and gathered up her arrows, only to fire them off again. Each successive shot came faster; she created a song of *twang* and *thump*, *twang* and *thump*.

"That is some of the best shooting I have ever seen."

With no more than a flinch, Geneviève spun round, bow and

arrow at the ready, nothing but the tips of her fingers holding off the shot as she turned toward the intruder's voice.

"Stop!" Sebastien cried, and threw himself to the ground, flattening against the moist earth. "Friend, friend!"

With slow suspicion, Geneviève collapsed the tension on the bowstring as the taut hold of alarm released the grip on her body. Her belligerent stare captured him, held him as securely to the ground as had her arrow.

"I find it hard to fathom that a member of the Garde Écossaise has never been taught not to approach an archer from behind," she said with impatience.

Sebastien stared at her from the ground; there was no mistaking his hesitancy to move as long as Geneviève held firm to her bow. "You are right, mademoiselle, of that I have been taught. I thought you were empty of arrows. It is my mistake. My apologies."

Geneviève dropped the stave to her side, putting the lone arrow back in the quiver, fiddling with the nutmeg-colored fletching on its tip. "Indeed, it is. But I am sorry to have drawn on you nonetheless," she relented honestly.

Sebastien pushed himself from the ground, wiping dirt and grass from his striped royal blue and moss-colored doublet, and his knees, where his blue stockings were blotched with moisture.

"I must surmise that my amazement at your proficiency chased away all common sense." He approached her and bowed with a tilt of his peacock-plumed toque. Geneviève curtsied, remembering she had left her crescent hood in her chamber. She raised a hand to her pinned-up hair, fearing what a mess it must be after her exertions.

"You look wonderful. Have no fear," Sebastien assured her with a charming, dimpled smile. "Tell me, how does a beauty such as you come to shoot like the most skilled of warriors?"

Geneviève shrugged, remembering to smile her courtier's smile as if it were all a merry jest, dousing the flutter his flattery ignited. "As a child, my only companions, other than my aunt, were the household servants, and I was a bit of a ruffian. I fear the men indulged me. They took me on the hunt with great frequency. Too often, I suppose."

Sebastien laughed. "I can imagine what a little rapscallion you were." He leaned toward her, his fathomless blue eyes glimmering with a spark of amusement. "I can see her there, in your eyes."

Geneviève turned from him, pretending to be the coquet, fearing he would see the true hunter in her depths, and diddled with her stave. He took it from her hands and studied it, running his palms over the smooth, polished surface.

"Belly of horn, the best for compression," he mused as he rubbed the inner curve of the bow. "Back side of sinew. An impressive weapon, Geneviève."

"*Merci*," she acknowledged with a prideful nod, entranced by his slow caress upon her bow. With a small shake, she turned away, striding to the crest of the archery butt and returning her arrows to their place in the quiver.

"Did you come to shoot, Sebastien?" She straightened, realizing he had no weapons of his own.

"Ah, no, I did not." He joined her at the small mound of earth, helping her retrieve her arrows. "Though I would like to pit my skill against yours sometime. I know—" He slapped his muscular thigh with the shaft of an arrow. "You must join a hunt. I insist you be my guest when next we ride. The king would be delighted with your prowess."

Geneviève racked her mind for some feasible excuse, but as Anne and her ladies often took part in the festivities, nothing sufficiently logical suggested itself. "I look forward to it," she told him, denying the many ripples of truth in the reply. She would look forward to hunting again. And she would anxiously await a return to this man's company, though to herself at least, she would pretend otherwise.

"Wonderful," he announced, stepping intimately close as he

put the arrows in her quiver, his chest brushing against her shoulder.

Geneviève inhaled the manliness of him, the leather of his gloves, and the musk of his hair.

"You must return to the château, Geneviève," he said with reluctance. "Your mistress looks for you."

Geneviève's eyes bulged in concern and she grabbed her bow, slinging it with her quiver once more upon her back.

"No need for worry, it was not urgent. But I assured her I would send you along at your leisure."

"Then I thank you for your errand." Geneviève gathered her skirts in one hand and set off at a trot.

"*Au revoir,* Geneviève. I will see you soon, I hope," he called after her.

Without turning back, she waved her free hand.

As she rushed from his side, Sebastien prowled the top of the knoll, finding every small fragment of the targets the astounding archer had left behind. They were not large pieces nor corners clipped from the edge; they were no more than slivers, the targets smashed into smithereens. Direct hits—hit after hit—produced such complete devastation. He looked up at Geneviève's fast retreating form as it shrank away from him, no longer a dashing smile upon his lips or a glimmer of charm in his eye.

She sat at the large vanity, the triptych looking glass showing all sides of her face. Diane stared at each of her reflections, looking for impurities, any signs of the age she fought against like a crusader. The graceful line from jaw to narrow chin seemed a tad droopier and she vowed to increase her cold-water soaks from two to three a day.

Henri lay sprawled upon her bed, his youthful beauty framed by the royal blue curtains and tester. He stared as Diane brushed the reddish gold of her long hair. He adored how it looked blond in the sunlight, but then here, in the ochre light of her candlelit chambers, it looked rich and deep, as if he could lose himself in the gently curled locks.

If Diane could know his mind, she needn't have worried overmuch about her passing years. In Henri's eyes, she would always be that magnificent woman of thirty and three who had befriended the fourteen-year-old when no one else had. A sullen and stormy youth, he had allowed his petulance to segregate him, not only from the father who had used him so heinously, but from the rest of the court as well. The pugnacious adolescent cared not that France was falling apart, that François had been given little choice in his actions. Diane became the beacon of light in his dark world and he had loved her—with his body and his mind—ever since; she would never grow old in his eyes.

"Did you do it?" His whisper held but a touch of accusation.

Diane swiveled on her embroidered cushion, brush poised in midstroke, and stared blankly at her young lover.

Henri raised himself up on an elbow, his sculpted chest glistening with beads of sweat, lingering evidence of the throes of their passion. "Did you begin the rumor of Anne and Beauville?"

With controlled movements, she placed the gilt-edged brush upon the table and rose, the silhouette of her body visible through her thin shift as she stood in front of the candles, stopping at the edge of the bed. "Do you think I did?"

Henri stared up into her eyes for a brief instant, salacious gaze dropping to the curves tantalizing him so, then shook his head. "No. No, I do not," he said, and reached out a hand for her.

With a harrumph of relief and irritation, she sat by his side. "The woman plagues me, I cannot deny it. But this was not my work, I assure you."

He smiled at that, amused by all she did not say.

Carine brought the tray into Geneviève's room and placed it upon the small table by the bedside. Stars glimmered beyond the windows in a sky long fallen to night; a diminutive fire crackled and spit in the grate.

"Are you sure I cannot attend you further?" She tutted with obvious disapproval; no other maid in the palace was as unused as she, and she thought her mistress's independence annoying indeed. "There is no need to bathe yourself."

As if arriving on cue, four more maids entered the chamber: two hefting a large open-topped wooden cask between them, two others lugging buckets of steaming water. They placed the barrel before the fire and poured in the hot liquid with a splash.

"*Merci*, no, Carine. I shall be fine, I assure you." Geneviève rubbed her forehead, wanting nothing more than a soak and some solitude.

Carine waved the other women from the room, muttering beneath her breath, "Self-sufficient nonsense, if you ask me. That aunt of hers did not teach her the ways of a civilized lady."

Geneviève dropped her head back upon her shoulders, smiling up at the plain painted ceiling. "Good night, Carine. Sleep well."

"*Bonne nuit*, mademoiselle," Carine called with little pleasure.

Before the door closed behind her, another young maid rushed in, a thick, folded linen towel in her hands, her modest white cap bobbing as she ran.

"To dry yourself, mam'selle," she said as she laid the white material on the bed.

"*Merci*," Geneviève thanked her dismissively.

As the latch clicked behind the girl's scampering form, Geneviève stripped off the last layers of her clothing, leaving the smelly shift in a heap on the ground. She had had no opportunity to freshen herself before attending Anne, and the rigors of the morning and the duties of the day had left their stain and their residue upon her undergarments.

With a deep, contented sigh, she lowered herself into the tub, surrendered herself to the soothing, steaming, lavender-scented water. She closed her eyes in bliss, her body finding its ease, her mind wandering to the events of the day.

How good it had felt to shoot again, and yet already the muscles along the back of her arms ached. Geneviève vowed to practice more often, to keep up her skills, for the satisfaction and exercise it offered. She needed to stay as ready as ever, both in mind and body.

Hearty voices and merry laughter ebbed and flowed, the sound slinking through the crack under her door; footsteps advanced and receded as courtiers made merry. Geneviève's thoughts skipped to Sebastien. She could not deny her attraction, nor could she risk indulging it. He was the king's guardsman and thereby her enemy. And yet he was the most beautiful man she had ever seen, his masculine handsomeness far outshining that of the pretty Pitou, and worthy of her most lustful fantasies. In the stables of her aunt's château, in the arms of the lads who toiled there, Geneviève had learned much of the pleasure shared between men and women, but she had undertaken those lessons as dutifully as all the rest. Her body tingled as her thoughts strayed to the charm of Sebastian's smile, to the pull of his warrior's physique. She knew there would be nothing dutiful about pleasure found in his arms.

She soaked until the water turned tepid and her ardor cooled. Rising up, the fluid dripping from her body like rain into a bucket, she stepped out and grabbed the linen, unfurling it with a snap to wrap about her body.

The small round package flew out of the linen and sailed across the room. For a moment, Geneviève stared at it, dumbfounded.

"Mon Dieu," she cried with delight as understanding dawned.

With great haste, she swathed her moist body, dripping hair matted against her face and back, wiping the water from her eyes with an impatient, trembling hand. Her bare feet left wet prints as she rushed to retrieve the box. Her legs curled beneath her as she dropped on the spot and grabbed greedily at the parcel. Smaller than her fist, a plain hemp string bound the thick, buff-colored ball of velum.

Geneviève laid the package gingerly in her lap, untied the string, and opened the package with the tips of forefingers and thumbs. Her curled lips formed a silent O of delight as the treasure revealed itself, as she found the ring within, and beneath it, the small square of parchment. She brought the ring up before her eyes; the square amethyst jewel mounted upon a simple band of white gold twinkled in the candlelight. Geneviève held it to her, clasping it in both hands, holding it against her chest, feeling the heavy thudding of her heart beneath skin jeweled with beads of water. She kept the trinket imprisoned in the palm of her left hand, the hard metal biting the tender skin, as she deciphered the message.

Once more, the words spoke of gratitude and blessing. Her king compared the purple jewels of her eyes to the purple jewel in her hand. Leaning her back against the corner post of her bed, Geneviève read the message over and over, closing her eyes to memorize its every word, those which gave instruction on how next to send a message, and those conveying Henry's care and tenderness.

Exhaustion crept upon her with the stealth of a thief, and in the half-conscious state—in the strange world between sleep and wakefulness—Geneviève's dreams took flight. Her father came to her, alive and magnificent, bearing gifts. If he were alive, he would have done as the king did, showering her with his love through thought, word, and deed.

In the last hazy moments perched on the precipice of sleep, Geneviève tossed the king's message upon the embers, watching it burn, without regret. She needed no paper to remind her of his fealty. She had his gift and his love; she needed nothing more.

❧ 13 ❧

It is better to act and to regret,
Than to regret not to have acted.

—Mellin de Saint-Gelais (1491–1558)

There was no mistaking the genuine gladness upon the king's face as his son cantered into the cobbled courtyard of the stable. It was as apparent as Anne's disgust when Diane de Poitiers rode in beside him, Montmorency and two members of the House of Guise in their company. The duchesse wiped the revulsion from her face as with a thick, rough cloth when the king called out brightly, "My son joins the hunt," and turned to her with his broad smile.

"What a wonderful surprise," she said loud enough for all to hear, and a rousing cheer rose up from the large gathering of courtiers.

Geneviève mopped the thin film of sweat forming on her forehead. At its apex in the brilliant azure of the afternoon sky, the sun glowed like a ball of flame while cicadas buzzed in a heat that was more like midsummer than late spring. She studied the heir apparent with a squinty-eyed gaze.

There was little denying the beauty of the Dauphin, his black hair glinting like steel in the bright light, his black eyes dazzling and dangerous. In his early twenties, he was at the peak of his manhood and it exuded from him with every movement, with every brooding look. How hard he fought to strut and flaunt his gloom for the sake of resistance itself, always struggling to maintain the control over his own existence that had been lost to him as a child prisoner in Spain.

"Father." He dipped his head at the king, bearing little resemblance to François or his happiness. But the child's coldness could not dampen the father's spirit.

"I am pleased to see you, my son. We shall have a fine day of sport." His words reached for his child, though the young man lay forever out of his grasp; the father he was now, had not yet—and perhaps never would—replace the father he had been. "Madame." François greeted Diane with a turn of his black stallion, the jewels encrusted upon the saddle blanket and bridle sparkling as did his smile.

The pale beauty was the perfect foil for her lover's dark good looks; together they formed both ends of light's spectrum.

"*Majesté.*" She rose up on the stirrups of her saddle and bowed to the king, not acknowledging Anne with either word or gesture. Anne's eyes turned deep emerald as she stared at her rival, as she watched Diane interact with the king, always leery of any form of discourse between the two.

Diane's father had been a part of the Bourbon affaire; her husband had been among those who revealed the treason to the king. From that moment, Diane had known a bud of hate for her husband from an arranged marriage. It soon eclipsed any affection burgeoning between them, and her marriage's demise brought the angst of her father's action upon her twofold. Was her guilt, in truth, enough to impel her to the king's bed, to beg for forgiveness with the most precious commodity she had to offer . . . herself? Most of the court believed it to be true. Neither had ever denied it.

"You have picked the perfect day to join us." Sebastien chuckled as he pulled his horse up beside Geneviève's; the animals neighed and tossed their heads as they recognized each other. He followed her gaze to the two couples at the center of the congested courtyard. "There will be all types of sport today."

Geneviève averted her eyes, but could not keep the conspiring grin at bay. "I made you my promise, sir, and it is my pleasure to keep it."

Leaning toward her in his saddle, Sebastien gave her his scintillating, half-dimpled smile. "You are a flower in full bloom today, mademoiselle," he said, taking in her eggplant-colored riding costume hugging her feminine curves. "But there was no need to bring your weapon." He gave a nod to the bow and quiver slung across her back. "We will hunt *à vénerie* today. The mastiffs will bring the beast down. All we need are our spears and our daggers."

Between the king and his great courtiers, they boasted more than five hundred falcons with which to hunt herons and kites, but today's sport would be a boar hunt, as preferred by François.

"I always carry my bow when on any hunt," Geneviève returned with the same jaunty air. "A hunter can never tell what quarry may cross her path."

Sebastien barked a laugh at her double entendre, the deep, creamy sound rising over the merry tune struck by the musicians of the *écurie*. The flageolets and trumpets, sackbuts and hautbois trilled a sprightly song befitting the day. The brothers who so amused Geneviève would not be among their number; they would be disgraced to be in the company of the socially inferior musicians of the stable.

From behind Geneviève another horse approached with a playful whinny, Sebastien grinning broadly at the rider.

"Albret, you have returned," he cheered. "How well it is to see you."

"And you, Sebastien." The marquis de Limoges dipped his red head at him and turned his pale blue eyes to Geneviève. "*Bonjour,* mademoiselle. It is a pleasure to see you again."

"Monsieur," Geneviève returned with natural ease. "I hope your journey was fruitful."

"I have found my holdings to be in fair condition," he replied. "A man can ask for no more."

"It is all well if it allows you to return to court," Sebastien offered with genuine delight. "And I am well surprised to find you know Geneviève." He smiled her way with ill-disguised propriety. "We will make a jolly day of it together."

Albret forced a smile in return, disappointed gaze moving between the two companions. "The very best of days."

Geneviève heard the note of discontent in the mammoth man's voice, and scoured his features. But the large lord offered no more than a wistful smile and she remained puzzled.

Horses chomped at the bit, voices rose in excited clatter, the anticipation grew deep and heavy in the air as the time to begin grew closer. What the common man did to feed himself and his family, these nobles looked upon as their most cherished sport. Lines began to form at the edge of the vast courtyard. In the front rank of the crowd rode the king, flanked by a hundred or more riders, like the lead goose in a V-shaped gaggle crossing and filling the sky. Riding closest to him, fluttering around him like petals around a stamen, came his fair band of ladies, the chosen group of the most beautiful, most amusing ladies at court. The noblemen and princes sat straight-backed yet with masculine casualness on their warhorses and stallions; the ladies graceful and fine in their colorful plumage.

The hounds came in with a cacophonous braying, straining against the reins and the whippers-in who held them, as if they would choke themselves with the effort to be loose.

"Are you ready?" Sebastien called, but his knowing smile said the question was no more than rhetorical.

Geneviève's cheeks burned with thrumming blood; she hitched in the awkward saddle she had at last mastered, as anxious to be off as the hounds themselves. She answered with the widest of smiles, dazzling him with her naked joy, all the more astounding for its rarity.

The bells chimed thrice and the beasts were loosed; at least forty hounds surged forward. With a giant yell, the king dug in his heels; his stallion reared and dropped as though he were the flag that began the joust. Like the surge of a tidal wave, the company broke forward, their cries drowning beneath the thunder of hooves.

Side by side Geneviève and Sebastien rode, their horses huffing and snorting. As the contingent broke the field, the assemblage fractured as well, one large party heading off behind a group of hounds, more hunters following another. Geneviève and her companions stayed behind François and his son Charles as they followed the loudest and most aggressive pack, and she felt the surge of the hunt, as if, like the hounds, she could smell the beast.

From the corner of her eye, movement captured her seeker's vigilance. More riders broke off into smaller parties of two; Geneviève watched their shift for a moment, confused, but turned back to the hounds and the pursuit.

Nearly an hour passed before the dogs slowed their pace, before they lowered their noses to the ground, picking up the scent of the boar. The riders slowed but the excitement built; the prey was near at hand. As Geneviève intently searched the forest, she found a few of the couples who had left the crowd. Hiding under trees, bent behind shrubbery, they clenched each other in the throes of passion—a man here with one woman, his wife there with a different man, their carnality furtive and extreme, as if the greater possibility of discovery intensified their pleasure. Now she understood the lewd tapestries so prevalent at every palace.

"They have other conquests in mind than the thrill of the chase," Sebastien bellowed.

Geneviève blushed, not at the wanton acts, but at her own naïveté.

"I can s—"

Four horn blasts from the left put all other thoughts aside. Riders yanked upon their reins, spinning their horses to the sound. Geneviève's horse leaped to the front behind the king, spurred on by her mistress's heels and the exhilaration coursing through her body. The prickly brown animal stood far ahead, halfway up a low, grass-covered rise on the horizon, his blackness a blemish on the speckled yellow and purple meadow. Its flat, ugly snout rustled in the ground beside its cloven feet.

"Magnificent!"

Geneviève heard the king yell at the massive size of the beast. Even from this distance, they could see the grotesque proportions of the animal. In all her years of hunting, Geneviève had never seen one quite so large. She turned to smile at Sebastien, galloping upon her heels. They brought up their horses a safe distance from the beast, before their movement and sound spooked him away. It reared its head, snout twitching at the new scent in the air, revealing huge tusks curling up over its top lip. From here, the spear-armed men would approach the prey on foot, following behind the hounds.

"He is mine!" The cry came from a small grove of evergreen trees on the right. From their camouflage, a group of riders shot forward, the Dauphin and Diane at the lead.

"He's mine!" Henri cried again, cutting off the pursuit, his enormous gray charger veering in front of his father's mount.

The king checked his descent from the saddle, no one but the few nearby catching the slight gesture. With a jut of his chin, he sent the mastiffs forward. The black hairy beast upon the hill froze for a fraction too long, beginning his ungraceful gallop as the horde of hounds bore down on him.

The dogs reached him with triumphant, horrifying yelps, sinking their teeth into his neck and hindquarters, pulling him down to the ground. The beast struggled for freedom, stunted legs waggling in the air as he tried to right himself and flee, blood running like a river of scarlet from his wounds, the smell dank and primal in the air. The mania of the kill shone in the hounds' eyes, but they knew their duty, knew no meat would reach their bellies did they not hold the beast for the master to kill.

Henri slid from his horse before it came to a stop, a long-shafted, short-bladed spear glinting in his hand. The other riders circled closer to watch, no one more attentive than the king himself. The Dauphin swaggered up to the beast, mounting the small hill like a victorious warrior. No more than a few steps away from the animal, he raised his spear and . . .

The beast screeched with one last push of ferocious strength, flinging off the dog at its neck, rising to its feet with the others upon its tail. Blood dripped from the open gash at its throat. Black, dying eyes found Henri; the Dauphin's feet were manacled to the ground with surprise. The boar lowered its tusks and launched. The Dauphin's body jerked back, his feet failing to follow, and fell to the grass, the jolt knocking the spear out of his hand. The king bellowed. Diane screamed. Men launched their spears, but they were too far away. The cumbersome close-range weapons hit the ground feebly. Defenseless, Henri struggled to stand, but there was no time. The beast was upon him.

The boar jerked back, propelled by the force of the arrow as the barbed tip struck him below the right eye and sunk in. With one last twitch, it expired, no more a threat to the heir of the French throne.

Every eye, every gaze, every incredulous expression spun round.

With calm certitude, Geneviève lowered her empty bow to her side. Cold, violet eyes found the king's and she dropped him a curtsy.

She stood beside the king, who stood beneath the center of the pristine white canopy, its gold-tasseled ends waving in the late afternoon breeze, the slanting rays of the sun casting long shadows beyond. Within minutes of the beast's death, a contingent of servants and carts had appeared as if by magic. A cold banquet of meats, fruits, and salads was spread out on the hastily erected tables. Courtiers jostled each other for food, wine, and a better position, all straining to get closer to the woman who had saved the life of the Dauphin.

The very picture of the reluctant hero, Geneviève longed to be any place but at this hub of commotion. Her ghostly smile and skittering gaze gave every indication of impending flight. The close proximity of the grateful king, the duchess, the Dauphin, and Diane kept her rooted to the spot. She berated herself silently for her rash actions, but they had been as instinctive as taking a breath. She prayed her true liege would not be angered by her impetuosity; Henri was a much greater friend to England than was his father. It was her only hope of salvation. How easy her life would have been if it had been the king the beast bore down upon; how easy she would have found it to keep the bow from her hand.

From beyond the crowd gathered round her, she glimpsed the smiles of Sebastien, Arabelle, and Albret as they looked on joyfully, vicariously enjoying her triumph. How tragic it was that Geneviève took solace in Sebastien's possessive pride and Arabelle's hopeful friendship.

"Mademoiselle Gravois, I wish you to take this as token of my gratitude." Henri cocked his head at a servant, who brought forth the cloven hoof of the slain beast, gloved hand drenched with the fresh dripping blood, and bowed before her as he offered it up.

The Dauphin had been the first to react to Geneviève's swift kill. With a horrendous roar at the dead beast, perhaps in anger that it dared threaten him, or perhaps in humiliation, Henri whipped out his jeweled dagger and slashed off the front right foot, blade grinding into bone, holding the trophy up over the beast as if to taunt it, though it be demised.

"No, Your Highness." Geneviève curtsied as she raised her hands in supplication. "Your courage has earned the prize. I would never have dared bring myself so close to such a ferocious beast." She played the part of a skittish female, realizing the embarrassment she may have caused the sullen young man by saving him.

She plied her compliment with the same skill as her arrow, and Henri bowed with a small if genuine smile, waving at the grooms-man to remove with the foot.

François banged the handle of his dagger against his golden jeweled chalice, and every mouth shut in anticipation. Raising his goblet toward Geneviève, he looked to Anne first.

"With your permission, madame, I wish to welcome Mademoi-selle Gravois to *ma petite bande*."

No one dared raise their chalice until the duchesse gave a sign of agreement, for she alone approved the members of the exclusive sorority. Such accord came readily, eagerly in fact, and with a nod to her lover, Anne raised her own chalice at her lady-in-waiting.

"You have stolen my very own thoughts, Your Majesty." She smiled at Geneviève with genuine warmth. "You have saved the king's son. You have my thanks and those of a grateful nation."

"To Mademoiselle Gravois!" the king cheered.

"To Mademoiselle Gravois!" rang the rousing chorus of courtiers.

Geneviève smiled at the accolades, wishing more than anything to crawl into the nearest hole and hide.

∂∂ 14 ∂∂

Women are never stronger than when they arm themselves
with their weaknesses.

—Madame Marie du Deffand (1697–1780)

"Is it true?" Anne slapped her hand upon the table and the
angry sound escaped out the open wings of the butterfly-
style windows, echoing down the long loggias and out into the
dreary gray and humid morning. Dogs barked in the distance as if
sensing some looming danger. "Are you having an affair with that
awful leach Narbonne? I won't have it, do you hear me?"

Geneviève cringed with embarrassment, knowing every curious
and intrusive gaze in the room stared as the duchesse chastised her
like an errant child. The chatter wasted away to whispers as the
hangers-on listened to the titillating conversation. The fame
brought about by Geneviève's damnably stupid if arguably ad-
mirable actions of the previous week had begun to subside, and
here she was yet again, bringing further undue notice to herself,
and this the worse of its kind. Of all days for this harangue to happen, on the first damp day in a fortnight, when bored courtiers
looking for amusement filled Anne's audience chamber to overflowing. How hungrily they drank of it at her expense.

Geneviève bowed low in a curtsy, but would not hang her head.
"No, madame, I assure you, there is nothing but the thinnest of acquaintance between the gentleman and myself."

Anne chaffed with cutting laughter, bounding to her feet, tipping her chair precariously backward as she took two quick menacing steps toward her attendant. "The man is no gentleman, Geneviève, I can assure you. He is a goatish and conniving cad of the worst kind. What is more, he is *her* agent and always has been."

There was no need to ask to whom Anne referred; there was but one woman in the kingdom she would speak of with such contempt, her voice rising to a painful shrill.

"I swear to you." Geneviève rose up to full height and took two steps closer, so that Anne might better see her truthfulness. "Yes, I danced with him, supped with him, but once, no more. He is nothing to me."

Anne hesitated in her rage, the cutting edge of Geneviève's voice halting her tongue, casting a look of doubt across her delicate features. The mistress studied the maid; the room held their collective breath.

"Very well, mademoiselle, I believe you." Anne capitulated with a nod and returned to her seat, her screech subsiding to speech. "But you must learn to be wary of such a man. He is tall, dark, and dashing, but he is a man who only plays at love. His greatest satisfaction comes not from actual lovemaking, but from making you want to want him. Once he knows you do, he will want you no more."

Geneviève shook her head. "I do not want him." She pictured herself convincing the man of her lack of ardor with the pointy tip of her dagger. "It will be my pleasure to set him straight."

"Now, now"—Anne clucked her tongue, sensing Geneviève's smoldering enmity—"I know you are new to the court, but you must learn the ways of a courtier. If displeased by a man, a lady does not whine and harangue, but turns her attentions elsewhere to show she has forgotten that which has displeased her."

Anne swept up and twirled across the room, running playful fingers along the shoulder of one handsome courtier who lounged upon her couch. He reached out for the duchesse, who whirled away to caress the cheek of another, who leaned against the marble hearth. The men reacted to her power as if unable to fight it; their eyes grew dreamy and their lips curled flippantly in seductive smiles.

"Indeed, to grandly, amusingly dismiss him, as if it is your greatest joy to do so, is the most stinging cut of all."

"And . . . and if I should care for someone's attentions?" Geneviève bristled at the asking, but it was an undeniable compulsion. Pulled into Anne's alluring power and the aura it created, Sebastien's magnetic eyes flashed in her thoughts.

"Well then." Anne continued her dance through the room, the men and women catching her pretend desire as if it were contagious, coming together to dance to their own tune, to flirt and smile as if part of a play. "Then it is all pretty words and charming smiles. It is all flattery and letting him know, without saying so, that you are his for the taking. Reveal—without a word—that he must conquer you, but that his quest will be victorious."

Geneviève looked askance at her and the twittering court. "You make no sense."

Anne fluttered back and took Geneviève by the hands, forcing her to twirl. "What elsewhere may be folderol, at court makes perfect sense."

With amused surrender, Geneviève laughed with the duchesse, her gaiety undeniably genuine. She allowed herself to be swept away as two gentlemen took to their lutes, replacing the make-believe music with lilting, spirited notes. The women pranced together, cutting through the crowded room as they danced.

"Please, madame," Geneviève whispered to Anne as they trounced about the room. "Will you tell me from where such slander came?" She was vexed by the thought of the nasty rumor linking her name to Narbonne's, incensed at the threat it posed to her mission.

Anne's green eyes slithered sideways to where Jecelyn stood with two handsome *gentilshommes*. "Be careful of her. Her heart is as black as her eyes."

Geneviève's jaw clenched as she gritted her teeth. "So it would seem."

"I have forgotten the matter. As should you." Anne recognized a malicious expression such as Geneviève's. "Have not a care."

Keeping one of Geneviève's hands in hers, Anne grabbed that of another lady, and within minutes a crooked circle formed and they danced a *branle* around Anne's furniture, the simple country dance becoming trickier with the added skill required to avoid the settees, cushions, and ottomans scattered about. The courtiers laughed like children on the playground, bounding about with unfettered joy.

"What have we here?"

The booming baritone cut above the music and the laughter.

Women dropped into curtsies, men to their bows, while Anne rushed to François's side.

"We are teaching Mademoiselle Gravois to be a courtier."

The king found Geneviève in the middle of the playful group, her pale hair a bit askew, bright color on her cheeks from exertion and embarrassment. He smiled with indulgence.

"If she can play the part as well as she can shoot, then she should have no troubles at all."

The room laughed at the king's jest, but they ceased their music and their dance. The king waved a hand in a beckoning circle.

"Please don't stop. It is lovely to see such merriment on such a dreary day."

"Play on." Anne nodded to the lute players without returning to the dancers, remaining by the king's side. There was no doubt of the weariness upon his aging face. His wide, thin mouth refused the smile he tried to force upon it, and his broad shoulders, always so unyielding to the weight they carried, drooped over his barrel chest.

His melancholy was palpable, and though the musicians continued to play, they chose a slow, more sedate tune. With a wave of her hand, Anne shooed away the courtiers upon the couch and led the king to it by his giant, paw-like hands.

"Sit, *Majesté*, and tell me how it goes." The duchesse sat beside him, all her attention focused on her liege. "Mulled wine for the king," she called without taking her gaze from him.

Jecelyn jumped to do her bidding, bringing not one but two pewter mugs of the warmed beverage to the table.

The courtiers scattered themselves about the room, taking their places upon the couches and footrests, whispering softly to one another so as not to disturb the king and his greatest confidant.

François raised the mug to his lips, sipped, and closed his eyes with a satisfied smile. He brightened a bit as the warm liquid infused him with comfort.

"I have not yet heard from the emperor." It was a bitter complaint.

"Our ambassadors confirm he has received the messages?" Anne asked.

François nodded petulantly. "They have. He actually flaunts it, letting them know each time he receives one but giving no indication if he intends to answer."

"He toys with us," Anne hissed crossly. In matters of foreign affairs, Anne's political views were broadly in line with her personal sympathies, those tainted by her dislike of the king's Spanish wife, and she leaned toward England. However, her ability to see the landscape for what it was, always ruled her tongue.

From the table by the windows, not more than a few feet behind the couch where king and mistress sat, Geneviève peered down at the open book in her hands, the words meaningless, the letters blurring on the page, as she strained to hear every word of the conversation. A crinkle of a frown formed between her brows as she reflected on the trepidation in the sovereign's tone, a vulnerability inconsistent with the reputation of the mighty King François.

"Agreed," the king said, rubbing the heel of one palm hard

against his brow. "But I cannot for the life of me think why. He has severed all ties with England. Henry's behavior with all those wives and his conflicts with the pope have seen to that. It is only natural we should align."

Anne watched as he tried to push the pain from his head. Putting her hand on one of his broad shoulders, she pulled gently, scooting farther down the end of the couch and lowering his head into the cradle of her lap. François relinquished his care into her bidding, but continued his diatribe.

"After all these years, he continues to hold Milan over my head like a master teasing a dog with a hearty bone," he said as she began to stroke his hair away from his worried face.

Having lost the territory in the Treaty of Madrid—a humiliation compounded by the disgrace, defeat, and his subsequent imprisonment at Pavia—reclaiming the birthright had been his lifelong obsession, one competing only with that of Hely herself. François craved all things Italian, a result and a symptom of his obsession, yet it permeated every facet of his life—his dress, his food, his home, and the art hanging on his walls.

Anne stared out the window as she caressed him. "And yet Charles knows he needs you. If the English king decides to ride out against him, the emperor will need you." Her words supported François's position, encouraged him to keep to his path, but to Geneviève her mistress sounded irked to speak them.

François's eyes closed against the succor of her touch. "You are right, I do know, but it takes so long. The road stretches out in front of me by half as much as it does behind. That's why . . ."

Anne looked down at him. "Why . . . ?"

"Why I have asked Eleanor to help me."

His wife's name hung between them like the smell of spoilt milk; Anne's lips curled in distaste.

"She is his sister, Anne," he said as if by apology, and sat up to face her.

Geneviève dared a glance at the couple, shocked to see the

king's face look so old, so weary with worry; she hardly recognized him as the man she had come to hate.

"I must use every weapon at my disposal. I'm sure you can understand. Our country needs this victory, but I will not—cannot—make our people suffer another war."

He appealed to her devotion to nation, one as strong within her as him.

"Of course, *Majesté*, you are right, as always," Anne conceded with courtly grace and acumen, the very kind in which she had tutored Geneviève. "We must do whatever it takes."

The king smiled broadly, appeased, lowering himself back into his lover's embrace.

"You have read something enlightening?"

Geneviève flinched at the question and spun to find Arabelle standing at her elbow. She looked at her in confusion.

Arabelle grinned, refusing to surrender the flimsy bond of friendship between them. "You appear a bit dumbfounded. I thought perhaps you had read something confusing."

"Oh, ah, *oui*." Geneviève played along and gazed down at the book in her hands, but she saw none of the words printed there. Her mind whirled with the words of the message she would write to her king, one filled with all she had learned. "It is some of the most intriguing I have read in a long time."

Queen Eleanor held her head high as the king escorted her into the great hall; she looked like a different woman from the one Geneviève had seen in all the weeks since coming to court. As she must, the duchesse d'Étampes followed behind; François would abandon Eleanor as soon as the meal ended, but the notion did little to quash the mistress's resentment. The queen preened, aware that the court—especially Anne—would know by now of her king's request; she basked in the glow of her husband's need.

No matter how triumphantly Eleanor strutted, her pudgy body encased in her dowdy gown, she could not eclipse her rival's beauty, looking more like Anne's mother than a contemporary nigh on but ten years older. Anne glowed in pale jade silk, trimmed in creamy lace and pearls as was her crescent headdress; she looked every inch the greatest beauty of the realm, despite her features scrunched in a mask of displeasure. It would be a long, tedious banquet for everyone with Eleanor so smug and Anne so annoyed—especially for the king.

When the musicians struck a *gaillarde* between the meat and fish courses, the entire room heaved a collective gasp as Eleanor took to the floor, none other than Montmorency as her partner.

"This cannot be happening," Anne hissed under her breath to the ladies seated around her, Geneviève among them. She smiled at François as he caught her eye in obvious apology from across the room.

The growing rift between the king's two most intimate councilors—the two Annes—became more and more evident with each passing day. Many wondered who would emerge the victor and who would fall. Anne grabbed her jeweled goblet and drank the liquid in one long gulp.

"She is his pathetic puppet," Anne continued to grouse. "Can she really believe this one event will change her status? The king uses her and she cannot see it."

Jecelyn leaned toward her mistress, the very devil looking out from her black eyes. "She makes a fool of herself," she jeered. "Look at her—she flounders like an ox."

They watched the queen as she attempted the complicated steps, turns, and hops of the dance, but her bumbling brought the duchesse little ease.

"Shall we return to your room, madame, and take our entertainment there?" Arabelle suggested kindly.

Anne spun on her with fury. "I will not retreat. I will not surrender to . . . to . . . that," the duchesse spit.

Arabelle's tawny skin turned crimson and she hung her hood-covered head. "My pardon, madame."

Geneviève felt Arabelle's anguish. She had made the suggestion to be helpful; the lady-in-waiting was perhaps one of the kindest people Geneviève had ever met. There was no need for the fuming mistress to take her anger out on the devoted servant.

"Look at her, she can hardly breathe." Geneviève threw out the insult at the queen, wanting only to divert the attention away from Arabelle.

"God's blood," Anne cursed, Arabelle's misstep forgotten. "Ladies, take partners. Fill the dance floor, please. Fill the space so I might not see her."

The women jumped. Arabelle, Jecelyn, Lisette, and others reached out to the first man they found, rushing onto the dance floor and forming a barrier around the queen and her partner.

Geneviève floundered, lost and unsure, searching the faces for someone familiar to partner, uncomfortable with the forward behavior of the ladies at court.

The powerful hand spun her around before she recognized the face of the man who brought her to the dance floor, imposing his lead with such mastery, she had no choice but to follow.

Geneviève found her footing and looked up, unable to keep all relief and delight from her features as she found the roguishly handsome face of Sebastien smiling down at her. Clamping down on her emotions, she found herself stepping a little lighter, hopping a little higher, as they pranced in the lively and strenuous routine.

"You are one lucky man." The dashing blond youth approached his friend as he stepped off the dance floor and handed Sebastien a pewter mug of frothy ale, slapping him indelicately on the back.

Sebastien chugged down the quenching liquid, wiping white foam from the corner of his mouth with the back of his hand, and smiled at his companion. "Is that so, Dureau? And why is that?"

Dureau's honey brown eyes flitted back to the dance floor,

caught and held upon Geneviève as she partnered the marquis de Limoges in a *courante*. Together the men watched with appreciative stares as she ran across the dance floor with the agility of an athlete, the light catching the auburn satin of her gown and her hood and the shimmering daffodil yellow of her hair, as she skipped beneath the chandelier. The fiddlers' bows flew across the strings, the hautbois players' puffed cheeks reddened, the drum beats raced. She smiled at her partner as they turned a particularly difficult maneuver, while Albret tripped, clearly besotted, and Sebastien cringed a little at the sight.

"She is a great beauty," Dureau said, nudging Sebastien with a pointy elbow. "And you seem to be her favored friend."

Sebastien's gaze never wavered nor did his mouth smile in reply. "She is striking, I grant you. But tell me this: Why and how does any woman come to shoot so well?"

"Did you not tell me she was raised in a manly household?" Another gallant had joined their ranks and the study of Geneviève.

"I did, Edgard," Sebastien conceded. "But somehow it does not ring with great truth. Dureau here was raised in much the same way, and he couldn't hit a dead stag two meters away."

The trio of cavaliers laughed, but Sebastien's smile faded away long before the others'.

"With all that is perfect and fine about her, there is something not right there," Sebastien said with deathly seriousness. "I will make it my duty to keep a close watch on her."

The two men by his side guffawed uproariously, their bawdy laughter drawing glances of curiosity from the surrounding men and sighs of desire from the women.

"I bet you will." Edgard threw back a mug of spirits.

Sebastien tried to keep the sheepish blush from his face, but failed. "It is only logical," he defended himself. "I already have an acquaintance with her."

"Like I said," Dureau teased, "you are her favorite."

Sebastien cuffed him on the shoulder, and the man tripped as the group swaggered from the room. "Be off with you then," he said. "Let us play some cards so that I may take your money."

Sebastien brought up the rear of the merry triumvirate as they left the hall in search of some private game. Try as he might, he could not stop himself from looking back, from taking one last glance at Geneviève.

The argument begun in his head some days ago grew louder, and he did not know which voice to heed: the one urging him to seduce her or the one insisting he keep to his duty.

❧ 15 ❧

Better to laugh than weep, then, if we can,
For laughter is the special mark of man.

—François Rabelais (c. 1494–1553)

They filled the narrow pathway between the tall conical shrubs flanking both sides of the garden corridor like sentries at post, their bright afternoon gowns luminous against the evergreen. There would be no hunt or other sport to entertain them this afternoon; it was a day for deputations, and the king would be imprisoned in his public chamber all day—his gentlemen with him—giving audience to the people of the region, and listening to their appeals.

Anne had worn a path upon the hearth rug all morning, pacing like a caged animal, seething as the day for Eleanor's meeting with her brother approached. The queen had departed three days ago to travel by horse to Marseilles; from there she and her entourage would travel upon a stately barge to Nice and attempt to convince Charles to meet with François. The importance of her errand eclipsed the joy of having the dowdy queen gone from court; if she was successful, who knew to what lengths François's gratitude would take him? For Anne, the possibilities were not to be borne, and she had flung herself from the confines of the room, looking for any distraction available.

Like a general taking point as he besieged a battlefield, Anne led her half dozen ladies through the symmetrically patterned gardens, oblivious to nature's artistry, stomping upon the gravel and grass as if she were stomping on Eleanor's head. The ladies had long since surrendered their attempts to divert her, and spoke amongst themselves in hushed whispers.

Geneviève followed obediently, Arabelle by her side, as devoted as ever, perhaps more. The door had opened a crack and Geneviève knew it, yet she did nothing to close it again. The fear and the worry assaulting her from every direction felt like the pummeling of fists, and though she knew her duty took precedence above all else, she needed the small succor of a friend. It could never be a true friendship, for such intimacy required a baring of the soul, and she guarded hers with a steely determination. But the isolation was no longer all encompassing, and for that, she was grateful. Geneviève could not deny the guilt she felt; it was the same when dancing with Sebastien, but she could not gate them out any longer. Her true king indulged himself, she rationalized; he would not begrudge her a little of the same.

The lovely but doleful procession passed through the archway shorn through the shrubbery, and entered the courtyard beyond, taken unawares as they stepped into the midst of a great brouhaha. A clamorous cluster of servants fussed around one man and his horse, packing his saddle bags, handing him his gear, readying his mount. Geneviève had never seen the man before; though no doubt of middle age, the man's sharp nose, pointed chin, and overlong swath of gray hair spoke of preeminence, affording him a dashing air.

"What's goes on here?" Geneviève asked Arabelle over the clip-clop of their heels upon the cobbles.

Arabelle turned her blue eyes to the man and shook her head. "I'm not sure. He could be one of the king's *chevaucheurs* making ready. The king keeps these messengers forever on the move."

Geneviève felt the tremble as it crested through her body. Questions about the French king's messenger had come up twice in her communiqués with England, so desperately did King Henry want to know the identity of François's message riders. As much as they could surmise the nature of the discourse between France and Spain, England needed to know the details, needed to prepare if an attack was soon to be forthcoming. By cutting off the dispatches between the two sovereigns, such information might be gleaned firsthand.

"Do you know who he is?" Geneviève asked Arabelle and the miniature, mousy Lisette, who had joined them.

Once more Arabelle shook her head, but Lisette giggled. "I do not know him, either. Do you find him attractive? He is quite debonair."

Geneviève smiled indulgently at the small woman. She had come to realize how deceiving this pocket-sized woman's quiet demeanor was; in truth, Lisette was one of the most unbridled among them.

"No, not attractive," Geneviève said, feigning nonchalance. "I merely find all the fuss curious."

"Well, if he is a messenger, it must be quite an urgent dispatch to send him forth during the day. They most usually leave at night, when there is less chance he will be followed."

Geneviève ground her teeth, wishing to moan aloud at the disobliging information. She had to find out this man's name; she could not let this opportunity pass.

Without another word for her companions, Geneviève skipped to Anne's side.

"You have forgotten your fan, madame, and you are flushed with the heat. I will run and fetch it for you," Geneviève announced, and scampered off.

"It's not necessary," Anne called to the swiftly retreating form, but to little avail. Geneviève continued on unabated.

"I'll be no more than a moment," Geneviève tossed over her shoulder. "I'll cut through the kitchens and catch up quickly." She disappeared into the small wooden door leading to the kitchens and the quartermaster's station.

Her eyes took a moment to adjust to the dim interior of the low stone hallway, and Geneviève staggered about, unsure of which direction to travel.

"Oof!"

Bumped into from behind, she hit the wall to her left, scraping the palms of her hands on the rough stone as she braced herself.

"Beg pardon, mademoiselle," the youthful squire called as he rushed past.

"Of course," she assured him, brushing the dirt off her hands and silently thanking him for becoming her unwitting guide.

"Can you tell me, please, who is that man in the courtyard?" She trod on his heels like an obedient pet, heading toward the scent of curing meats and the clang of pots and pans.

The youth took the last step out of the confining hallway and into the cavernous kitchen. As large as the great hall itself, the sooty stone walls rose far above their heads. The chamber clamored with frenetic activity. The hundreds of servants who kept the king and court fed and happy, rushed about their work, calling out and talking as they did. The staff of the *paneterie*, who baked the bread in the stone ovens, and the *échansonnerie*, who dispensed the wine, worked beside the butchers and the pastry chefs while the scullions dashed about every which way. Geneviève almost forgot her purpose as her mouth salivated, assaulted by the enticing aromas—the warming dough, the sizzling meat, the juice-soaked fresh fruit—coming from every corner of the room.

"Beg your pardon, mademoiselle?" the young man asked, moving toward the scullery maid who held out the bulging sack toward him.

"The man in the courtyard," Geneviève repeated. "Can you tell me who he is?"

The squire took the package and stared at Geneviève with ill-disguised suspicion upon his long, horselike face. She forced a kittenish mask to fall over her features, one she had seen Lisette and the other women adopt so often when they plied all the weapons at their disposal on some handsome gallant.

The kitchen maid wiped her hands on her dirty apron and pushed back the lace-edged cap upon her forehead. "It is Monsieur de La Bretonnière, is it not?"

The young man suffered the loquacious servant a remonstrative gaze, but the damage had been done.

"Ah, *oui*, it is he, Pierre de La Bretonnière, the seigneur de Warthy," he said reluctantly.

"*Merci.*" Geneviève dipped the young man a fine curtsy with a bat of her exotic eyes and he willingly dismissed the departure from procedure. With a wink to the kitchen maid, who smiled broadly back at her, Geneviève rushed from the room before the youth's mind cleared and any questions came her way.

By no more than a good sense of direction did she find her path through the castle to Anne's deserted rooms. Locating the seed-pearl-embroidered fan her mistress favored, she composed her next message to King Henry in her mind, so anxious to send the most profound information she had garnered yet. She imagined his happiness, his pride at her work done so well. As she curled the finger brandishing the exquisite amethyst ring, Geneviève wondered if perhaps he would send her another token of his affection. Far better, perhaps he would soon send for her to live by his side, as did his daughters, Mary and Elizabeth.

"This package has been delivered for you, mademoiselle," Carine said with a flick of her pert nose toward the vanity, as she lay out her mistress's outfit for an evening at the king's salon. The maid smoothed the lavender and cream brocade, and beside it the matching bejeweled hood. By the foot of the bed, she had placed the cream, lace-covered shoes with their dainty wooden heels.

Rushing into her chambers with little time to spare, Geneviève pulled up short. This could not be one of her clandestine transmittals; it would never have been left with such lack of consequence. Yet she could not fathom who but King Henry would send her anything.

Geneviève scooped up the small square wrapped in periwinkle silk and untied the scarlet ribbon as she sat with a thump upon her embroidered stool. Carine bustled about, done with her work on Geneviève's clothing, flitting like a hummingbird over to the dressing table with forced insouciance, and taking great interest in the organization of Geneviève's brushes and perfumes. Geneviève smiled at her maid's obvious curiosity; Carine would make the clumsiest of spies.

Geneviève curled her shoulders and spun away, out of no grave concern to hide what lay within but to tease her exceedingly inquisitive maid.

Her small, bow-shaped mouth fell open as she revealed the dazzling pair of amethyst earrings sparkling upon the small swath of black velvet; the teardrop-shaped stones as large as the pad of her thumb hung from clasps of perfect white gold. She fingered them with timid awe and took up the folded square of parchment.

> *Mademoiselle Gravois,*
>
> *Though I can never thank you for the life of my son, I offer these as a small token of my esteem and gratitude. I have had them wrought especially for you. As beautiful as your eyes, I thought they would be the perfect complement to the ring I have seen you wear so often.*
>
> *François*

Carine gave an astounded gasp, unable to restrain herself from peering over Geneviève's shoulder. "They are exquisite, mam'selle. You have garnered the best of the king's favor."

Geneviève turned with agitation; Carine had dared sneak a look at the gift and read its accompanying missive as well. Geneviève brushed aside her annoyance for the meaningless irritant it was, while Carine attached the jewels to Geneviève's ears. She turned to face the looking glass and laughter snagged in her throat. The earrings did indeed perfectly match the ring on her finger, as if they were created simultaneously.

"How exceedingly considerate of the king," Carine remarked.

Indeed it was, and yet Geneviève could not reconcile the gesture with the man who had made it.

Carine laughed as she glimpsed the bewildered amazement on Geneviève's face. "You *are* pleased," she cooed. "What a wonderful gift."

Was it wonderful? Geneviève was unsure. She knew only that life was a twisted journey, and hers more than most. Irony was assuredly God's deranged sense of humor.

Silks, satins, brocades, and velvets lay draped upon every available surface of the duchesse d'Étampes's audience chamber; iridescent primrose silk fell across the settee, crimson flowed over the ottoman, royal blue velvet hid the corner chairs.

Like half-blossomed roses, the women pranced about, scantily clad in frilly petticoats and shifts as the maids measured them for their new gowns, tossing the yards of exquisite fabrics around their shoulders to see how the color might highlight their own particular beauty. No one could choose before the duchesse herself had discarded any selection, but there was more than enough fabric to please all of her attendants, to send them twittering with squeals of delight as the contingent of merchants brought out each new bolt of cloth and each new style pattern.

Federico II of Gonzaga had returned from his latest visit with his mother, Isabella d'Este, and his trunks overflowed with Italy's most current fashions and cosmetics. François loved for the ladies of his court to be adorned with nothing but the finest couture the world had to offer, and he made sure the Italian brought them on a regular basis.

A knock at the door brought scarcely a notice, and little more as the adolescent serving girl opened the door to the messenger. She took the parchment he offered her and closed the door quickly. The mousy girl stepped sprightly through the dithering throng and delivered the small square with the red wax seal into Geneviève's surprised hands.

A pang of fear gave Geneviève's heart a squeeze, but she cast it off. No message from King Henry would be delivered in such a public manner; she need not fear exposure.

Unfolding the parchment, she was well aware of the prying eyes and the women who grew closer about her, but she wanted them to see, wanted the normal events of her life to appear as transparent as possible.

"Hmm. Very well then," she said as she finished the message. Her reaction, though genuine, was nothing more than diluted surprise.

"What is it, Geneviève?" Monique asked, having not been able to read the complete missive, though she had craned her neck the most.

"My aunt has died," Geneviève said as if she reported the condition of the weather.

"Mon Dieu," the woman responded. "I am so very sorry."

Arabelle and others rushed to her side, ready to make a fuss, to either join her or support her as she fled into the dramatic bliss that could be mourning at court. But Geneviève would have none of it.

"Please do not concern yourselves." She stood and busied herself with hunting among the fabrics once more, as if to put a punctuation mark on her feelings. "She had been sick for a very long time. It was to be expected."

"But she raised you," Sybille insisted with a frown. "You spent your entire childhood with her. Will you not miss her?"

Geneviève gave the question a moment's thought. The passing of Madame de Montlhéry did affect her profoundly, though not in any predictable manner. With her aunt's death there was no one in the world who knew her true identity—the person she had been born as—save for the king of England. There was something liberating and yet surreal in the notion.

Geneviève turned to Sybille with a straightforward violet stare. "She did her duty by me and for that I shall always be grateful."

Her dispassionate candor astonished more than one woman, but only Béatrice made to remark upon it. "Will you trav—"

"Madame, madame!" Lisette rushed in on her little feet, crashing the door open in her haste to find her mistress, cutting off all other conversation.

"Here, Lisette," Anne called, stepping out of the cloth being held against her and away from the bevy of servants surrounding her, put on guard by the urgency of her lady's tone.

"Oh, madame, you . . . will . . . not . . . believe . . ." Lisette struggled with words and shortness of breath. She gained Anne's side, bending in half, one hand on her chest as it heaved to find air while the other reached out for her mistress's arm.

"Bring her a drink." Anne snapped her fingers. "Some ale, please."

The women jumped to her bidding, crashing into one another as they moved in a different direction. Arabelle was the first to latch onto the jug of ale and sloshed some into a pewter mug.

"You will excuse us?" Anne tossed a pointed look toward the merchants posed before their wares, ears and eyes as wide as their lidless trunks. "We will call for you again in a moment."

With reluctant bows the men took their leave, disappointment evident on their polite expressions, frustrated they would not be present to hear what astounding news the diminutive lady would impart.

Lisette threw back the beverage and gulped, drew a huge draught of air, and suppressed an unladylike belch with one fisted hand.

"Now tell me, Lisette"—Anne wheedled like a parent to an overstimulated child, but with a distinct lack of patience—"what is the matter? Is anyone hurt? Is the king well?"

"I'm sure the king is fine, madame," Lisette finally said and, as one, the women inched forward to catch every word. "Though he may be embarrassed by what has happened to the queen."

"What has happened?" Anne beseeched her, pulling her roughly by the arm and throwing them both upon the settee, the others gathering close around them, the lustrous fabrics and ingenious patterns forgotten like yesterday's stale bread.

Lisette's round cheeks flushed with high color. "The queen and her train had finally reached Nice and the day had dawned for her to meet with her brother."

"Yes, yes, it was to be three days ago." Anne spurred her on, having little tolerance to receive information she already knew. "But no word has yet come from the encounter."

"Oh, but it has, madame." Lisette giggled. "And it is most delicious." She took the last swig of ale, keeping her captive audience on edge for as long as she could.

But Anne tired of her drama. "Lisette," she growled, and the silly girl needed no further prodding.

"The day was rather fine." Lisette launched into her story with hands thrashing theatrically. "And the emperor decided to wait for his sister at the end of the dock in Nice. Much show was made as the queen's boat pulled up to the pier. There was music playing, and the emperor stood there accompanied by his guards."

Here Lisette turned to the women hanging on her every word. "You know how handsome those Italian men are. I can only imagine how debonair they must look in their uni—"

"Lisette!" Anne barked, patience stretched to the breaking point.

Geneviève was grateful for the duchesse's intervention. Had she not stifled Lisette's aimless prattle, Geneviève was quite sure she herself was about to pummel the flighty woman.

"Oh, ah, *oui*, madame," Lisette mumbled, contrite. "They had erected a fine wooden ramp with unique railings, especially for the queen, to make it easier for her to disembark. You know how ungainly she can be. And they had moved it up to her boat. The music grew louder as she descended, three of her prettiest ladies behind her. The emperor waited patiently, himself splendid in velvet and gold, or so I was told. He reached out his hand, the queen and her ladies stepped onto the dock and . . . and . . ." Lisette took a deep breath, her mouth open, the words hanging in the air.

"And, and?" the voices rang out, as if the chorus to Lisette's solo.

"And the dock collapsed. Each and every one dropped into the water like a stone!"

Hands flew to mouths stunned into silence. But only for a moment. The laughter, when it came, rang from the rafters, trembled the tapestries on the walls and the glass in the windows. Such a vision her words created . . . resplendently attired royals flaying and sputtering in the water, the queen floundering like a fish.

"You jest?" Anne laughed as hard as the others did, unable to lower her hand from her drop-jawed mouth. "Surely, you jest?"

Lisette shook her head, her shoulders quivering with unabated laughter. Geneviève turned, quaking with suppressed mirth. She stared out the window as if to see the humiliated nobility far to the south.

"Was anyone injured? Was the queen hurt?"

"No, madame, though it took many soldiers to fish her out of the sea. Of course, everyone made quite the fuss over her, concerned over her delicate sensibilities, worried she would become ill from a little dousing."

"And the emperor. What of him?" Anne asked.

"He was not injured, either, except for his pride. It is said he roared with rage, calling everyone imbeciles—the mayor, the governor, all of them—for not insuring his safety and that of the queen of France."

"*Mon Dieu,*" Anne whispered as she pushed herself to her feet and came to stand beside Geneviève near the sun-saturated windows, as if she could see the comedic scene in the distance beyond. "What will the king say? He will be so angry." Though she spoke of doom, her smile grew wide and her eyes glinted with satisfaction.

"She is returning in four days. Who knows what else will happen when next they meet," Lisette said, enjoying her fame as messenger.

Anne spun as if struck. "What's that you say?"

Lisette cowered; perhaps she had said too much. "The queen, madame. She is to meet with her brother once more."

Anne's green eyes narrowed and their spark of pure delight dimmed appreciatively. The room held its collective breath as the women waited to see how the mistress would take this news. Ever so slowly, the duchesse began to shake her head, and a glimmer of a grin once more tickled her rosy lips. Geneviève watched in wonder as the woman threw off the despondency as if she discarded an old soiled gown.

Anne threw back her head, auburn curls dancing against her back, and laughed riotously. "Oh, but for all the gold in the kingdom, would I have been there."

❧ 16 ❧

You have no enemys except yourselves.

—Francis of Assisi (1181–1226)

"The king is playing tennis with the duc de Montrichard, but we will not attend the match. His rooms will be empty, and I wish to surprise him." Anne held the white silk garment out to Geneviève. "Bring this to his privy chamber, and lay it out on the bed. Display it prettily, would you?"

Geneviève accepted the shirt and recognized it as the one the duchesse had worked on for the past fortnight. Sewing was not her strong suit, and Anne had anguished over each stitch in the silky fabric, the intricacy of each full, flouncy sleeve, and the detail of lace at collar and cuff. The king was a man of fashion, and his mistress's gift would appeal to his distinct sense of style.

"Put this on top once it is all arranged." Anne handed her an aromatic lily, dappled pink flesh edged in white and centered by golden stigma. "He will know from whence it came."

With a curtsy, Geneviève took the bloom by the stem, unable to keep her nose from inhaling the powerful fragrance.

The aroma followed her like an invisible tendril as she hiked through the vast château. Geneviève approached the king's chambers, inured to the sight of the halberd-brandishing gentlemen of the guard resplendent in blue and gold, who stood forever at the double gilded doors.

"From the duchesse." Geneviève held up the shirt and flower as explanation for her presence, but she need not have bothered; her face had become a part of the court tapestry and the men presented her with a nod of recognition as they turned the brass handle and allowed her entry without question.

Geneviève tiptoed across the colorful tile flooring of the audience chamber, each little step loud in the vast empty suite. Never had she seen it so deserted, so vacant of roisterous courtiers and obsequious servants. How different it looked, the beauty of its architecture and décor especially striking without competition from any inhabitants.

Another set of guards stood at the single door separating the public room from the king's privy chamber. Geneviève stood at the aperture, and though once more afforded unquestioned entry, she hesitated at the threshold. To enter a king's private rooms, or anyone's for that matter, was to peel back layers of armor, to see beneath that which the person chooses the world to see and to peer deep within them, to their very truth. Geneviève did not want to look so closely at this man; she wanted only to see him for what she knew him to be. She admitted her fear and wanted nothing more than to spin on her heels and run.

"Mademoiselle?" The tall guard who held the door open beckoned quizzically.

Geneviève shook off the apprehension. *"Excusez-moi."* She dipped her head and stepped through.

The door clicked to a close behind her, but she did not move. Her astonished gaze rose from the marbled floor to the gilded frescoed ceiling above, to rest, in the end, upon the crowning glory of the room . . . the artwork hanging upon the limestone walls.

Geneviève circled the room, studying each breathtaking painting in its gilded and scrolled frame.

From the inauguration of his reign, François had used every

treasure at his disposal to tempt the world's greatest artists to his court. Michelangelo and Raphael had turned him down but had sent many of their works in their stead, canvases now forming the centerpieces of France's growing collection. Here the most cherished were displayed; in one bearing Raphael's name, St. Michael slayed a demon; in another, a most delicate beauty in magnificent maroon velvet stroked her long locks.

Raised for a time in his father's home, a man who took food from his own plate to give to artists who found sponsorship under his roof, François had inherited this artistic passion and made it his own. It was rumored the king of France had threatened to choke Benvenuto Cellini with gold, and that his warning had worked; the artist had answered the call and would soon make his way to the court, following the footsteps of Primaticcio, Andrea del Sarto, and, of course, Leonardo da Vinci.

Geneviève arrived at the far wall, against which stood the king's mammoth bed, royal blue and gold curtains hanging from the golden columns at each corner. One—and only one—intriguing painting held the place of honor above the head of the bed. Not as large as the others, this was a portrait of a woman who smiled amidst the earth-toned landscape with the most captivating and curious of expressions.

"He called her *La Gioconda*."

"*Merd—!*" Geneviève yelped, spinning round, losing her balance, and falling upon the bed.

The king stood in the threshold, his large silhouette outlined in the bright light of the presence chamber at his back.

"Your Majesty"—Geneviève dropped into a curtsy like a felled bird—"please forgive me."

"Fear not, mademoiselle. Rise up," François said blithely. "The guards alerted me to your presence. And I can see by the possession you clutch so tightly that you have come upon an errand."

Geneviève remembered the shirt and flower in her grasp, both a bit crumpled by her stumble. She straightened her shaky legs, took a step toward the door, remembered her errand, turned back to the bed, but hesitated under the king's scrutiny.

"Do you like the painting?" he asked casually, but there was a note of such deep sadness in his voice it startled her, and she did not hear the words for the anguish of it. "I saw how you looked at her. You think it fine, *oui?*"

"Yes, Sire, I do," Geneviève answered honestly, turning back to gaze once more at the small portrait at the head of the bed.

With his long strides, François crossed the room.

"What is it that speaks to you?"

Again, that note of bleakness in his voice. Geneviève turned to look up at his face. His hollow eyes had grown more so since she had first seen him, and more frown lines punctuated each side of his wide mouth. In the slanted sunlight of late afternoon, he looked like someone else altogether, an older and disheartened version of the once young, hubristic king. As if he felt her scrutiny, he looked down at her, one brow rising expectantly.

"I . . . um . . ." she floundered, tilting her head to one side. "I am sure most say it is her mouth that captures their attention. But for me it is her hands. They are so very graceful and lifelike, and her eyes. They seem to hold me in their sway."

François chuckled. "You have a keen eye, mademoiselle. I feel her eyes on me often, but they do not condemn me. And for that I am grateful."

Did he bear a heavy burden of harsh public opinion? Geneviève found it hard to believe a man of such noted arrogance would allow civil judgment to affect him. Many alleged that he never said a foolish thing yet never did a wise one, but Geneviève struggled to think he would feel the sting of such barbed arrows. And yet so much of what she had seen of this man in these past weeks spoke of humble defeat.

"It is not for my pleasure alone that I gather these treasures." François shuffled to the high-backed wing chair awaiting him in the corner. He lowered his large frame into the dented blue brocade cushion. From this perch, he could view every piece in his collection or gaze out the leaded glass window to the front gardens and the rolling hills of the land beyond. He put his elbow in a depression in the chair's arm and his head in his palm. "I want my people to open their minds to this genius, this beauty. Our artists mark the trail to enlightenment, if we can only learn how to read the signs." He turned back to the woman's portrait standing guard over the chamber. "Da Vinci taught me this."

Geneviève knew not what to say; she felt as if she had never met the man before her, and she struggled with the awkwardness of unfamiliarity. "I have heard he was a very learned man, Sire. That he knew of many things besides art."

" 'Tis true," François nodded. "I have never known a man as thirsty for knowledge as he, or as willing to share such with the world. The hours I spent with him I count as the most precious of my life. Never before or rarely since has my intellect felt so challenged, or my eyes opened so wide." He shook his head and a deep furrow formed between his brows. "I will never forgive myself for not being there at the moment of his passing."

Geneviève had heard the artist had died in his patron's arms, but it seemed the story was no more than rumor, another myth surrounding this enigmatic king. The king's own words dispelled it, and the naked anguish in his almond-shaped eyes could not be denied. It resonated deep within Geneviève, touching the pain of grief buried in her core.

"It was your bed upon which he lay? Your physicians who attended him?" Geneviève whispered, breaching protocol with such intimacy.

François dropped his hand into his lap and looked at her, perplexed. *"Oui."*

"Then you held him as tenderly as if it were with your own arms."

The elderly man's need for succor was compelling and she responded to it, in denial of all she had been taught. These days of close proximity had revealed so many of this man's cracks; despite herself she felt a sudden urge to fill them, perhaps because they mirrored her own fragmented existence.

The king rubbed at his forehead, seeing Geneviève's perplexed pity as if she wore it on her sleeve. "Complete your task, mademoiselle, so that I may tell the duchesse how well you saw to your duty."

With a quick dip, Geneviève turned to the high bed and laid the shirt upon it, fanning out the sleeves to display them at their best, and placing the flower at the end of one cuff as if an invisible hand held it.

She faced the king once more, gave a full curtsy—skirt opened wide—and made for the door. As she grasped and turned the cold gleaming knob, she heard his whisper.

"*Merci,* my child."

The ladies stood like pretty flowers all in a row along the rail of the grandiose spiral staircase in Château Blois, an artistic architectural achievement renowned throughout all of France. An exterior spiral-shaped incline, at each floor a landing overlooked the courtyard below. It had become tradition for the courtiers and nobles to rest at the rail, as if from a balcony, and watch the jousts and plays in the common, another place to see and be seen. Looking up from below, the spiral rose up like a five-story monument, the exterior of the pale stone balustrade festooned with a sculpted garland of crowned salamanders.

Here the ladies awaited the duchesse as she spoke with the king on the landing above, the sun once more shining bright upon the hordes milling below them, multicolored sparks bouncing off jewels and swords. With so much to look at, the women chatted amiably as they bided their time.

"I hope it is not forward of me." Arabelle reached out a tentative finger and touched the back of Geneviève's hand resting on the railing, and the discoloration upon it. "But how did you come by this mark?"

Geneviève looked down at the stain upon her flesh; it had been there as long as she remembered. It was a splotch more than a scar and could have passed as a birthmark. "It is a burn," she responded dispassionately. "Acquired the night of the fire that killed my parents."

"Oh, *mon Dieu*, my poor Geney." Arabelle's fair face flushed behind a hand raised in shock. "I had no idea. Forgive me, it was wrong of me to ask."

Geneviève reached out and lowered Arabelle's finger with a small squeeze. "Not at all. I remember nothing of the event and never has the wound pained me."

"But there are other scars," Arabelle whispered, "and other pains. *Oui?*"

Geneviève's silence revealed far too much, and her gaze skipped away from her friend's intuitive vision.

"I wager my scars would best any that delicate damsels such as you might boast." The king's cajoling voice echoed along the twisting, cavernous staircase and the ladies dropped into their curtsies.

"I have this one." Lisette held up one elbow, and the women craned around the king to see.

With a patronizing chortle, the king dismissed the small crescent-shaped disfigurement, no larger than a fingernail, on the back of her plump arm. "Why, I can barely see it. How did you come by it?"

"I fell out of bed as a child," Lisette pouted prettily. "And landed on a ewer."

François chucked her under the chin. "I see you survived well enough."

"Indeed, Sire."

"Where is the duchesse?" Jecelyn asked, having watched the stairs, waiting for her mistress to appear.

The king looked sidelong at his cousin. "She felt a need to freshen herself." The cloud passed over his features. "Perhaps you might see to her?"

"Of course, Your Majesty," Jecelyn said with a bob, and set off.

The king turned back to the expectant faces before him. "Can no one do better than this paltry contestant?"

Geneviève felt Arabelle's glance but would not rise to its bait; she would not show this man the scar on her hand, nor discuss how it came to be there. But a childhood spent learning how to use dagger and arrow had left more than cunning upon her. She pulled up the short puff sleeve of her almond-colored silk gown.

"Now here we have a contender." The king peered in, as did the other women, at the inverted V-shaped gouge upon the uppermost part of her arm, the thick line a putrid reddish purple. "Did you crash through a window?"

"No, Sire," Geneviève said with a jaunty shake of her head. "I was struck with an arrow."

The women gasped, pulling back with alarm, but the king stared at her, a glint in his tired, bloodshot eyes, as if Geneviève had thrown down a pair of gauntlets at his feet. With a glimmer of a smile, he doffed his feather-plumed toque, and pulled up the hair on the left side of his head. There a thick, white, hairless line ran through his full dark hair like a road running through a dense forest.

"Was it received in battle, Sire?" Arabelle asked with awed timidity.

The king chuckled. "No, at play. Though I have plenty enough gouges gained in battle. No, this one came from a day of fun. I was a young man, no more than a pup, though already king. We were visiting the estate of the comte de St. Paul for Twelfth Night and he had prepared the most marvelous mock battle for us to participate in. He had actually erected a model town upon his grounds, complete with a moat and a gun battery." The king looked out across the courtyard and the years. "It was the duc d'Alençon and I against St. Paul, Vendôme, and Bourbon."

For the briefest moment, the fondness in the king's eyes

dimmed and the small vertical crease between his brows deepened.

"It was a marvelous fray, one of the best ever. We pummeled each other with snow balls, apples, and eggs, but my squad and I soon gained the upper hand." The king laughed at what was to come and the ladies with him. Though they didn't know the story, they were charmed by their sovereign's self-deprecation. "St. Paul ran out of ammunition and thought it would best serve him to throw a burning log out of a second-story window. It struck me dead on."

Every one of the women stared at him, openmouthed and with bulging eyes. Geneviève lost herself, swept away by his story.

"I could have had him hung." François laughed. "But it was far too amusing. Except, of course, when they had to cut off all my hair to seal and cauterize the wound."

"Is that how you came by your current style?" Lisette asked.

"Indeed," he answered. "How surprised I was to see others boasting the same fashion within days. I couldn't very well change it back at that point."

The women all agreed.

"So what say you, Mademoiselle Gravois—do you concede?" He pushed back his heavy mop to reveal the scar once more.

Geneviève peered at it with mock seriousness. "Well, I don't know. It is large, but it does not look very deep." She pulled up her sleeve. "While this struck bone."

The king and the lady-in-waiting moved close together, a bare shoulder revealed, a head leaned down, a laugh between them.

"Well, whatever do we have here?"

Geneviève jumped back at the sound of her mistress's snide voice, tugging her sleeve down.

"There is my love now." The king dropped his hair and turned to Anne with an outstretched hand. "Nothing more than a battle of scars, *ma chérie*, one I fear I have lost."

Geneviève dipped at the offered victory, but with little gladness. The thunderous gaze from the duchesse did everything to dispel any triumph. How well Geneviève remembered her first conversation with Anne, how keenly she saw anger and suspicion in the woman's squinty-eyed gaze. All would be lost if the duchesse should dismiss her.

Anne placed her jeweled hand on the king's offered arm. "I am glad you have kept yourself amused in my absence." No one, especially the king, missed the derision in her tone.

"No, indeed, I was highly entertained. And I thank these ladies and especially Mademoiselle Gravois for that."

He gave them all a bow and Geneviève cowered at how the duchesse might interpret his words.

"You have brightened my day, mademoiselle." He took up Geneviève's hand with his free one and bowed over it. "You remind me a great deal of my beloved Lily."

It was as if he chanted a magic spell. To mention his dead daughter banished any qualms Anne's imaginings had caused her. For Geneviève, to be likened to a daughter, and a king's at that, caused her only more doubt.

No bird can ever fly
Like a heart can rise so high.

—Mellin de Saint-Gelais (1491–1558)

The dust rose up in great clouds; so dry was the earth, so thirsty for moisture, it lay parched and cracked, misused by the drought prevailing over the sweltering summer. The horses' hooves kicked up great puffs of particles and the wagon wheels left tracks in the powdery roads.

Today, like yesterday, the first day in the court's next progress, the king traveled beneath the gauzy curtains of his litter. Geneviève envied him; her eyes stung from the dust, and the taste of gravel lay thick upon her tongue.

"He must not be feeling well." Sebastien rode beside her in the group trailing the royal conveyance. How natural it seemed that they would seek out each other's company on the journey. From the moment the king announced he and his library were ready to make for their next home, thoughts of the guard had come to Geneviève's mind. The informal intimacy of travel allowed her to enjoy his companionship so much more than at court.

"I wish to go home," the king had said, and so to Fontainebleau they made their way, the palace the king longed for more and more with the passing years. There he would bring his beloved books and rest awhile.

"Perhaps it is his souvenir from Spain. I hear the illness plagues him with greater frequency these days," Dureau offered from atop his charger on the other side of Sebastien.

Lisette shook her head as she bobbed upon her clopping mare. "Nay. It is a gift from one of his many paramours." There was little note of churlishness as she gave voice to the rampant rumor; she simply relayed what to her were well-known facts. "It's been said that it may be the end of him."

"Truly?" Geneviève winced at the shrillness in her voice and cleared her throat. "He is that often ill?"

Sebastien frowned. "No one knows for certain what illness tortures him," he said with a stern sidelong glance to the small woman riding beside Geneviève. "But it does seem he is more and more frequently bedridden."

Such thoughts burst into Geneviève's mind. That King Henry would be keen to learn of François's declining health was understandable; that she should be bothered by it was not.

"I'm sure he will see his other physicians once we are closer to Paris," Albret offered, eager to soothe. "They will b—"

His words were lost as the thunder of galloping hooves roared up around them like a wave crashing against the shore and they no more than helpless pebbles in its path. A great posse of courtiers rushed by, whipping up the dirt and the dust, hats flying off their heads in their urgency forward. Those overtaken wrestled with their reins, fighting to keep their skittish mounts from bolting.

"Whatever is happening?" Arabelle squealed with fear from between the duc de Nevers and Sebastien's friend Edgard.

"Look!" Lisette pointed a chubby finger and all eyes followed.

Not far ahead, down a gentle slope, lay a small orchard abutting meandering farmland. Not as lush as it should be, it was the healthiest vegetation the cortege had seen along a dusty trail lined with dehydrated, yellowing oak. Trees heavy with bright green leaves dotted with coral peaches and purple plums stood in symmetrical rows, and sugar beets poked their lush leaves up toward the sun.

Sebastien smiled at Geneviève and she caught hold of his mischievous spirit. Together they kicked at the horses and set off, not to be outdone or denied the spoils of the road.

As the king looked on in amusement from the open curtains of his stretcher, the nobles descended upon the small demesne like starving locusts, tripping through the foliage and vegetation as if it were a great dance floor, hanging from the tree branches like acrobats on the stage. They plucked the fruit with little regard for ripeness, like snatching pearls from the neck of opulently dressed ladies. Bees, fat with nectar and pollen, hummed in agitation and birds squawked, protesting the disruption.

The farmer and his family raced from their home, begging the nobles with pathetic cries of outrage to cease their pillaging, mollified into a semblance of silent acceptance when the king's representative handed them two brown leather pouches jingling with coin. The courtiers paid them no mind, flitting from fruit to fruit, frolicking with joyful abandon and childish exclamations as they stripped the trees of their bounty, as they trampled tender tendrils beneath their stomping feet, as they robbed the farmer of his living, all in the name of entitlement.

They reached the small village of Fourneaux in the early evening, a little before dusk began to threaten the day, unable to make Orléans for the night as intended, their progress slowed by the king's mode of transport. As they passed the small hovels on the outskirts of the tiny town, mothers ran out of their ramshackle homes holding their children aloft, husbands assisted weak and decimated wives, all crying for the touch of the king.

Geneviève saw the pale and drawn faces, the small bodies limp in their parents' arms, and felt a rush of sympathy couched with a stab of impatience. These desperate people clung to their conviction of the healing power of the French kings, a belief as nonsensical as the royals' faith in soothsayers. The long-standing legend of the curative ability of the sovereigns seemed like false hope to her, one that opened the heart to a fair chance for heartbreak. Geneviève assumed François would ignore their pleas and continue on. He did not.

"Are you all right?" Sebastien pulled hard left on his reins to keep his mount from colliding with Geneviève's as she drifted toward him.

Geneviève pulled up and nodded. "Yes, I . . . I'm fine." She ticked her chin toward the scene before them, as the guards lowered the king's litter and the sluggish man hefted himself out from its confines.

The villagers rushed about him, circling him, his large head and broad shoulders rising far above the reaching, pleading hands. With great patience François reached out a bearlike paw, taking great pains to touch upon each head bowed before him, with a merciful pat.

"I did not expect him to heed their calls," Geneviève said.

Sebastien smiled. "He always has and always will, for as long as he is able, I'd wager."

Geneviève stared at the king. It was the same long, horselike face, the same slanted eyes, long nose, and wide mouth, and yet she did not know him, and the inconsistency ate away at her like scrofula itself, the disease most sufferers came to the king to cure.

"Are you feeling ill?" Sebastien asked. So many on the journey had contracted a stomach flux; the drought had dried up the wells, forcing the courtiers to drink from polluted waters. The duc d'Orléans suffered badly, as did Lautrec, who ran for the trees with great frequency.

"I'm fine, I said," Geneviève snapped, unable to contain the uneasiness and anger her tumbled thoughts caused. She regretted her sharp words the instant they left her tongue. "My apologies, Sebastien. It seems I am much more tired than I myself realized. A long night's sleep will stand me in good stead once more, I'm sure. I will make for my pillow as soon as we stop."

"I am sorry to hear that." Sebastien shrugged off her truculence, not batting an eye at Geneviève's astounded expression. He leaned over in his saddle and drew on her reins, pulling her and her horse as close as possible. "I have made the acquisition of a rare bottle of Bordeaux and was hoping you would share it with me this evening." His gaze slipped for an instant to the gathering of courtiers around them. "It is a very small bottle. Not enough to satisfy this rabble."

Geneviève lost the battle with her smile and leaned in as well, a coconspirator on a mission of entertainment. "Well then, I think I can make a change in my plans. For the sake of the Bordeaux, of course."

Sebastien's mouth spread and his dimples came out to play. "Of course," he said, and straightened in his saddle.

With a flurry of activity, the court spread out over the town and the surrounding territory. The king would stay at the abbey, high on the hill overlooking the river and the town proper, as would the queen and the duchesse alike. The *maré chaux des logis* scavenged to find sleeping quarters for the hundreds in the caravan, following the strict rules of conduct but forced to make unprecedented accommodations. The ladies of the queen and the duchesse would take the rooms of the two small inns while other nobles were forced to billet with the town's residents. Many of the king's gentlemen had chosen to forge on, to ride through the night and make for the estate at Orléans rather than bed down under tents or in the open air. Sebastien was not among them.

"That large tree there, do you see it?" he whispered to Geneviève as he took her reins and began to lead their horses away.

She followed his gaze and saw the lone weeping willow perched at the top of a rolling hill beyond the edge of the town square, its pale green, feathery fingers reaching down to tickle the earth as they swayed in the feeble breeze.

"May I see you there as soon as the sun has set?"

She could deny his hopeful gaze no more than the flutter of excitement in her belly. Suddenly shy before this man with whom she felt so comfortable, Geneviève nodded with a bashful grin.

Geneviève joined the procession of Anne's maids as they crossed the narrow wooden threshold of the Four Horsemen's Inn and climbed up the winding stairwell to a closet of a room in the peak of the wooden structure. Four narrow beds for six women meant two must sleep upon the floor, and the ladies drew straws to see who would get the cots. Béatrice accepted her fate with grace, while Jecelyn grumbled viciously about seniority, and birth having greater influence than any straw, short or long.

The dark-haired vixen continued to grouse as the group made their way back down to the common room for victuals. Only when she took a seat among three handsome cavaliers who plied her with a mug of ale, did her griping cease.

Geneviève picked at her food, tearing small pieces from the overcooked partridge and nibbling on it with little enjoyment. The room filled with the sounds of clanking mugs, plunking daggers upon wooden trenchers, and hurried footsteps of harried servants. Pungent aromas filled the air as did raucous voices, but Geneviève found all her concentration was on the small, unshuttered windows flanking each side of the door. The gray of dusk took its reign over the yellow glow of the sun with slow, agonizing triumph, until, at last, the sun conceded and dropped below the horizon.

Geneviève jumped up, startling the ladies at her side.

"Is everything all right, Geneviève?" Lisette asked as she tore off another piece of crusty bread and popped it in her mouth.

"Yes, yes, I am fine. I am so very warm." She wiped her hand on the back of her neck; the thin film of sweat was no feigned illusion. "I think I need a bit of air. Perhaps a walk will help."

Arabelle stood. "I'll accompany you."

"No!" Geneviève stopped her with indecorous haste, and laid a calming hand upon her friend, easing her back down to her seat. "You have begun your meal. I'll be fine on my own, I assure you."

"Very well," Arabelle acquiesced. "But please do not go far. We don't want you to become lost."

Geneviève tossed a smile and a tease over her shoulder as she made for the door with haste. "Yes, Maman."

She skipped through the portal, pleased to see Arabelle's smile and indulgent head shake.

The lopsided door banged to a close behind her and Geneviève stopped just beyond. A few noblemen lazed about the small town square, leaning chairs back against stone and wood buildings, voices low with exhaustion and relaxation.

Though the air had cooled but a few degrees with the absence of the burning sun's rays, the smidgen of relief was a gift, and Geneviève heaved a deep sigh of relief. A faint breeze stroked her, tingling on her moist skin. She put a hand upon her stomach, smoothing the thin linen, hoping to squelch the flutter of anxiety and anticipation beneath.

She ran then, thinking to dash up the stairs and bury herself in her bed. Sebastien was a king's guard and she a king's enemy. And yet the thought of him as no more than a man and she nothing but a woman, pulled at her with greater force than her fear could counter. Geneviève set her sights on the tree, a fuzzy round shadow upon the hill, and set off, lifting her skirts to hike up the narrow meandering trail through the grass and weeds. Her silhouette became a ghostly specter hovering up the side of the mound.

"In here, Geneviève."

The whisper came from the tree itself. Geneviève ducked down, looking through the curtain of feathery leaves, where Sebastien's mischievous smile found her. He moved forward on his knees and drew back the branches, as if opening the drapes of a hidden room. Geneviève gathered her skirts and scurried in on bended legs. Once within the burrow, she took his hand and straightened.

"Are we in a fairy tale?" she asked him, as he led her to the large trunk and she turned round.

It was a different world in the nook of the tree; the heavy heat of the day had not inveigled its way into the space formed by the gnarled trunk, the roots that buckled up out of the ground, and the verdant branches that reached down. Looking out, the real world beyond appeared like an opaque illusion through the haze of green, as if it were no more than a painting on the wall of a room—their room. The blurry vista made it impossible to see the black-haired woman who stood at the corner of the nearest building and peered at them from around its brown wooden frame.

"My very thought," Sebastien replied in wonder. "Come. See what I have for us." He conveyed her around the back of the tree with the smile of a playful child.

Geneviève brought her hands together and then to her mouth at the sight of his cloak spread out on the ground, snug between two burgeoning roots, the bottle of wine and two mugs sitting beside a small picnic of fruit and cheese and bread.

"Sit, Geneviève, and rest ye here awhile," he beckoned poetically, and she floated down beside him. She found the most comfortable seat in the very crook of the tree and he joined her. They giggled as he removed the cork from the bottle with a bright pop and the pungent, fruity aroma joined them in their secret hollow.

Geneviève hummed as the delicious beverage slithered down her throat. "How did you say you came by this?"

Sebastien waggled his brows at her. "I didn't, but I will tell you now. I won it at cards, much to the anger of the marquis Fontage." He laughed as the memory returned, broke off a piece of the warm bread and gave them each a portion. "He did not have enough coin to cover his bet and floundered for something. I had heard of his purchase of the expensive wine that very morning. I think I had it in mind all along to win a bottle of it."

Geneviève held up her tankard for him to fill once more. "Your thoughts made it happen."

Sebastien laughed. "It would seem so. My cards trounced his and he stalked away from the table with many a curse upon his tongue."

"But he lived up to his bargain?" Geneviève giggled, picturing the jowly marquis's fat, cracked lips blubbering as he swore oaths upon Sebastien.

"Most certainly." Sebastien chortled. "He may be a braggart and a leach, but he is honorable."

They guffawed at the dichotomy of his words; how well they summed up the true nature of a courtier.

The stars poked through the clear night sky as darkness pushed away the gray, as twilight triumphed over dusk's fleeting dominance. They spoke of everything and nothing at all. They shared their favorite poems, marveled over their love of art, but said not a personal word about themselves, as if neither wanted reality to join them in their secret place and ruin the magic of it.

They were of a similar mien—not as riotous as most courtiers, but quiet souls who kept their truths close to themselves. And yet they shared this laughter, this intellectual curiosity without haughtiness or grandeur, without fear of reprisal for their thoughts.

"I am glad you are here, Geneviève." Sebastien's voice purred like a satiated kitten, the sentiment bursting from him with unpracticed spontaneity.

"I am glad as well," she responded with a shrug, as if unable to deny her reply. She threw back her goblet and swallowed a mouthful of wine with a large gulp.

As he closed the space between them, his smile faded and his gaze grew intent upon her. He lingered, his face inches from hers. Her breath quivered as his lips drew near, and she parted her own in silent welcome.

Sebastien's lips were soft upon hers, his breath sweet and warm upon her face, his nearness alone a delight for her senses, his closeness bringing her to another place from where she usually dwelled. Here in this state of being there was no stark aloneness, no avaricious anger. There was only the two of them and the chirping of the crickets in the warm night air.

He explored her mouth as if it were an undiscovered land and he its first conqueror, yet there was nothing demanding or insistent about his expedition. His lips brushed against hers with a delicate sweep, a gossamer touch, as he gently moved his head back and forth. With an indrawn breath, he nuzzled her face with his, yet with hardly a touch at all; his eyelashes fluttered against the apple of her cheek, his lips against her forehead. It was the most intimate embrace Geneviève had ever felt and she swayed with its intoxication, opening her mouth as he returned to it again and again.

"I do love kisses," he whispered, and her eyes flashed open in surprise.

"You do?" she asked, her voice rising, bewildered.

Sebastien laughed huskily, and pulled back a bit. "Does that surprise you?"

Geneviève had the decency to wince with embarrassment. "Well, yes, a bit. I thought only women enjoyed kisses. Men would rather . . . well . . ." she faltered, feeling the heat rise upon her cheeks. "Well, I think most men would rather arrive at the destination, as it were, than enjoy the journey."

Sebastien threw back his head and laughed aloud, his eyes sparkling, his dimples deep and full of mysterious shadows. "I suppose you are right, Geneviève. Many a man would rather have his belly full of wine, but not I." He wrapped his strong arms around her waist and pulled her close. He opened his mouth, grazed it along hers with a promise. "I would rather taste the moist sweetness upon my tongue for as long as possible."

Geneviève felt her heart thumping against his and she reached up, allowing the tips of her fingers to caress his dimples and the slight cleft in his chin as she had wished to do for so long. His lips took hers again, and together they drank.

* * *

They whispered their good-byes in the early morning, neither realizing how long they had been gone, neither caring. He kissed the wrists of both her hands as he saw her to her door, leaving with a quiet rumble of laughter as she shivered with the touch.

Geneviève passed the door of the common room, tiptoeing in swift silence, doing her best not to disturb those within, their heads dropped upon the scarred wood tables, snoring and snorting in their drink-induced slumber. The winding stairs creaked and she longed to hush at them but knew it would do her no good. She slipped into the room, the sound of soft, restful breathing greeting her, the lumps of her roommates indistinct in the muted moonlight filtering through the lone window at the gabled peak.

With great stealth, she made her way round two of the beds and the curled-up form of Béatrice on the floor, then pulled up short. Her bed was not empty; a long, slender body filled its space, a head of thick black hair covered its pillow. She stood over the form, arms akimbo, considering for a moment how good it would feel to reach down and throttle Jecelyn until the aggravating woman fell from her perch.

"Oh, I'm sorry, Geneviève. I have taken your bed, haven't I?" The counterfeit sweetness cast such fantasies aside. "We did not think you were returning, with such better company that you found this night."

Geneviève's jaw tightened. How like the conniving woman to have found her out. No wonder no one had come looking for her as she had expected. There was little Geneviève could do about her now, no matter how strong the urge to yank the woman out from the threadbare sheets by her hair. She found some space at the end of Arabelle's bed and gathered up someone's discarded gown, rolling it into a ball, hoping it was Jecelyn's as she smashed it into the shape of a pillow. As she tried to find some comfort on the thin ticking put down for Jecelyn's benefit, she felt hands reach down and loosen the laces at her back. Once released from the tightness of the stays, she took a breath of relief, rolled onto her back, and smiled into Arabelle's sleepy face, giggling softly as her friend sent a stuck-out tongue in Jecelyn's direction. Rolling back onto her side, Geneviève closed her eyes and dreamed of a fantasy world of wood nymphs and kissing satyrs.

❧ 18 ❧

All strangers love her, will always find her fair,
Because such elegance, such happiness,
Will not be found in any town but this:
Paris is beyond compare.

—Eustache Deschamps (c. 1346–c. 1406)

"Come with me, ladies!" the king yelled to Geneviève, Arabelle, and Jecelyn as they crouched behind the hitching posts.

The bright fruit careened across the courtyard, whistling by as the men and ladies of the court hurled them at one another, splatting with juicy collisions and a bursting of citrus. Out of ammunition, the three women took refuge behind the thick beams, trying to hide the red ribbons on their arms that would give away their location to the blue contingent. The battle of oranges—one festivity in the days' long homecoming celebration—had ensued. The custom, begun in the twelfth century in Ivrea in the north of Italy, had become a favorite pastime of the king from his earliest days, calling for the contest whether it was carnival or not.

Returning to Fontainebleau proved the greatest elixir prescribed for the king, and he rebounded, taking part in every celebration, both day and night.

Rushing past the women, François seized an abandoned shield and crossed in front of them. "Stay behind me as much as you can, but grab those oranges. We need weapons, my soldiers!"

His enthusiasm was infectious and the women jumped into it, scooping up any fruit not smashed open on the cobbles or the stone walls. Jecelyn gave hers to the king, who launched them with incredible accuracy. Arabelle and Geneviève hurled those they gathered at the opposing team, closely following the king as he cut a swath toward the "enemy" with great guffaws of laughter and whoops of delight.

More who wore the red arm bands joined in their siege, and Arabelle and Geneviève fanned out from the king to cover more ground. From the right Geneviève caught sight of three or four blue bands and swiveled toward them. Lisette, Sebastien, and two other members of the opposition fell in her sights as they tried to flank the red team.

Geneviève cocked back her arm.

Jecelyn stepped up to the king with more oranges, jumping directly between Geneviève and her shot at Lisette.

Geneviève hesitated, barked a laugh, and launched her weapon.

The juicy orange hit Jecelyn squarely on the side of the head. The fruit burst upon impact. The left half of her face became a mess of stringy pulp. She dropped to the courtyard with a cry of pain and indignation.

"I believe you have hit one of our own team, Mademoiselle Gravois," the king yelled, but not without a peculiar expression contorting his features.

Geneviève batted her eyes, all innocence and coyness, fighting hard against the volcanic laughter in her gullet as she dodged another hurtled fruit. "Oh dear, have I?"

Beside her Arabelle roared, not able or caring to hide her hilarity at Jecelyn's expense.

"Did you see her go down?" she howled, doubling up with laughter as she grabbed at Geneviève's arm. "She dropped like a stone! Marvelous!"

Geneviève turned, allowing the mirth to finally burst forth. The two ran off, weak from laughter and no longer useful. Jecelyn stared at their retreating backs with pure evil upon her orange-stained face.

François sprawled back inelegantly in his chair, rubbing his large full belly, eyes soft and satiated. Strewn about the chamber in the east wing of the palace were his greatest lords and physicians; his almoner, Jean Le Veneur; and his confessor, his squires, and gentlemen of the chamber. The same pages who had delivered his lunch now cleared the remnants of it away, the clanking of pewter plates and golden chalices challenging the melodic voice of Monsieur du Chastel.

"A little louder, if you please, monsieur," the king requested, and the bishop of Mâcon raised his beautifully modulated bass voice. Pierre du Chastel had been François's *lecteur du roi* for the last three years, and these lunchtime readings were atop the list of the king's favorite moments in a day. Most often of late, he would request something from Rabelais, at other times passages of Roman history or heroic tales of antiquity. Some days it was not such weighty material but a romance instead, and Du Chastel would read from *Destruction de Troie la Grant* or perhaps *Le Roman de la Rose* with his perfect diction.

Beyond the double doors of the main entry at the far end of the rectangular room, a great rumbling of voices coalesced behind the gilded wood, as if an orchestra warmed up for a performance. The king sighed, knowing the time of such midday relaxation drew to a close.

"That will be all for today, I fear, monsieur." He dismissed his royal reader in midsentence, and the small, cassock-clad man closed his book and retreated with a slight bow.

"I wish to speak to the room before we open the door, La Barre." The king stopped the *premier gentilhomme de la chambre* from beginning the day's deputations, the first since their arrival at Fontainebleau, with a raised hand.

The noblemen returned to their seats at the now clean table,

Montmorency and Chabot among them, though on opposite sides of the table. The bitterness between them had reached new heights as Montmorency's investigations into the allegations of Chabot's malpractices continued. Like children vying for the love of a parent, the two men jostled for preeminence in the king's council, though neither gained much ground.

"I have two things to share with you this day," François announced, his ashy, aging skin glowing with a joy few had seen of late. He rubbed his hands upon the high-gloss mahogany table before him. "First, I would tell you that I have decided to sojourn at this most splendid of palaces for the majority of our time."

Mixed responses met his pronouncement, most of surprise, few of pleasure. Those nobles who would travel with the progress to check their lands, would now need to do so on their own; it was costly to travel, though far more costly to be away from court. Many had foreseen the king's decision; his desire to lead a less nomadic life had been instilled in him by his mother and her family. François was at last bringing their desire to fruition.

"It is not only for the pleasure of the hunt in this bountiful forest surrounding us, but for the beauty and splendor that is Fontainebleau." The king opened his arms in a wide gesture, offering the marble, gilt, and art of his own room as evidence.

The great kings of France had long since made a home for themselves on this magical spot. Legend held that here a babbling spring and the goddess who watched over it had been discovered by a hunter name Bilaud. The fecund spot, washed by the spring, became known as the fountain of blue. What had begun as a primitive castle in the twelfth century, oval in shape with a gatehouse, a square keep, and flanking towers, had become the pinnacle of French architecture. François had torn down all of the original structure save the old dungeon, rebuilding it in its current variation, one of the greatest palaces in all of Europe, envied by kings far and wide.

"I can think of no better place to rule our great nation, to bring to bear the full force of our nation's strength, than here at Fontainebleau." François grew more serious; some feared his words hinted at war, which they could neither afford nor support. "This brings me to my second announcement. But perhaps I shall let Monty tell you, as it was his work and guidance that has led us here."

Montmorency narrowed his small, bag-rimmed eyes at the king, perplexed; to take credit could bring one great acclaim, or make one the scapegoat if the plan should fail. Monty shrugged off his diffidence; his efforts were well-known. He could not very well turn from them now.

"We have heard from the emperor." His pronouncement set off a riot of shock and sound; the cries filled the room to the top of the vaulted, frescoed ceiling. "Indeed, it is true."

"Bretonnière has at last returned?" Chabot petulantly asked about the king's first messenger, finding no delight in his rival's success.

"No, he has not, though he should have, and days ago. I have sent others out in search of him," Monty replied. "No, this message came by way of La Forest. Our ambassadors have been hard at work and their efforts have not been in vain." The chancellor stuck out his weak chin, holding his words until the silence held them all captive. "Charles, the king of Spain and the Holy Roman Emperor, will be the guest of France and its great king within a few months' time."

François sat back in his chair, a wicked smile of triumph on his wide mouth, as a cacophony of jubilation rose up around him.

"How?" Chabot asked, one of the few quiet voices among the raucous many.

The king leaned in, anxious to tell. "We had learned the emperor soon needs to reach the Netherlands. What swifter path to take than through our lands? Monty saw it for the opportunity it is and began the negotiations. I will issue the formal invitation this very day."

"But what of Henry?" Chabot continued as the voice of cynicism.

"Ah *oui*, Henry. *Mon ami* Henry," François said with the far-off look of introspection. "How much I feared him. Once. Now I fear him not at all. He is far too busy killing off his wives and his own people. He cannot see how much it weakens him."

Chabot would not let it lie. "But if he and the emperor align, it could be catastrophic. We have not the arms to defend ourselves, nor the funds to build such arms."

François looked upon the admiral with a closed face of skepticism. "The chance of our most pious Charles taking the hand of the sinner Henry is beyond reason."

"But there is a chance," Monty interjected. "And all the more reason to court Charles, all the more reason to look upon the emperor's coming visit as a great triumph."

Most in attendance agreed, and the acclamation wafted through the room; some men clapped each other on the back, while others broke out in applause. Chabot bit his lips; he had offered Montmorency fodder for his own cause, something he had not intended to do.

A laughing king gave a nod to La Barre. "I think we are ready," he instructed, and the chamberlain opened the door.

The horde of those who would hope for the ear of the king congregated far beyond the door and the long staircase leading to it, their fetid body odors, heightened in the heat of high summer, entering the room first. But the pleadings of the door today were unlike any the gentlemen of the court had ever seen, as the king called more and more of the plaintiffs into the chamber, allowing them to approach and beg their case while in the same room.

They would talk of the change in the king and the events about to take place at every table and every salon. Many would learn of it, and they, in turn, would tell others.

* * *

The knock upon the door roused her from an afternoon's slumber, and Geneviève muttered a mild complaint as she crossed to the door, irked at the interruption. Sleep had become an elusive companion, and she felt slighted to have it chased away by a visitor. She opened her door but there was little welcome in the gesture.

"My, but you look a bit of a mess."

"Lodovico!" Annoyance vanished and Geneviève burst with joy at the sight of her friend. The artist had not made the same journey to Fontainebleau as she, having been sent by the king to capture the image of his sister in Navarre, whom he had not seen in a while.

"Ah, that's better." Lodovico laughed as he took her hand, bowed over it, and presented her with an enthusiastic smooch.

Geneviève bobbed a quick curtsy. "I am so pleased to see you. When did you arrive? Will you be staying long?"

She had indeed missed the artist and the flighty, untroubled distraction he afforded her.

"I fear I have come with some disturbing news." The stick-thin young man barreled his way into her chamber, and plopped himself upon her bed as if it were the most natural thing in the world.

"What? Tell me. Are you to be sent away again?" Geneviève rushed to follow, confused by the strange expression on his narrow face.

"I'm afraid you must resign yourself, *cara*." He looked up at her with a sad gaze, but a smile broke out across his lips as bright as the morning sun. "I have officially become an *artiste du roi*."

"Oh, how wonderful, Lodovico. You must be so very pleased." Geneviève took his hands in hers and gave them a fond squeeze, trying to deny how delighted she herself was, trying not to allow another bittersweet bond to form, but the moment to steel herself had long since passed. She released their embrace and took herself to her vanity chair. "Tell me of your journeys."

The young man rolled his big eyes camouflaged by the crop of shaggy hair grown bushier since last she saw him. "Ah, *cara mia*, every court is a mirror of the other—the intrigue, the gossip. The music may be different but the song remains the same."

His laughter died away on empty air. Lodovico's lips pursed as he stared at her.

"How do I find thee, Geneviève? I have been so busy posturing about my own greatness, I have yet to ask after you. Have you been unwell?"

Geneviève shook her head and turned away, busying herself with a sudden necessity to straighten the bottles and potions upon her vanity. "No, no, I'm fine. It is . . . it is a difficult adjustment to this way of life, always on the move, always bustling here and there. It is far different from the life I've always led."

"A better one?"

"How could such a life not be? There is nothing but the finest of everything at the court of King François."

He took her chin between his thumb and forefinger, brown eyes scouring her face as he leaned close. "You have become a courtier."

Geneviève thought to obfuscate, but abandoned the notion; it was not easy to hide from the discerning eye of one who captured the essence of life with brush and paint. "I have. It was what I was sent to do."

Lodovico straightened, a troubled line forming on the smooth skin beneath the tousled bangs.

"*Si*, it is, but make sure you do not lose yourself in the process."

"Now that you have returned, I have no fear on that score." She spun to him then, a sudden thought dawning. "Will you grant me a favor, Lodovico?"

He smiled his charming, boyish smile, pleased to see his friend cheered once more. "Anything for you, *cara*."

"Will you paint my portrait? A miniature?"

He plunked his hands on his hips, eyes sparkling. "I have been waiting for you to ask."

* * *

Through the many and varied courses, through the astonishing performances, through every moment of the great gala, Geneviève had followed every move of Thomas Cheney, the English ambassador, newly arrived at court. It was in his honor the banquet was named, though all knew it was a celebration of the king's negotiations with the emperor that lay behind the most splendiferous of events the court had seen in many a month.

Far more dazzling than any great hall, as majestic as the most imperious cathedral, the ballroom of the Château de Fontainebleau dazzled the eye; it was the supreme context for the world's most glamorous nobles. Styled in the manner of an Italian loggia, the open arches covered by rich, colorful frescoes and intricately carved stuccoes, were topped by a coffered ceiling the color of rich chocolate. Though dressed in their finest, replete with jewels, the courtiers were but bits of ornamentation in this exquisite chamber.

As she entered the circle of Sebastien's arms, as she felt the thrill found there—the memories they invoked, the promises they offered—Geneviève's stare followed the stick-thin, angular ambassador about the great hall. How adulterous she felt as she danced with the dashing guard, as if she betrayed Henry by finding pleasure in another man's arms, as if having the Englishman in their midst would reveal her perfidy to his king, or behavior she perceived as perfidy.

There had been other such moments for Geneviève and Sebastien since the first magical night beneath the tree, and yet her agony over her actions would not yield. No matter how often she argued with herself that pleasure had little to do with loyalty, the nagging guilt pecked away at her like a crow upon a dead, rotting carcass along the side of a deserted road. Her feelings for Sebastien, her loyalty to Henry, her changing impressions of François raged a battle within her, the war the most rampant when alone at night, and she found little ease in slumber.

"Would you care for some wine, *ma chérie?*" Sebastien asked with a bow as the rousing *volte* came to a close.

Geneviève began to nod, but the motion became a shake as the orchestra struck the slow, ponderous notes of a somber *pavane*.

"Will you pardon me, Sebastien?" Already she walked away from him. Rumor held the Englishman was not much of a dancer and only took part in the less vigorous of dances. Here was her chance and she would not let it pass. "I have promised the duchesse to partner the ambassador, and I see he is at his leisure."

Montmorency and the queen had stepped away from Cheney, and for the moment, he stood alone. Geneviève scampered across the room before another captured his attention, Sebastien's words of regretful forgiveness fading away behind her.

"My lord," she called out in that most English of greetings as her prey began to step away.

The tall man stopped and turned, eyebrows rising on his pasty white face.

"Mademoiselle?" He bowed as he spied Geneviève's flustered approach.

"Gravois," she informed him. She did not expect him to know the name. Her identity was secret to all save the king, Henry had assured her time and time again, and the convoluted streams of communication between them—cryptic messages passed between four or five hands before reaching each other—guaranteed it. "Would you care for a dance, sir?" Geneviève curtsied as she reached him, hiding the flush of her forward actions.

Taken aback, Cheney sputtered with an inelegant accent to his simple French. "I . . . well . . . I . . . but, of course, if you wish. It will be my pleasure, Mademoiselle Gravois." His whiny tone made it clear that it was not his pleasure at all, but it would be unseemly to deny a lady of the king's court.

The odd pair strode onto the dance floor and took their place at the end of the slow-moving line of couples. The stiff ambassador led her through the simple steps—three forward then one back, one forward then two back—with little grace.

"You have recently come from your own court, monsieur?" Geneviève asked with all the feigned casualness she could muster.

"I have," Cheney responded, pale blue eyes fixed upon his feet and the intricately configured parquet floor, as if to move his gaze would surely send him spilling upon the multicolored wood squares.

"And how is your king? Well, I hope?"

"King Henry is not much himself these days," Cheney responded without thought, too distracted by his own awkwardness to guard his tongue.

Geneviève frowned at the nebulous response. "Whatever do you mean?"

The ambassador shrugged his pointy shoulders. "Do not misunderstand me, mademoiselle. King Henry is a powerful ruler who has done a great deal for his country. But I am afraid his health and his recent . . . disappointments have left him in foul temper. To say he takes it out on his courtiers would be to state the case mildly."

"You mean to say he treats them badly?" Geneviève wanted to stop where they stood and shake the man until he gave her details. Then she remembered he was a diplomat, a master of speaking much and saying little.

"I would never say such a thing at all. But he . . . he keeps us on our toes, demanding no less effort than that which he is willing to give himself." There was more to his prettily phrased words; it rang in the sudden sharp edge in his voice.

"I am sure his insistence is to honor a worthy cause," Geneviève said as the pair dipped at the end of the line and turned to the left, where the couple before them had gone right, to return to the beginning of the promenade.

"A king's glory is always considered a worthy cause, at least by the king."

Geneviève fell silent as she mulled his words.

"But why so many questions about my king, mademoiselle?" Cheney asked, daring to take his eyes off the dance floor.

Geneviève smiled her muted, courtly smile. "Would you believe I saw him once? Oh, it was a very long time ago." She had expected the question and had the answer well rehearsed, yet she had not foreseen how hard she would have to work to keep the disappointment from her voice. "I was a very little girl at my father's side at the field where my king met yours, where the great golden tents rose up in the air. I remember your king." Here she giggled with practice. "Though I suppose I remember his grandness and bright hair the most—they would be the most memorable to a wee child."

"A delightful story." Cheney was charmed, as intended, with no more thoughts as to the bounds of her curiosity.

The slow song came to its end and Geneviève dropped his hand before the last note faded away.

"Thank you, monsieur." Geneviève dipped a shallow curtsy, hands fisted into tight balls by her side, and turned on her heel. She left the ambassador bewildered by her brusque dismissal, but she paid him no further heed. She had come to him in search of the fortifying testimony she craved, for the words of a regal and righteous king to bring her back into focus. Instead, she had gotten nothing but more confusion, and the company of this festive crowd chafed her like a scratchy wool cloak. She quit the room with imprudent haste, under more than one concerned and discerning gaze. At this moment, Geneviève longed for nothing so much as to be gone from this court, this life, this world, and she ran as if to escape it all.

❧ 19 ❧

A slight flame comes out of the emptiness and
makes successful that which should not be believed in vain.

—Michel de Nostredame (Nostradamus) (1503–1566)

"What do you mean, I cannot see the king?" The duchesse
d'Étampes stood toe-to-toe with the mammoth halberdier who stood at the door between waiting room and council chamber. Though the man had no doubt seen the ravages of many a battlefield, he squirmed beneath this powerful woman's wrath, beads of sweat forming on his upper lip.

"My apologies, Madame la Duchesse, but the king has insisted he not be disturbed."

Anne crossed her thin arms over her chest, porcelain skin mottled by fiery splotches. "I am quite sure the order did not extend to me."

The soldier pinched his lips as if to seal them forever. "No one is to disturb him. Those were my orders."

The heat of outrage wafted off the woman in waves, as if to scorch everyone around her. Thwarted, Anne snarled once more at the soldier—bestial, with dire threat—and huffed over to the small grouping of chairs, dropping onto an embroidered cushion like a stone.

With a shared roll of their eyes, Geneviève, Arabelle, and Sybille took their posts around their infuriated mistress, knowing if she did not find satisfaction soon, they would feel the sharp edge of her ire.

"Oh, good Lord," Sybille muttered, and her company followed her gaze to the room's entry.

On the threshold stood the Dauphin; by his side, as always, Diane de Poitiers.

Anne rose to her feet, as she must to greet Henri, though it pained her greatly.

"*Bonjour, Majesté.*" She dipped him a fine curtsy.

"Madame," Henri countered with a graceful side tilt and short bow of his head.

The women's gazes met, equally impervious. Without a word, each gave the other a most perfunctory obeisance.

"I wish to see my father." Anne forgotten, or perhaps ignored, Henri approached the guard, as had the duchesse.

With a bow, the soldier—by now cursing the name of the man who put him on duty that day—turned the king's son away as he had the king's mistress.

"I am sorry, Your Majesty, but the king insists he not be disturbed. By anyone."

Henri scowled, as he had most of his life.

"Madame la Duchesse already awaits him," the soldier offered, as if to deflect any further reprimands from the Dauphin.

Diane's eyes flashed with a devious glint. "Then we should wait as well." She leaned toward her lover as if to speak confidentially, but it was intimacy for appearance's sake; she wanted Anne to hear.

With a nod of agreement, Henri followed her to the settee across from Anne. There was little mistaking the salacious grin of satisfaction on Diane's face. Tension choked the room; Geneviève opened her fan, unable to breathe in the stifling air. Like combatants across a battlefield, the two groups sat, neither attempting to breach the silence with polite conversation.

Diane and Henri whispered between themselves, the woman's laughter grating on Anne's already strained nerves.

Sybille tried time and again to distract her cousin with conversation, but the frustrated duchesse would have none of it, answering with one-word grunts.

"I hear Monsieur de Gonzaga has returned from his moth—"

The latch clicked, the door inched open, and the anxious bevy in the waiting room jumped to their feet, as if they would rush the door to be the first to enter.

But no one moved, all progress denied in the face of those who came to the threshold.

Catherine de' Medici wore a smile on her plump face the likes of which few had seen in many a day. Henri stiffened to see his wife leaving his father's inner council chamber. Any smugness on the haughty features of La Grande Sénéschale's face disappeared as if scrubbed away with a rough cloth.

"Good day to you, Your Highness." Catherine curtsied and crossed into the waiting room, her step faltering at the sight of the group awaiting her. It took her but a moment's recovery for her surprise to turn into hauteur.

"I thank you, Catherine, and you, monsieur."

Though he was not visible, the king's deep baritone inched out into the room, full of sincere congeniality and gratitude.

Anne and Henri shared a look of concern; there was enough of a struggle vying for the king's favor; they had no wish to share it with Catherine or whomever she had brought to meet François.

All such considerations were forgotten when the man stepped into the room. Geneviève felt her breath hitch in her chest, and one quick glance at those around her revealed they felt the same sudden rush of apprehension.

The tall young man wore the all-black cloak of an apothecary or physician, a four-horned black felt hat upon his long face. His presence filled the room, a spirit not to be ignored or denied.

"Husband." Catherine paid greeting to Henri, ignoring the woman who stood by his side.

The Dauphin responded with a silent bow. "Pray introduce us to your companion."

"Oh, of course, wherever are my manners," Catherine responded with effusive politeness. Turning to the man by her side, she gave name to the nobles in the room.

The enigmatic man greeted each with a very deep, very silent bow.

Catherine held the stage with great superiority. "And this is Monsieur Michel de Nostredame."

The name meant nothing to them, but it seemed as if it should.

"Welcome to court, monsieur," the Dauphin said.

"*Merci*, Your Highness." The raspy voice was thick with secrets.

"What brings you to the palace?" There was little polite equivocation to Anne's query.

The intense gaze turned to the duchesse and Geneviève felt the onslaught of it as she stood beside her.

"I am a guest of the Dauphine's," Nostredame replied, giving no real answer.

Henri's smooth brow crinkled. "I see. And what—"

"Come, monsieur." Catherine stepped upon her husband's words mercilessly. "We must be off. There is much to do this day."

If she had intended her words to incite further concern, the future queen of France could not have done any better.

The apprehensive assemblage watched the odd pair until they turned into the corridor and out of their sight. As if in a dance, all eyes turned back to the king, poised in the doorway; all hearts beat quicker at the enraptured look upon the aging sovereign's face.

"*Bonjour, mesdames.*" The king entered Anne's spacious presence chamber as the morning sun began its climb to midday, its rays finding no flesh as it streamed in the gaping wall-length windows. The ladies had run from its scorching touch, hiding in the shadowy, cooler corners of the vast room. The fingers of the fiery orb found nothing more than robin's egg blue and sunflower tile, matched in the rich fabric on the walls, walls graced by the long, tapering limbs of the caryatids that flanked the gilded artwork.

The royal wing of the château consisted of two pavilions joined by a gallery. Like those of the king himself, the rooms of the duchesse d'Étampes were found in the Pavillon des Armes. François had had them designed to her unique and elegant tastes, and they rivaled those of any queen.

"Good morning, Your Majesty." The ladies rose and curtsied. Anne moved to her lover's side, her sage silk and the layers of taffeta beneath rustling as she skittered on her tiny, ribbon-festooned slippers.

"You look luminous, *ma chérie.*" The king bowed over her hand and brushed his full lips across her flesh. "I burn with your touch. It was a night I will always remember."

Though the king whispered his endearments, Geneviève heard them from her nearby perch, recognizing the contentment of well-served passion in his husky voice.

"Will you take a walk with me, dear Anne?" François asked. "The hydrangea is in full bloom and the sun has not yet reached the garden."

Anne gleamed. "It will be my pleasure," she purred. "Ladies, if you please."

Though she had spent the night in the king's arms, decorum called for chaperones when upon a public stage.

Arabelle rose, as did Geneviève and Lisette, and they formed a train behind the regal couple. Jecelyn joined them from the far side of the room, sneering as she passed close to Geneviève with a discourteous bump of her shoulder, the faint smudgy remnants of purple and green bruises visible beneath the layer of powder around her left eye. Sybille would remain in the chamber with Béatrice, who had yet to recover her full strength after weeks of battling the flux she acquired on their progress.

They strode through the golden gallery connecting the pavilions, the crowning glory of the most lavish palace in the land, with slow admiration. Breathtaking stuccowork skirted the long passageway marked by chandeliers and windows; this carved plaster and powder of marble were topped by frescoes painted directly upon the wall, image after image intended to glorify royal power and prestige. Everywhere were symbols of the king's wisdom and courage, some drawn from antiquity, and always the salamander and the fleur de lis.

Passing out of the Cour du Cheval Blanc, the troupe entered the more pristine and formal back garden. Not as ostentatious as the Grand Parterre, nevertheless it embraced its visitors in nature's calm stillness.

The king plucked a huge round blue blossom, a perfect ball of petals, from a bursting shrub and handed it to Anne. "I hope you will not be surprised to hear that I need your assistance, *ma chérie.*"

Anne accepted the gift and plunged her pert nose within its soft foliage. "You know there is nothing I would rather do than help you."

François smiled, patting the delicate hand resting in the crook of his arm. "Then I wonder if you would be inclined to some travel?"

"You wish me to leave court, Your Majesty?"

"For a few days at most." The king stopped and turned to Anne, her ladies hovering a discreet distance away. "It has come to my attention that England's King Henry will be passing close to our border very soon. I would like for you to bring him my regards."

"Has the meeting with the emperor fallen out?" Anne asked.

"No, on the contrary. Plans proceed beyond my expectations," François explained. "But I would not be doing my due diligence to my people were I not to take every advantage, and pursue every opportunity as it rose up before me."

"Does this have anything to do with your conversation with that man yesterday, that Nostredame?"

François raised his chin. "You know well I take advice from many quarters. He has offered some theories for me to ruminate upon, some prophesies to ponder."

Anne searched her lover's face, chewing on all said and unsaid.

"But . . ." Anne blinked her green eyes, pale in the bright light. "Me? You wish for me to take the meeting with Henry?" For years, the duchesse had been one of the king's greatest advisers, on both domestic and foreign issues, but she had never conducted negotiations on her own.

"Do not look so surprised. The women of this nation have often brought about its greatest accomplishments in diplomacy. If it were not for the efforts of my mother and Margaret of Austria we might still be at war with the emperor, my children might never have been returned to me." He shook his long head in naked adoration. "*La paix des dames* gave us the Treaty of Cambrai and the chance for this land and its king to heal."

"If it is what you wish, then rest assured I will do my best." Anne raised her chin and threw back her shoulders, but the gesture did not obscure the caution in her voice.

The king smiled with pleasure. "Then I will tell the council of it. I hesitated to do so until I had your accord." François put his pawlike hands upon her small shoulders. "You are one of the most brilliant women I have ever met, Anne. You will handle yourself splendidly, I am quite certain of it. And you'll find an additional treat upon arrival." He grinned mischievously. "My sister will be waiting for you."

Anne brightened. "Marguerite will be there?"

The king's sister had forever been a stalwart supporter of the duchesse, for they were alike in both political and religious philosophies. It had been many months since the women had shared company and Anne would delight in a visit with the woman who had helped raise the king, who was as devoted to him as she was herself.

"She learned as much of diplomacy as I. Marguerite will help lead you through any difficult moments, on that you can rely." Anne put her hands over his where they rested upon her shoulders, lifting up on tiptoes to nuzzle his nose with her own. "I won't let you down, my liege. You will see."

He wrapped his long arms around her small waist and pulled her against him. "You never do."

"But you have already told the king you will make the trip, have you not?" Sybille strode beside Anne, as Arabelle, Jecelyn and Geneviève rushed to keep up. From the main wing of the château, they crossed the Cour Ovale to the small wing beyond. Here the lesser nobles made their homes and here, in the bleakest corner of the ground floor, Madame Arceneau awaited the arrival of her mistress.

"Yes, of course." Anne begrudged the response.

"Then what possible difference could it make what Madame has to say about it?" Sybille huffed with a crass familiarity only a relative would dare.

Anne crossed the cobbles and entered the far building with the prowess of a gladiator rushing at the lion upon the Coliseum floor; no shortness of breath plagued the fit woman, as it did her cousin and Arabelle. Geneviève kept pace, invigorated by the physical exertion, feeling so very lazy after all these months at the pampered court.

"I know she will give me affirmation." Anne turned a dour stare on her cousin as they plunged through the quiet corridor. "And I need to hear it."

Geneviève thought it might be the first time she had ever heard an inkling of fear in Anne's voice.

Anne knocked on the knotted wood of the small closed door

with three quick raps, showing little patience in the request for admittance.

"Come," the distinctive voice called, and Anne needed little else. She flung the door open and stepped in.

"You are here, Madame Arceneau?"

The sinister shadows inhabited the room; it belonged to them, and they allowed the mystic access to it. Subdued golden candle flames cast wavering light, pale circles of illumination, and their fumes mixed with those of incense, spices, and something sinister and untamed.

Everywhere Geneviève looked there stood bottles of potions, jars of herbs, talismans and amulets of the soothsayer's craft. It was difficult to find where to stand among the collection of mysterious objects.

From the farthest corner of the room, the aberrant, girlish squeak beckoned them. "I am here, Madame Duchesse."

Anne crossed the room, stepping, nearly tripping, over the books and charts scattered upon the bare floor. Her ladies hurried after her, Geneviève reluctantly, as she tried to discern the strange markings on the stone beneath her feet. Black marks against gray granite formed the shapes of pentagrams, stars, and moons; a strange language formed incomprehensible sentences.

Without invitation, Anne dropped herself into the chair at the small table covered in the same maroon velvet Geneviève had seen on her first glimpse of the mystic. The woman appeared as pale as ever across the small expanse, a wraithlike face glowing from out of her looming hood; white eyes staring out from the translucent skin like two glowing crystals.

"Tell me of the days to come, madame, for I would know my path."

Madame Arceneau fixed her gaze on Anne, but neither moved nor spoke in response to the demanding duchesse, as if she gazed into her soul rather than her eyes. Shifting slowly as though time held little consequence, unconcerned by her mistress's tapping fingernails upon the tabletop, the soothsayer reached into a hidden pocket of her cloak and pulled out her long, narrow deck of cards. As she splayed them out across the surface, their colorful and grotesque pictures formed a message, one for her eyes alone.

"You will be traveling soon," she said with a rising lilt, as if she herself was surprised.

Anne looked back at her cousin with a supercilious glance. No one knew of the plan save the king, Anne, and her ladies. There was no possibility the mystic had heard of it from anyone.

"Correct, madame. Can you tell me how I shall fare on my journey?"

Madame Arceneau dealt three more cards, peering down at them as if from a distance. She shuffled the cards and dealt them again, grabbing small bits of herbs and tossing them over one shoulder, a pinch of powder over the other, and studied them once more.

"You will return with treasure, Duchesse." The mystic looked up. "I see no more."

"Hah!" Anne slapped her hands down upon the table and thrust to her feet as if shot from a cannon. "I knew it. I shall be successful," she cried. "Nor will I make myself a joke of the court as the ill-mannered cow did." Anne danced around the close room, untying the small pouch at her wrist and tossing it to the clairvoyant. "My thanks, madame."

Arceneau offered a small dip of her head and hid the jangling purse away in a flash.

"Perhaps your ladies would care to hear of their future."

"Oh, yes." Annie laughed. "What a splendid idea. Arabelle, would you care to have your cards read by the gifted madame?"

Arabelle hesitated, but her eager smile spoke her truth. She sat in the chair Anne vacated and, within minutes, the visionary forecast a bright and sunny future full of love and children for her. Arabelle rose from the seat, glowing with bursting confidence in the perfect days of her future.

"Come, Geneviève, it is your turn," she said, holding the chair out.

Geneviève raised two hands and shook them. "No, thank you. I'm sure someone else would rather enjoy the opportunity."

"Come, come, Mademoiselle Gravois," Anne insisted. "I don't believe I have ever seen you ask the advice of my mystic."

Geneviève choked on a response. To call the drivel Madame Arceneau offered *advice* was kind but also blind, yet she would not overtly chide her mistress's beliefs.

"Perhaps the young lady has no faith in my words," Madame Arceneau said, the vaguest hint of a smile upon her hard-edged face.

Geneviève dared to gaze into the strange eyes and saw the challenge in them. She grabbed the back of the chair from Arabelle's hands and dropped herself upon the seat, pulling closer to the table with a shriek of the wooden legs as they scraped across the stone floor.

"Tell me, madame, tell me all the wonderful things in my future." Geneviève clenched her hands together and thumped them upon the table in front of her.

With an arrogant waggle of her head, Madame Arceneau took up her cards and shuffled them, pale eyes never leaving Geneviève's face. At last she dealt them out into a cross, and placed the deck by her side.

Geneviève waited—leg twitching beneath the folds of her heavy skirts—for the happily-ever-after tale of her life she was sure was forthcoming. She longed for the woman to look down at the cards, spew her nonsense, and end this travesty, but no such movement came.

The woman's wraithlike skull fell to her chest as if struck, her chin lolled against her breastbone.

Arabelle gasped. Anne and Jecelyn stepped back in fear.

"What is this?" Geneviève asked, and turned to the women behind her, but they shook their heads and shrugged their shoulders.

They leaned forward, realizing the low, rumbling hum came from the mystic, from deep in her throat; it was the sound of the devil crying out from the depths of hell.

All of a sudden, as if revived, Arceneau's head jerked up. Her eyes rolled in their sockets till they latched onto the face in front of her.

"Beware!" A deep male voice came from out of the small skeletal mouth of the mystic, and for the first time Geneviève shook with palpable fear. No matter the talent of this fraud, a voice could not be so altered by any human means. This was the voice of someone—or something—else.

Geneviève put one hand on the back of her chair; she had had enough, she was done with this, and turned to bolt. The cold digits felt like bones as they strangled her other hand, as the frigid fingers of Madame Arceneau reached across the table, latched on and pulled.

"Oomph!" Geneviève cried as the table stabbed her in the ribs, as the force yanked her upper body across the table. Her face was no more than inches from that of the mystic. Geneviève shuddered to see the blankness of the woman's face, as if she were no more than a vessel for the truth, a blank canvas awaiting the painter's brush.

"There is a beast around you, one that could consume you," the guttural voice groaned at her. "You must beware."

The last syllable spoken, a last rattling gasp of air emitted, and the woman collapsed into unconsciousness, slithering out of her chair and onto the floor with a dreadful thump.

Anne pitched herself forward to grab for her. "Help me," she cried.

Arabelle and Jecelyn jumped round, helping the duchesse pull the mystic to her feet. Dragging her across the room, they laid her upon the small blanket-covered cot in the opposite corner.

"A drink, Geneviève. Get her a drink, quickly."

Geneviève stood, confounded, slack-jawed, and dazed. Her

mistress's order loosened the blight of fear clutching her and she shook it away. She searched the mayhem of the room, found jug and ewer, jumped to it, and splashed whatever liquid the jug held into a dented and scarred mug. Crossing to the bed, she held it out to Anne, keeping her distance from the mystic.

Anne tipped the mug to Madame Arceneau's lips, clear fluid drizzling out from her gaping mouth. The woman swallowed, coughed, and sputtered. With a deep breath, her lids fluttered and her eyes opened.

For one pregnant moment, she stared at the faces bent over her.

"What has happened?" She tried to sit up, but her eyes began to roll once more and her head wobbled precariously upon her shoulders.

"Lie back, madame," Anne insisted with a gentle push. "It would seem as if your . . . reading for Mademoiselle Gravois has left you ill."

The cold stare of the mystic found Geneviève over Anne's shoulder. In silence, the mystic studied her. A faint flush of color brushed across her cheeks. "I remember it not at all."

"It is of little concern," Anne told her with a pointed glance at Geneviève and the other women; there would be no mention of the confounding incident in front of the mystic. "We will leave you now to rest. But I will send my physicians to attend you at once."

"There is no need, Duchesse. I have everything I need here."

"Be that as it may," Anne countered, shooing the other women from the room with her waving hands, "I will feel more assured if I hear from them."

"As you wish," the mystic conceded, sounding tired as the group crossed the threshold and Anne closed the door behind them.

Out in the passageway, every bulging eye lit on Geneviève.

Arabelle reached out and took her hand. "I am so sorry, my dear."

Geneviève cringed. "There is no need to be sorry, Arabelle. It is all folderol."

"We will seek the advice of another," Anne continued, as if she had not heard Geneviève besmirch the powers in which she so deeply believed. "I am sure Catherine will allow us an audience with her mystic. I hear he is a great power."

"It is not necessary, madame," Geneviève assured her.

Anne rushed down the corridor, pulled up, and turned, a pointed finger thrust at Geneviève. "No, there is a need. Rest assured you will be protected. The king will see to it."

Geneviève would not argue with such vehemence, but gave a small nod in thanks. As Anne stalked off, Geneviève caught Jecelyn's intense scrutiny and averted her gaze. There was nothing in her depths she wanted this vindictive woman to find.

The tapers were nothing more than nubs in their pewter and bronze candlesticks, and yet the release of sleep had not blessed her. Geneviève thrashed in her bed as she had all night, the linens no more than a tangled, knotted mess. She sat up and threw them off in frustration. She quit the bed and its dissatisfaction with a huff. The generous chamber she had been so grateful for when she had arrived at the château had become a confining prison cell, and she needed to escape it. She threw a laced silk cloak about her shoulders, pulling its concealing hood over her jumbled blond hair, and flung open her door.

Out in the dark corridor, Geneviève pulled up, hovering by her door, looking down the long, abandoned passageway, thinking twice about wandering the castle in the middle of the night. The silently plodding pages had extinguished most of the wall sconces, as they did most nights, but here and there a few lone flames cast weak and wavering light. She could fell great beasts with a single arrow shot, gut and clean them, cipher and decipher the secrets of a nation, and yet fear of darkness remained hidden in her depths, as if she were that small child, abandoned by parents so cruel as to die, unloved by an aunt who claimed filial connection but offered no affection.

Geneviève pushed herself away from her door and crept along the hall in her thin slippers. She needed a drink, a powerful draught of heavy wine or brandy to slay the beast of her thoughts, to quiet it long enough to allow her some peace and somnolence. Perhaps she would find a poultice left on the stove to steep, to ease the pain splitting her head in two.

She found no one in the kitchen save two scullions, asleep in the ashes of the hearth, but gratefully located a full bottle of *eau de vie* and, though fruitier than her tastes preferred, she threw back a large gulp, satisfied by the immediate trail of warmth burning from throat to gullet. Geneviève made to steal away, thought again, turned and grabbed the whole bottle off the stained sideboard, and slipped out of the quiet room, the low crackling fire the lone witness to her thievery.

As she crested the landing of the second flight of stairs, the effects of the powerful beverage struck her; the tingle of relaxation nipped at her fingertips. She longed for her chamber now, and the small goblet that would bring her another portion of the fluid. Geneviève turned to the right—and froze.

The scuffling step came from back around the bend. All her senses were alert. She dare not turn, dare not stay, and she began to move forward once more. But the shuffling continued, inching closer. If the footsteps belonged to another insomniac, Geneviève mused, he or she would make no great pains to keep their presence concealed—might, in fact, look for company when a night's somnolent embrace refused them.

Geneviève drew closer to the next corridor, the one leading to her chamber. She could not allow her pursuer to follow her there.

Geneviève slowed her pace, as if she strolled without a care, humming a lulling tune low in her throat. She put her hand in her pocket and withdrew it, opening her clasped fingers.

"Oh dear," she murmured idly, looking down at the tile floor in front of her as if she had dropped something. She bent her knees and squatted down, her nightgown and cloak ballooning around her. In their concealment, she reached beneath the fabric and pulled her dagger from the sheath strapped to her leg. With the small weapon hidden in the palm of her hand, she rose again and continued on, turning the corner that would take her to her room.

Once beyond the edge of the wall, Geneviève threw herself flat against the stone and waited, allowing herself no more than a shallow breath, fearing to give her presence away. The furtive footsteps grew closer. She braced her left hand on the wall, raised the right with its drawn dagger.

Like a hunter intent upon its prey, Geneviève caught the scent of the body, one of muskiness and herbs, before she saw it. Every muscle clenched in readiness. The form crept round the bend. Geneviève stepped out and grabbed. A half second of fumbling, a squelch of surprise, and she grabbed a throat, squeezed and pushed, forcing the hooded form back against the wall. With her left forearm against the interloper's neck, Geneviève pinned the intruder to the stone with the tip of her dagger.

Two cold, bony hands fought against her, but they struggled ineffectually.

"Who are you?" Geneviève hissed and, with the dagger still in hand, used her palm to push back the concealing hood.

She gasped at the pale face, the white eyes gleaming out at her, releasing the tension of her hold in shock. Madame Arceneau lunged forward, trying to take advantage of the opportunity. Geneviève recoiled and pushed back again, thudding the mystic's head against the wall, holding the tip of her weapon to the woman's vein-threaded throat. The sharpness of the misericorde—a battlefield weapon used to end the life of a mortally wounded enemy with merciful swiftness—nipped at the thin skin.

"What do you want of me, woman?" Geneviève felt the creature of hate and anger that lived in her raise its head, so quiet it had been of late. This woman and her strange eyes brought it out like a randy *chevalier* in a roomful of virgins.

"I've come to tell you the truth." The childish voice struggled through the hold upon her throat.

Geneviève felt her upper lip curl in revulsion. "Truth. What truth?"

"Your truth."

Geneviève pushed the small woman harder against the wall. "Then tell me if you dare."

The mystic bared her teeth at Geneviève. "You are the beast I saw. I know you are up to no good."

A flash of fear and revelation squeezed at Geneviève's gut, but she swallowed it back. This woman was nothing if not clever; those eyes may not see the future, but they saw everything else, and the rest she inferred. But inferences were not enough to be hung upon.

"Tell me, old woman, what will I do?"

Madame Arceneau lowered her inhuman gaze to stare down at the dagger point sticking into her ribs. "You will kill."

Geneviève sniggered from between clenched teeth. "That is not a particularly intuitive assumption at this juncture. Now is it, madame?"

"Not me," the soothsayer sneered with impatience. "Another. One of high importance." She leaned into the dagger, taunting, her face closing toward Geneviève's. "A royal."

Geneviève felt her teeth gnash and the ache in her jaw as the muscles hardened. "And what's to stop me from killing you now . . . from silencing you and your nonsense forever?"

"It is all written down and entrusted to my greatest ally." The fin of flesh hanging from the center of the fortune-teller's throat wobbled as she spoke. "It will be delivered to the duchesse should I meet with an untimely demise."

Geneviève's hand squeezed the handle of the dagger until it

shook. Visions of the woman's slit throat oozing her life's blood were brilliant in her mind's eye. She lowered the weapon.

"What do you want?"

"Money," the mystic said with a sickening smile, "and a home of my own, one on the rue de Turenne."

Geneviève raised her eyes to the coffered ceiling. "You're mad. I have no such funds, no such influence at court to get you such things."

Madame Arceneau would tempt fate and Geneviève's hesitation no longer. She stepped away from the wall, sliding off down the dim, empty corridor like a ghostly specter wafting along on its nightly haunting. "Then you had better find a way."

Geneviève threw the empty bottle against the stone of the hearth, where it crashed and shattered into pieces. All its fluid gurgled in her gut and her head swam with its intoxication. But there would be no sleep for her tonight. The words of the mystic haunted her, screaming in her head until she longed to pull her hair from its roots if it meant they would leave her alone. The fear and anxiety refused to release her, making her sick as it rung all breath from her lungs.

She paced a worried circle from door to bedside and back again, looking at the treasures she had strewn upon the cold linens. The jewels the kings had given her were all she had of any worth and yet she didn't know if they would garner her enough to placate the blackmailing mystic.

Geneviève dropped to her knees by the bed, laying her head against the soft mattress, rubbing her forehead back and forth as if rubbing away the pain and worry. The thought of their loss was more than material, and it sickened her.

As the sneaking, slithery light of dawn smudged the leaded glass of her window, Geneviève stared beyond it, startled to realize she did not know which jewel she would miss more.

It is far safer to be feared than loved.

—Niccoló Machiavelli (1469–1527)

The brown and brittle grass crunched beneath the horses' hooves as the troupe rode out, hats pulled low against the glare of the sun, the cacophony as loud as the crackling of a massive fire. Geneviève burned with her own frustration and disappointment; the eager anticipation of the king's falcon hunts was dampened by the augury following her like the long shadow that rushed over the sun-dried ground behind her. She found no joy in this day. Her doubts and fears plagued her as they had for more than a week, ever since the night the mystic had hunted—and haunted—her; all else seemed trivial and meaningless.

Fifty or so birds were tethered today; most rode on the arms of the falconers, the bells on their legs jangling, their eyes covered by the pointy white caps. Others rode upon the wood bar and leather strap contraptions the falconers braced against their bodies as they walked behind the mounted cortege. On each litter, these men carried three or four falcons, all belled and capped.

The assemblage reached the vast meadow and those on horse quit their mounts. The tall oak and maple trees lining the perimeter of the field stood lush and motionless in the breezeless air. The nobles gathered round the falconers, grateful for the lack of wind that might dare pull the birds of prey away once released.

Geneviève stood on the outskirts of the anxious circle; Anne and many of the other ladies of the king's little band gathered deep inside near the king, but nothing impelled her to join them. The sweat poured down the slim line of her spine and she longed to rid herself of the heavy hunting costume, longed to jump her horse and ride, to feel the wind pull her hair out to stream behind her and to jiggle her cheeks with its cleansing force.

Clad in full red regalia, the grand master of the hunt stomped into the small space at the center of the circle and raised his arms. The crowd quieted, breath held in expectancy.

"Release!" he cried, and the birds were launched, the flapping of their wings furious in the quiet. Feathers flew off their powerful bodies with the force of their ascension, and tumbled down like snowflakes onto the crowd below. Like a living cloud, the birds rose into the air as one. Then, as if in a choreographed dance, they broke apart, each hunter intent upon finding its own prey. Like the falcons, the courtiers scattered, small groups following their own particular birds or those upon whom they had placed a wager.

Geneviève followed not a one, finding the opportunity in the chaos to escape. She ran off to the outer east edge of the field, gathering her skirts and crouching low beneath the branches of an evergreen, finding a small chamber within a grove of redolent pine. She kicked at the brown needles carpeting the floor, as if they alone were responsible for her angst. A fallen birch lay across a clearing in the middle of the grove, and Geneviève sat upon it, oblivious to the tacky sap covering the thick trunk like frosting upon a cake and sticking to the back of her skirt.

Jolly voices and laughter found their way through the leaves and branches, but she ignored them, perching her elbows on her knees and dumping her head into the basket of her hands.

As she had for days, she worried about the extremes of her life. . . .

So much had gone as planned, and so much had happened that she had never foreseen. It could have been the greatest moments of a life well lived, and yet it held more threat and fear than any life should ever know. She could no longer see the path in front of her; it had become muddied and dense with prickly bushes. She held her future in the balance of her choices, and yet she could not decide how to proceed. The vagaries pulled at her from all sides and she felt ripped apart by them, felt the hot tears of them in her eyes, and hated herself for her weakness.

"What is it, Geneviève? What has happened?"

With a gasp, Geneviève pulled her face from the shelter of her hands and found Sebastien on the other side of the copse. How like the soldier he was, to make his way through the thicket undetected.

She rubbed at her face as if to wash it. "Nothing, Sebastien. I am fine." She pushed errant strands of pale hair from her face and forced her shoulders up.

Sebastien stepped toward her with a small smile and a shake of his head, a lock of his shiny black hair falling upon his forehead as he looked down on her. "You may look as beautiful as ever, but you do not look *fine*." He stood beside her and she raised her grief-stricken eyes. His brow furrowed at her distraught expression and the smile vanished. "May I sit by you?"

Geneviève nodded and turned back to the sun-dappled ground.

"Talk to me, Geneviève," he said, his whisper thick with sympathy and tenderness.

His commiseration added fuel to her gnarl of discontent.

"I am a bit fatigued today."

"It is not only today." He took her hand from her lap and captured it in both of his, holding it atop his knee as if he held a fragile bird fixed on flight. "You have been distracted for days. I've never seen you like this."

He reached up a thumb to her face and brushed away a stray tear. She bit her lip at the compassion of his touch.

His restrained, sweet smile returned, dimples peeking in and out. "You are usually so . . . so . . ."

Geneviève met his gaze, her curiosity getting the better of her. "So . . . ?"

Sebastien shrugged comically. "So stoic."

Geneviève laughed, but there was nothing pretty in the sound.

He took her by the shoulders and spun her toward him, his deep blue gaze beseeching her. "Let me help you."

She could fall into that gaze, tumble away, and never return. She shook her head and broke away from the oasis of his eyes. He lay open to her, to whatever she had to say. Perhaps there was some assistance to be gained here after all; perhaps Sebastien might help her acquire the funds to fend off the soothsayer.

"It is . . . Madame Arceneau." Geneviève faltered, violet eyes shifting off to the left, away from him. She needed time to conjure the story—a logical, credible story that would allow for her torment and garner his help. "She has threatened me."

Sebastien frowned with angry curiosity. "Threatened you? How? Did she try to hurt you?"

Geneviève waggled her head; another curl tumbled down in a corkscrew. "No. She would have no power over me there."

"Then what is it?" he coaxed, picking up the fallen curl and tucking it gently back under her hat.

Her aunt had taught her to keep her lies as close to the truth as possible. "She claims to have had a premonition about me."

"What kind of premonition?"

Geneviève's chest heaved as she took a steadying breath, as the notion jumped into her mind and off her tongue. "She claims she has seen me . . . with the king." She allowed her voice to fall away, to let him infer a far more devious meaning. The cloud crossed his face and she knew he understood. "What's more, she claims to have seen my future standing beside him and she threatens to tell Anne, to tell her everything."

Sebastien met her pronouncement with stony silence. Geneviève pulled her hand from his grasp, so tight it had become painful. He forced away his tension and drew her hand back, lightness of touch returning.

"She is asking for money, a great deal of money," Geneviève continued. No need for her to act desperate; it clung to her with clammy truth. "She asks for a home. As if I could ever conjure such a thing."

"She is mad," Sebastien whispered.

"Most certainly," Geneviève agreed, her voice cracking with desolation.

He jumped to his feet and paced around the small thicket, hands thrust hard upon hips, treading heavily upon the pale green shoots of creeping vine that dared to search for life above the pine needles. "We cannot let her do this," he mumbled as Geneviève's gaze followed him. "This would be disastrous."

Sebastien rushed back, taking her in his arms as if the threat bore down upon her at this very moment and he was her shield.

"The duchesse will have you sent away from court. Or worse."

Geneviève nodded her head where it lay against his hard chest. Never would she have believed she would long for the protection of a man. She believed she would never need or desire it, and yet there was such a pull to his embrace.

He pushed her off him to look hard into her eyes. "What will you do?"

Treacherous tears blurred her vision, try though she might to deny them. "I do not know."

Sebastien's face crumbled; her agony became his own. He kissed her then, her lips, her eyes, her flushed cheeks. She closed her eyes to the feel of him. He pulled away from her and she fell forward into the empty space, opening her eyes in surprise. She heard it herself then, the voices and caterwauling drawing closer to their seclusion.

"We will talk more of this soon, *ma chérie*." He brushed her lips once more and rose to his feet. He would leave her then, hoping to separate before they were seen, before their clandestine meeting sullied her reputation.

"Know that I am with you, always," he said, and with one last squeeze of her hands, he left her.

The perpetually peeved woman dogged Geneviève's heels as they returned to their rooms, the dust and odor of the stables clinging to their tailored riding costumes. Jecelyn's hot ire jabbed her back like the tip of a knife. They rushed on unhindered in the sparsely populated corridor.

"You were seen, you know," Jecelyn said at last, as if she had been taunting Geneviève with her penetrating silence, a predator poised for the kill.

Geneviève's shoulders knotted, creeping up closer to her ears, but she refused to take the bait.

"In the woods." Jecelyn's pronouncement kept time with the hard clicks of their boot heels upon the stone floor. "With Monsieur du Lac. The whole court knows what you were doing."

"*Merde.* Enough!" Geneviève stopped with no warning.

Taken by surprise, Jecelyn walked on, barging into Geneviève's back. Geneviève spun and shoved out with her hands, connecting with Jecelyn's shoulders. The stunned woman tumbled backward, tripping on her long skirts, reaching out to the wall to stop her fall.

The smattering of courtiers kept moving, but every gaze fell upon them, every ear listened for their bickering words.

Two long, quick steps and Geneviève was in her face, the late-day sun streaming in sideways, throwing harsh, scraggy shadows upon a beautiful face twisted with frustration. "The court knows nothing. It is all pretense and posturing. It is all make-believe."

Geneviève spoke of deeper meanings, but Jecelyn had not the insight to follow her. "You cannot deny it. Everyone knows you are lovers."

"And what of it?" Geneviève shook her head at the insignificance of this conversation. She narrowed her eyes at Jecelyn, at the black eyes staring at her with such contempt. If they must speak, then she would speak to the heart of the matter. "What have I ever done to vex you so? You have hated me from the moment you met me."

Jecelyn's anger propelled her forward. Geneviève recoiled as she hissed in her face. "You think to take my place. You think you can come to court, a veritable stranger to this life, when I have given every moment of mine to it, and become Anne's first." Spittle flew off Jecelyn's lips; her cheeks burst with splotches of fury. "You, with your strange eyes and your prowess with a bow, yet you are nothing compared to me."

Geneviève laughed—a cruel, harsh sound—and Jecelyn's spewing tongue fell silent. Geneviève shook her head with the disappointment. This was nothing more than petty jealousy, the greatest weapon women used on each other. While men fought for causes and crusades, women quibbled over beauty and privilege. Such envy would be the downfall of their gender.

"Very well. *You* are the most intriguing of Anne's ladies. If offered the position of first, I will decline. I concede wholly and completely . . . to you." Geneviève threw up her hands and dropped them to slap upon her thighs. "There. Are you happy now?"

She spun on her heel and barreled off and away from this trivial annoyance, this petulant child of a woman. "I have no time for this nonsense."

Like the specter of a haunted house, Geneviève had become a nightly prowler of the darkened halls of the château, as if searching for the ever-elusive sleep in the shadowy corners where lovers met and lowly servants swept.

She had waited for word from Sebastien, for a note with a time and place to meet, certain one would come after their words in the glade this afternoon, but one hadn't, and she could not bear any more hours of soundless worry. She could not read *Pantagruel* another time; its words had become far too familiar to distract, and the tome served to remind her of all to be won, or lost.

Geneviève held the candle out—lighting her path but not blinding her sight—with her left hand, her dagger gripped in her right as she crept up the one flight of stairs to the floor above and the library situated over the gallery. Among all the books the king had brought from Blois, there must be something to engage her mind and silence the braying voices screeching at her from within. There was escape in the pages of books; she had found it there so often during her childhood and knew it would be there for her again.

The large gilded door gave way at her push, and Geneviève entered the long rectangular room that fell away from the portal. She stepped over the threshold and breathed deep, inhaling the sublime and soothing scents of leather and parchment, an aroma that eased more effectively than the incense of a church. She moved cautiously into the unfamiliar chamber until she came upon the first in a long row of double-sided desks running parallel to the windows at the back of the chamber. With her small flame, she lit the five-branched candelabrum poised upon its smooth surface. In its light, she found the next such desk and flambeau, lit it, and the four that followed as well.

Once she had them aflame, the center aisle of the room glowed with light and Geneviève glimpsed the giants rising up on each side. The shelves soared from floor to ceiling, the rich wood cases waxed and polished to a high gloss. Each flame multiplied ten fold in the reflections, shimmering prismatic echoes of light, and books stood upon every available space on the towering shelves.

Fears forgotten, she flushed with an eagerness to find another world; the wondrous choices laid before her proved enough to pull her out of time and place. She walked along the right side, her fingers brushing across the leather bindings and their gilt letterings.

Here and there, she found other treasures, strange objects hidden in niches formed in the shelves, square hollows hosting intricately carved busts, a terrestrial globe, and other small works of art. She squealed at the menacing eyes of a crocodile's head and smiled at the miniature portrait of François as a child. Pulling out book after book, some closed by intricate locks and clasps of silver, Geneviève ran her hand over the embossed Moroccan leather, turning the gold-tipped pages, unable to decide which to choose, wondering what other delights lay on the shelf of the next aisle.

She turned a corner, heading toward the outer wall, and froze, her heart slamming against her chest. A hulking shape of a human form rose up in silhouette against the moonlit sky beyond the glass. Like an animal locked in the sight of a deadly weapon, Geneviève couldn't move, her hunter's prowess abandoning her.

"You are a creature of the night, Mademoiselle Gravois." The king's voice was unmistakable, as was its gloominess.

Geneviève dropped like an arrow-pierced bird, her legs trembling as she curtsied.

"Forgive me, Your Majesty. I did not mean to intrude. I . . . I . . . did not intend any harm." She kept her face bowed. Her trespass was undeniable; only those with permission from Mellin de Saint-Gelais, the king's keeper of the royal library, or the king himself, could gain access to the chamber. She had neither.

"Do not worry yourself. I know you to be trustworthy. I have no fear you would hurt any of my precious books." The king did not move from his seat at the desk, but beckoned her forward with the wave of a hand. Geneviève saw the gesture in the glow of the moon and answered its call, giving no pause to the irony of his words.

She stood on the opposite side of the desk and placed her candle between them. In its wavering light, she saw the face of the king, a ravaged face cut deep with hollows and crevices. He wore no courtly mask here in this refuge in the middle of the night, did not bother to don it, though he was no longer alone. A book sat on the table in front of him, opened to pages nigh invisible in the pale light.

"Is it a passion of books that has brought you here, Geneviève, or an inability to sleep?" He sat back in his chair and his face became shrouded in shadows.

Geneviève shrugged. "A little of both, Your Majesty. I do love to read, but would prefer to do so in the light of day."

The king laughed at her quip.

"Is it a romance you come to find?" François crinkled his nose as he prodded her, but shook his head before she could answer. "No, I do not think so. It would be the obvious assumption, but an incorrect one, I think."

Geneviève worried that the man saw her so clearly. "I prefer adventures, Your Highness."

François nodded. "Ah, now *that* I can see." He sat up and reached for her candle, using the flame to light the candelabrum sitting on the desk between them. Like her, he wore his evening clothes, his face deathly pale against the maroon and gold mantle. "Come look at this."

With a long, lithe finger, he summoned her around to his side of the desk, and opened the book before him. "Have you ever seen a book with such text?"

Geneviève looked down at the formation of the letters on the page, anchoring her loose pale curls behind both ears. The text was a unique style, with long extending lines and small interior spaces. "No, Sire, I have never seen it. It is quite pleasing to the eye."

"Indeed," he agreed, grinning. "Garamond has created it especially for my books."

He fell into a heavy silence, save for the rasping of his dry skin as his hand rubbed circles on the page.

"Our words, our stories will live long after we're gone."

Regret drenched his words; his sorrow held Geneviève captive. He turned and looked upon her, all his truth laid bare. This was not a king, just a man.

"Like you, I find sleep elusive." He pulled out the chair beside him, and Geneviève sat, no other action conceivable, and he leaned in close, his chair creaking as he shifted his large form. "The ghosts, they keep me awake."

"G . . . ghosts," Geneviève sputtered, eyes wide, mouth agape. She could well believe the palace was possessed; she had often felt the oppression of angry spirits in the halls, late at night, heard their footsteps or felt the rush of air as they passed her.

He nodded and pushed back the strands of black and gray hair falling across his face. "I have led a selfish, greedy life, and my greed has given birth to them."

He turned back to the book, began to turn the pages, as if he saw a ghost on each surface, and recounted them.

"The friends I lost in the war and in prison"—he flipped a leaf—"my sons' youth"—he turned another. "Semblançay groans at me." He spoke the name of a man he condemned to death. "My strong and proud François." This one he named for his son, not long dead, poisoned by an Italian. "My . . . my darling Lily." His voice broke; his hand trembled on the thin sheet of parchment.

He closed the book with a hard snap and thrust it from him. "Every one of them dead, because of me." François turned to her as if she would confirm or deny it, his face twisted and malformed, scourged with grief, eyes flooded with tears.

Please stop, she wanted to beg him. *Do not take me into your confidence, do not take me into your heart, for my own cannot bear it.*

"You did your duty as a king to his country," she whispered, compelled.

He shook his head back and forth so hard his whole body moved with the force. "No, no. It was my need for my own brilliance, to feed my own ego. Greed made me weak and my weakness infected us all. My country would have prospered had I simply treated it with loving care."

He pushed against the arms of his chair as though to stand, looking as if he would run from the room, ghosts snipping at his heels. His hands slipped from the perch, his shoulders curled and slumped, and he dropped back upon the seat.

"Lily, oh my Lily." He whispered his daughter's name, his Madeleine whom he called his flower, Lily, dead less than two years, a weak and sickly woman who lasted no more than a few months after her marriage to the king of Scotland, after leaving her father's court for the coldness of her husband's land. "She was so fragile. I knew it was wrong, knew it. I do not think I can bear to live without her." He grabbed the edge of the desk, knuckles turning white as if he would break off a piece of it, hanging his head between his trembling arms.

Geneviève turned from the ravaging sight, her own frustration pounding in her head. Would that a father trembled with love for her, that such a man existed, willing to give away his life for her own. The pain of the wanting dug a hole in her gut and tears for them both filled her eyes. A sob stuck in her throat.

She turned back to the grieving man, his shoulders shaking with his sobs, his hands trembling upon the varnished wood. Little by little, she reached out and laid her fingers upon the age-spotted skin. His fingers clutched at hers, the lifeline of a drowning man, and held.

❧ 21 ❧

If you grant to your soul all the things it covets,
it will pay you back in your enemy's satisfaction.

—Ignatius de Loyola (1491–1556)

Anne sat at her writing table; haphazard piles of parchment, unanswered letters, and lists of tasks to prepare the palace for the visit of the Holy Roman Emperor covered the top of the finely carved *bureau-plat,* mounted on the H-shaped stretcher. The duchesse stared vacantly down at the chaos, her gaze vague and unfocused, her ladies' questions ignored and unanswered.

"I need to speak with Madame Arceneau," Anne said, an untethered remark that silenced all other conversation.

Béatrice was the first to react. At last recovered from the illness that had plagued her through the summer, she was anxious to be of service to her mistress once again. "Of course, madame, I will accompany you."

"No, no, bring her to me," Anne commanded brusquely. "I have no time to scamper about the palace."

Béatrice dropped a quick curtsy at the harsh imperative and ran for the door, Sybille fast on her heels.

"Thank you, *ma chérie,*" Anne called, recanting her own callousness. Béatrice replied with a grateful smile upon her gaunt face and the two women scuttled from the room.

Geneviève squeezed the needle in her hand; not one stitch had she taken since the mention of the soothsayer. She scoured her mind for any reason to be gone from the chamber before the mystic made her appearance, but nothing of any credence came to mind. She and Arabelle alone remained with the duchesse. Jecelyn and Lisette were already off on Anne's errands—delivering a lengthy note to the *grand maître de d'hôtel* concerning the menu for the finicky Charles V, asking the *maréchaux des logis* about the state of the visitor's rooms. Geneviève had no choice but to remain should another such task crop up; she prayed that one would, and soon.

Anne knew the queen would be busy with similar arrangements, certain that in many cases their instructions would contradict each other. She also knew with confidence that hers would take precedence, and the success of this visit weighed heavily upon her slim shoulders. There was little question who was the mistress of the king's heart and his castle.

Geneviève stuck the needle into the thick fabric of the pillow coverlet; Anne had launched the project to make gifts for the emperor, and the ladies stitched night and day to complete the task in time. If current negotiations held, the emperor would arrive in less than two months. Geneviève pulled the thick magenta floss through the sumptuous ecru fabric, her stitches crooked and awkwardly plied. She jumped at the sound of every footstep as it neared the door, cringed at every voice slithering through the cracks.

"Where in heaven's name are they?" Anne's patience had thinned with every tick of the clock, so many had sounded since the cousins set off on their errand. She slapped her hand upon the table, papers flying up in the breeze, Arabelle and Geneviève recoiling in fright.

"Madame Arceneau does not move very well." Arabelle made the excuse, a flimsy one at best.

Anne gave it no consideration. "Geneviève," she barked, "see if you can find my mystic and my maids. Perhaps you will have better efficiency in seeing to my wishes."

All the moisture in Geneviève's mouth evaporated and her tongue caught on the dryness. She gave herself a mental kick, chiding herself to be careful what she prayed for, always. "I . . . uh . . . *oui* . . . but—"

"Madame!" The door burst open, pounding against the inside wall with a stony crack.

Béatrice grabbed it as it dared to kick back upon her and her sister, hanging onto it as she gasped for breath. Sybille hung upon her sister's arm, her other hand on her heaving chest.

"What? What is it?" Anne rushed forward; only bad news came on such panting tongues as these.

"She's . . . gone . . . ," Béatrice groaned.

Anne's face puckered. "Gone? Who is gone?" Her green eyes gaped with comprehension. "Madame Arceneau is gone? Gone where?"

"No one knows, madame," Sybille said, recovering faster than her sister did. "All her clothes, all her possessions, are gone as well. Her room has been stripped clean."

Arabelle and Geneviève exchanged stunned glances. Geneviève dropped her stitching, squeezing her hands into fists, her knuckles turning white.

Béatrice picked up the story. "She has moved on with but a cursory note to her sister that she is well, that everything has worked out as she hoped, but she has chosen to start a new life in another town."

"Which town? Where?" Anne prodded, disbelief and aggravation a double edge in her tone.

"The note did not say," Sybille replied.

Anne stood immobilized, a seething statue.

"How very bizarre," Arabelle mumbled as she leaned toward Geneviève.

Her own mouth agape, her tongue vacant of coherent speech,

Geneviève nodded in agreement. The woman who posed the greatest threat to her had now vanished, and in such a way as to bring none of the mystic's threat to bear. It was astounding, too astounding. Geneviève tried to imagine all the possible explanations, but one word—one name—rang out again and again. Sebastien.

"This can go on no longer." Giuseppe stood with arms akimbo before the gathering of musicians that included his brother, his foot tapping with flagrant impatience.

Geneviève tossed her gaze his way, balking with surprise. The young handsome man appeared as normal, pale skin topped by raven curls, but this night his lips were black, as if he had decided to try his hand at cosmetics, with disastrous results.

Eliodoro batted innocent eyes as he clamped his lips between his teeth, fighting against the laughter bubbling in his throat at the sight of his brother's indignant, comical face.

"I do not know of what you speak," he managed to eke out, but the blush across his ruddy complexion told another tale.

"You have inked my wine!" Giuseppe launched himself across the chairs at his annoying sibling.

Eliodoro jumped to his feet, chair flying out behind him, fists raised, ready to defend himself. "You stole my clothes!" he countered with his own indictment, and lunged.

Fellow musicians jumped between them, pulling the brothers apart before the fight was engaged.

"Behave yourselves," the hautbois player admonished with a roll of his eyes, as if he were their appalled parent.

On any other night Geneviève would have delighted in the antics of the feuding siblings, would have pulled up a chair to watch them as she would any of their other performances, but not tonight. Tonight she could think of nothing but finding Sebastien, to learn if he had anything to do with the disappearance of Anne's mystic.

She had not seen him in many a day, their duties keeping them apart, but she could wait no longer. She wanted answers, desperate to know if he had had anything to do with the disappearance of Madame Arceneau. It was like a gift from God, but Geneviève's cynicism feared the ease of attainment and did not trust it, feared the price such a lagniappe would reap. If Sebastien had done anything to precipitate the woman's leave-taking, his actions might serve to exacerbate the situation, and Geneviève feared what repercussions they would bring.

Geneviève searched the packed room, circling the perimeter like a soldier on parade, then skirting between the tables, swerving between the hundreds of courtiers grouped together, eating and drinking, their laughter raucous in her ears like the condemning caw of perturbed crows.

"Monsieur!" Geneviève shrieked a bit as she found and grabbed onto the arm of Sebastien's friend Dureau. "Have you seen Sebastien?"

"*Bonsoir,* Geneviève." The young cavalier bowed in genuine greeting, but Geneviève would not be deterred by pleasantries.

"Is Sebastien here?"

Dureau nodded, head swiveling about on broad shoulders. "*Oui.* He was standing right here." He rose on tiptoe to search above the heads of the crowd around them, amber eyes flitting from face to face. "Ah, there he is."

Geneviève followed the man's outstretched finger, seeing the dark hair and ruddy complexion of the face she had searched for at the far side of the room.

"*Merci,* Dureau," she said with another grateful squeeze of his arm, but scurried off without awaiting his reply.

Geneviève tumbled through the crowd, the hunter intent on the prey through a thickly treed forest.

"Sebastien!" she called at the very moment the mischievous musicians surrendered their petty bickering and struck up a rousing song. Her voice was lost in the crescendo.

She neared him and he turned, as if sensing her approach, and his face broke into an expression of pure joy—eyes crinkled, dimples deepened as his mouth spread wide.

"Geneviève!" He held out his hands and she caught them. "How wonderful to see you. I have missed you so." He kissed her on both cheeks, impervious to the prying gazes of the courtiers around them or the crestfallen expression of the marquis de Limoges by his side.

The opening chords of the song gave way to the melody, and a cheer rose up through the crowd.

"A *farandole*," Sebastien cried. "Come. We must dance."

Geneviève shook her head, pulling back on the strong arms leading her to the center of the vast room. "No, Sebastien. I must speak with you."

"Yes, of course." He smiled dashingly. "After."

Geneviève tried to resist but failed, unwilling to cause a scene by running off the dance floor. They clasped hands with the people beside them and launched into the spirited circle dance. Geneviève completed the steps with precision, as she always did, but with little joy. Sebastien's grin slithered off his face when he saw the furrow between her eyes, the downward turn to the delicate curve of her lips.

Within seconds of the long song's last note, Sebastien grabbed her hand and drew her off the dance floor, down the long corridor, and into the inner foyer outside the gray cobbled courtyard. Beside the tall glass doors looking out onto the rainy night, he pulled up short, and swung round to face her, grabbing her by the shoulders and pulling her close.

"Are you all right? Has Madame Arceneau threatened you again?" His gaze searched her face.

Geneviève's bow-shaped mouth formed a stunned, silent moue.

Sebastien gave her a shake. "Tell me, what has happened?"

"No, no, she has not bothered me again." Geneviève found her voice, surprised by his response. She brought her hands up to her face, her fingertips pushing on her forehead as if the pressure forced her to think more clearly. "I found you. I searched for you, to ask about her."

"Me?" Sebastien recoiled. "Why would you ask me about her? I d—"

"She's gone." Geneviève silenced his words with her own. "We are not sure when she left, but she has left court. For good."

Sebastien's hands fell from her as she told him the entire story, repeating the words in the note the mystic had left with her sister. Her tale done, he sniffed a laugh as he pulled her into a tender embrace, arms circling her waist, hands rubbing the curve of her lower back evocatively.

"How wonderful," he cooed in her ear. "All your troubles are over."

Geneviève closed her eyes to the tingling sensation of his breath through her curls. "I thought . . . I meant to ask . . ."

"To ask?" he encouraged, kissing her forehead languorously.

She lowered her head, modestly chagrined. "I thought perhaps you were responsible for her sudden . . . departure."

"What a silly thought." He turned her around to face the rain-speckled glass, curling his body around hers, nuzzling his warm lips against her neck. "I have not an inkling of what the woman looks like. Perhaps she has acquired that home in Paris she desired so much, and needed nothing further from you."

Geneviève's hand faltered as it rose up to grasp his head, frozen inches away from the luxuriant waves of black hair. Had she mentioned Paris to him? Did she tell him Madame Arceneau craved a home in that city? She could not remember, and the question plucked at her as the scullion plucks the feathers from the slain chicken.

"Whatever has taken her from here, I am grateful for it." His tongue traced a line of fire from her ear to her shoulder, drawing down the edge of her gown to reveal the snowy whiteness of her flesh, plying his lips and his tongue to the sensitive skin.

Her legs quivered, her resolve weakened at the sensual assault; she became fluid in his arms. His mouth lifted, his grip grew tight, and he spun her around.

Sebastien looked down with true fire and passion burning in his eyes. "I will serve you, Geneviève," he said, his voice thick and husky. "I have made it my mission, but it has become my destiny."

His mouth ravaged hers, as if he fought against all he felt for her, and she was defenseless at its onslaught.

She closed her eyes, relinquishing her body to his kisses and caresses, but she could not release the questions from her mind.

❧ 22 ❧

Who naught suspects is easily deceived.

—Petrarch (1304–1374)

The two long-legged men circled the courtyard; the king with his hands clasped behind his back, Monty with his own crossed upon his barrel chest. These two childhood friends had ruled their country for decades, and yet the friendship had not survived as well as the land. So many disputes had wedged themselves between them, but they were ever united in their devotion to France.

"This is the second time in as many months we have encountered problems with our correspondence to Spain." The choler in François's voice belied the pleasant smile on his face, the public form he offered to the courtier-filled terrace.

The heat of the parched summer had at last broken, with a crash and a thwack and a thunderous lightning-filled storm that raged for two days. In its wake the air was fresh and clean, free from the ponderous humidity, but pleasantly warm. The court reveled in the stirring climate, finding every excuse to be out of doors. Men and women frolicked like children, playing a game of *l'escaigne* in one corner, hitting the large inflated ball with a stick shaped like a stool, the legs filled with lead. Across from them, courtiers fired darts at a wooden target affixed to the stone wall of the castle. The afternoon had taken on a festive atmosphere, a spur-of-the-moment fair in celebration of the crispness of autumn, and the king would not allow his agitation to besmirch the enjoyment of his people.

"Any word of Bretonnière?" he asked Monty, concerned both as a king and as the messenger's friend.

The constable's jowls trembled when he shook his head. "No, Your Majesty."

"*Merde,*" the king swore under his breath. "I do not understand it. We must assume he has been found out and captured, though I cannot surmise how his identity could have been revealed. The secret survived for so many years. But it is the only possibility."

"I agree," Monty mumbled.

"A missing messenger, missing and altered messages. What is plaguing us?" The king demanded answers.

"I have been making quiet inquiries," Montmorency stated with unnatural casualness.

"You have?" François turned a foreboding gaze upon his chancellor. "Why have you not told me?"

"I did not want to make any report until I could offer a complete one."

"Your desire for thoroughness is to be commended, sir, but I would have been appeased to hear that action, any action, was under way."

Montmorency took the rebuke with a silent frown.

"Well," the king prompted impatiently, "what have you found?"

The statesman turned his round face to his king, a flush of color rising on his grizzled cheeks. François had not often seen this opinionated man as hesitant to speak as he was at this moment, and the councilor's silence frightened him more with every moment it devoured.

"There can be but one answer, *Majesté.*" Monty's voice dropped to a cavernous octave. François hung on every syllable. "There is a spy in our midst."

The king stumbled, tripping over a stone as well as the calamitous concept, faltering at the thought of such a threat to his nation. He reached out to his friend and colleague, grasping Monty's arm to right himself, then dropping the hold before others witnessed his weakness.

"You are certain?" He hissed the question, the words tasting foul upon his tongue.

"It has been suggested by more than one source," Monty confirmed with irrefutable gravity. "Though my investigation is newly begun, there is more than one indication that it is the only plausible postulation."

François's feet shuffled to a stop, and he turned to look out upon the courtyard and the throng of playful courtiers. He knew each and every one by name, their faces as familiar as those of his own children, both living and dead. That one of them might have betrayed him so grievously sent bile burning up his throat. His hands trembled and he clasped them beneath his arms, holding himself as if to guard against the painful sedition.

"Find him, Monty." His voice trembled with violent wrath. "Find him and kill him."

The news of a subversive infested the palace, slithering through every crack and crevice like the unseen poison of the plague. At the king's bidding, Montmorency had let the news of his investigation slip, hoping to draw the illicit emissary out, forcing him to make a pernicious mistake. Gossip turned into mania and the courtiers looked upon each other with suspicion and fear. The court became a festering nest of mistrusting vipers, and Geneviève gasped for every breath she took inside it.

"Where's the lavender silk?" She sat at her dressing table, watching the sunset through her window, watching it blaze with magnificent colors—taking its last flourishing bow—before departing the stage of the day. Earlier and earlier, the light bid *adieu* to the day; more and more the darkness overpowered the light.

Would she exit this world with the brilliance of a setting sun?

Thoughts of the gallows had possessed her mind from the moment the rumor had reached her ears. Geneviève thought of little else save escape, but upon that path lay nothing but fear. If she ran, if she simply disappeared, there could be no greater indictment of her guilt, and the search would begin; they would hunt her down. She could not hope for a successful retreat without the help of King Henry. To stay, to continue the façade, might be the only way to stay alive, but the pressure it put upon her was more than she believed bearable. Geneviève saw herself clearly for the first time in her life; not in the mirror, but in life's reality. How different was truth from the reflection.

Carine fussed over the saffron gown spread upon the bed. "I'm afraid the gown had grown rank. I could not in good conscience allow you to wear it again."

Geneviève turned dispiritedly; she had asked for her favorite gown, to encase herself in the familiar dress and its safety.

Like all of the incredible couture worn by nobles the world over, this one had fallen to the frequent wearing, overuse of perfumes, and the inability to wash such fragile garments. Most women rarely noticed as one gown disappeared and another took its place, but Geneviève refused to dismiss her favorite with ease; she felt its loss and it showed on her face.

Carine frowned at her mistress's disappointment. "But I have saved the jewels, mam'selle, of course."

The maid knelt at Geneviève's feet, taking her hand, opening the palm, and gently dropping the purple stones into it, closing Geneviève's fingers upon them. "We will have another made."

"I thank you, Carine." Geneviève shook her head imperceptibly as she stared down at the sparkling amethyst stones in her hand. "But we can never go back."

"Perhaps it is true that we can never go back," Carine said thoughtfully, "but we can always begin again." She smiled with all her innocence and hope.

Geneviève raised her gaze to her maid's face. "Have I told you how grateful I am to have had you on this journey?"

Carine tilted her head, taken aback by such words of endearment from her aloof mistress, and by their tone of fatality.

"And will continue to be," she affirmed.

"Yes, yes of course." Geneviève nodded with a pale smile. "Come, help me into this beautiful dress."

The inner court dined quietly tonight, a subdued supper for no more than fifty of the king's intimates—his *gentilshommes* and his *petite bande*. Truffles and cheese preceded pheasant and quail, followed by marzipan biscuits and pine-nut cakes. But the main course of the meal was talk of the spy, and every mouth chewed upon it with great relish.

"I know that Monsieur de Brumagne has spoken contentiously for many months," the fastidious Guillaume du Bellay hissed to his neighbor, failing to inform the other man of his territorial dispute with the House of Brumagne.

Admiral d'Annebault leaned close to La Rochepot, Montmorency's brother, but did little to obscure his words. "Poncher has acquired *another* château. Certainly his own coffers cannot support such an acquisition. I've heard it said that spies are well compensated."

They bandied names about with cruelness, malicious and ambitious courtiers using the occasion to propel themselves up the ladder of the court with particular deftness. Geneviève strained to hear every name they passed across the table like platters serving up the next sacrifice. It appeared she clung to the gossip for the sake of salacious satisfaction, but she listened for no name but her own.

With studied nonchalance, she turned to the niggling feeling coming from her right. She found Sebastien's eyes locked upon her as he stood guard at the door. For a fleeting moment, Geneviève saw something alien in their depths, something frightful in the blue gaze, but it passed so fleetingly she wondered if she had imagined it. She threw back a gulp of hippocras, berating herself for seeing condemnation in every face. Sebastien's lips flickered with the scantest of smiles and one eye ticked with the flash of a wink; Geneviève relaxed at the affectionate gestures and took a bite of her dessert, finding further solace in the sugary treat.

"Might I have a word, Mademoiselle Gravois?" The gruff voice of the constable did little to support the politeness of his interruption.

Geneviève stared up at the tall man towering over her, throat pulsing as she swallowed the rush of moisture in her mouth. "Ah . . . yes, of course, monsieur. You will excuse me, Arabelle?" She began to rise, but her companion jumped up first.

"No, please, I wish to avail myself of more of those delicious tarts." She gestured to her empty plate and her now vacant chair. "Please, sir, have a seat. I will return shortly."

Arabelle cast a faint smile at Geneviève over her shoulder as she left.

The powerful man heaved his hefty form into the high-backed leather chair and sat back, sipping upon the small cordial held in his large hand. "You have become comfortable with your new life here at court, mademoiselle?"

Geneviève nodded, unsure where this conversation might lead, fearing the worst. "I have, monsieur, thank you. The duchesse is a good and kind mistress."

There was no mistaking the grimace of disagreement on the man's puckered face. "Be that as it may, I have been meaning to tell you how impressed I am with you."

Geneviève pointed a finger at her own chest, eyes wide with surprise. "Me?"

"Indeed," he said with sedate alacrity. "You are not like many of the other young females at court. You appear withdrawn, aloof at times, but I think not."

"No?" Geneviève asked with genuine curiosity as she leaned forward.

"No." Montmorency mirrored her motion, closing the space between them. "I believe you are simply more intellectual and intuitive than these other"—he waved his hand at a bevy of giggling girls at the center of the room—"ladies."

"Thank you, sir." Geneviève raised her pale brows in irritation disguised as surprise. "You honor me."

She studied the other women her age flitting about the room; perhaps she did not giggle enough, or flirt enough. Perhaps her affectation was not as well done as it should have been.

Monty tossed aside her gratitude to return to his purpose. "I know there has been much talk this night of the betrayer in our midst. But I have not heard anything from you."

The urge to vomit threatened to strangle Geneviève. "I d-do not have anything to say on the matter."

The man narrowed his gaze. "Is that because you refuse to be a gossipmonger or because you know nothing?"

"Monsieur?" Geneviève's voice squeaked, unsure of what he asked of her.

"I want to know, mam'selle"—he whispered now—"if, with your keen eye, you have seen anyone suspicious in the company of your lady?"

Geneviève shook her head, unable to conjure the correct answer, the right words to alleviate any shadow of discovery from falling her way.

Montmorency scowled. "Have any newcomers made themselves known to you, perhaps one without family or long-standing connection with the court?" He badgered her now. "Someone with no other family here?"

"No, monsieur, no one comes to mind." Geneviève thought of nothing but denial. She squirmed in her seat, certain every eye in the room studied them.

The hefty man sat back with an unsatisfied sniff, and took the last sip of his beverage. "Then I would ask a favor of you."

Geneviève raised her shoulders to her ears. "I am at your service, sir."

"You will keep your eyes and ears open and tell me should anything of consequence come to your attention." Montmorency put his empty goblet on the table between them and slipped to the edge of his seat, ready to take his investigation to the next person on his list.

"Of course, monsieur." Geneviève bowed at the waist, eager for his departure, ready to agree to anything to expedite it.

"Bon," he said with finality, rose, and took one step away.

Geneviève took in a great gulp of air. The chancellor spun back and she held it tight in her lungs.

"Forgive me, mademoiselle. I realize something." He hovered over her like a craggy mountain perched aloft the pale valley. "The very credentials I have applied to the potential conspirator could be applied to you. I hope I have not offended?"

Geneviève glared up at the man. He had called her intuitive, yet she had no idea if his concern was genuine or an intelligent ruse.

"No, monsieur, no offense has been taken."

"That is well, then," he said and turned away, striding off without a second glance at her.

Geneviève's mind screamed with alarm, paranoia tainting every thought. Did the grand master's words hold some inner meaning? Were they intended as a warning or a test of her reactions? She was certain only of her growing uncertainty.

It was an act of desperation, as illogical as the panic strangling her so decisively. Sending a message to the English king when every eye in France searched for a traitor and a spy was madness, but she was indeed insane with fear. For the first time, Geneviève was grateful for her inability to sleep, for only in the dead of night could she take the time to create her most covert message yet.

It had been little more than two weeks since she had received her last missive from the land across the channel, but she remembered its directives well. The apothecary in the bustling town surrounding the castle was her next contact; she had thought to bring any message there herself, concealing it amidst a list of articles she wished to purchase, but she did not dare wander from court. No, she would create the message but use one of the many servants of the palace to deliver it and acquire the items; it was an errand they ran many times through the course of every day. It was a natural part of court life and would garner no undue attention.

The message itself was not so simply done; Geneviève had to take every precaution, use all the knowledge of ciphering at her disposal.

As soon as Carine had left her for the night, she gathered the small bottles onto her dressing table, pushing aside the cosmetics and perfumes with a clank and a clatter of glass bottles and ceramic trinket boxes. She would compose the message using the more complex alphanumeric code, and she would do so with invisible ink.

She mixed the small dose of white wine with a few drops of vinegar and a few squeezes of lemon, the acidic odors burning her nostrils. Stirring the concoction with a small spoon, the *click, click, click* of the tiny silver utensil upon the thin glass blared in the hush of the dimly lit chamber. Hunched over the table, Geneviève picked up the water and the dropper and raised her hands over the bottle. She gritted her teeth, willing away the quiver in her hands. Here was the most important step in the concoction; too much water and the message would disappear, too little and it would appear before the intended recipient warmed the paper and turned the invisible words to light brown. She pushed the fear from her mind and focused, taking herself back to the hours she had spent practicing, formulating this very recipe.

Geneviève dropped the instruments on the table and sat back, heaving a ragged sigh. The mixture was perfect; she was certain of it. Now for the message.

She laid the sheets of parchment before her and began to write, first with quill and ink. Here she listed all the ingredients for a headache remedy, and one to relieve the pains of a woman's monthly courses. Putting that list aside, she took up another parchment and her concoction, but on this one she used the tip of her little finger to form the triplets of numbers, leaving behind no telltale scratch marks that would alert a vigilant gaze to the hidden message. She filled the parchment with the code, the message reiterating all she had done for the king's cause and asking for the sanctuary that had been promised, and waited for it to dry, staring at the vanishing wetness, willing the depth of her appeal to imbed itself upon the drying fluid. Once the code vanished, she would camouflage it a second time, writing another meaningless shopping list over the message, but this time, underlining some words to indicate this page held the cipher.

As the words disappeared, faces began to appear in her mind—Arabelle's and Sebastien's, those of Anne and King François himself, and she was not taken by surprise to see them. There was loss for her, no matter which direction she turned; she must follow the less dangerous course, though it may be the less desired.

❧ 23 ❧

Dirty water will quench fire.

—Italian proverb

The pale, bleak light of dawn beckoned and she was grateful for its call. She feared walking through the night as she had done so often in these past weeks, feared her nocturnal prowling would now be taken as some type of evil assignation. Geneviève threw her russet velvet cloak over her simple morning gown of marigold linen and crept from her room, slipping out of the palace as servants stirred, cleaning the refuse from the night before, preparing the food and clothing for another long day, and stoking the fires in the cool grates.

Geneviève stepped out into the Cour Ovale and her breath streamed up from between her lips, thin vapors released into the chilly morning breeze. Throwing the gabled hood over her platinum plaits, she quit the courtyard through the east opening and circled around to the stables and the sloping lawns of the large garden.

Animals stirred in their pens, horses neighed as they nuzzled their morning hay, and groomsmen stretched away the stiffness of the night with great groans. Geneviève wandered along the length of the barns and the tack rooms, mindless of any destination, wanting no more than to be away from the palace and the thick tension inhabiting every room, the wagging tongues filling the château with their grating noise.

Low fog clung to the ground, unwilling to give way, a reluctant departing lover's embrace, and Geneviève squinted in the dimness to see the path in front of her. The small, off-kilter, gray wooden door of the back barn came into view at the same time that she heard the creak of its hinges, but she paid little heed, until the petite woman stepped from its threshold.

Traipsing out into the watery light, hands up and rustling in her hair, the well-dressed, curvaceous young lady fidgeted with the pins as she tried to force the plain brown lengths back into the semblance of a smooth coiffure. Geneviève's steps faltered; she scrunched her eyes, trying to see through the morning fog.

The woman giggled and Geneviève knew without doubt that it was the merry Lisette; her laughter was as brightly distinctive as the woman herself. She opened her lips to call Lisette's name when thick hands and black hairy arms reached out of the portal to encircle the small woman's waist and pull her back in.

The name died on Geneviève's tongue as she watched Lisette lean into the embrace. Geneviève floundered feverishly for a hiding place, her head spinning back and forth, searching for a place of refuge to ogle the woman and her lover without being seen. The face of the statue off to her left pointed in the other direction, and Geneviève took it as a sign. Grabbing her skirts, she scurried away, praying the embracing lovers would not notice her movement.

She threw herself against the far side of the sculpture, took two deep, steadying breaths, and leaned her head ever so slightly around the cold curve of white marble. From this angle, she could see Lisette clearly from behind, lengths of her disheveled hair cascading down her back, and onto her crumpled maroon silk gown. The petite woman stood on tiptoes, her head tilted up, her lips reaching upward for the man who gathered her into his strong arms. Bent attentively to his lover's lips, the man's face remained concealed; only the long, wavy brown hair falling around his head was visible as he leaned over Lisette. Their kiss deepened, passion and tenderness laid bare in every fluid movement of their heads and each brush of their lips and lick of their tongues. With another breathless giggle, Lisette pulled unwillingly away.

"I must go, *mon cher.*" She put her dainty hand upon the man's chest, unable to retreat without one last caress.

The man raised his head then, and Geneviève beheld her first glimpse of his face. Swarthy and chiseled, his features were masculine, intriguingly handsome. She had never seen him before, she was sure of it, positive she would have remembered such a face had she seen it. He must be a newcomer to court.

Geneviève swiveled back behind the sanctity of the statue, thrust against the cold stone with the force of her discovery. A newcomer, the very sort Constable Montmorency had asked her to look for. But she had no name to give to the chancellor, no person to indict. She could tell him no more than what she had seen, for there was no better defense than the accusation of another. But to do so would implicate Lisette.

With a quick peek around the stone woman who stood guard above her—one swift glance confirmed the lady-in-waiting continued to lavish her affectionate good-byes on her lover—Geneviève turned and ran in the opposite direction, away from the palace and into the woods surrounding the sloping lawns of the garden.

She caught herself up on the fattest tree, resting her back on its far side, leaning against it as she recovered her breath. Geneviève willed herself to calm; only with cold calculations could she make this work without harming innocent people. Her breath steadied and she pushed herself off the tree. Trekking through the foliage, crunching the fallen brown leaves beneath her feet, she conjured her course.

The constable did not seek her out for information, she was sure of it; he intended to gauge her own loyalties by her willingness to be part of the investigation, and that she would be. If she told him no more than what she had seen, there would be no accusation, only the gesture of a loyal and vigilant subject of the king of France. The chancellor would investigate the man, find nothing, and then both he and Lisette would be free from all suspicion, as would she. Without proof, there could be no prosecution; with her cooperation, there could be no supposition. It was the perfect plan.

Geneviève watched as Montmorency fired arrow after arrow upon the archery butts, each one zinging off the string, the sound piercing the air, and striking its target with precision, shattering the plaster discs into smithereens. His prowess as a statesman had evolved through years upon the battlefield, and the adept soldier he once was echoed in the movements of the aging diplomat. Geneviève had rarely seen the chancellor on the practice ground, though she came often. Two men trained at the far left end of the grassy knoll, while the chancellor stood alone on the right. It was the perfect opportunity, and she seized it.

"Perhaps you might show me your method for such rapid fire, monsieur." Geneviève approached the constable after a few missed shots of her own; a calculated move.

The beady-eyed man sniffed as he turned from the field. "I find it hard to believe you should look to me for advice, mademoiselle. I have seen you shoot." There was no mistaking the respect in the man's voice, tainted though it may be with a hard edge of rancor.

Geneviève shimmied up to the firing line with an insistent shake of her head and said, loud enough for the others to hear, "No, monsieur, I eagerly welcome your tutelage." As she stepped up beside him she whispered, "I have something I would like to share with you."

Montmorency heard the urgency in her simple statement; he stared at her agog for an instant, flicking his gaze up to the two men standing at the other end of the line to see if they had heard her furtive whisper.

"Then it would be dishonorable of me as a gentleman not to share my knowledge with you, mademoiselle," he said, loud and stiff, a bad actor thrust unwillingly upon the stage. "Show me your stance."

Geneviève took her position at the line, the left side of her body facing the butt and the left arm straight up and pointing at the target, right arm drawn back as if to fire.

Montmorency stepped behind her like a lover snuggling close to kiss the back of her neck. With rough hands, he pretended to adjust her stave hand in one direction while pushing the elbow of her string arm higher. "You have learned something?" he hissed in her ear.

Geneviève shrugged, a small, meager motion. "I have seen something, monsieur, though I am not sure if it is at all helpful." With a low whisper and an economy of words, Geneviève described to the constable the early morning scene.

"If there is any perfidy in the man, I am sure Lisette is an innocent victim of his charms."

Montmorency must know, above all else, that her friend was no more than a puppet in the scenario she had concocted.

"And yet you say she was intimate with him, this stranger?" Monty grumbled, and then raised his voice. "Take your shot, mademoiselle."

Geneviève loosed the arrow, aiming to the left of the target, exactly where the projectile landed.

"Young women are often used as tools by men who are up to no good," she insisted with a potent direct stare at the older man, who stepped closer once again to adjust her already perfect form. "Lisette is the most faithful and devoted of servants, to the duchesse and to the king."

"We shall see. You may leave the rest to those who know of such things." He pulled her arm back, a tad roughly perhaps. "Another shot, if you please."

Geneviève had had enough of this man and his obnoxious superiority; the one he sought stood inches from him and he had not a clue. So much for his preeminent intellect. She launched her arrow, striking the plaster target dead center, shattering it to pieces.

"I have spent near to every day and night since my arrival with Lisette. She is guilty of nothing more than loving pleasure." Her voice was as sharp as her arrow's tip, and Montmorency frowned at its barb.

"We shall see," he sniped back again as she pulled another arrow from her quiver and set it to the string. "I thank you for the information."

He turned and strode away, eliminating any opportunity for her to plead the case of Lisette's innocence. Geneviève armed her weapon, her eyes on the statesman's back with lustful desire. She turned with a soldier's quickness and launched the arrow into the target, dead center.

ﻌ 24 ﻌ

Rarely do great beauty and great virtue dwell together.

—Petrarch (1304–1374)

It had been months since the king took part in a game of *jeu de paume* and hundreds of courtiers turned out to watch the match. François stood on the opposite side of the net from the baron de Florennes, a noble of a like age, though both moved at a much slower pace than in years gone by. But as was his wont, the king relished physical activity, preferring to reinvigorate his day with some midafternoon sport.

The morning's rain had dried up, its foreboding clouds scudding across the sky, revealing a deep blue expanse. With its brilliant appearance, the sun had brought a bitter wind, knocking away the colorful dried leaves clinging tenaciously to the trees and sending them scuttering across the lawns and gardens, rustling together as the wind caught them up into little eddies swirling along dusty lanes.

The biting chill forced the king's afternoon match indoors to the large great hall of the old wing. The king and the baron wore identical costumes, flounced shirts of ecru cambic that allowed for ease of movement, worn atop silk stockings and trunk hose of the same fabric and color. Each man brandished a wooden racket, volleying the small leather ball across the string net.

The boisterous crowd at each end of the court cheered as the king sent the ball skimming across the wall on his left to land with precision on the baron's square, skipping off and away before the huffing, lunging nobleman's racket could reach it. The king had forged ahead by two points; the momentum was on his side, and those who laid bets against him were now regretting their decision.

"Come on, Florennes," someone cried scathingly from amidst the rowdy spectators. The king turned toward the voice with a thunderous expression—one adopted in exaggerated jest—and the audience laughed and clapped in enjoyment. So loud was their applause and acclaim that few heard the clanking of the halberdiers as they marched into the vast chamber, led by Constable Montmorency himself.

The baron tossed up the ball, raising his racket to serve, but let the ball and his arm drop, paying no mind as the small sphere hit the ground and rolled away.

"What, monsieur, do you concede?" the king taunted him, a smile spreading his wide lips. But Florennes shook his head and used his racket to point at a spot behind François.

The king spun round, on sudden alert, and found the sight of his chief minister in the company of five stern and serious soldiers. His smile faded with painful rapidity; there could be no good bringing such an auspicious panoply of authority here now.

With a few quick strides, the king arrived at Montmorency's side, leaning down for the minister to whisper in his ear. All eyes watched in deathly silence as the king's face twitched and splotched with heinous fury.

Like the women around her, Geneviève gasped as the king's murderous gaze slid their way, but none of the queen's ladies were as terrified as she. The king gave no order, for none was needed. With a nod from Montmorency, the guards marched across the floor, their hard leather heels beating out an executioner's cadence. Geneviève felt a moment's gratitude that Sebastien was not among them, that her lover would not be one of those to bring her to prison and, perhaps, her death.

The panicked women trembled like an aviary of frightened birds; hands reached out for other hands; heads turned, desperate to find hope or another's guilt in the faces around them. Geneviève watched the guards approach with relieved fatality; days and nights of living a lie were over, gone would be the incessant apprehension haunting her every moment. Such release might well come at the end of the hangman's rope, and yet there was liberation in death, if God was indeed as merciful and forgiving as professed.

"*Mon Dieu*, Geney," Arabelle whispered as her fingertips dug into her friend's arm.

Geneviève turned soulful eyes to this woman she had attempted to avoid but now could not imagine a life without. "Fear not, *chérie*, they do not come for you." She gave Arabelle's hand a fortifying squeeze, unsuccessful in silencing the quake of emotion from her voice.

The soldiers were upon them. Geneviève closed her eyes, one last prayer given up to God for her safekeeping.

"What are you doing? I've done nothing wrong." Lisette's squeaky, childish voice screamed with anger and fear.

Geneviève's eyes snapped open. She leaned forward, gaping down the row of women to where Lisette stood on the other side of the duchesse. The halberdiers captured the tiny Lisette by the upper arms; she looked more like an adolescent than an adult in their mountainous midst. Their size was inconsequential to her spirit, and she struggled against them, her enormous efforts lifting her feet off the floor as she pulled and kicked, her full skirts snapping like sheets drying in a heavy wind, looking no more substantial than a rag doll torn in half by two bullies.

Geneviève raised her hand in protest, stepping forward to impede them, but it was as if she moved underwater, her motion heavy, slow, and unaffecting.

"No, stop!" she yelled, but her voice was lost in the chaos of the moment, in the guards' clanking armor, in the crowd's exclamations of shock.

As the soldiers marched Lisette past the constable, he looked down at her with ill-disguised contempt. "You are under arrest, mademoiselle."

"Arrest?" Her voice squealed higher with righteous indignation. "For what?"

"Treason!" Montmorency screamed, and the crowd roared with mass hysteria, half of them calling for her head, the other pleading for her life.

Lisette pedaled the floor with her tiny feet, their movements meaningless in the face of such commanding opposition. She craned her neck over her shoulder, pulling against the hands imprisoning her in their constraining grasp, her tear-filled eyes seeking out her mistress.

"I've done nothing, madame, I swear!" she vowed, her proclamation a defense and a cry for mercy. "You must believe me. I would do nothing to hurt you. Not ever."

Anne's face crumbled with anguish and heartbreak, but she turned away.

They dragged Lisette across the floor, as if parading her in front of the king whom she had served so loyally. Geneviève thrust forward, but Arabelle pulled her back.

"Let go, Arabelle. I cannot let them take her," Geneviève cried, but Arabelle would not release her and Sybille clung to her now as well.

"You will only endanger yourself," Sybille hissed at her.

"But Lisette is innocent!" She fought them, her entreaties falling on deaf ears.

"Your Majesty, it's not true. You must not believe them," Lisette implored of him, her words bleating through a strangled throat as she looked up into his tormented face.

François stared at her as he would a rabid animal, and yet

Geneviève saw compassion and fear for his subject, one for whom he cared. They all saw it, Lisette most of all. As they rushed her away and down the long corridor, her pleas echoed back to them.

"Never believe it, Your Majesty!"

Her pitiful cries fell away, leaving the room in a vacuum of turbulent silence. In it, the king stared at Montmorency, lips white in a snarl.

"There are other ways to have done this." His words slithered through his clenched teeth.

Montmorency tipped his head ever so slightly at the king's mistress, at his unstated enemy. "I thought to set an example, Your Highness."

François shook his head in disgust. His gaze found Anne's and they shared their heartache in the single glance. He bowed, perhaps in apology, and quit the room, Montmorency and his other advisers fast upon his heels.

"Please, help me away," Anne whispered to Béatrice, who gathered the other ladies in a circle around their mistress, a shield to the poignant and poisonous glances cast her way, and rushed her off.

Geneviève entered the darkened room. Miniscule rays of an orange sun, rushing toward the seclusion of the horizon, snuck their way through the cracks between the curtains, bringing ethereal form to the interior of Anne's privy chamber. Dust danced in their glow, but nothing else stirred. She found the indistinguishable shape of the duchesse in her bed, curled up like a ball and hidden by the silk counterpane, as if she had crawled into a hole and buried herself beneath the earth.

"Madame?" Geneviève whispered, not knowing if her mistress slept. It had been hours since Anne had retreated into this sanctuary, refusing to speak with anyone, refusing to come out. But her audience chamber began to fill with the evening's visitors, and her absence became more telling with each passing moment.

Geneviève crept up to the bedside. Anne's blank gaze stared at the brocade tester overhead.

"Your friends are eager to see you, madame," Geneviève said softly.

"They are not my friends." Anne spoke with a voice rough and scarred with tears. "They come to gawk and to berate me."

Geneviève sat on the edge of the bed, a familiarity dared because of the woman's suffering. "No, I assure you. Only those who are loyal to you, who love you, are here. Sybille and Béatrice have ensured it. They stand at the door this very minute, turning any away who would disturb you. They are quite the guardsmen."

A tiny flash of amusement crossed Anne's decimated features, and at last she turned her gaze toward Geneviève. "They will see me imprisoned."

Geneviève blenched. "Who will?"

"Montmorency and La Sénéchale," Anne hissed. "They have finally found a way to be rid of me. He will follow this line of treachery back to me."

"It cannot be, madame." Geneviève shook her head, her own fear rearing its ugly head, for the path to Anne could only lead her way. "Lisette is innocent."

Anne laughed bitterly. "Innocence makes no difference. Connecting me to this debacle is all they need to bring me down. Using an innocent is nothing to these people. It is how things work at court, how it has always worked."

Geneviève could not argue with her; Anne knew better than anyone the extent of the machinations plied to rule a kingdom. That Diane de Poitiers would want the duchesse gone from court was a foregone fact; she craved to rule the royal retinue, to be the most glittering jewel in the crown, and yet she was forever compared ignominiously to the duchesse.

"He hates me, you know. As much as she." Anne pushed herself up against the bolster, sliding her legs beneath her body as she leaned anxiously forward. "Because the king loves me more. Because he is Poitiers's puppet. Because Montmorency loves the queen and blames me for her pain. For this and more, he detests me. It is all a tangled, sticky web and I am embedded in it without hope of escape." Her hands flayed with each reason she recounted, the gestures wider and more fearsome with every accusation.

Geneviève reached out to the duchesse, capturing the erratic hands in her own and trapping them down upon the bed. "The king loves you, madame. Have faith in that love." Geneviève pitched forward, her face inches away from Anne's, the violet gaze piercing the green. "You must not let them triumph."

Her words struck a chord. Anne's agitation ebbed like the outgoing tide, and composure descended about the woman like a regal cape. Pulling her hands away, the duchesse squared her shoulders.

"Bring me my emerald gown, Geneviève," she instructed, pushing the vagrant strands of strawberry blond curls off her face. "And my finest jewels. I must look my best for my guests."

Geneviève smiled and turned to her chore, the grin fading from her face like dusk's last light. To Anne she spoke with conviction, but her own thoughts could not be more irresolute. Her plan had traveled so very awry; Lisette arrested, Anne in turmoil, and she to blame. She had ventured to distract any condemning finger from pointing her way, and she had brought destruction upon those she would least wish to harm.

They had held their heads high for hours—the king and his mistress—presiding over a subdued evening's salon. But now all their guests had departed, words of encouragement spoken, uncertain glances denied. In word and deed, François and Anne had assured their closest confidants that there was no truth to the outrageous charges, and that all would be put to rights. Though certain in their own truth, the efforts had wearied them, none more than the king, and age had rampaged across his face through the long, horrifying hours of this day, leaving it ashen and flaccid.

Anne sat on her couch, her eyes encircled by plum-colored sockets of exhaustion, and stared out into nothing. The king lay with his head in her lap, accepting the succor that she so often offered him, as servants tidied the remnants of the evening with their guests, gathering up the half-empty goblets and the crumb-covered plates strewn haphazardly about the room. The cleaning women went about their chores in unobtrusive silence, nothing more than the clanking of silver and the swish of a broom revealing their presence.

Anne's ladies sat in a circle around the king and the duchess—silent, vigilant, splendidly dressed guards on watchful duty.

"Did you ever suspect . . ." The king's tremulous voice broached the question, all façade of strength surrendered in the safety of their intimacy, his niggling fear unable and unwilling to remain silent.

"No, never." Anne was quick to slap at the suggestion, and her undeniable certainty slayed the dragon that was his trepidation. He reached a hand up into the air and hers found it. François clasped her hand to his chest, holding it dear to his heart with both of his.

In their unity against disaster, they formed a more perfect coupling, for that was indeed where true love lived—not in the moments of great passion and bursting joy, but in the strength with which it weathered any storm, no matter how harsh or violent.

Geneviève looked upon them with envy and wonder. How could these two of such notorious reputation find such love together? François may have strayed, taking lovers while having a wife and a mistress, but he always returned to her, his Hely. And if she had found forbidden passion in the arms of another, it was the king she craved, to whose heart she belonged. Did they possess a deserving nature she herself did not, that King Henry must not, for what this man and woman relished remained elusive to them both.

"I must allow the court to treat this situation as decisively as they would any other," François croaked. "I cannot impose any sort of intervention, though she may be one of your ladies."

Anne nodded silently, a balled fist pushed hard against her lips. The Swiss Guards had transported Lisette to Paris that very afternoon, delivering her to the dungeon of the royal palace on the Île de la Cité, where the Parlement of Paris would hear her case. It was a thickly layered judicial conglomeration presiding over, among other indictments, all those brought against any persons on behalf of the king. They were his voice in court, though they did not often speak for him.

"There may be action I can take once they have completed their case," François continued. "I will have some of my inner council looking into things as well, should it be required."

"I pray such action will not be necessary," Anne said from behind her hand. "Her innocence will win out. I am sure of it."

"As am I," François agreed. "In the meantime, you . . . we . . . must do all we can to dispel any notions of our own impropriety."

Though he spoke of them both, there was no doubt he meant Anne. She looked down at him, finding his amber eyes intent upon her. "What do you propose?"

He pushed himself up with a stiff, achy movement, and shifted over to sit close by her side. "You must keep your appointment with King Henry. There can be n—"

"I cannot leave until I know she is free," Anne argued doggedly, shaking her head with agitation. "I must be here should—"

"Of course, of course," the king placated her, large hands clasping her face tenderly, thumbs stroking her flushed skin until she calmed. "I would never suggest otherwise. I propose that we continue to make plans, no more. It will remind everyone of your devotion and willingness to work on our behalf. I am merely asking you to continue on as if nothing had changed, as if all will be well."

"All *will* be well," she hissed, and struggled against his embrace.

François held her tighter, allowing her to rail against him, to pound out her anger, frustration, and fear as she beat her small fists against his large chest. Her hands fell limply, all strength wrung out of them, her protests slurring to incomprehensible sobbing. The king pulled her to him, laying her head against his chest, stroking her head with the same loving succor she so often administered upon him.

"Of course, *ma chérie,* of course all will be well."

But to Geneviève and every ear who heard the words, the promise sounded like no more than a hollow echo of hope.

❧ 25 ❧

In me the fires abide.

—Mellin de Saint-Gelais (1491–1558)

The trial had begun, and the court whispered of it constantly. Talk of it seethed through the castle like the unrelenting hiss of steam. Riders were dispatched to and from Paris four or five times a day, returning with news brought to the king; yet every word found its way through the court, spreading with the same insidious contagion as an illness once breathed into life.

Like many others, Arabelle and Jecelyn had made their way to the great city, to hear for themselves the words spoken against their friend and colleague, leaving Geneviève, Monique, and Anne's cousins to see to the duchesse and her needs. Geneviève could not have borne one minute in the stultifying air of the judicial chamber; every word spoken against Lisette would have pushed and twisted the dagger of guilt piercing her heart, a cutting reminder of her own hand in the fallacious charges against the woman. Yet she could not have been more torn apart than she was, far away though she may be. She held her breath with every new report, unable to alleviate the nausea grinding in her gullet, no matter how many steamed herbs she imbibed.

Anne kept herself frantic with plans and activities, hiding her own desperate fear in action, and Geneviève was grateful for it. She left Sybille and Béatrice to the sewing and stitching, accepting every errand, running willy-nilly through the castle, borrowing hair notions from one comtesse, a jeweled and embroidered fan from another, anything to escape the duchesse's abandoned, tension-filled chambers. But such frenzy was futile; every salacious report found her no matter how fast she ran; eventually, she heard every bit of news as the breathless riders plunged into the palace.

Geneviève wrapped the small pearl-encrusted drawstring pouch in soft gauze before retrieving it from the chamber of the comtesse de Freyne, guarding the delicate accessory with exceptional care.

The white-haired woman pretended to help, doing no more than tucking in a corner of the cottony material, leaning in close to whisper to Geneviève as they worked together on either side of the round claw-foot table. "Have you seen any of them?"

Geneviève looked up at her with a puckered brow. "Seen any of what, Comtesse?"

"Any of the papers?" The elderly woman's cloudy blue eyes pierced her with vicious curiosity. "I'm sure you have been to her room. You would have seen the papers they accuse Lisette of possessing."

Geneviève felt her mouth open and close like a gaping fish, her blatant shock feeding the woman's hunger for scandal.

"You have not heard then? Oh, I am so sorry to tell you." But the small pointy-toothed grin on the noblewoman's face refuted her apologetic words. "It is said that substantial evidence was found in her rooms, messages passed between her and her foreign lover."

Geneviève gnashed her teeth against such unsubstantiated condemnation. "Love letters are hardly treasonous, madame. If they were, most of the court would long have been imprisoned."

The comtesse leered at her. "Perhaps, my dear, but where there is smoke . . ."

Geneviève tucked the package beneath one arm and dropped a curtsy before the malicious woman spoke again. "I thank you, Comtesse, as does the duchesse."

She did not mean to let the door slam shut behind her, at least not consciously. Geneviève rushed back to Anne's chambers as the echo of the crash chased her down the hallway. She hoped to deliver the latest dispatch to the duchesse before anyone else, someone who would be vicious in how they plied the propaganda. Geneviève rushed through the palace, the woman's words a gauntlet she must hurdle, and she tripped on them. She had called Lisette's lover a foreigner, and nothing else Geneviève had heard that day vexed her more. There existed no harsher a denunciation against Lisette than for her man to be from another land.

Geneviève dashed through the halls, bursting through the door, package in hand.

The reticence filled the room with dire gloom. Anne sat immobile on the green organza settee, Sybille by her side, one of Anne's hands in both of hers. Facing them, perched upon a small petitpoint hassock, Béatrice sat, leaning forward with elbows on knees to hold her cousin's other hand. Silent tears ran down Anne's face; they marred her beauty, but she cared not at all.

"You have heard then, about the papers found in her room?" Geneviève's whisper barely cut through the oppression, so thickly did it permeate the chamber.

Béatrice nodded. "And of the man."

Geneviève rushed forward and flounced down onto the floor, inveigling her way into their circle to cast her lot with this small group of apprehensive women. "What of him?"

Sybille shook her head as it fell to her chest, her bottom lip quivering. "He is an . . . an Italian." She said the word as if it were the most licentious ever to pass from her lips.

Geneviève's befuddled gaze rose to Anne's face.

The woman's pert nose stood out like a red cherry on her pale visage; her delicate chin quivered. "He will be helpless to save her now. It is too soon after his son."

Geneviève recoiled incredulously. "Do they infer a connection between Lisette and the Dauphin's death?"

The Italian count, Sebastian de Montecuculli, had come to France in the retinue of Catherine de' Medici, and had later come to serve as the young François's secretary. He had also been convicted of the murder by poisoning of the king's son, and had been executed for it in a most vicious manner, one in keeping with the king's fury. Drawn and quartered, they hung the four parts of Montecuculli's body at the four gates of Lyons, his head skewered on a lance and placed on a bridge over the Rhône. But there could be nothing to associate Lisette to that man or the heinous act; it had taken place three years ago.

"No connection would be needed," Anne said with a calamitous monotone. "All know of the king's unrelenting bitterness. If Parlement should find her guilty, he cannot intercede. It would be an obvious act of favor and not of justice. They will expect him to be hideous with his punishment."

"But there are hundreds of Italians at our court. Hundreds of noblemen have Italian mistresses. What of it?" Geneviève snapped.

"But the man did not make himself known to the court or to the king," Anne bawled. "He kept his presence secret and she her involvement with him. Why?"

Béatrice rocked as she nodded. "It is always our secrets which give us away in the end."

Geneviève flicked up a wary gaze, but saw nothing to fear except the words' truth.

"We must have faith," Sybille intoned with little of her own conviction. "And pray for God's mercy."

Anne nodded with a quaking sigh, rising to cross to her large writing table. "Let us continue our work, ladies."

The three women shared a moment of concern, but they rose to their mistress's command.

Long into the night, Anne had Geneviève fetching and carrying, copying plans and lists, and bringing them to the king for his approval, though they were of such little consequence the approval was unnecessary.

She returned once more to Anne's chambers, this time finding it dark, a lone, three-branched candlestick casting a pale glow in the center of the room, leaving the ravenous gloom to devour the corners. Evening had fallen without fanfare, and a murky night reigned supreme. Béatrice slept curled upon a couch, Sybille slouched in a chair, and Anne was nowhere to be seen.

"We gave her a sleeping draught and put her to bed," Sybille explained with a whisper. "Go to your room, Geneviève. Find some peace if you can."

Geneviève nodded; there was nothing more any of them could do this day.

Her feet dragged as she passed through the deserted corridors toward her room, her head aching with disruptive thoughts. She had lost her purpose and the strength it gave her, no longer certain who she was. Perhaps only God should wield the sword of revenge, as the Gospel proclaimed, for look at the harm she had done by brandishing it herself. The need to avenge her parents pumped through her veins, but the part of her that wanted to forget, if not forgive, to live in untroubled peace, grew more insistent with each passing day. The dichotomy of desire fought inside her like a parasite intent upon assimilation of its host.

Geneviève reached her door, placed one hand upon its latch, and pulled away. She could not go into that room, could not be alone with herself and the voices in her head refusing to cease their prattling, could not lie quietly while the fight raged inside her, or she would surely go mad.

Geneviève ran; the desperation chased her. At first she was unmindful of where her rushing feet took her, until she clattered down the flight of stairs and through the great hall to the rooms on the far side of the castle. As soon as she turned the corner and saw the heavy wooden door at the end of the dimly lit stone hall, she knew what she needed . . . whom she needed.

She ran until her body fell against the portal, the flat of one hand rapping upon it.

Sebastien threw open the door, features contorted in confusion, dressed in nothing but the tight breeches and hose of his uniform. In the moment he saw her, his confusion changed to concern and again as quickly to desire. Geneviève fell into the space, fell into his strong arms, which opened without question and caught her.

"Sebastien, I . . ." she groaned, but she needed to say nothing more. His lips covered hers with his own greedy lust, his hands touched her everywhere, as if he could not believe in her nearness. They rubbed her back, pulled at her arms, held her face captive like a delicate dove in a tender, loving cage.

Geneviève threw her arms around him, felt the smooth, hard nakedness of his back, and latched onto it, her fingers digging into his flesh as she surrendered to his kisses. He led her toward his bed, or perhaps she moved on her own. Her laces came untied in a flurry of motion. Her gown dropped to the floor; her shift loosened as his hands found her breasts and paid homage to them.

Geneviève threw back her head, all painful thought abandoned in the escape found in Sebastien's touch. The air filled with the musky scent of them and their rasping, harsh breaths.

Sebastien raised his lips to hers and took possession and she groaned like a petted cat. He raised his gaze and stilled, brows furrowing at the tears on her face. The passion raging through him simmered at her sorrow. He kissed her cheeks with small, tender kisses, like the touch of a butterfly's wings, and laid her gently on the bed.

But she would have none of it. Geneviève grabbed the back of his neck with one hand, the hard curve of his shoulder with the other, and pushed, rolling them over until she lay on top of him, her legs straddling his.

For a fleeting moment, Sebastien's stunned gaze stared up at her. His soft smile spread, his dimples came out to play, and a low, husky laugh rumbled in his chest. They came together then, in the frenzy that held her, in the impassioned violence she prayed would hammer away all her fears and sorrows.

She curled herself in a ball and he surrounded her, his warm, moist skin clinging to hers, his body the shield with which he kept the world at bay. He kissed her shoulder, caressing her soft flesh with his warm lips. One hand rose to her face, to push back the gorgeous mess of blond curls draping it, and felt her tears.

"Did I hurt—"

"No, oh no, Sebastien. That . . . we . . . it was wonderful," she said, and rolled onto her back, her violet gaze confirming the truth of her words, pale skin blushing with stunning beauty at the delight she took in their lascivious lovemaking.

Sebastien rose up to brace himself on one elbow. "Then why do you cry, *ma chérie?*"

Geneviève turned her head and looked away from him, looked back at all she had lost and all she had become, looked forward to a future filled with nothing but uncertainty.

"I do not know my path ahead nor my own heart." Her voice cracked on the words.

"None of us can know the future." He kissed her full bottom lip and the tip of her nose. "We must do whatever is intended for us, no matter how difficult the challenge may be."

Geneviève stared up into his penetrating eyes and saw a struggle in them she had never noticed before. With the tip of one finger, she followed the hard frown lines she had never seen around his lips.

He gave her a smile, though it did not seem to come easily. "We can take one step at a time and hope that God will give us a sure footing."

Geneviève's worry eased. His doubts echoed her own uncertainty, and she found great succor in his empathy.

Sebastien brushed his lips across hers, moving them down her throat, and she tipped back her head to open herself to him. He took her gently then, with all the peace and tenderness she needed so desperately, loving her until she fell into a deep, restful sleep.

Sebastien jumped as the pounding struck the door, ungraceful with his slumberous movement, sleepy but splendid in his naked-ness, grabbing his sword from its sheath hanging on the arm of the chair. Geneviève jolted up, blessed slumber cracked into jagged wakefulness. Smudgy gray dawn light hovered through the open curtains of the window, throwing their faces into shadowy masks of surreal specters.

It came again: explosive hammering that shook the wooden door in its frame, hinges and latch jangling in protest. The lovers stared at each other, confounded in their apprehension.

"Geneviève? Are you in there?" The fretful voice found its way through the cracks, and they jumped at its familiarity.

"Arabelle?" Geneviève leaped out of bed and wrapped the rumpled linens around her naked body.

Sebastien dropped his sword and grabbed his breeches, tum-bling as he tried to walk to the door while pushing his legs through the slim openings. He made it to the door, threw up the latch, and yanked it open.

Arabelle stood on the threshold, face grubby with tears, lovely features decimated by exhaustion and turmoil. Geneviève rushed to her, grabbing her by the arm and pulling her into the tiny cham-ber before any inquisitive courtiers wandering the halls found them.

"You are here?" Geneviève thought of nothing more to say. When she had fallen asleep, when emotional and physical exhaus-tion had overtaken her, Arabelle had been in Paris.

Arabelle nodded, throat bulging with a hard swallow. "We rode through the night. We did not want anyone else telling the duchesse."

Geneviève's chin dropped to her chest and her jaw hardened as she looked up at her friend. "Tell the duchesse what?"

In that wretched moment, she knew what was coming, but she would deny it to the last minute.

Arabelle reached out and grabbed Geneviève's forearms as her knees began to give way.

"They've found her guilty," she sobbed. "Lisette. They are going to hang her. They are going to hang Lisette in two days."

Geneviève shook her head back and forth and back again, refusing Arabelle's words, but such anguish was undeniable. The friends slipped to the ground and fell together in their sorrow.

❧ 26 ❧

The smile is a weapon as well as the sword—
And just as dangerous.

—François I (1494–1547)

Every one of Anne's ladies came to her chamber that morning, creeping in long before dawn's first light. As the day faithfully came, undeterred by their deepest hopes and fervent prayers, Jecelyn and Geneviève sat beside each other on the settee, pretending to sew, yet doing nothing more than holding the wood frame and linens in their hands without taking a stitch. Their senseless feud was forgotten, abandoned in the face of life's bleak cruelty. There was no place else to be but here, no other people to be with.

Arabelle sat alone in the window embrasure; no words consoled her, no embrace called her away, but neither could she face the moment in solitude. Huddled in a ball, skirts wrapped around her knees as she rocked, Arabelle stared out at the bright sunny morning as if unable to comprehend its cheerfulness.

Sybille and Béatrice sat at the table with Anne. Not one of them had touched a single bite of the morning's fare, not even Béatrice, for whom a good meal was of sacred esteem. The large corner clock in its walnut cabinet beat out the minutes left in Lisette's life and the women listened to each tick, willing it to stop.

The door opened without a knock and the women jumped,

fearful the Grim Reaper himself had come calling; the ravaged apparition standing in its frame could well have been.

The king hovered on the threshold, an elderly man beaten by a life that had piled hardship and loss upon suffering and grief. Geneviève stared at him, at the deep crags upon his once handsome face, at the inward slump of his once broad shoulders. She had come to his court to destroy him and, in a manner, she had succeeded; but at what cost?

His presence here, now, meant one thing; the time for a pardon had passed. Lisette's fate was sealed.

Anne stood and for a long moment made no move toward her lover, her life's mate. Temper clouded her features; they all saw it, the king most of all. He curled further inward, as if struck in the gut by a powerful fist, and began to turn away.

"Wait!" Anne cried, rushing to his side, a choked sob rising above the rustling of her skirts. She threw her arms around him, clutched him near, her cheek flat and tight against his chest.

Relief flooded François, his wide mouth trembling as he lowered his lips to the top of her head, closing his eyes as he leaned upon her. Their silent, intimate embrace, one offered to each other as freely as if they had been alone, healed any fissure daring to insinuate itself between them. Anne lifted her face, offering him a tender smile, an expression infused with love but tinctured with their shared grief. The large man returned it in kind. Taking his hand, Anne led him silently into the room.

Out in the courtyard the drums began to beat, echoes of those in the courtyard of the Louvre, informing the king of what took place at the city's judicial center. François and Anne fell onto the couch opposite the settee—listless, shocked victims of a ruthless trauma. For an instant, the king's gaze caught Geneviève's and her heart thudded against her chest. Did he know of her hand in this catastrophe? She did not believe it would serve Constable Montmorency to tell him, but she feared his censure nonetheless. His empty stare passed over her, and she knew he was ignorant.

Yet the hammering in her chest would not yield. As the beat of the drums grew faster and faster, so did her palpitating heart. She stared at the defeated king, but there was no joy in a battle won. It should have been a moment of triumph, at the very least one of enormous relief, but it was neither.

The drum beats became a furious roll, a never-ending roar.

The king threw himself into Anne's arms.

Arabelle sobbed.

Sybille and Béatrice began to pray, beseeching God for intervention.

Geneviève gasped for air, unable to breathe.

But she must.

She had to tell the king to stop it.

He had to save Lisette.

The drums thundered.

She jumped to her feet.

The words formed on the tip of her tongue.

The drums crashed.

And then . . . they stopped.

"God be with her," Sybille sobbed.

Geneviève crumbled, unconscious, to the ground.

Her gowns hung upon her, so much weight had she lost in the last fortnight. Carine had no choice but to hastily ply needle and thread to make Geneviève presentable before she returned to the duchesse's chambers and resumed her duties.

The duchesse had insisted Geneviève take time to recover. The king's physician, the same who had scooped her off Anne's floor and rushed her to bed, had told them she suffered a physical malady, one whose symptoms included weakness, lack of appetite, and an inability to keep food in her gullet. In truth, the symptoms had been extreme, the nausea debilitating, but no one knew her illness bore the name of heartbreak and confusion.

Carine's hands brushed her mistress's skirts. "It is not the best I have seen you looking, but it is far better than some." She offered the backhanded compliment as she looked up at Geneviève's pale face with a smile. "All shall be much pleased to see you, mam'selle."

Geneviève gave a small nod. Day after day, Arabelle had been to visit her; Sebastien came as often as his duties would allow. The duchesse had sent her tokens, as had the king, both his sons, and Diane de Poitiers as well. Yes, she was a well-liked courtier, for all that she was a murderer.

She looked at herself in the cloudy looking glass, or was it her essence that was cloudy and not the glass? How much of herself had she lost? The blond ringlets flowing from the jeweled crescent hood, the waiflike body encased in beaded lilac: It was her, but it wasn't.

The knocking upon her door did little to rouse her from her self-examination, and Carine jumped up to answer it.

"Oh look, mademoiselle, another posy to cheer you," Carine trilled as she retrieved the delivery from the page and dismissed him with a *denier* to his palm and a polite *merci*. "And English ivy, no less. It must be a deep pocket to afford such a token."

Geneviève jerked round, eyes wide at the sight of the two small pink rosebuds surrounded by the trailing, three-pointed green leaves.

"Who sends it, Carine?"

Her maid used her fingers to hunt among the leaves and petals, but found no note or card. "It doesn't say," she said dubiously. "How very odd."

Geneviève rushed to retrieve the small bouquet from Carine's hand. "Very odd, indeed, but beautiful all the same. I will treasure it in the spirit it was given."

"Will you take it with you to the duchesse?" Carine asked casually, clearing her sewing notions from the floor where she'd left them, and missing the vexation sweeping across Geneviève's face.

"No. I believe I will keep it to myself," Geneviève replied.

"You may leave me now, Carine. I think I will take a few minutes' more rest before I go."

Carine looked hard at her mistress. "Are you all right? Do you feel a return of the illness?"

"No no, have no fear," Geneviève assured her, deciding again to use truth to perpetuate deception. "I'm a little nervous, if truth be told. I would gather myself before seeing the duchesse."

Carine tilted her head and smiled at Geneviève with the sympathetic indulgence of a mother. "Of course, mam'selle, I understand." She took up her sewing basket and made for the door. "I will not be far, should you need me."

"*Merci*, Carine," Geneviève said.

Before the door latched closed behind the servant, Geneviève pulled at the ribbons on the posy, tearing the shoots and tendrils of the plants apart in her hands. There, at the very center of the greenery, was the small piece of parchment she expected to find. No one but King Henry would send her a bouquet of English ivy, and the irony had not been lost on her.

It was a tiny rolled rectangle of paper, with no more than a few words on it. It took Geneviève a few scant minutes to decipher it. But it required more time to accept its meaning.

I need you where you are. You are safe.

The message could not be clearer for all its brevity. Henry needed her to stay at the French court, needed her to continue her mission, but would see to her safety. Geneviève dropped the papers into the fire, those that held the coded message as well as its translation. As she watched the flames devour the words, she worried upon them. She had broken King François, she was sure of it. What more he would do worthy to report to King Henry, she could not fathom. As to Henry's assurance of her well-being, that was as intangible as the smoke rising up the chimney; she was alone here, and she felt it more with each passing day.

* * *

"Geneviève. It's Geneviève!" Arabelle's delighted cry greeted her as soon as she entered the bright presence chamber. But a few steps across the threshold and they all flocked around her, Sybille and Béatrice, and Jecelyn as well; they had shared a great loss and in it found a place to coexist in peace if not friendship.

Geneviève accepted their welcome with modest grace, unable to deny the cloak of warm affection they piled upon her. Stepping out of their circle, she made her way to the far corner of the room, where the duchesse and the king sat side by side at the head of the table. They broke their solemn counsel as she approached.

"It is quite wonderful to see you, Geneviève." Anne stood and pulled her attendant out of her curtsy, gracing each side of Geneviève's face with the brush of a kiss. "You had us worried, *ma chérie*."

"Far too worried." François reached out and took Geneviève's hand, bowing over it in a chaste and tender gesture. His clasp upon her hand was weak, the fingers tremulous. "I could not have borne to lose another daughter."

Geneviève dropped to a deep obeisance, her face to the floor in undeniable respect and necessary artifice, hiding the strong reaction his words wrought.

"We will be on the hunt this afternoon," the king told her gladly. "I hope you are up to the challenge. It is not the same without your skilled bow at the ready."

"It will be my honor, Your Majesty," Geneviève assured him.

"Then make ready with the ladies," Anne told her, dismissing her from their side.

Geneviève gave a quick dip and returned to the circle of women who eagerly waited to chat with her.

"You have missed so much," Sybille twittered as Geneviève sat among them.

The women launched into a tirade of gossip, reporting on every illicit love affair, every bastard child conceived, every marriage match that had taken place in the two short weeks of Geneviève's absence. Not once did they mention Lisette's name; their wound was too raw for anyone to poke at it.

Geneviève listened with halfhearted consideration, indulging a catty interest in the outrageous comings and goings of the nobles at court, but she strained to hear the discussion of duchesse and king, listening to each conversation with diligence. When the king spoke the name of the Holy Roman Emperor, Geneviève shut out the twitterings of the ladies around her and focused on the words passing between the ruler and his adviser.

"The timing has been confirmed by his ambassador." A glimmer sparked in François's serious stare, one not seen in a long while, and for a moment, the dashing cavalier once more reigned. "The emperor will arrive at the end of November, no more than a month and a half from this very day." He reached across the table-top and gripped Anne's hands as if they began a dance, his anxious delight apparent in every movement, in the breadth of his wide smile.

Geneviève denied the nagging desire to jump up and protest. How could the king consider keeping his appointment with the emperor? How could he continue on the destructive road to domination, one that might well bring France to war with England and wreak the deaths of more innocent people? Had he learned nothing from all his losses?

Geneviève longed to argue aloud; instead, she nodded distractedly as the women continued their frivolous lecture. She had been a fool to think Lisette's death would have changed the king's attitude, for if he believed Lisette's Italian lover was a secret agent bent on evildoing, then the man could only have been an emissary of Charles V's. Had they tortured the man before executing him? Perhaps he *had* incriminated himself and Lisette. How could it not have changed François's strategy with the emperor?

The ways of a king remained a conundrum. She could not attempt to persuade him against his plans nor could she abandon her quest. As much as François's weakness and affection captured her sympathy and touched her heart, she could not allow him to gain back any former glory. If she could not have her parents back, he could not go unpunished. If he did not show remorse and allow it to change him—for only with remorse, can true forgiveness be granted—then she would not show mercy.

"Time to make ready, ladies," Anne called out.

The women around Geneviève jumped up and she followed.

"Take yourselves off and change into your hunting costumes." Anne released the hand of the king as he stepped out of the chamber, then she turned back to the room. "Return soon. The king is anxious to be off."

Like fish up a stream, the women rushed for the door as Anne's servants made her own riding outfit ready.

"Geneviève, could you stay a moment?" Anne gestured to two winged chairs in front of the windows.

"Of course, madame," Geneviève replied, waiting for the duchesse to sit before taking her own seat.

The rising afternoon sun was warm on their backs, the autumn as preternaturally hot and dry as the spring and summer had been. Geneviève felt beads of moisture form on her upper lip and wiped them away.

Anne leaned toward her companion, a devilish smirk spreading on her dainty face. Geneviève did not know whether to fear it or be amused by it.

"I have a surprise for you," Anne said. "A pleasant one, I hope."

Geneviève replied with a half smile, "I am most eager to hear it, madame."

"I have decided you will accompany me on my upcoming journey," Anne announced, and flounced back in triumph.

Geneviève's small mouth formed a perfect O.

Anne laughed. "I knew you would be surprised."

"To see the king of England?" Geneviève found her voice, be it no more than a hushed whisper.

"Mais oui!" Anne leaned forward and took Geneviève's hand. "It will be grand, yes? I knew such a trip would cheer you."

Geneviève's heart burst with joyful astonishment, and she did little to keep it from showing on her face. If she had searched for a sign, if God answered her prayers for guidance, the intention could not have been clearer.

ॐ 27 ॐ

So you must always remember
That time ends the beauty.

—Mellin de Saint-Gelais (1491–1558)

The caravan arrived in Calais with far less fanfare than had launched it from Fontainebleau, and it was a somber cortege awaiting the duchesse d'Étampes and her train of ladies and outriders. The burghers of Calais stood together in a quiet reception line, looking none too pleased to have their town host such a turbulent meeting, concerned that should it sour, they would somehow be to blame. This gaggle of gentry offered no more than shallow bows and mumblings of welcome. One voice in the crowd offered a rousing greeting.

"Anne! Anne! You are here!" The dark-haired, sumptuously dressed woman ran out of the crowd gathered in the cobbled town center, her arms flung wide in greeting, familiar features bursting with joy.

The duchesse abandoned her posture of aloof pretention at the sight of Marguerite de Navarre, launching herself into the tall woman's arms.

"Oh, *ma chérie*, how wonderful to see you," Anne twittered. "How I have missed you."

"Dear sister, what a delight you are for the eyes." Marguerite held tightly to the *maîtresse en titre* of France, her brother's official mistress and her dear friend. "We should not allow years to pass between our visits."

Anne's retinue looked on as the two women greeted each other with poignant affection. Geneviève had never seen the king's sister prior to this moment, but there could be no denying their kinship, for Marguerite's appearance was a mirror of François's; they shared the same tall build, the same long face, the same wide mouth and prominent nose. What projected as masculine beauty on the king was not quite as attractive in its female form, and yet Marguerite showed none of the signs of age that so beleaguered her brother. Her quieter, more peaceful life gave her an appeal and a healthy glow the king had long since lost.

Since her marriage to the king of Navarre more than a decade ago, Marguerite had spent much of her time with her own court and her residences at Cognac, Alençon, and Nérac. Though far away, she continued to support the brother she adored, producing some of the most erudite missives in support of his reforms and initiatives in the land, for Marguerite was nothing if not a prolific writer. And yet her distance had saved her from the angst of her brother's turbulent life.

The duc d'Orléans swaggered up to his aunt and they paid each other fond, affectionate greetings, the elder woman tousling the handsome young man's hair. He revealed the adolescent he was, embarrassment warming his cheeks, but he smiled at the motherly affection he knew so little of.

"What has happened to the naughty child I have missed?" Marguerite cajoled, without letting go of his hand.

Eyes so like her own twinkled back at her. "The child is gone, but the naughtiness remains." Charles laughed, as did his aunt and the duchesse.

"And how does my brother fare?" Marguerite asked, leading them toward the large main building anchoring the square to the north.

"He is doing better of late. He is finding renewed vigor in purpose." Anne smiled. "He sends his very best to his darling sister."

From their childhood days together, François had called his sister "darling" and she warmed at the affectionate endearment. "King Henry does not arrive until tomorrow, but I have arranged a wonderful night of entertainment for you. I have brought my most favored musicians and linguists, all for your diversion and amusement."

A true patron of the arts like her brother, Marguerite was forever in the company of scholars and poets, musicians and painters.

"Then we shall have a jolly time of it, at least for one night." Anne offered the sarcasm with the snidest of grins, and Marguerite laughed at the king of England's expense.

The food was perfectly prepared, the music magnificent, the readings rousing, and yet the night stretched on interminably. Geneviève nipped at her food, neither cognizant nor comprehending of the poetry, so fervent was her anticipation of the meeting to come. She would at last be in the company of the man whom she had thought of as her father for most of her life, whose dimensions of power and authority had evolved into nothing short of godlike in her esteem. The occasion could be no more momentous were she to travel to the gates of heaven.

At last they had retired—to the soft beds at the top floor of the inn, in the quiet that wrapped them in slumber—and yet she still could not find her ease. She sat up on the feather ticking, back against the headboard, eyes out the window and on the moon as it rose in the clear sky, watching it through the long hours, until it began its descent.

"Are you unwell, Geneviève?" Arabelle roused, half-conscious, her speech slurred by sleepiness.

Geneviève found her friend staring at her in the moonlight, perched on one elbow in the bed beside her own.

"I am fine, fear not."

"You must get your rest. Many busy days lie ahead."

"Go back to sleep," she told her friend, nodding.

Arabelle needed nothing more; she flopped back onto her pillow and mattress and within minutes, Geneviève recognized the slow, even breath of sleep. How she envied her.

"Please bring these gifts to the king's lodgings." The duchesse handed Geneviève and Arabelle the brightly wrapped parcels, bouquets of pastel silk linens tied together with golden taffeta bows.

Geneviève did her best to keep her hands from trembling as she accepted three such packages. The traditional exchange of tokens played a vital part in any noble meeting. But having never taken part in such a ritual, she did not know if she would present them directly to King Henry, or to his representative. *The* moment could be upon her, and she quivered with anticipation and apprehension. She scrambled after Arabelle as the woman scampered off to do her mistress's bidding.

They stepped out into the bright courtyard, the slanted rays of early morning light streaming through the thin alleyways between the stone and spire buildings that formed its periphery. A cacophony assaulted them—the quiet, largely abandoned square of the previous night now teemed with people, animals, and conveyances. Though the king of England had just arrived, his essence dominated the town. Squires groomed the long line of exhausted horses, the animals snorting two streams of vapor from their long noses. Servants grunted as they hefted trunks from the backs of wagons, and maids scurried to follow as they claimed each for their particular masters and directed them to the appropriate lodgings.

Fog and smoke filled the air, blending with the aroma of small fires and cooking food; so many attendants had arrived with the English contingent, many were forced to take their accommodations out in the open, and they prepared their morning meal over small makeshift stoves, the meat sizzling and spitting over the small grates. Their strange language, so hard and guttural, lent the whole scene the spirit of a barnyard filled with braying and barking animals.

Geneviève and Arabelle took a twisted path from one end of the courtyard to the other, skipping around a smiling group of breakfasting cavaliers here, avoiding a large, steaming pile of horse excrement there. They made their way past the enormous oak tree dominating the center of the courtyard; large russet leaves clung tenaciously to the thick, gnarled branches, unwilling to concede to the undeterred march toward winter. Geneviève's eyes rose to the top thin twigs crowning the tree like fuzzy hair, marveling at how many hundreds of years this magnificent plant had survived, how many storms it had weathered, how much of man's evolution it had witnessed.

When at last they entered the large four-storied main hall at the south end, their arms ached with the weight of their cargo and they looked about, confused and leery, at the hordes of people bustling about.

"May I help you?" The tall, lanky man stepped out of the crowd, no sign of friendly welcome on his pasty face, dressed in the expensive but simple clothing of an attendant.

Geneviève understood his English well enough, but it had been far too long since she had used the language to explain their errand. She dipped a curtsy, as did Arabelle. "*Bonjour*, monsieur."

"Ah *oui, bonjour*," the man replied, his stiff tongue mangling the lyrical greeting as he continued in French. "You have brought the gifts, I see."

"Yes, monsieur." Arabelle stepped forward, thrusting the parcels out toward him, only to be abruptly forced aside as Geneviève stepped in front of her.

"They are for King Henry," she squawked.

The man frowned, raising one eyebrow in disdainful disapproval. "And I will see he gets them."

Geneviève opened her mouth to protest, but Arabelle cut her

off, handing the man her packages and grabbing those in Geneviève's hands. The attendant made a small motion over his shoulder and two young pages rushed to his side, relieving him of the gifts. There was no chance to see the king, nothing Geneviève could say that would not be an unseemly breach of protocol. With reluctance, she made her obeisance beside Arabelle and followed the woman back out into the sun-drenched courtyard.

"He is very unattractive, isn't he?" Arabelle laughed, once safely out of the attendant's hearing. "He quite resembled a horse, don't you think?"

Geneviève mumbled her agreement, throbbing with disappointment at not seeing King Henry for herself.

"Do you think all Englishmen are as pompous as he?" Arabelle asked.

"I would ima—"

She slammed into the bent, wizened woman who appeared before her like an apparition, so small and slight, Geneviève sent her crashing to the ground.

"Oh no! Oh, madame!" Geneviève and Arabelle cried out in alarm.

Geneviève rushed forward, grabbing the tiny form and hefting her up, brushing the dirt from the woman's threadbare skirts.

"I am so very sorry. Are you al—"

Geneviève's words froze on her tongue as the old woman straightened up.

The purple scars covered most of her, the raw, reddish splotches bright under the wiry gray and white hair surrounding it. No more than a small wrinkled portion of the woman's forehead and one crinkled eye were untouched by whatever trauma had decimated her face. It took all of Geneviève's control not to cringe outwardly at the deformed visage.

"Are . . . are you all right, madame?" Geneviève asked with unvarnished concern.

The elderly woman stared at the young face before her. The

jagged opening that was her mouth moved a fraction, but no words came forth. Geneviève looked helplessly at Arabelle, but her friend shrugged her shoulders feebly.

"Do you need a doctor?" Arabelle asked, but received no reply, and turned back to Geneviève. "Perhaps she is English and doesn't understand us?"

Geneviève nodded and searched her mind for the words studied so long ago. "Doctor?" Her brows rose with the upward lilt of her voice and she pointed to the woman's body. "You are . . . *qu'est-ce que* . . . injured?"

But not a word came in response. Geneviève looked down at the woman. The steady blue eyes, their brilliance shining out of the decimated skin, had not moved from her own face. The woman stared at her as if she looked through her.

"What do I do?" Geneviève appealed to Arabelle, but the befuddled young woman offered no more than another shrug.

Geneviève untied the small drawstring purse from her waist. Reaching out, she lifted the old woman's hand and dropped the purse and the few coins within it, into the flaccid palm. "This is all I have." She spoke once more in French, not knowing if the woman understood her, but unable to find the right English words. "If I can help you otherwise, get you a doctor, please come and find me."

Geneviève pointed at the smaller building where she stayed with Anne, and then back at herself.

"Look for me there. Ask for Geneviève, Geneviève Gravois."

"G . . . Geneviève?" The raspy whisper eked out of the old woman's throat.

"Yes, that's right. Geneviève." She smiled, feeling better; at least she had not knocked all coherence out of the deformed, decrepit creature.

The woman watched Geneviève walk away; her gaze locked upon the slender, graceful form as the mademoiselle strode the entire distance of the courtyard and entered the building on the far side. Once Geneviève looked back, as if she felt the gaze so firmly fixed upon her. Geneviève threw back a small wave and a tender smile, the gestures of a caring soul.

As soon as the young lady disappeared from her sight, the old woman's sob broke from her lipless mouth, the remaining flesh slashing wide as the crying burst from her. She dropped where she stood, unable to take a step away, collapsing onto the sun-warmed stone.

All this time, all these years of searching, and here was her daughter, discovered when she no longer looked for her. She may call herself by a different surname, but there could be no other Geneviève with the same luminous pale hair, the same jewellike eyes.

Those months and months after her recovery from the fire, they had told her that her daughter was dead. She had begged them to show her Geneviève's grave, but they claimed there was none, that the child's remains had never been found. She knew then her daughter lived, and she had spent more than fifteen years looking for her. How could she have given up? How could she have let the cough that plagued her day and night for the last few years stop her from continuing her search?

The old woman raised her scarred face to the heavens, the warmth of the sun drying the tears from her haggard cheeks. She looked up into the face of God and offered her thanks.

The long, narrow table ran from one end of the great hall in the burghers' common house to the other, the silver trenchers lined up along each side like flowers spaced precisely apart in a formal garden, sparkling against the pristine white linens swathing the table. The flames in the three fireplaces, each large enough for a man to stand in, burned low but bright, their glow reaching up to kiss the gilt-edged ceiling coves.

From morning until afternoon, the debate over the order in

which the attendants arrived persisted, though there was never any question of the outcome. Protocol and precedence were the dictates of the day, and each player knew his or her part well.

The duchesse d'Étampes was the first to cross the threshold, preceded by her ladies and her guards, her gracious entrance performed for the town's nobles and the servants who awaited the arrival of the evening's honored guests.

Geneviève walked beside a tall soldier, a flash of yearning for Sebastien tugging at her. In truth, she was glad her lover did not attend the assemblage. Their intimacy had revealed much of her soul; he would know the conflict raging within her. Better to miss him than to face questions she would not care to answer.

The duc d'Orléans sauntered in, his dashing cavaliers beside him, the marquis de Limoges among them. Geneviève felt a moment's pleasure at the sight of his round, freckled face, but it fluttered away as her anxious gaze returned to the wide entry arch, breaths quick and shallow as she waited for the king.

Marguerite de Navarre entered next, her quick and informal entry more regal than Anne's, for its lack of any pomposity announced her as a true royal. Her attendants took their place at the far right end of the table, joining Geneviève and Arabelle and the other attendants from Fontainebleau; Marguerite sat beside Anne, Charles, and the burghers at the other end.

Minutes passed, the vaulted room filled with spirited conversation and enticing aromas, until two heralds, in plumed hats and tabards in black and gold, entered the chamber and blared the arrival of the king of England. Every man and woman in the chamber rose to their feet and turned to the wooden arches of the entry. Situated on the far side of the table, Geneviève jostled the woman to her right, unable to see around the rather robust man who stood between her and the door, until at last she caught her first sight of the man who had dominated her thoughts and dreams for most of her life.

There was no mistaking the king, though he hobbled in upon a cane, followed by the handsome, haunted Duke of Suffolk, the somberly clad Cromwell, and a contingent of ministers and soldiers. Tall, rotund, and dictatorial, Henry's small, bow-shaped mouth puckered firm and tight into a sour expression. This king owned the room but was not pleased by it.

Geneviève grabbed the table before her, thighs pressing against the hard edge. She glared at the prodigious man with impudent astonishment. She had expected an altered visage, his physique affected by the years since she had received his miniature portrait, since she had grown from child to woman. But she never imagined such a drastic transformation. The broad shoulders remained, enhanced by the puff-sleeved gold and maroon mantle; but the bulbous cheeks, the red-veined complexion, the wiry white hairs poking out from the sparse auburn remnants on his head and chin, and the hard coldness in the beady eyes shocked her.

Geneviève tore her gaze from the disappointment. A person's physical appearance meant nothing; beauty often blossomed behind ugliness; ugliness often masqueraded as beauty. Geneviève reminded herself that this king was older than François and she saw for herself every day what age and hardship had done to that once fine-looking man. Henry's leg wound was no secret, nor its lasting effect. All this she would dismiss. She would know this king for the sanctuary he had given her, and for the wisdom and kindness she was sure would come from his words.

The two long rows of courtiers remained standing until King Henry took his seat at the very end of the table. Geneviève leaned forward to catch a glimpse of him and frowned; there was little hope of hearing any of the sovereign's words from this distance, indeed she could barely make out the movement of his lips. She flounced back in her chair, all appetite for the meal and the night buried beneath layers of discontent.

The servants placed course after sumptuous course before her, Arabelle and the courtiers around her offered conversation, musicians performed entertainment, yet Geneviève was no more than a shadow in the midst of such activity.

"Do you feel ill?" Arabelle whispered her concern. "Does the food not agree with you?"

Geneviève shook off her worry. "I am fine. Overwhelmed perhaps."

Arabelle nodded with a relieved smile, casting her bright blue eyes down the long table. "The king is quite . . . quite imperious, I think, *oui?*"

"Indeed," Geneviève agreed wholeheartedly.

"But look at our lady." Arabelle encouraged Geneviève to glance again down the far end of the table.

Anne sat to the king's left while Marguerite took the place of honor at his right. Geneviève watched the duchesse smile and banter, green eyes sparkling, hands gesturing with ease and grace. She was at her most charming, her intellect and vivaciousness suffering not at all beside the dominance of the king and the perspicacity of Marguerite.

Geneviève could not deny nor comprehend the sense of pride she felt watching her mistress. As if Anne felt their gaze upon her, she turned from the king and glanced at them, returning the fond smiles she found there. They watched as the duchesse gestured one curling finger at the thin adolescent page behind her, as she and the queen of Navarre gave him their instructions and he scurried down the table toward them.

"Oh my," Arabelle trilled.

Geneviève turned in question, but had not time to give voice to it.

"The queen and the duchesse request a moment with their ladies." The scrawny young man gave a most regal bow as his voice gave a raucous crack.

Arabelle jumped to her feet, as did the two women who sat across from them.

"Come, Geneviève," Arabelle hissed down at her. "We are to be presented to the king."

Geneviève felt the small fingers as they pulled gently on her upper arm and followed their direction, rising slowly. A sense of the surreal cloaked her as she followed the women along the breadth of the vast table, as each pair came to stand beside their mistresses.

The humming in Geneviève's ears grew louder as she stood a mere foot or two away from King Henry, and yet such proximity did little to dissuade her of her initial impressions; verily, he appeared more despotic than ever. The hard, heavy lines cut deep around his mouth, and displeasure gleamed from his eyes.

"Your Highness"—Marguerite smiled and extended an open palm toward the women beside her—"pray make the acquaintance of my attendants, Mademoiselles d' Alincourt and de Nemours."

The two young women curtsied deep and remained so.

"Nemours," the king mused with a low throaty voice, eyes upon the raven-haired beauty. "Was not your father once an ambassador at my court?"

The attendant daringly raised her caramel eyes. "That would be my grandfather, Your Highness."

Henry snorted a half-amused laugh, affected more by what the young lady's glance said than her words. "Ah yes, I remember him well." He shifted to the edge of his seat, animated and attentive.

"Your Majesty"—Anne took her turn in the conventions—"may I present Mademoiselle Gravois, and Mademoiselle d'Aiguillon—the daughter of the comte de Vandreuil."

Like Arabelle, Geneviève dropped into her deepest obeisance, but dared to look up, peeking at the king.

Henry turned to them with a perfunctory gaze and an indiscernible grunt. Geneviève shivered from the empty chill of it.

"Your Highness," Arabelle intoned as she and Geneviève rose.

Geneviève said nothing, nor did it matter. She had sat for weeks as Lodovico had painstakingly captured her likeness onto the miniature, and she had sent it to King Henry as requested. And yet his gaze passed over her without the barest glimmer of recognition. He had heard her name without a tincture of reaction. He gave all the ladies the same cold, cursory greeting, save Mademoiselle de Nemours. To the exotic beauty—a woman young enough to be his granddaughter—he offered a lecherous smile and asked after her journey, his rheumy eyes rarely straying from the rounded globes of her breasts spilling from her jewel-trimmed square neckline.

"Thank you, ladies." Marguerite pleasantly dismissed both her attendants and Anne's, sharing a cynical roll of her eyes with the duchesse.

The four women dipped a quick curtsy, taking themselves back to their own seats, but not before a last knowing look passed between the king and Mademoiselle de Nemours.

Geneviève rushed back to her place, grabbed the full goblet of wine before her, and drank deeply, her mind tumbling with thoughts of the encounter and the king's complete lack of acknowledgment, thoughts fraught with the sting of devastation.

Her breathing slowed; she raised her eyes heavenward as she chided herself, as understanding dawned. Henry VIII was a cunning man, one of the most powerful in all the world; he knew better than to show any sign of recognition of her, for it could be disastrous for them both. She fought with herself over the logic of it, struggled to believe this was the reason for his arrogant dismissal. Part of her clung to her rationale with all the inner tenacity she could muster. The other said far less but spoke much louder.

೪ 28 ೪

A fool may well teach a wise man.

—François Rabelais (c. 1494–1553)

She circled the square in the gloaming, her heels clacking upon the cobbles, losing herself in the anonymity of the smudgy light. Fires crackled around her amid the grumble of those who sat in their warmth, but few paid her any heed; she had become another of the nameless who began to settle down for the night. Geneviève counted the steps as she passed the buildings a second time, filling her head with the useless words, pushing out those intending her harm.

"Geneviève?" The whispered call was lost in the whistling wind meandering through the courtyard. "Geneviève, *s'il vous plaît?*"

Geneviève spun toward the sound of her name and the ill-spoken French, finding a huddled shadow beckoning to her from beyond the corner of the next building. There was something familiar in the small, bent form and she inched toward it. Only when she came within a few steps of the shadowy figure, when the form turned outward and the mangled profile caught the torchlight from the pole above them, did Geneviève recognize it as the old, scarred woman.

"Are you well, madame?" A sudden chill rippled across her flesh and Geneviève pulled her cloak tighter about her shoulders.

"Well enough." The woman's voice warbled with age as she tripped over the unnatural language.

"I am surprised to hear you speak in my tongue." Geneviève stepped closer; it was easier to look upon the woman in the dim light, when the gloom concealed the ravaged skin. "Why did you not converse with me this morning?"

The bent woman shrugged a single shoulder in a lopsided gesture. "I could not find the words, then," she said portentously, and Geneviève frowned at her.

"Do you need a doctor? Is that why you call for me, madame . . . ?" Her question hung in the air. Geneviève would know this woman's name before they spoke any more.

"Hainaut. I am Millicent de Hainaut." The woman straightened her shoulders and raised her chin as she offered her name. Her face appeared serene as the light from the fire grazed it from below, and yet somehow horrifying.

"It is my pleasure to meet you, Madame de Hainaut," Geneviève said, but no such polite response came her way. Instead, a strange silence rose up between them.

"Does this name mean nothing to you?" Madame de Hainaut asked finally.

Geneviève shook her head, brows high. "No, nothing. Well, only that I am surprised to hear it is a French name."

The woman stepped back farther into the alleyway, to the fire that kept her company, and her companion followed along.

"Yes, it was my husband's name. My French husband."

Once more, the thick hush bundled them in a stultifying embrace.

"Are you sure you do not require a physician's care?" Geneviève asked. The woman showed no discernable physical ailment, but her strange behavior was beyond reckoning.

"I know your mother."

The words cut the heavy oppression like the hard edge of a cleaver.

Geneviève stared at the apparition across the wavering light with a dropped jaw. Not since she was a very small child, when she had watched them lay the earth upon her parents, had anyone spoken of her mother. Though Geneviève cherished the small portraits of them, she had never asked her aunt more about them, for it could only bring more pain. It was far easier to pretend such a love had never existed, than to know it had been lost.

"I fear you are mistaken, madame. I have no mother," Geneviève responded with a harsh bitterness. The shield she had brandished all her life rose up to protect her heart once more. "My mother is dead."

Madame de Hainaut fell back against the stone wall behind her. Geneviève rushed forward, grabbing her by the arm before the elderly woman fell to the cobbles.

"Who told you that?"

Geneviève craned to hear the harsh whisper reaching out for her.

"Come stand before your fire, madame." Geneviève felt the scrawny limb trembling beneath her grip, and pulled the woman gently back to the flames.

"Who told you your mother was dead?" the frail woman repeated, teeth chattering with chill or fear or dire insistence. Geneviève could not tell which.

"I have always known it. She died in the fire of the great meeting of the kings." Geneviève did not falter against the piercing stare of the woman's pale eyes. "I saw her body, saw it buried with my father's. I saw the stone carved with the name of Gravois, with my own eyes."

Madame de Hainaut clamped her hands together, fingers pointed to the sky, pressing them against her lips as if in fervent prayer. The chattering of the old woman's teeth grew so loud it rose above the crackling of the kindling at their feet. She tottered and swayed on legs Geneviève did not think would support her much longer.

"Do you have a place to sleep tonight, madame? Do you have a bed?" Geneviève would not relinquish the arm in her grip, though she shivered in aversion at the feel of the bones so fragile beneath the thin flesh.

Madame de Hainaut answered with a shallow nod and eyes pleading for something unfathomable. Her hands moved not an inch from her lips, but the fingers folded together into two clasped fists. She began to walk, allowing Geneviève to keep her hand upon her arm, not telling her where to go but leading her on with her wrathlike silence.

Together the women entered the courtyard, the older woman leading the younger in a diagonal direction, toward a small but well-kept establishment in the corner, near the large stately manor in which the king stayed.

"Have you eaten dinner tonight?" Geneviève asked, receiving nothing more than another silent nod in response. "Are you sure you do not require the attention of a physician?" She grew more concerned with the woman's unrelenting silence. Geneviève felt her weakness growing with every step they took.

The hinges of the door squeaked as they entered the small building, already veiled in darkness and the somnolence of sleeping inhabitants. The stairs groaned as they tread upon them; so slowly did they ascend, each creak fairly announced a minute as it passed.

Madame de Hainaut led Geneviève to the top landing, stumbling as she breached the last stair and entered the angle-ceilinged room opposite. Without word or sound, the old woman, seeming far older than she had been when the night began, floundered in the pale light of the small window, found the tattered ticking in the corner of the closet-sized chamber, and threw herself down upon it. In the shadows, Geneviève found a rough blanket and laid it gently upon the small frail form, tucking in the ends.

Geneviève knelt down beside her, unable to leave this strange woman, touched somehow by the depth of emotion emanating off her in waves. Without consideration, Geneviève followed the urging of her own feelings and reached out a hand, smoothing the wiry gray hair upon the pillow, stroking this unknown troubled soul, until the woman's breathing grew slow and her trembling ceased.

"I will visit you on the morrow, madame," Geneviève whispered, coaxing her to peaceful slumber. "We will talk more then."

With one last caress and another tuck of the blanket, Geneviève rose and crept from the room.

Madame de Hainaut said not a word. She turned to watch the young woman as she left her side, as she vanished beneath the stairs, reaching out a hand, trembling with her silent tears.

The scream pierced the pallid, slumberous dawn like a screeching banshee wailing in pain. Geneviève fell as she jumped from her bed, stumbling on feet not yet awake, legs tangling in her white cotton nightdress. Arabelle yelped as she flung herself up and the two women spoke at once, their words falling one on top of the other.

"*Mon Dieu*, what was that?"

"Heaven help us."

They stared at each other, faces swollen with sleep, contorted in fright—eyes bulging, mouths gaping.

More screams, more yelling rose up from below.

"The duchesse," Arabelle hissed, and the women launched into movement, shedding their nightclothes, throwing themselves into gowns, lacing them as they rushed from the room.

They clattered swiftly down the stairs, unsure footing slipping on worn runners. They pushed against the door to Anne's rooms, shoving it open with a bang and a crash.

Anne stood by her raised bed, clad in her nightgown, sheet

clutched to her chest as if it would ward off the evil knocking at the door. "It is not I," she assured them.

Footsteps banged on the stairs behind them as people rushed from the inn; voices rose in alarm in the courtyard beyond the windows. Anne jumped to the leaded glass.

"Something is out there." Her eyes cast furtively about. "Everyone is running toward the center of the courtyard, but I cannot see what draws them."

Arabelle and Geneviève needed to share no more than a half second's glance and they rushed for the door.

"Help me get dressed, and I will—" Anne began.

"You will stay here, madame." Geneviève whipped around, one finger pointed sternly at her mistress, like a general directing his troops into battle. Threat brought out her soldierly training, and she instinctively applied it to one for whom she felt responsible. Anne parted her lips as if to argue, but Geneviève did not move, pinning her mistress in place with her finger and a squinty-eyed stare; her powerful command brooked no argument.

Anne frowned at her, for an instant unable to recognize her maid, seeing something—someone—unknown to her, antithetical to the stoic and devoted servant she had come to know. The duchesse offered a quick nod of agreement; she would acquiesce no further to one lower in rank, but it was enough.

Geneviève whirled away, sprinting to catch up to Arabelle, hot on her heels as they raced down the stairs.

Hazy light spilled in the doorway left open by the last person to run across the threshold, and they aimed for the rectangle of suffused illumination. Arabelle stepped out and hugged herself fast, her breath streaming from her mouth as she turned to the woman behind her.

Like their own, every door on the square hung open as people streamed from the dark interiors, creatures escaping from out of the blackness, their mouths gaping maws in pale faces, their eyes wide in fright. Arabelle and Geneviève joined the rush as the pack around them surged forward, many still in their nightclothes, heading toward the center of the square where a large, noisy horde gathered. The rumble of distressed voices grew louder as they approached, and the newcomers searched among the rabble for the source of the ruckus. Only Geneviève thought to look up.

She tripped at the sight, a choked, garbled scream caught in her throat. Arabelle reached out and grabbed her a second before she tumbled to the hard stones at her feet.

"What is it? Are you all right?" Arabelle's fingers dug into the soft flesh of her upper arm, golden, untethered hair spilling into her eyes.

Geneviève spoke not a word; she could not. She raised her hand, one tremulous finger pointing up ahead. Arabelle's eyes followed, though she pulled back and away, shoulders curling round as if to guard against what lay in the distance.

The body hung from the lowest thick branch; small and frail, it looked like no more than a rag doll spinning on the end of a thick, grimy string. Long, wiry gray hair hung over the face, splotched black from the coagulating blood behind the diaphanous skin.

With a whimper of repugnance, Arabelle jerked her head from the sight, thin hands rushing to her face to guard against the vision. "Who is it? Do you know who it is?"

"I . . . don't . . . think . . ." Geneviève began. "Oh God, no . . ."

She ran, lifting her skirts, heedless of the leg she revealed. She ran, leaving Arabelle calling out behind her, struggling to catch up. She ran, until she could see the face for herself.

In death, the old woman's purple scars were no longer visible; her putrid skin was nothing more than an ill-begotten memory. The wind pitched and the body spun on its tether, the rope creaking as it twisted back and forth. The breeze brushed Geneviève's face, and only then did she feel the moist tracks upon her cheeks. One shoddy slipper had fallen to the ground below the body, the exposed foot petite, the toes perfect and bluish white. The crate she had used as a weapon against herself, lay overturned and cracked, perhaps kicked as the woman's last thoughts railed against her own assault.

"We must cut her down," one man called to the paralyzed crowd huddled around the woman's feet.

"Does anyone know her?" a woman sobbed from the cradle of a strong man's arms.

"I do," Geneviève said, but it was an incredulous whisper, and no one heard it. She felt as if she had known this woman, not as one person passes a stranger along the divergent path that is the road of life, but as though a connection existed with her, albeit one too intangible to comprehend. She meant to make her way forward, felt compelled to speak for the woman, but her grief shackled her to the spot.

Arabelle tumbled into her from behind, breath ragged, gaze frozen on the lifeless body as she grabbed onto Geneviève. "Is that . . ."

Geneviève nodded before she finished. "I must tell them who—"

A cry rang out. "The king comes!"

The crowd parted, all eyes turned from the appalling sight to the powerful ruler, as King Henry barreled into the square.

In a simple black suede jerkin and trunk hose, he looked no less imperious as he took in every facet of the grisly scene with one sweep of his intent gaze. He circled around the tree until he stood beneath the hanged woman, an arm's reach away from Geneviève.

"Who is she?" he barked, his indignation sweeping the crowd with a hard bristle.

Arabelle nudged Geneviève's back, hissing in her ear. With a stern, tight shake of her head, Geneviève pushed against it; she could not speak to him, not now, not of this.

"She is one of your staff, my lord." A pudgy bald man stepped forward; his fine dress and distinctively accented English revealed him as man of Calais, and one of some import. "A scullion, I am told, with the name of Hainaut."

Henry gave the man a hard stare in reply, jaw muscles convulsing on a hard cast face.

An adolescent page ran up to the chubby man, thrust a torn and ragged piece of parchment into his hand, and melted back into the crowd.

Before the man looked upon it, Henry snatched it from his hand and lifted the parchment closer to his eyes, squinting at the scraggly writing in the dim light. Geneviève inched closer, pushed against an obstructing shoulder, and rose on tiptoes to see over the king's shoulder. A few English words sprawled across the page:

I cannot live, if I am already dead.

The bizarre inscription was no less troubling than the self-destructive act itself.

King Henry dropped his hand, the note clasped within it, his piercing gaze scanning the expectant crowd around him. His head swiveled on his short, thick neck, and he scrutinized those behind him. For a fleeting instant, his glare snagged on Geneviève's face and she gasped at the hard touch of it. It moved on in a flash and she wondered upon it; so much of this moment stank of delusion.

The king turned back to the paper in his hand, and without a glimmer of remorse, tore it in half, and in half again, tore it until it was no more than shredded scraps of nothing.

"Cut her down," he barked rancorously. "Cut her down and bury her."

Geneviève shivered from the cold radiating from this harsh man. This woman was nothing to King Henry, a nameless, faceless kitchen servant—he could have no animosity for her, and yet he showed nothing but rancor toward her, though death be her master. How starkly his actions compared to those of King François, whose heart had been torn asunder by the execution of someone convicted of betrayal against him. There was no resolving the divergent behavior and Geneviève's mind screamed with the disparity.

As cold and immobile as stone, Geneviève stood and watched as men cut down the body of Millicent de Hainaut and carried her away. Like a stalwart boulder in the midst of a rushing stream, she moved not a step as the crowd dispersed around her. As the square emptied, she moved, stepping forward to pick up the discarded, forgotten slipper. She would take it with her. Whenever she looked upon it, someone, somewhere would remember this woman.

∂ 29 ∂

My lord, if it were not to satisfy the world and my realm,
I would not do what I must do this day for none earthly thing.

—Henry VIII (1491–1547)

"You pester me, Master Cromwell." Henry turned his back on his drably clad minister and limped away. The journey had done much to aggravate his illness-plagued body and his fiery disposition; he looked eagerly to his familiar throne and its promise of relief.

"And for that I do humbly apologize." The dour-faced adviser bowed deeply, but dared to shuffle forward nonetheless, raising his eyes to his ruler, who glared thunderously down at him from the dais. "But the situation grows dire with every passing moment, Your Highness. The evidence of collusion between the emperor, the pope, and the French king has become more resolute and powerfully incriminating."

"They have taken no firm action against us." The hard-edged pronouncement came from Charles Brandon, the Duke of Suffolk, the diamond-patterned lead windows at his back, arms folded across his hard chest, silhouette enlarged by the fur mantle set about his powerful shoulders.

Cromwell spun to his adversary with his lip curled in an expression of distaste. The tension between them grew as thick as a

317 SERVE A KING

bear's fur as winter's hibernation drew near. "They have withdrawn their ambassador for a second time, and the emperor travels to France in a fortnight. Your own spies confirm it."

"A visit means nothing. Our king's recent travel confirms it." Suffolk scoffed at the minister's argument. "The entire visit was a sham, intending to obfuscate any hint of our own agenda. For all we know, François does the same, a magician's sleight of hand."

"We know the French king will do anything for the Italian territory. Who knows how far his longing will take him. And we know that Cardinal Pole has paid King François another visit. There can be no greater condemnation."

"England has nothing to fear," Suffolk barked. "The queen of Navarre and the duchesse d'Étampes made it very clear."

"And a marriage to Cleves would bring with it the financial and military support of the Schmalkaldic League. They have made it very clear. A triumvirate such as the one that forms across the channel would be extraordinarily powerful," Cromwell argued. "England would be powerless against such an alliance, on its own."

The men glared at each other across the short expanse, their discourse at an impasse.

Henry's lips curled into a snarl, beefy hands gripping the carved arms of the chair, knuckles blanching with the grip. How often in his life had the question of eminence risen among the three kings? He refused to fall by the wayside; such a thought tormented him.

"Very well," he grumbled with a dismissive wave at Cromwell. "Call her to us."

A smirk slithered across the minister's face and he bowed, backing out of the chamber before the king changed his mind.

With long, purposeful strides, the Duke of Suffolk rushed to the king's side, leaning down upon the throne's arm. "Are you certain, Sire? I fear this action will only bring the wrong sort of alliance, for you and for our country."

Henry reached up to squeeze the beefy shoulder of his lifelong friend and adviser. "It would seem I am forced to act. But it shall not be my only maneuver."

Brandon answered him with nothing more than a quizzical expression.

A devious light sparked in Henry's eye. "Send the message, Charles." The king breathed the decree as a priest would whisper the last rites. "Give the final order . . . to them both."

Brandon blinked as if in defense, a small tick the other advisers in the room could not see. He whispered as well, his words for the king alone.

"I have been your man for all my life. I have been your hand of justice, staining my own in your name." Brandon crouched low, his eyes level with Henry's, his stare penetrating the king's, laying bare the haunted shadows lingering within them. There could be no question, no second guessing. "This time, above all others, I would question you, and beg you to consider for a moment more. Only if there is no hesitancy in your mind, should you tell me again."

If Charles Brandon thought to see a glimmer of doubt in Henry VIII's eye, he could have more readily asked for the moon.

Henry leaned over, his head no more than inches from the duke's. "Give the command, Charles." Henry waggled his large head, jowls set firm. "If this plan should prove successful, it may save me from this woman and all who would rise against me."

With a hard swallow, but a deep obeisance, the Duke of Suffolk rose and strode from the room, set upon his master's course.

The king of France himself stood upon the steps of Fontaine-bleau, waiting to greet them as the entourage of women and guards returned home. Servants fanned out on each side, poised to relieve the tired travelers of their possessions and their horses. As the procession turned onto the approaching lane, his shoulders straightened and his smile spread, brightening his pale face as the sun did the earth when thrust from behind a gloomy cloud.

The duchesse rose in her saddle, stretching her hand into the sky to beckon to him, as anxious to return to her lover's arms as he was to have her there. She nudged her horse forward and the mare broke into a spirited canter, the horses around them taking up the pace, large nostrils flaring as they smelled the scent of home. Before Anne's mount had ceased its clomping, the king was by her side, pulling her down and into his arms. In silent reunion, they held each other, unmindful of the many eyes observing them.

Geneviève's lips twitched as she gazed upon the scene; whatever rumors prevailed of these two eccentric lovers, their devotion to each other was to be admired . . . and coveted. She lifted her gaze and searched the crowd gathered in welcome, daring to seek out the one face offering but a taste of what these paramours had shared for decades.

There, in the gathering of soldiers beyond the massive doors, she found him. His twilight eyes twinkled at her, his dimples flashed for a split second. It was not the embrace the king gave to his mistress, but it would serve. Turning shyly away, Geneviève basked in the warmth of Sebastien's greeting, succor for her forlorn soul, and stepped up to stand obediently behind her mistress.

"Your sister sends her fondest regards, Your Majesty," Anne said, released from the king's firm embrace, though he refused to release the small hand in his. "She bids you prepare for her for she will arrive shortly."

The king's happy countenance glowed. "She will be here for the emperor's visit?"

"Indeed she will," Anne assured him with a tender smile. "I have much else to tell you, Your Majesty, but I would rest awhile first, if I may?"

François raised the tiny hand enveloped in his large one, and brushed his lips across its soft flesh. "There is nothing that cannot wait, madame. I would have you rested and well, above all else."

Together they turned and made for the tall doors, Anne's ladies but a few steps behind.

The king looked over his shoulder at them. He tilted his head in a dashing nod to Arabelle; to Geneviève he offered a smile and a tender, "Welcome home, my child."

She felt the warmth of it upon her cheeks and she beamed with all absence of guile and disguise. And yet she hesitated, trudging feet growing heavier, as she mounted the stairs; this palace was her home and yet it wasn't; she longed for it and to run from it with equal yearning. Her gaze roved over its splendid façade as if to see her truth upon it.

A curtain moved in a second-story window and her eye jumped up. Looking down at the warm scene of homecoming, lips puckered with bitterness, stood Queen Eleanor. The stalwart figure by her side, as ever, none other than Catherine de' Medici. These two women, more than most, would recognize the resentment burning in her heart, the unrequited, opposing existence with which she must grapple. Yet she could not bring her trepidations to share at their table; she could share her true heart with no one.

"Look at you." Carine stood with arms akimbo just inside the door to the chamber. "You are a mess. Mademoiselle d'Aiguillon did not take as fine care of you as she had promised."

Geneviève shook her head with a chuckle. She need not miss a mother, for here one stood, her maid's nagging as fine as any pestering parent could offer.

"Arabelle was a wonderful maid to me, as I was to her." For all Carine's frenetic energy, Geneviève was gladdened to see her servant. "But pray tell me, is this how you greet your returning mistress?"

Blushing and contrite, Carine bobbed a deep curtsy. "*Pardonnez-moi*, mam'selle. Welcome home, of course."

"And a good day to you, Carine. You look well."

Geneviève pushed farther into her chamber, happy as well to

see the familiar furniture and most especially the thick, silk-covered mattress; how she had longed for it through the many sleepless, uncomfortable nights on thinly stuffed and smelly ticking.

"I am quite well. A bit restless, if truth be told, bored by the idleness of the past few days." Carine dove into work with enthusiasm, emptying Geneviève's trunks, separating the gowns needing an airing and a pressing from those soiled beyond repair.

"Shall I have a bath drawn for you, or would you rather rest for a while?" Carine asked.

"A bath sounds perfect, thank you, Carine. I am more sore than tired from so many hours in the saddle."

"Then be so kind as to tell me all about your trip, mam'selle. What was Calais like? Is it as beautiful as they say? Were the people nice? Were there any handsome men about?"

Geneviève chuckled again, but strove to answer each one of her twittering maid's questions, removing her own riding boots as Carine worked, too anxious for her toes to be unbound to wait for her maid's assistance.

"What a magnificent casket. I do not remember packing this." Carine's hands caressed the large rectangular box of tooled, thatched leather she retrieved from the bottom of Geneviève's trunk, the bright afternoon light shimmering on the glossy russet finish. "Did you purchase it in Calais, mam'selle?"

Geneviève lurched up and crossed the room as if thrust by a cannon, snatching the chest from her maid's hands with rude brusqueness. "Yes . . . yes, I had forgotten about it."

Carine stared up at her mistress, empty hands aloft in the air.

Geneviève turned away, shoulders curling over the chest clasped firmly in her hands, like a miser over his pot of gold. She had never seen the unique casket before. It must have been put in her trunk while in Calais; it could be from Henry and no other.

"Perhaps you are right, Carine. Perhaps it would be best if I took some rest after all." Geneviève placed the small chest on her bedside table and pretended to ignore it as she plopped herself down upon the bed. "It seems I am more tired than I first imagined."

Carine came to stand by her, watching cautiously as Geneviève rubbed her forehead.

"Are you well, mam'selle?" she asked tremulously, wary at Geneviève's abrupt change in temperament.

Geneviève did her best to offer Carine an assuring smile, taking the young woman's hand and giving it a playful shake. "I am well as can be for someone who has traveled many leagues and back again in a matter of days. The fatigue has come upon me with the relief of homecoming. That is all, I swear."

"Then I shall leave you to your rest," Carine agreed, but did not quit the room until she had seen Geneviève tucked tenderly under the soft coverlet and the curtains drawn against the glare of the afternoon sun.

The door at last clicked shut behind her, and yet Geneviève lay utterly inert beneath the covers of her bed, listening to the small fire crackle and pop in the grate and the voices that ebbed and flowed outside her door. If she never moved, if she never opened the chest, then she would never receive his message. Perhaps she could stay thus and hide forever.

But she knew such a fantasy could not become reality; sooner or later her truth would find her and do its bidding.

Geneviève thrust the covers from her body and spun upon the mattress, staring at the casket upon the table as if it were offensive. She imagined throwing it upon the fire, unopened, the leather and all it held disintegrating in the hungry flames. In that moment, the tide of her heart turned toward France and she would sell her soul to the devil to ride it into shore.

Her hands balled into fists as she struggled, but the misguided teachings of her youth and the first wound in her heart ruled victorious. She picked up the box, placed it upon the bed, and opened it.

Leaning over, Geneviève peeked into its depths, inhaling the smell of leather and wood released from the confines. Two smaller boxes sat within the larger one and on their tops sat a folded golden piece of parchment. She deciphered the message with haste, wanting the deed done. Upon this paper were two lines, one each to describe the contents of the smaller boxes.

Geneviève swallowed back the bitter tears as she retrieved and opened them. In the first, a miniature unsigned landscape of some unknown place, but by the technique of the brushstroke and uniqueness of hue she knew: It was her father's work. She had seen others like it in her aunt's home. She laid the palm-sized square gingerly upon the coverlet and reached back into the casket, hand trembling over the second box. Steeling herself, she snatched at it and opened it, as if pulling a binding from an open wound.

The sapphires glittered up at her; one large teardrop suspended by the three round ones. She had seen this magnificent piece of jewelry many, many times; seen the eyes hovering above that matched the color so perfectly, but only in a portrait. This was the very necklace her mother wore in the miniature she had treasured since childhood. One hand caressed the jewels as she would her mother's face; her head dropped heavily into the other.

When the wave of grief passed, as Geneviève made to hide her new belongings and the casket in which they came, she looked once more into it. On the very bottom of the chest, as if no more than an afterthought, lay another parchment.

With a tired hand, Geneviève transcribed the cipher. With a heavy heart, she accepted the fate awaiting her.

> *The time to avenge them has come. Take your action*
> *while the emperor visits. The blame will fall upon him and*
> *his people. Set yourself free. Come to me.*
> *Henry R*

She fell asleep with her mother's necklace warm against her chest and her father's painting clutched in her hand. It was a deep, exhausted sleep.

*   *   *

But the escape of slumber did not last long. Like a jagged edge of shattering glass, the voices in her head began to scream once more, their arguing haunting her as they had for so long now. She sat up, one hand over each ear as if to muffle the incessant screeching. Geneviève would do anything to shut them up once and for all. She would do what she must.

The tide turned back.

❧ 30 ❧

Shallow men speak of the past;
wise men of the present;
and fools of the future.

—Madame Marie du Deffand (1697–1780)

The entire country groomed itself, washing away dirt ignored
for years, sprucing up what had grown disheveled, and don-
ning itself in its best finery; there was no greater urgency for tidy-
ing up than the anticipation of visitors.

King François dictated every facet of the preparations with a
meticulous eye, but his body failed to keep up; the weakness laid
him low once more and tethered him to his bed. He ignored the
resurgence of illness as best he could, working from his privy
chamber as candles gutted and their light flickered and waved in
their last bursts of life.

The sputtering light cast unbecoming shadows on Montmorency's unattractive face as he stood at the king's bedside, the
heavy velvet navy blue curtains drawn back and tied with gold tasseled ropes. Monty's tight jaw flinched with growing impatience.

"You are sure the instructions were clearly writ and properly dispersed?" François asked for the fifth time that day, his legs rustling
under the silk linens, hitching himself higher upon the blue and
gold bolsters at his back.

Montmorency bit the inside of his cheek—better that than to

roll his eyes. "I am quite sure, Sire. I wrote them with my own hand and entrusted them to our very best riders." He heaved a heavy sigh, for a moment abandoning the gnawing impatience with his sovereign; the strain that the illness and the stress of the moment had placed on his childhood companion wrought undeniable sympathy. He reached out and clasped the king by the shoulder, feeling pliable flesh and bone where there had once been hard muscle. "You have arranged all to perfection, François. Have no fear."

Tired eyes rose gratefully to the minister's face, and in them, a touch of regret. Ruling a nation would always strain those who held the reins of power, and these two had not been exempted from the fracturing acrimony of divergent principles. The last few years had found stiff wedges thrust between them—the religious conflict, the investigation into Chabot's malpractices, and, most especially, Anne. François wanted only for his greatest companion and adviser to love whom he loved; that Montmorency did not, had become the hardest wedge of all.

"Merci, mon ami," François whispered, lament touching his words. "I could not have done this without you."

Montmorency answered with a squeeze, his small mouth set firm with the unpleasant taste of the angst living between them. "It is my duty and my honor, Your Majesty."

A light knock upon the door broke the intimacy of the moment, and the two men turned to it ruefully.

"May I come in?" Anne poked her head round the edge of the door.

"Of course, *ma chérie.*" Small bursts of color brightened the king's ashen face at the sight of his mistress.

Anne dipped a formal curtsy, paying tribute to the formalities in the presence of the minister, but her simple, pearlescent gown was not meant to be worn for long.

Montmorency bowed stiffly. "By your leave, Sire, I will return in the morning."

François nodded, gaze full with the sight of his love.

The duchesse passed the minister, exchanging a cool greeting, no more than a polite, ghostly gesture of tolerance. Anne watched covertly over her shoulder as the lumbering man crossed the threshold and closed the door behind him. The instant the latch clicked into place, she climbed upon the king's bed, burrowing herself beneath the soft covers and into the crux of one of his large arms, purring like a satiated cat.

François smiled, lowering himself into her nuzzle and further down upon the softness of his bed, his body cumbrous with age and illness. He was too tired and weak to do more than hold her, and she knew it, but it was enough for them both.

"Charles will speak against my continued relations with Suleiman and the Turks." It was the king's most pressing thought, now that the moment of the Holy Roman Emperor's visit was upon them.

Anne spoke from the sanctuary of his embrace. "You must listen to his intentions carefully. He may well rail against such an allegiance, but what will he offer to abolish it? That is the most important question." Anne hitched herself up on one elbow, lifting her head out of the crook of his arm and placing one hand softly upon his heart. "This is *your* moment, *mon cher* François."

François closed his eyes, chest filling and rising with his deep indrawn breath. When he opened them once more, they sparkled, clear and focused.

"This is *the* moment."

Charles V, king of Spain and Holy Roman Emperor, entered France with a small retinue of ministers and servants in the south, near Bayonne. There to greet him were the king's two sons and Constable Montmorency. The country welcomed him as the great dignitary he was, but what is more, they courted him, plying him with the best food and wine the nation had to offer, each town showering him with costly bribes wrapped as splendid presents. In

Poitiers, he received a silver sculpture of an eagle and a lily on a rock, in Paris a life-sized silver statue of Hercules holding two pillars.

King François joined the cavalcade in Loches, arriving in the city by way of litter. Mustering his strength to mount his great white warhorse, he then traveled with the emperor under a bannered and tasseled canopy. Their public conversation, surrounded by servants and ministers, consisted of no more than pleasant platitudes—a dialogue between any two educated men of the age, filled with talk of art and the great explorations taking place, the expeditions revealing more of the New World on the other side of the ocean.

From Loches the itinerary led them northward, a circuit specifically devised to display the artistic achievements of François's reign. Charles visited Chenonceau and from there Chambord, the *château* Madrid, the Louvre, and on to Fontainebleau in preparation for Christmas celebrations. At each stop along the route, great festivals and galas were held in his honor, but none so great as the one awaiting him at the grand palace.

Garlands of holm oak leaves, ivy, and bay festooned the pale stone corridors and pillars throughout the castle like layers of necklaces on a magnificently dressed lady, the red berries bright like jewels on the deep green leaves that linked them. Outside, a dusting of snow had fallen, a sprinkling of sugar clinging to the gardens and buildings. All had been made ready for the emperor, now comfortably ensconced in the Pavillon des Poêles, specifically decorated for him by Rosso and Primaticcio. From his window, the king of Spain could look down into the vast Cour de la Fontaine, and the tall pillar erected in honor of his visit. Upon his arrival the pinnacle flame had been lit, burning day and night while water and wine flowed from the sides of its base.

Geneviève rushed into Anne's presence chamber, throwing her back against the door as if barricading against a rampaging beast.

"It is utter madness out there," she breathed, but if she had hoped to find sanctuary here, she was soon disappointed.

The ruckus of preparation throughout the palace matched the commotion within this room. Not a woman looked up at her as they fussed and preened over gowns and fans, lace and ribbon. Every one of the ladies of Madame la Duchesse was present, and their twittering rivaled that in a dove coop at mating season. Jolly laughter vied with lilting trills; a song of anticipation and celebration. The castle now hosted some of the world's greatest thinkers and diplomats, artists and musicians, all brought together in honor of the meeting, and the women tingled in anticipation of the festivities.

Geneviève remained untouched by the tumult, firmly intent upon her own agenda and the spirit of separation it forced upon her. She walked through the milieu as the lone fox walks through a deserted forest, unseen and perhaps nonexistent without a witness. Geneviève curled up onto the window embrasure and wrapped her skirts about her, shielding against the cold December air leaking through the rattling glass. Her gaze flopped to and fro, as if she watched a game of *jeu de paume*, alternating between the frantic, colorful scene within and the serene, sparkling grayness beyond the window. Most often her glance flicked back to Arabelle, like a bee intent on a particular flower, and with each glimpse, a small tear grew in her heart. She had been raised without human attachment, taught not to need it, and yet she could not deny her bond with this woman. Geneviève bristled at the first pangs of sadness as she contemplated her departure.

As if the attention grazed her with its touch, Arabelle raised her head, and finding Geneviève's gaze upon her, smiled a worried smile.

"Is all well with you, Geney?" Arabelle approached the embrasure, hands crossing upon her arms with a shiver.

Geneviève's mouth ticked up at the sound of the silly nickname. "Well enough," she assured Arabelle. "I had thought to help, but with so many hands in the till, I think I would only be in the way."

Arabelle swung her gaze over the large room and the riotous activity. "I do not think there is anything else to do." She laughed. "We are all so excited. We are inventing chores to make the time pass quicker."

"I'm sure all will be perfect," Geneviève said, "though the duchesse does not look nearly as festive as do her ladies."

A covert glimpse at Anne found her a stiff statue at her table, paying no attention to the papers before her or the twittering birds of her court, fingers drumming upon the polished wood surface with an impatient rhythm.

"She is a bit miffed by the emperor's attitude toward her," Arabelle whispered as she leaned close.

"Do you mean to say that her lover's wife's brother does not fawn over her?" Geneviève's brows rose in feigned shock. "Scandalous."

Arabelle laughed, but clamped her mouth closed with one hand, shaking a chastising finger at Geneviève with the other.

The panes rattled with a gust of wind and Arabelle shivered once more.

"Come away from the window and sit by the fire," she urged. "I will join you soon."

"I think I shall return to my room." Geneviève unfurled her skirts and her legs and stood, placing a gentle hand on Arabelle's forearm. "Will you come visit me once you are finished here? I have something for you I think you may want for tonight."

"A present?" Arabelle giggled like a little girl.

"Perhaps." Geneviève waggled her brows at her. "Come when you can, and see for yourself."

"I'll be there in minutes."

As good as her word, no more than a quarter of an hour had passed when Geneviève heard a soft knock at her door and the latch opened without call or permission.

"Here I am and all aflutter." Arabelle launched herself into Geneviève's chamber. Finding her friend seated at her table, she crossed the room and gave Geneviève's shoulders a fond squeeze. "Where is my present?"

Her cheerful blue eyes blinked with a child's innocence, scanning the tabletop and the nightstand, but finding no gaily wrapped package upon them. Her search stopped as she spied the magnificent gown splayed across the bed cover.

"Are you wearing this tonight?" Arabelle asked with a gasp, skipping across to the bed, fingering the stunning creation upon it.

Of iridescent sapphire brocade, the square-cut bodice tapered to a narrowly tailored waist to a scoop at the hips. Soft rainbows of color glistened from the magnificent fabric but paled in comparison to the rows of diamond-shaped lapis lazuli jewels adorning the edge of the bodice, the bottom of the skirt, and the pointed tip of the sleeve. With the gentlest kiss of light, the gown shimmered like a twirling snowflake. It was the most stunning dress Arabelle had ever seen, and she had fawned effusively over it upon the one occasion she had seen Geneviève wear it.

"No, I'm not wearing it tonight," Geneviève answered with a beatific smile.

"Oh, but why not?" Arabelle lifted the sleeves as if she danced with the gown itself. "It is so very splendid."

Geneviève rose and came to stand by her.

"I cannot wear it, because you are."

Arabelle's head spun; her eyes flashed. "I are? Uh . . . I . . . I mean, I am?"

Geneviève laughed. "You are. In fact, I want you to have it."

Arabelle's mouth formed a startled moue. "You cannot mean it?" she whispered.

"I can. I know how much you love it." Geneviève's tone grew somber. "It seems the least I can do."

"The least you can do? But what have I done to deserve such a gesture?" Arabelle tilted her head.

Geneviève raised her intent gaze and trapped Arabelle's with it. "You have been my friend when I offered little in return."

"You needed me," Arabelle said with plainly spoken truth and a one-shoulder shrug. "It was enough."

Geneviève sniffed a rueful laugh through her nose. She put her arms around the surprised woman and gave a squeeze. Arabelle's brows shot up and she moved not an inch. For all the times she had offered Geneviève physical affection, it had never been returned.

"I will always be your friend," she whispered through the platinum curls into Geneviève's ear.

Geneviève released her and picked up the heavy gown from the bed, laying it across Arabelle's eager, open arms, her dispassionate demeanor once more at the fore. "Go. Make yourself ready."

Arabelle raised her shoulders in girlish delight. "Thank you, my dear friend. It will most assuredly be a splendid night."

Geneviève watched her skip from the room, her smile fading like the waning moon in a starless sky. "A splendid night indeed."

Geneviève called the messenger to her chambers herself, requesting that a scullion who had come to stoke the fire bring him to her instead of Carine. She would have her devoted servant ignorant of this.

The young page, scrawny in a blue and gold velvet tunic and hose, arrived with haste and took the thick fold of parchment from her with a bow.

No name covered it, only a circle of wax set with the distinctive seal.

"Please take this to the emperor's chambers," Geneviève instructed the young fellow, pressing two large gold coins into his hand, satisfied by the incredulous bulge of his blue eyes.

"The duchesse . . . uh . . . I mean, I . . ." Geneviève stammered obnoxiously. "I, yes, *I* am most grateful."

She quickly pressed another coin into his palm, and the youth looked as if he would faint from the glory of the largesse.

"For your silence," she implored with a deathly look.

"Mam'selle." He bowed and scampered off, quick to his errand and to squirrel away his reward before the woman could change her mind.

Geneviève watched the door swing closed behind him. She had taken the first step upon the road from which there was no return, but whether it was the path to redemption or to hell, she knew not.

31

Yea, I will laugh and leap and dance away,
And drain at last the brimming bowl so deep,
I care not if it end in merry madness.

—Olivier de Magny (1529–1561)

The festive music reached out of the grand ballroom, the chamber resplendent like a fiery planet. Thousands of miniature candles hung overhead in wrought-iron circles, twinkling like the stars in the twilight sky.

Geneviève recognized the cheerful refrain of "Çà, Bergers, Assemblons-Nous," the song calling the shepherds to the place of the Messiah's birth, as the duchesse d'Étampes and her entourage of divinely costumed ladies approached the broad archway. Arabelle glowed in her new gown, her eyes sparkling brighter than ever above the shimmering jewels that reflected the same blue luster.

The duchesse radiated all beauty and brilliance in a gown of gold cloth, her high crescent hood constructed of formed gold strands, tipped with diamond and topaz. She resembled a work of art, outshining every other woman in the palace, and she knew it. Inside the great hall, the king and his sister stood in conversation with the emperor and Constable Montmorency, the mundane presence of Queen Eleanor hovering by their side. Anne advanced upon the powerful consortium with not one iota of reticence.

King François's eyes burst with pride and admiration at his first sight of her, making not the slightest attempt to hide his pleasure at the vision that was his mistress, heedless to the presence of his wife and her brother by his side.

Queen Eleanor shrank into her confectionary pink gown encrusted with pearls. She had been so proud of its beauty; now she looked down upon it with ill-concealed disappointment. Perhaps the emperor saw her deflation or felt the rancor and heartbreak no doubt radiating from the woman, forever second—forever needless—in the life of her husband and king. He took his sister's hand and wrapped it protectively in the crux of his arm.

Stooped and slight, he stared at Anne through heavy-lidded, round eyes sunken into his skull. Charles V wore all black, enhancing his natural pallor, the only adornment the thick heavy gold chain of office and the amulet hanging from his neck. Though six years his junior, the emperor appeared much older than François; his dismal aspect aged him beyond his years. Vestiges of illness tainted François's face, yet the dapper king of France stood regal in royal blue velvet, gold peeking out of his slashed balloon sleeves, and glittering jeweled embroidery adorning his broad-shouldered mantle.

Anne stood before François, lowering herself into the deepest curtsy, as if she would sit upon the ground, her eyes never leaving his as she performed the most graceful courtesy, Marguerite smiling fondly as she looked on.

"Welcome, duchesse." The king raised her up, brushing his lips across her hand, and turned to present her to his guest. "My brother, here is a beautiful lady who advises me to atone in Paris for the work of Madrid."

Their eyes held for a moment longer and Anne moved on, a quick dip for the queen as she stepped spryly to the emperor.

But Charles's bleak gaze remained upon François. "If the advice is good, you ought to follow it."

Anne ignored his dissonance; she offered another deep obeisance, as did the cluster of women who gathered behind her.

"Your Excellency." The duchesse smiled, stiff with forced gaiety. "I hope this evening finds you well. May you enjoy every luxury and entertainment this night has to offer."

Anne thrust her arms wide in a gesture of welcome, as if she, and not Eleanor, were the hostess. It was no more than the truth; the brilliance of the hospitality was hers to claim.

King Charles tilted his head, his muffin-top velvet hat hardly moving as he paid her a diluted salutation.

"Madame Duchesse," he said, the full lips of his small mouth hardly moving.

A gaggle of courtiers—early arrivals already jocular with imbibed spirits—rushed out of the room, brushing close to the circle of nobles. One man bumped into another, who bumped into the duchesse, who bumped into the emperor. The king reached out as if to stop the momentum, a scowl for them all.

Apologies rang out from all the young miscreants, a beleaguered chorus of contrition, but the injured parties waved them off and away, François dismissing them like shamed children.

One *chevalier* hesitated, the last in the accidental line of dominoes, and bent down to retrieve something from the floor next to one of Anne's beribboned shoes.

"I believe you dropped this, Madame Duchesse." He bowed as he held up the blue velvet drawstring bag.

Anne looked down her pert nose at him and his offering. "It is not mine. I know it not at all."

"I think you are mistaken, madame." The emperor startled them with his somber insistence.

"No, monsieur." Anne shook her head, though she took the small purse in her hands. "I have never seen it."

"Are you quite sure, madame?" Charles's small eyes narrowed. "Perhaps you should check the contents."

Anne's fingers closed upon the circular shape of the bag in a tactile examination, delicate features puckered unbecomingly. She lifted the pouch, inserted two fingers, and gently pried the ties apart.

Every neck craned forward, every gaze strained, but hardly a one gained more than an obstructed glance, nothing but an impression of something round and sparkling.

Anne closed the bag quickly and tucked it away in her palm. Under the weight of so much curious attention, she forced the merry expression upon her features as if she threw a mask upon her face.

"As I said, it is not mine," the duchesse said to the emperor, raising her voice for all to hear, "but I will see it to the hands of its rightful owner."

The grimace Charles used for a smile touched his wrinkle-rimmed lips. "I am quite sure you will."

Something had passed between them; there was no denying it. Yet if the emperor had thought to make a covert gesture toward the duchesse, he had done everything to make his actions as overt as possible.

Giuseppe and Eliodoro were on their best behavior this night—hair groomed, and dressed in their finest velvet doublets and pansied slops—and no arguments or pranks passed between them. All the musicians played with brilliance, and the compositions filled the room with their spirited genius; the performances dazzled and entertained. Geneviève sat at the table, in the very place she had taken at the start of the night, abandoned by most of her companions, who had moved on to socialize and cavort; but she could not conspire in the festivities, could not complicate herself more with these people. Now was the time to build up the wall, and she did so, brick by painful brick.

As one rousing song ended, Montmorency rose from his seat at the queen's table, thudding his jeweled goblet on the linen-covered wood. "The emperor wishes to dance with the queen," he announced with as pleasant an expression as ever he mustered, and the room responded with appreciative applause.

Charles led Eleanor to the floor, and eager dancers lined up beside them to participate in the stately parade. The musicians launched into the sedate melody of the *pazzamento*, an odd choice of song, rarely heard at the French court, learned in anticipation of the less-than-athletic emperor's visit. The agile dancers surrounding brother and sister contained their naturally exuberant spirits, adjusting to Charles and Eleanor's small and hesitant steps.

"Will you dance with me, Geneviève? I believe I can keep up with such a performance."

The marquis de Limoges stood by her side, having come upon her with no warning, and Geneviève smiled with pleasant surprise up into his handsome, always cheerful face. His ungainly soldier's grace had become an intimate jest between them, though never had she told him how much she admired his thick and muscular build. He possessed a warrior's stature worthy of Michelangelo's trowel, and yet always exhibited the most affable of demeanors. He would kill when he must but would take no deviant pleasure in doing so.

Geneviève answered with a subdued shake. "I fear I am not in the dancing mood this evening, monsieur."

The tall man bent at the waist to look upon her more closely. "You are not unwell, are you?"

"No, Albret, a bit overwhelmed and overdone, no more," she said lightly. "I am content to watch at this moment."

"Sebastien will be relieved of duty soon." A slight blush touched the apples of his cheeks and connected the array of freckles upon them as he straightened. He had lost the prize to a fellow soldier and had done so with impeccable courtesy.

"*Oui*, in another hour."

He bowed and started off, but on impulse, Geneviève grabbed his hand and held him back, amused to see the riot of freckles as thick on the back of his hand as on his pleasant face. "Take good care of yourself, Albret."

The wiry red brows knit upon his forehead. "I'm not leaving yet, silly one." He laughed and chucked her softly under the chin. "You will see me yet. Mayhap we can all share a toast once Sebastien has joined you."

Geneviève responded with no more than a shadowed smile, and watched him walk away from her as the music wound to a close.

The emperor returned his sister to her chair, forsaking his own beside her. Instead he shuffled to the next table, where sat the king and Admiral Chabot and the duchesse d'Étampes, as well. Ignoring the others, he came to stand by the king, silent but commanding, until the room stilled and every eye fell upon the scene unfolding at the front of the room.

François heaved himself up from his gilded blue velvet chair, the legs scraping against the cool stone beneath. He smiled with grace at his guest but not without a crinkle of uncertainty in the corner of his eye.

"*Mesdames et messieurs,*" Charles announced with his thin, lilting accent. "I have never been made to feel more welcome than in your beautiful land. I wish to thank Constable Montmorency, Cardinal de Lorraine, and of course, my dearest sister, for their magnificent hospitality."

A rousing round of applause met his proclamation, though from the duchesse d'Étampes, having been left off his list, acclaim was not as enthusiastic. The emperor raised his hand; he had more to say. Geneviève took no greater part than that of witness; to conclude her business in such a scene would be a bold and decisive statement, but the thought was no more than madness. She must wait for another time, another place.

"To the great François, my brother, I am most grateful. He has opened his doors and his arms to me, and I bask in the warmth."

François bowed gallantly amidst the applause, raising his golden goblet by the jeweled stem. "You honor us." He bowed to the emperor and turned outward to the assemblage, most of whom raised their chalices. "To King Charles," he coaxed.

"To King Charles!" came the rousing reply, and in the anonymity of the ruckus, Geneviève escaped.

He threw open the door, gaze cast downward, intent upon the gold buttons of his doublet, hands working furiously to undo them as he rushed forward. The last undone, Sebastien shrugged off the heavy vestment, revealing the thin cambric shirt and muscular physique beneath, and made to discard the uniform upon the bed.

"*Mon Dieu!*" he cried as he stumbled back, startled by the ethereal form perched upon the bed in stony silence.

"Geneviève." He breathed her name. "What are you doing here? I was hurrying to change and come find you at the fête."

With legs tucked under her chemise, her pale hair unpinned and flowing in an iridescent cloud around her, she looked like an angel come down to earth to pay a visit upon the pitiable mortals.

"Are you not pleased to see me?" she whispered.

A lustful grin played upon his lips. Sebastien slithered up to the bed with the stalking, graceful gait of a panther sneaking up on its prey. "I have never been more pleased to see anyone."

His strong legs scaled the foot of the bed and he came to her on his knees, towering above her. Sebastien reached down and captured her face in his hands, lowering his lips upon hers. Geneviève sighed with pleasure, hands brushing up along the back of hard thighs and buttocks, to tangle in the shirt. Sebastien groaned. His mouth . . . his touch grew masterful and rough, demanding and wanton. Geneviève's hands came round to the pearl buttons of his shirt, to the tawny skin and hard muscles beneath. Sebastien moved one wide hand up her back, another to her neck, and lowered her slowly upon the bed, sinking down into the bliss beside her.

The candles gutted, their flames extinguished in the pooled molten wax. The fire in the small arched hearth had dwindled to no more than glowing embers; only moonbeams danced with the dust motes.

Geneviève watched them twirl above the bed, listening to Sebastien's sure and steady breathing from beside her. Her legs quivered with satiated exhaustion, but her hands felt bound by the ties of deception. By force she must cast off both, and rise to the purpose of her life.

She turned her head, silky hair shushing against the pillow fabric, and studied the man who lay so near. In sleep as in wakefulness, his beauty was undeniable. There was but one way to leave such a gift behind.

With the stealth of a thief, she raised the coverlet and slipped her legs around to the side of the bed. Hitching forward, her feet searched the dark abyss for the floor below.

"Where are you going?"

The groggy whisper held her fast, toes poised an inch above the wood.

Geneviève cringed, unable to face him. She had wanted nothing more than to slip away from his arms and his life without another word between them, a coward's retreat. "Dawn beckons. I must make ready to attend my mistress."

A rumble of a chuckle met her words. "Your mistress will be in the king's bed for many more hours to come. Won't you stay in mine a bit longer? It is warm and welcoming here."

The promise of his words was undeniable, and it plucked greedily at her, but she must away.

Geneviève spun round and threw herself upon him. In her kiss burned all the heartbreak of separation. She kissed him until she could bear the taste of him no longer. She pulled her lips from his, hesitating as their moist, warm flesh brushed with hers. With eyes closed, she whispered, "*Adieu, cher* Sebastien."

She thrust herself off his chest and off the bed, two steps away . . .

He jumped to his knees, bed linen falling in a low puddle at his waist, chiseled torso revealed in all its glory, as one powerful hand reached out to grab her arm and pull her back.

Geneviève's legs bumped against the bed, but no more would she yield.

Sebastien stared at her, a deep furrow forming between his brows. "*Adieu?* You bid me *adieu?*"

"I must, Sebastien. I fear I must."

He shimmied closer, pressing his flesh against hers, no more than a thin layer of brushed silk between them. "No, we do not say *adieu*." He shook his head resoundingly. "To you I will only say *à demain*, for I will see you tomorrow and the day after that." He kissed the tip of her nose and the apple of each cheek, his voice an impassioned whisper. "And if I may hope, if all should go well, every one of the days to come after."

Geneviève closed her eyes to the emotional onslaught and lowered her forehead against his, allowing the tip of one finger to caress a dimple and the strong, square jaw.

Without a word, she rushed from his embrace, grabbed the heavy brocade robe from the floor, and ran from the room.

Sebastien fell back upon his haunches, helpless to do more to stop her. He could only watch with a determined and pleased expression as the door swung shut behind her.

32

'Twas then I warned thee to beware,
Of one as false as she is fair.

—John Thomas Mott, *The Last Days of
Francis the First, and Other Poems*

"There is little for me to rejoice about," François whispered from the abyss of the deep-cushioned chair drawn close to the mammoth hearthside, the warmth of the crackling flames reaching out, warming his pale cheeks until they flushed red.

"I disagree, Your Majesty," Montmorency murmured.

They spoke discreetly, as if they would guard the secret of their words from those around them. But in truth, the room was preternaturally empty; after last night's soirée, few courtiers possessed enough energy to attend an evening's salon. A few of the king's closest advisers and companions slumped about the perturbed sovereign—Chabot, though his influence had begun to wane, Lorraine and others of the Guise family with him—but most were there out of necessity, not out of any desire for social intercourse.

Anne curled at her lover's feet, her head upon his lap, lids fluttering against the onslaught of fatigue. A smattering of female courtiers drooped about the room—those who had passed the darkest hours of the night in bitter loneliness, and craved company to dispel it and the disappointment of a party ending without an assignation.

Geneviève sat unaccompanied in the small grouping of chairs not far from the king. She had not come to banish isolation or from any duty to the duchesse or the king of France, nor did she come to hear secrets worthy of passing along. The time for messages and codes and ciphering had ceased. She had packed her bag and hidden it in the garden. She had drawn her path on the map, to the address given her with King Henry's last message. She came to finish what had started all those years ago, to finish it decisively once and for all. Her dark-circled eyes fixed upon François like the drawn arrow locked upon the heart of the target, chin tucked to chest as she sipped a heavily watered mug of wine.

The emperor had not stepped one foot from his chambers at any point in the day, adding fuel to the king's frustration as he ruminated on another missed chance for negotiations.

"These days with the emperor have done much to solidify the friendship between you." Monty continued to plead his case.

François stared at his minister, lips clamped in a tight white line, nostrils flaring as though assaulted by the scent of something grievously distasteful. "Friendship? Do you think I have done all this for the sake of friendship?"

"It can on—" Monty began, hands raised in supplication.

"You assured me inroads would be made."

"And I believe they have been," Montmorency countered. "Your conversations with the emperor have brought accord on many topics."

François waved a spotted hand with agitation, as if to brush away a pesky insect. "Oh *oui*, we have talked of the Turks and his disapproval, and we have gone on ad nauseam on matters of faith, but there has been not one word of Milan."

"I'm sure gi—"

"Not one word!" François banged a fist on the arm of his chair, his vehemence startling the sleepy Anne at his feet and the others gathered around him.

"I am sorry, *ma chérie,*" François muttered apologetically as he gave her silky hair a caress.

Anne shook off his regret with a tender pat on his knee. "I think I will take to my bed, though, if it would not displease you."

"Not at all, dearest." The king rose with arduous effort and pulled her up. With a chaste kiss to the forehead, he sent Anne off, her lady Monique not far behind to attend her.

"You may retire at your leisure," the duchesse said to Geneviève as she passed, though Geneviève had not come to attend her.

Geneviève had stood with the royals, as had all the room's populace, and offered Anne a quick curtsy. "*Bonne nuit*, madame," she replied, but made no move to leave the chamber.

Geneviève turned to the full chalice on the small, round, clawfoot table, giving it far more attention than it deserved, her mind conjuring any excuse to speak with the king alone, ready to offer her body if need be, though certain the gesture would disgust François as much as it would her.

François stood in silent argument with his constable; he did not release the man from his side and yet he spoke not a word, simply glowered at him with arms akimbo.

Chabot yawned noisily behind him. "My apologies, Your Highness."

François spun round, remembering the others in the room. "No, it is I who should apologize. I have kept you all overlong. To your beds, everyone."

With sleepy salutations and dragging feet, the courtiers filed from the room, heading east, to the double doors that opened onto the main corridor. At the very tail, Geneviève shuffled along, her head turned upon her shoulder to keep the king in her vision.

François stared down at the fire as if he ruminated upon all the regrets of his life in the orange and blue flames. A log popped, and it seemed to break the hypnotic hold of the blaze. With a slump of his shoulders, he turned to the west end of the room, toward the door to his privy chamber and the two guards flanking it.

With fists balled in frustration, Geneviève lingered no longer, and made for the door, stamping her feet as if in a tantrum. Time was running out; the emperor would be in residence for another few days at most; if she did not make her move, all would be lost. She had t—

"I would take a turn about the castle before I retire."

Geneviève skidded to a halt at the king's words.

She changed direction, scurrying to her chair, picking up her abandoned tankard and tossing back a gulp as though she couldn't continue without one last drink.

"As you wish, Your Highness." The large halberdier gave a clipped bow of his head and took a step forward.

The king strolled away, turning back to the guard with a raised hand. "Your companionship is not required. I'm sure I am safe within the corridors outside my room."

"But, Your Hi—"

"I would accompany you, *Majesté*." Geneviève's voice squeaked with audacity and fear, but she could not let this moment pass. A sign could not be more apparent had it been chiseled in stone and laid at her feet. She cleared her throat and dropped into a deep curtsy. "Though I cannot offer protection, I can offer companionship. If I may be so honored."

The king smiled with pleased paternal charm. "Nothing would please me more." François beamed. "But are you not as fatigued as all my other courtiers?"

"No, Your Highness. I believe I took to bed much earlier than most."

François narrowed his eyes, but the squint did not fail to conceal the keen, amused gleam.

"Then if you will not be bored by such older company"—the king bowed to her as he would to his queen, and held out his hand—"I would be honored to take a turn with you, mademoi-selle."

Geneviève smiled despite them both; it was hard to deny his charm, though there was nothing licentious about it. He had played the lothario long after his body could keep up with his lust, but with her, his intentions had always been chaste. She had been foolish to think it could ever be otherwise.

"I find your company quite inspiring, Your Highness," she said with blatant candor. "You are as well-read a man as I have ever met and I would discuss great works with you whenever able."

With her hand upon his, the king of France led Geneviève out into the corridor and turned her toward the gallery, no doubt an oft-trod path.

"I have recently finished *The Tales of Priam and Hector*, in the *Iliad*, and would ask your opinion of it," Geneviève said, her voice slithering up to the top of the vaulted stone-and-beam ceiling of the silent castle, the vibrato growing as the words echoed away from her. Geneviève took her hand from his; she could not let him feel the quaking that shook it, nor the dagger that lay up her sleeve.

She had him alone.

"You read Homer?" François asked with pleasant astonishment as they turned onto the *galerie*. The long golden arcade stretched out before them like the never-ending road to hell; it glittered with beauty and elegance, silent and abandoned by any other liv-ing soul.

He shook his head as he sniffed. "I am most impressed, young lady. Did your father teach you this love of literature?"

Geneviève stumbled upon her skirt. The king's quick arm movement saved her from sprawling upon the parquet floor. She gathered her composure, reclaiming her arm from his grasp. He could not have asked a more virulent question.

"My parents died when I was very young." Geneviève spewed the venomous words with a jagged whisper.

François stopped and turned. "I am so very sorry, Geneviève." His wide mouth drooped; his large Adam's apple bobbed a swallow. His sentiment was no polite obligation, but undeniable compassion.

Geneviève turned from it.

"I, too, lost my father when I was very young, but I had my mother for many, many years. She was a blessing in my life." He reached out a large hand and took Geneviève gently by the shoulder, giving it a benevolent squeeze. "No child should be without a parent."

Geneviève avoided his gaze, unable to respond. His words mocked her, this man who wore the stain of her parents' blood, and yet his empathy touched her.

She took herself from his grasp and recommenced their stroll down the vacant hall, forcing her thoughts to the task at hand. In the large, barren passageway, her deed would go unnoticed for many long minutes, more than enough to make her escape via the far pavilion's stairway, and out into the night.

"How did they die?" he asked.

Her gaze burned holes onto his face, and she longed to cry out *You! You killed them!* but she could not, not without revealing the monster trapped within her, a fiend about to pounce.

The king pulled back, stung by her rancorous glower. "Perhaps I have overstepped my bounds. Pray forgive me."

But Geneviève would not allow his umbrage to pass without counter. He would know the truth, in a sense, if for a short time.

"They died upon the great golden field, when you met with the English king. There was a terrible fire and in it they perished."

François's eyes bulged and his steps faltered.

Geneviève thought what a great thespian he was. She gave her right arm a discreet shimmy and the tip of the dagger inched lower down her arm, slipping into her waiting cupped fingers, edge sharp against the soft skin.

"*Sacrebleu,* you astound me, mam'selle." He stood below the large center chandelier, one hand to his head, as if pained. "I remember that night so well. We saw the blaze far across the valley from our camp. It was as if the fi—"

Geneviève's hand flashed out like the stinging venomous tongue of a snake, and her fingers dug sharply into the king's velvet-covered bicep. So abrupt, so intent was the clutch, that the king looked indignantly down at the white-knuckled fingers biting him.

"Across the valley? You . . . you *saw* the . . . the fire from *across* the valley?" Geneviève stumbled on her words, unable to process her thoughts fast enough.

François's gaze flashed from her hand to her face, brows knitted thunderously across his wide forehead. "*Oui.* It was so near King Henry's structure, we feared for his safety."

She didn't release her unpardonable breach of propriety on his royal person; she could not. "King Henry's encampment? You say the fire was at the English camp? Are you sure?"

"Yes, quite sure," he sniped. "I may be old, my dear, but I have not yet become completely senile. I remember it as if it were yesterday. Monty and I, Chabot as well, as I recall, dressed in haste, and with a large contingent of guards set off to assure Henry's safety. What we found . . ." All malice evaporated. François's large head fell upon his chest; his gaze fell away and filled with sadness. "The smells, the chaos . . ."

Geneviève dropped her hold upon him, tumbling backward, crashing against the wall behind her. He spoke the truth; it lay bare upon his naked expression, resounded in the grief of his words. He would have no cause to lie to her, not to Geneviève Gravois. But how could it be? She had been told, time and time again, that the fire had been in the French camp, that she and her family were there, that her French father had been a member of the king's envoy, that the fire had been set by this man's orders. Yet two truths of the same event could not exist.

"Oh, *mon Dieu*." The king rushed forward, grabbed her by the arms, and kept her from falling. "What have I done? How callous I have been to speak of it thus. I did not think. I am sorry. I became lost in the horrific memories, but they can be nothing compared to your own."

But Geneviève did not hear him, did not care one whit for his apology. His words had torn her world asunder, had thrown the truth of her life—of her very existence—upon a blazing fire.

The words of her aunt screamed in her head and she threw her hands upon her ears, but she could not block the sound out. *He's a liar and a murderer. Never forget what he has done to you. Never forget who he is.* And yet Geneviève could not deny all she had learned for herself about this man, how open his broken heart had become. Did a fissure await the sharp, cold tip of her dagger?

"Henry did all he could for his people. He tended to the wounded himself. I saw it with my own eyes."

Henry, King Henry, her Henry. He had done so much for her, but had it really been for her? The bud of suspicion broke ground, the voices screamed, but she knew not which to listen to. The time had come to listen to her voice alone.

"You must not think of it anymore." François whispered to her as he would a frightened child. With great tenderness, the powerful man pulled her into his embrace.

It was the perfect opportunity, his nearness the perfect opening. Before her jumbled thoughts could delay her any longer, Geneviève slipped the hard, cold handle of the dagger down into her palm, the glinting blade protruding and ready to strike as she lay her head against the wide, welcoming chest, as his arms held her tight, as his hands rubbed her back with slow, soothing gestures. He mumbled words of sympathetic consolation in her ear.

She half listened as she took a step backward and created space between them, as she raised her hand and the dagger. She would do this; she could do this. The darkness that had always lived within, urged her on, as if its own existence depended on it.

And it did. Geneviève knew it did. Knew that if she killed this man now, it would not rid her of her hate, but bind her to it eternally. It would devour her whole.

"I know your sorrow for my own. You have lost your parents and I my dear children," he crooned in her ear, raw emotion in his voice, soothing them both. "But God has seen to bring us together, perhaps for that very reason. He would give me back a child, and . . . and you a parent."

He grew shy and timid, craning his neck to look down at her. This man who had conquered kingdoms lay vulnerable to her in a way no one had ever been.

"Perhaps, if you would let me, if your heart could allow . . . I could be your father? Mayhap you will let me love you, as a father?"

The words thrust a sword up into the darkness, and the sharp foil cut the soft underbelly of the dragon, slaying it once and for all.

In her mind's eye, two kings stood side by side; each wore only the clothes she herself had seen them don. In that instant, she knew which was true.

Geneviève gripped the weapon in her cold hand, blood rushing from her fingers, limb shaking with the fierce grip . . . and shoved the blade back up into her sleeve.

Relief flooded her like a crashing wave. She sagged against the king, tears allowed at last to fall, shoulders quivering.

The king's jaw fell; he did not expect such a reaction, especially from her. He held her tighter, with not a word, rocking her in his arms until the silent sobbing passed into sniffling.

"I can only hope those are tears of joy," he said as the emotion ebbed, "or I would throw myself upon my sword in mortification."

She laughed through her tears then, laughed at the irony of his words and the comical, embarrassed expression upon his face. She could not tell him of the long journey that had brought her to this place, but she would tell him of what lay in her heart—the truth of it.

Geneviève stepped back so he could see her as she spoke.

"All my life I have longed for a father, lived each day as if I could create one. I have longed for nothing as I have longed for a place to belong." Geneviève listened to her revelation, hearing it as he did. "And here I find both, where I least expected. I am most grateful to God and to you. Your love is the greatest gift I have ever received." She dropped herself into the deepest curtsy, her quivering legs bent until her knees touched the ground.

King François's sharp chin quivered and his eyes shined bright. He held his hand out without a word, for there was none worthy of this moment. Both so intent within the moment, neither saw or heard the man as he slipped from the edge of the corridor. Geneviève took the king's hand, gladly, eagerly, accepting the fate it offered. In this fulfilled, exhausted silence, they returned together to the end of the gallery, to the threshold of his door.

François faced her. "I feel as if I shall sleep deeper and sweeter than I have in a very long while."

Geneviève sniffed a laugh. "None of nightmare's ghouls will bother either of us this night, Your Majesty."

He looked old and worn, and yet there was a light in his eyes that had not been there an hour ago, a light she herself had lit.

He reached up with a large, clumsy hand and wiped one last tear from her cheek. "Sleep well, *ma* Geneviève. *Ma fille.*"

❧ 33 ❧

Men are always wicked at bottom
unless they are made good by some compulsion.

—Desiderius Erasmus (c. 1466–1536)

How often had she walked these corridors late at night, shadows as her sole companions? No more light illuminated the passageway than on any other night, and yet the umber was not so deep and the only shadow was her own. Geneviève had made her choice, *her* choice, and she recognized this moment as the one where her life began. She turned a corner, making her way to her chamber with a craving for her pillow and a sense of belonging she had never felt, her smile a sweet kiss upon her tear-swollen face.

Hardships fell away with the echo of each step, and yet the path before her remained shrouded and unclear. How she would extract herself from King Henry's employ, she did not know. One misstep and she may well yet reach the ultimate end, but for now she would revel in this triumph. She would allow the embrace of reprieve, allow herself serenity in the quiet . . .

The quiet. Geneviève stopped. The weak echo of her clicking heels died away. Her head tilted and she listened. The silence in the castle matched the silence in her mind . . . the voices were gone.

She raised her hands to her face, tingling with astonishment and joy. She skipped then, like a schoolchild on the way home, and turned the last corner onto the last corridor.

"Geneviève." The whisper found her as the man stepped out of a patch of darkness, a void between two torches where their light could not reach.

She slipped as she flung her body back, a cry of surprise and fear escaping her throat.

"Be not afraid," he said, turning his head with an odd smile. A veil of pale light found one deep dimple.

"*Mon Dieu,* Sebastien," Geneviève grumbled, one hand flattened against her palpitating heart. "You almost frightened me to death."

"I have been waiting for you." He offered no apology. "We mus—"

"Never mind, never mind." Geneviève gave him no pause, flinging herself into his arms. "Seeing you, having you here, it is perfect, perfect."

She stood on her toes and ravaged his face with her kisses, her hands caressing his arms, his chest, as if feeling him for the first time, mumbling with incoherent happiness. "Everything is different now, do not ask me how, but trust it. What I feel for you—all that I feel—I can allow. There is nothing to stop me, not even myself."

Sebastien looked down at her, brows furrowed, accepting her affection with neither struggle nor contribution.

Geneviève pulled back, saw his face, and laughed, a low throaty chortle that spoke of lustful amusement. "I'm sorry, so sorry. I make no sense, I know." She brought her curved mouth closer to his, her body brushing against him with slow, provocative movements, her lips caressing his as she spoke. "But know this: We have much to celebrate, so let us begin."

She kissed him then, all restrained passion liberated, as if the laces binding her heart had been ripped away. Her tongue fought to conquer his mouth and, with a ravenous groan, Sebastien surrendered.

His hands wrapped around her waist and squeezed; the air rushed from her lungs as he yanked her against him, his hardness mastering all her soft roundness. Their clamorous breathing grew loud in the quiet, their bodies damp. Sebastien's mouth ravaged her—her lips, her face, her neck—he took her with a brutal passion she had never felt, as if her enticement had freed a beast buried inside him. The passionate onslaught brought her to heights of exhilaration she had never known or imagined, as it mingled with lascivious danger.

With arms clenched as thick and hard as steel bands, he picked her up and thrust forward, shoving her back into the stone wall.

Sebastien's chiseled body trapped her against the cold rock; any air left in her body rushed out, until she gasped with pleasure and fear.

"Sebastien . . . Sebastien, wait," she wheezed, trying to contain his frantic onslaught, her hands thrust upon his shoulders.

But he heeded her not. His hands tore at her bodice, grabbed at her breasts as he buried his face in the deep hollow between them, his mouth nipping painfully at her soft, pliable flesh. Alarm overtook arousal and Geneviève wanted it to stop, wanted him to stop. She clamped one hand on each side of his head and yanked.

Geneviève felt a scream rise in her throat at the face unmasked. Lust burned naked in his eyes, but so did something else, something sad and brutal and terrifying she had never seen before. She shut her eyes to it and Sebastien plunged his mouth onto hers, pressing his lips upon hers until they shred upon her teeth and the foul, acidy taste of blood burst in her mouth.

She shook her head, struggling until she freed her mouth.

"What is this madness, Sebastien?" she entreated. "What are you doing?"

His hard jaw thrust forward, his hands tore a path upward from her breasts.

"Why did you not do it, Geneviève? It would have been so easy. We would have had such a life together, but you've changed everything."

Geneviève's mouth fell, words and thoughts a tumble. "What are you talking about? What do you me—"

A tear formed in his eye, one ray of sadness in the face of a fiend. His hands moved up farther, the long fingers wrapping around her throat.

"I have no choice now, Geneviève, don't you see that?" With slow fatality, his hands began to squeeze. "Above all else, I must serve my true king—my cousin."

Beautiful face contorted with devastation, Sebastien brought his lips to her ear.

"I must serve King Henry."

One moment of crippling incomprehension . . . shattered upon horrific realization. Geneviève kicked her legs, banged her fists upon the arms squeezing the breath from her. She had always fought. Now she must fight for her life. She tried to push forward, to reach down to the dagger returned to the leg strap, but he jerked her backward.

I am always with you, I am always watching. How many times had King Henry written those very words? This man had been his eyes, his presence. He was her keeper, her lover, and now her executioner.

"If only you had done what you were meant to do." His hands shook as they tightened their grasp upon her throat. Tears slipped from his eyes and down his cheeks. He shook his head, as if he denied the act he committed. "We could have married and lived under my cousin's love. But now it cannot be. I must do what you could not. And then I can never go home. Never!"

Stars burst in Geneviève's eyes. Rushing blood thrummed in her ears.

"You . . . love . . . me." The words croaked out of her closing throat, their certainty irrefutable.

Sebastien's hands quivered. For a fleeting instant, Geneviève hoped.

"Of course I love you." The words of pure anguish fell from his lips. His head dropped under the weight of it. His whole body shook.

Geneviève made her move. She dropped her hands to the wall behind her and pushed.

But he did not yield.

Sebastien pushed back, his grip tightened, her throat closed.

"I am sorry," he sobbed as he choked her.

Geneviève's vision blurred. The face before her swam in the darkness that had come at last to swallow her, as it had threatened to do her whole life.

She felt her body slipping down the wall, felt herself rising above it, and she reached out to grab at the release.

Suddenly I laugh and at the same time cry,
And in pleasure many a grief endure.

—Louise Labé (c. 1524–1566)

The whirring hum of the dagger cut through the air; the squish of spurting blood and fractured bone screamed in answer.

Sebastien's eyes flew open, his jaw slumped, as the dagger sank into his flesh and found his heart.

But Geneviève did not see it, did not feel it as her assassin's body fell forward and to the ground with her own.

At the cornerstone of the corridor, King François's arm dropped to his side. He had killed and knew it, but was it too late?

Like the three guards behind him, he broke into a run. He reached them first; the bodies splayed upon the ground, scarcely discernible in the dim light. François grabbed the body of his once loyal guard and tossed it aside with the brutal force of his youth.

"Geneviève, Geneviève." He chanted her name as if he prayed to God.

Two guards grabbed the flaccid body of Sebastien and flung it over with disrespectful viciousness as the third kept his sword point fixed on a spot in the center of the man's chest. One felt for breath as the other checked for pulse. They found neither, with a condemning sense of delight.

The king held Geneviève's limp body cradled in one arm, rocking her as he gently patted her face, as he shook her as if to impel the life back into her.

"Dear God," he prayed, "please do not take her. Do not ply my punishment upon her as well."

He dropped his forehead onto hers and there he felt it. Breath. Her breath, tickling his face ever so lightly with its faint vapors. But it was enough.

"Loosen her laces," he commanded, and the closest guard dropped his weapon to the floor with a thunderous clang, dropped to one knee, and untied the laces along the side of the prostrate woman's gown.

Geneviève sucked the air into her lungs with a rattle; her eyes fluttered as they struggled to open.

François raised his gaze heavenward, a silent, rushed prayer of gratitude. He muttered as the deathly white skin on her face flushed with the palest pink blush. "Something compelled me to return to you, to make sure you were all right. Thank the good Lord. Thank you, God, for bringing me here."

Geneviève drew in each breath with deliberation, her body pulsing once more with life. Her filmy gaze scoured the scene before her . . . the king of France, the man she was raised to kill, had become her savior. She raised a weak hand to his face, to touch him with her thankfulness. François thrust the hand to his cheek with his own and closed his eyes. Geneviève turned her regard to the guards, the bloody body of Sebastien lying within arms' reach, and all she had forgotten returned.

She struggled to sit up, but François held her back. "No, do not move. I do not know how badly you are injured."

She shook her head, writhing as she clamored for breath to speak.

". . . speak . . . you . . ."

"Do not talk, Geneviève. Just breathe."

But she would not calm, would not stop. She grabbed the king by the clothes upon his chest, and yanked him toward her with unaccountable strength.

"I must . . . speak to . . . you." Her gaze beseeched him, the imperative transparent.

He opened his mouth to argue, but in the end, acquiesced with a frown and a nod.

"Help me," he said, as he struggled to his feet, struggled to pull her up beside him.

The men jumped forward, two of them wrapping each of Geneviève's limp arms around their shoulders. With a contemptuous look, François ticked his chin angrily at the body of Sebastien.

"Dispose of him," he demanded of the remaining guard, and began to lead the others away, back down the corridor toward his own chambers.

"No no, wait," Geneviève said, no longer gasping for breath, but her voice was the feeble bark of a sick dog and her throat burned with the flames of hell. The whites of her eyes were red with broken veins, and a purple necklace of bruises weaved around the porcelain skin of her neck.

"Please, Geneviève, we must get you to a physician." François chastised her as he would any of his children in his care.

Once more she reached out for him, grabbing him by the arm and pulling him toward her until her lips grazed the flesh of his ear.

"Swear them, my lord. Swear them all to secrecy. You . . . must." The weakness threatened to overwhelm her, but she would not release him.

The cloak of fear he had thought to dispel wrapped itself about his shoulders once more. There was much afoot here, the king knew it now for a certainty; he would question her no more.

"You are all sworn to secrecy," he brayed, "by your lives."

The three men bowed, soldiers' hard faces set in a pledge of honor.

"Your Majesty," they intoned, the two holding Geneviève bowing their heads, the third thrusting his fist to his chest.

Geneviève released herself to the soldiers' arms and allowed them to rush her down the corridor, the king at the prow, her feet dragging along the stone floor.

At his chamber, the king flung open the door and took Geneviève in his arms.

"Allow no one entry." He flung the command over his shoulder. "Tell them nothing."

"Your Majesty," the men repeated, each taking a stand on either side of the door, impenetrable statues at guard.

"I have been told of a disturbance in the castle. I must see the king. I must ensure he is well." Wrapped in an unattractive chartreuse silk evening robe, Montmorency rushed toward the king's door, blustering with anger as the guards stymied his admission.

"The king has ordered that no one shall pass."

"What?" the constable barked, with unmitigated annoyance. "You speak nonsense."

"What is this of nonsense?" Chabot joined them and Cardinal Lorraine as well, all dressed for sleep, sleep bloating their faces, roused by servants whose tongues twittered with nefarious rumor.

"This guard refuses me entry," Monty told the men, pointing at the soldier as if he were an insolent insect at their feet.

Admiral Chabot stepped up, hands on hips. "I order you to allow us entry, sir. We must see to the king."

"No one shall pass." The soldier kept his eyes straight ahead, fixed on an empty spot before him.

Chabot bristled with anger. "I said, I order—"

"No one shall pass." The other soldier took up the chant with a growl. "The king demands it."

For all their power, these ministers and councilors knew defeat when they tasted it.

They began to trudge away, when Montmorency swung back, a finger pointed at the soldier like a threatening dagger tip. "You will come for us the instant the king allows."

The soldier said nothing, answering with a stiff bob of his head. As the fuming contingent crawled off, he dared a shift and a roll of his eyes to his companion, who answered with the tick of a smile.

François stood at the window, thick thighs pressed against the embrasure, one long hand pressed against the cool glass. A gray glow glistened on his moist, wrinkled face; tenderness and longing showed in the sad tilt of the almond eyes.

His mind chewed on the unfathomable tale, now tucked away in his mind, never to be shared with another. He had been the king of a great nation for decades, and yet he had never heard a story like the one Geneviève had told. He knew with a certainty that the voice of his youth, the one who spouted superiority and entitlement, was nothing but a blustering fool.

His heart tore as he watched her and her companion leave him, as their horses brought them to the edge of the forest. In the murky light of a coming dawn, the man's red hair fairly glowed like a beacon. The only decision had been the right one, hard though it may be. François had entrusted Geneviève's keeping to his loving care; for with the marquis de Limoges it was love; he had seen it in the man's face for himself.

King though he may be, he could not escape the pangs of separation. He could not help but feel the loss of a daughter newly found.

As he watched them vanish into the arms of the naked trees, he saw her turn back, knew her gaze found him as it rose up the wall of the castle and searched the windows. He smiled a tremulous smile and she answered with her own. She would know his love, for he would send it often and for as long as he lived, through the ciphers she had learned so well.

The couple disappeared, and he turned from the window with a sigh. There was but one place he longed to be at this moment.

* * *

She turned away from her last glimpse of her king, but did not urge her horse forward, holding back on the reins, her body bobbing in the fringed saddle as the animal shifted its weight. Geneviève's violet gaze stared off at the twisting, light-dappled path that lay before them, a bittersweet smile upon her rosy lips.

"Is all well, Mademoiselle Gra—" The marquis de Limoges cleared his throat and dipped his large, pleasant face. "Is all well with you, Madame de Veu?"

Rousing herself from her introspection, Geneviève turned her attention upon her companion. She had often seen that look on Albret's face, his masculine, agreeable features soft with warmth and kindness, and always a glint of something more. She had never been as grateful for it as she was at this moment.

"I often knew I would leave this court, that my days would not end here, but never in my wildest fancy did I imagine such leave-taking," she croaked in a thoughtful whisper.

Albret's brow furrowed and a crimson blush broke out on his freckled cheeks. "It is not all bad, is it?" he murmured.

So much lay in the question. Geneviève's mouth thinned with a tender smile. "It is not bad at all." She liberated an incredulous laugh. "And upon that I am most surprised."

With an expert hand, she pulled her reins to the right and her horse sidled over to Albret's. A shaft of soft sunlight sneaked through the canopy of branches above her head, turning her porcelain skin near translucent; it caught the smudges in the hollows of her face and the circlet of purple around her neck.

"Though I am most sorry for how my path has changed your own." Her face scrunched in apprehension.

"Fear not, *ma chérie*, for I serve not only my king, but my heart." Albret reached across the small space between them and placed his wide, powerful hand gently upon hers.

She allowed it to rest there, his flesh warm and welcoming.

"We can never know the path ahead," he offered, "but we can move forward with hope."

Geneviève smiled again, and heaved a deep, cleansing draught of fecund forest air. "Then forward, Monsieur de Veu, with hope."

He clicked the secret door shut and it faded away into the molding of the room. With his long legs, François rushed to the outer door of his presence chamber and threw it open.

The guards spun round, relaxing at the sight of their king, well and unharmed.

"Messieurs, you have done your duty with great honor this night." The king of France straightened his shoulders and stepped across the threshold. The men swiveled their heads to peer into the room, glances scattering in confusion about the empty chamber, meeting in perplexity.

François smiled but a little. "By your oath." It was a command and a question.

The two soldiers straightened, faces set firm. "Your Majesty." They bowed.

The king returned the gesture with respect, spun on his heel, and strode off down the corridor.

Slipping through the empty hallways, he silently passed the guard at her door. With the ungainliness of a large, aging man, he sneaked past the sleeping attendants in her presence chamber, shrugged off his heavy outer clothes, and stealthily slipped into the sheets upon her bed.

Like a nuzzling kitten, Anne turned to him, wrapping her delicate arms around his broad body. "Is all well?" she asked, voice groggy with sleep.

François pulled her embrace tighter about him. "I have had to send Mademoiselle Gravois from us."

She stirred then, raising her head, a mess with a crown of tousled hair, to gaze upon him with a glimmer of fear and sadness.

"Will we see her again?"

A poignant melancholy tugged at the mighty king's heart. He would forever remember the brilliance of the violet eyes and the woman who had spared him his life and helped save his nation, a daughter who had served her king well. He would guard her name as he passed from this world to the next and, in doing so, lift her from out of the grave.

"No, I'm sorry, *ma chérie*. We will not. But we will know she loves us, now and forevermore."

AUTHOR'S NOTE

There is no lighter burden,
nor more agreeable,
than a pen.

—Petrarch (1304–1374)

Though Geneviève and the events of her life are all fictitious, the treachery of her setting, the struggle for power and glory at all levels, is based on fact and only a smattering of the events of the age are touched upon. It was called the century of giants, and the games these royals played with one another were of colossal proportion.

Anne de Pisseleu d'Heilly, the duchesse d'Étampes, remained by François's side until the moment of his death. Within days of his passing, rumors abounded that she had been involved in a covert relationship with the Holy Roman Emperor, Charles V— that he had paid her with, among other things, a gargantuan diamond. A messenger confessed to carrying secret letters from Anne to the emperor during his stay in France. Such letters, it was said, detailed all the duchesse knew about French military tactics and strategic points of defense.

Though never convicted, Anne's detractors were merciless. Montmorency, the widowed queen, the new king Henri, and his mistress Diane de Poitiers did everything to humiliate her. She was exiled from court and rejected by her husband. Henri confiscated all Anne's holdings—save one—giving them to Constable Montmorency. Her jewels, including those King François had had made to match her green eyes, Henri gave to Diane, who had coveted them so. Hely, this favorite, had loved and been loved by a king for more than twenty years, and will be forever remembered as having betrayed that love. Anne died in such obscurity, the exact date of her death in 1580 is unconfirmed.

From the moment Henri II became king, he elevated his long-time mistress to the rank he believed she deserved. Diane de Poitiers became the duchesse de Valentinois, wherein he restored the duchy that had belonged to her family. What is more, he pronounced her head governess to the royal children and insisted she be present for all meetings of the *conseil des affaires* and the *conseil privé*. Diane had been the single greatest influence in Henri's life.

After Henri's fatal wound on the jousting field at the age of forty, Catherine de' Medici banished Diane de Poitiers from her lover's deathbed, his funeral, and from court. Catherine ruled as regent for her young sons until the time of her death, becoming one of the most famous, and infamous, rulers in the country's history.

Despite all of Henry VIII's fears, an alliance between Charles V and François I never materialized. In actuality, the meeting between Charles V and François I did little to advance the relationship between the two rulers. Military conflicts continued in 1542 and 1544, with England falling in with the emperor. Neither were decisive, Milan remained out of François's reach, and *status quo ante* was established in 1544.

After the death of his wife, Charles V, Holy Roman Emperor and king of Spain, grew weary of struggle and glory, and eventually abdicated all titles in 1556. He died two years later.

Henry VIII died on January 28, 1547. Some rumors claim a great celebration took place in the French palace. François's public statement professed his grief over the loss of his "good and true friend." A grand legend has it that the dying king of England sent a message to the king of France from his deathbed, reminding François that he, too, was mortal. The mythology holds that, in response, François became depressed and fell ill to a sickness from which he would never recover, dying on March 31, 1547.

Perhaps it was the loss of his nemeses that brought about François's abrupt demise. He was deeply affected by the withdrawal of his two adversaries. There was no enemy left worthy of his attention. Each the equal of the other in pride and ego, the three kings had hated each other with a passion kindred to love, because it drew them together in constant relationships that amounted to a kind of sentimental fidelity. They had been ever trying now to destroy, now to charm one another.

As much is said in praise of François I's reign as in condemnation. His enormous strides in the arts and humanities and in forging a more defined nationality are tainted by his fiscal irresponsibility, his obsession with war, and his love of lust. He brought his country out of the uncivilized and uncultured Middle Ages, and yet set stepping stones on the nation's path toward revolution.

François has been called the Renaissance Warrior, for few other rulers can compare in leaving a more notable and lasting cultural legacy. By establishing the *lecteurs royaux* in 1530, François laid the foundation for the Collège de France. His compilation of books evolved into the Bibliothèque Nationale. And, most noteworthy of all, his trove of art became the nucleus of the world-famous collection now held at the Louvre.

ACKNOWLEDGMENTS

This book was written during a time of great struggle; a time to try my soul. In fact, I thought my pen had dried up for all time. Yet it is during the most egregious moments of existence that we see not only our true character, but also that of those around us.

To the many who gave freely of their love, their patience, their understanding, and even their finances, I am eternally grateful.

I stand on two feet,
perhaps not quite as tall as before,
but standing nonetheless.
Or perhaps I have grown taller than ever imagined possible,
Bowed but not bent.

BIBLIOGRAPHY

Books:

D'Orliac, Jehanne. *Francis I: Prince of the Renaissance.* Translated by Elisabeth Abbott. Philadelphia: J. B. Lippincott, 1932.

Grunfeld, Frederic V. *The French Kings.* Chicago: Stonehenge, 1982.

Hamel, Frank. *Fair Women at Fontainebleau.* London: Fawside House, 1909.

Knecht, R. J. *Renaissance Warrior and Patron: The Reign of Francis I.* Cambridge: Cambridge University Press, 1994.

Miltoun, Francis. *Royal Palaces and Parks of France.* Boston: L. C. Page & Company, 1910.

Mott, John Thomas. *The Last Days of Francis the First, and Other Poems.* London: William Pickering, 1843.

Pardoe, Julia. *The Court and Reign of Francis the First.* New York: James Pott & Company, 1901.

Somervill, Barbara A. *Catherine de Medici: The Power Behind the French Throne.* Minneapolis: Compass Point Books, 2006.

Tomlinson, Richard. *The Big Breach: From Top Secret to Maximum Security.* Global Press, 2001.

Internet Sources:

National Museum at the Château Fontainebleau
http://www.musee-chateau-fontainebleau.fr/

Château Royal de Blois
http://www.chateaudeblois.fr/spip.php?article5

Oxford Dictionary of Quotations
http://www.askoxford.com/dictionaries/quotation_dict/?view=uk

Museum of National Antiquities
http://www.musee-antiquitesnationales.fr/

TO SERVE A KING

Donna Russo Morin

ABOUT THIS GUIDE

The following questions are intended to
enhance your group's reading of
TO SERVE A KING.

DISCUSSION QUESTIONS

1. The novel's opening chapter quickly sets a distinctive tone. What is it and what does it reveal about the lives of the main characters? Does it expose the relationship that will form between Geneviève and the two kings? What does it disclose about the political condition of the era?

2. Discuss the dichotomy of the relationship between François I and Henry VIII. How did it affect their dealings with each other throughout their lives and at their deaths? How did it affect their personal, political, and religious decisions? What are the similarities and differences between the two sovereigns themselves, and how does this ultimately affect Geneviève?

3. In the monastery, Geneviève must face a confessor, even though "She had not practiced the sacrament of confession often in her childhood; perhaps her aunt had known it for the hypocrisy it was in a life meant for such iniquities. Geneviève had found neither succor nor blessing in the act." What are the iniquities of her life? Why does she feel that God may forgive her "for just cause"?

4. Rumors and opinions about Diane de Poitiers, La Grande Sénéchale, abound. Discuss those mentioned in this book. How does the image of the woman portrayed in *To Serve a King* compare to those offered in other works?

5. Discuss the irony of Sebastien's position as a Garde Écossaise. In what ways does his position affect his relationship with Geneviève?

6. Why does Geneviève feel that her budding relationships with Sebastien and Arabelle are the same? What underlying

emotion and motivation underscores all of her associations at court? Which associations change, and why?

7. Discuss the similarities and the disparities of the circumstances between the queen, Eleanor of Hapsburg, and the Dauphine, Catherine de' Medici. How are their reactions to these circumstances alike and different?

8. Geneviève is plagued by many demons and divergent emotions. Discuss them, their source and motivation. Do they change as her time at the French court continues? In what ways? What ultimately affects her? Who, or what, is her true enemy?

9. Discuss the reasons for King François's longing to possess the territory of Milan. To what lengths is he willing to go to obtain it? Why does he seek out the assistance of Queen Eleanor and how does it affect the duchesse d'Étampes?

10. Though she had spent many weeks and months with the king of France, Geneviève feels, as they travel to Fontainebleau, that she does not recognize him. "It was the same long, horselike face, the same slanted eyes, long nose and wide mouth, and yet she did not know him." Why does she feel this way, and what happened to her that may have caused these feelings?

11. Discuss the royal obsession with mystics, fortune-tellers, and soothsayers through the ages. What is it about the lives of nobles that would cause them to give credence to predictions and prophesies? How does this predilection relate to the teaching of Machiavelli? Who was the mysterious Michel de Nostredame? Why did Geneviève fear Madame Arceneau and her threat, though she professed no belief in her gift?

12. What does Geneviève mean when, in chapter twenty, she silently pleads with King François, "*Please stop. Do not take me*

into your confidence, do not take me into your heart, for my own cannot bear it." Why does the king reveal his innermost feelings to her?

13. What went wrong with Geneviève's plan to use Lisette's lover as a subterfuge to her own covert actions? Were her efforts a success, and if so, at what cost? Why was François unable to save Lisette?

14. Discuss the meaning of Madame de Hainaut's suicide note. What did Geneviève infer about King Henry from his reaction to the event? How did it change the path of Geneviève's life?

15. At the last moment, Geneviève changes the course of her life, refusing to complete the ultimate act. Discuss the reasons for her altered behavior. Is the most apparent reason the true reason? How does this relate to decisions made by most people throughout their lives?

If you missed Donna Russo Morin's previous two novels,
treat yourself to more of her delicious and
distinctive brand of historical fiction.
One story is set in the glittering and dangerous court
of Louis XIV's Versailles, the other in the fascinating world
of the famous Murano glassmakers. Read on for a little taste of . . .

THE COURTIER'S SECRET

and

THE SECRET OF THE GLASS

Kensington Trade Paperbacks
on sale at your favorite bookstore.

From *The Courtier's Secret*

She stood before the cloudy mirror wondering if the distorted reflection she saw in it was her own or if it had magically captured the image of another, one of the perfectly mannered, perfectly obsequious courtiers clogging every inch of Versailles. The sage-green silk bodice hugged her tightly, fitting to the exact form of the binding corset beneath it. Satin ribbon trimmed the low-cut bodice, elbow-length sleeves and hem and created bows embellishing the full skirt and slight train. The large felt hat in the same sage green boasted one fluffy white ostrich feather.

Jeanne peered more closely at her face; her eyes looked darker, deeper, and her skin glowed with tawny effervescence.

"Hmph," she grunted to the woman staring at her, acknowledging that her mother did know how to dress to bring about the best in one's appearance.

Jeanne, neither familiar nor comfortable in such elegance, had promised her mother a few hours ago that she would try harder, and she would. With a determined flick of her chin, and a giggle as the aigrette wiggled high above her head, she left the unfamiliar reflection behind.

*   *   *

Exiting through one of the many doors of the lower gallery into the back courtyard of Versailles, Jeanne hid her face in the large shadow cast by the brim of her millinery. The sun blazed white, and her eyes squinted in defense. Through narrowed lids, a colorful mosaic appeared before her—red, blue, green, yellow: every color of the spectrum blurred in her vision. Slowly her pupils adjusted to the light and her full, wide mouth turned up in a bow.

Courtiers. Like petals fluttering around the pistil, these creatures, prodigiously garbed in every color of the rainbow, blazed brightly in silk, satin, and brocade. Women with piled-high hair adorned with all manner of hat and lace, and men with their long, flowing curls blowing in the breeze and topped with plumed hats, vied for prominence.

Jeanne inhaled deeply, nostrils quivering in delight at the freshness of both air and water. She took her first step toward the entourage as they assembled between the two grand pools of the Water Parterre, the first section of the immense gardens spanning over two hundred and fifty acres. Her heart beat wildly, and she felt moisture forming under the layers of clothing she wore. This was her first social outing since her return, her first time among the gossiping courtiers, and she anticipated a cold reception.

"*Ma chère, ma chère* Jeanne!" A high-pitched call reached her ears. Jeanne turned, and her heart burst with joy.

Pushing and shoving, two young women struggled out of the cluster of courtiers, rushing toward her, arms and smiles wide and welcoming. Jeanne became enveloped in silk and satin, pressed between two strong bodies, perfume, soap, and musky female scents engulfing her.

"We heard you were back."

"Why have you not come to us sooner?"

Jeanne laughed, putting one arm around each of the women, relishing the acceptance she felt in their embrace and heard in their words.

"*Pardieu!* I am sorry," Jeanne giggled. "But I am here now. Come, let me look at you."

Jeanne released her friends and stepped back. Powdered and beauty-marked, Olympe de Cinq-Mars, daughter of the Marquis de Solignac, stood afire in brilliant red silk. Her jet-black hair and eyes burned with intensity. Paling in visual impact, Lynette La Marechal, daughter of the Duc du Vermorel, shimmered sweetly in yellow brocade, long blond curls pulled back softly to reveal her delicate skin and pale blue eyes.

"How I have missed you both," Jeanne almost sobbed as the emotional reunion with her two dearest friends overwhelmed her. Heedless of prying eyes, she kissed each one tenderly on the lips. Here in their arms, she found consolation in returning to Versailles.

"How do I find you, *mes amies?* What is about?" Jeanne asked, taking each woman by the hand.

"I will marry soon." Olympe was the first to answer, no surprise to Jeanne. "My father is in negotiations with quite a few hopefuls. Papa says many vie for my hand, but he will not concede to just anyone. *Maman* says every courtier in the country will attend my wedding. Well, the ones who matter, at least."

"How wonderful for you, *ma chère.*" Jeanne smiled at Olympe, seeing how little her friend had changed. Even as a young girl, Olympe's thoughts and dreams had dwelled on court intrigue, fashion, and to one day making the perfect match.

"And you, *ma petite.*" Jeanne turned to Lynette, swinging the hands of her friends as they headed slowly toward the bevy of courtiers. "Is there a handsome young cavalier waiting for you?"

Lynette hid behind lowered lids, a pink flush spreading across her pale skin.

"*Non, chère* Jeanne, it is not a conventional marriage which I seek. My papa has petitioned the King to allow me to enter the Convent de La Bas Poitou."

Jeanne stopped, arms pulling ahead of her body as her friends took another step or two.

"Truly?" Jeanne asked Lynette.

Unlike Jeanne, Lynette had completed her education at the abbey near Toulouse. Her letters had always been a window into the depth of her piety.

"It is what I desire above all else," Lynette assured her, chin jutting out.

Jeanne smiled at her friend's conviction.

"When will you know?"

"Soon, I hope."

Jeanne hugged her, face close to her friend's comely countenance.

"Do you feel well? Have you been ill?" Jeanne blurted her thoughts out, one of her least appealing habits, but Lynette's pale skin and the purple smudges under the familiar orbs troubled her.

"No. I am fine and have been." Lynette patted Jeanne's hand still clasped in her own. "Have no fear, dearest."

Jeanne smiled, nodding her head, but felt a niggling of lingering concern.

"And you, you rascal." Olympe pulled Jeanne along to continue their stroll, looking sideways through narrowed dark eyes at her friend. "Is all we have heard true?"

"Too true, I fear." Jeanne tried to look contrite, but the feigned repentance was an unconvincing mask before these two friends.

"You are the chatter of the château," Olympe chided. "Could you not contain yourself for one more year?"

Jeanne shook her head vehemently, one long curl coming loose to fall blithely down her neck.

"It is a miracle I did not get ousted sooner." Jeanne's mouth turned up in a devilish grin, a decidedly malicious spark lighting in her sable eyes. "In truth, my dears, I did everything I could to get evicted."

"*Non*, shh, do not say such things." Lynette surreptitiously cast her gaze about. "Why? Why would you wish it to be so?"

"Why would I not? The place was abhorrent, the instruction was trivial nonsense, the girls were brainless twits, and the nuns were naught but veiled monsters."

Jeanne closed her eyes tightly, repulsed by the memories. To revisit her seven years at the convent was to recall a nightmare that lasted all night. Just speaking of it brought the horrors quickly back; even the smells, the harsh lye soap, the burnt porridge, and the sickeningly sweet incense, came back to clog her sinuses. But it was the blind, slavelike obedience demanded from the sisters that she could not abide.

"How can my love of God be measured by how deeply I curtsey to the nuns?" Jeanne demanded self-righteously.

Olympe giggled loudly; Lynette shushed her again.

"You really must watch your tongue," Lynette warned softly, teeth clamped tightly together. "You are a part of Louis' court now. There are ears everywhere. You must control your words."

"Ha!" Olympe barked, holding her chin a smidgen higher and flashing a sensual smile at two young soldiers as they passed. "Advising Jeanne to hold her tongue is like advising the world to stop turning. It cannot be done."

Jeanne giggled, joyful at being among those who knew her well, yet accepted and loved her regardless.

"What will you do?" Lynette stopped and turned to face Jeanne, searching her friend's face under tightly knit brows.

"She will marry, of course." Olympe rolled her dark eyes at Lynette.

Jeanne remained silent but shared a telling look with Lynette. She longed to pour her heart out, to tell of all the unrequited dreams fermenting in her heart. Lynette put an arm around her friend, stifling the barrage about to burst, and turned Jeanne toward the large group. They were but a mere few paces away; to speak would be for all to hear.

The three young women arrived at the edge of the clustered courtiers. Jeanne held firmly to her friends, trepidation tightening her grip. A few of the gaudily plumed beau monde turned to glance at her; a few whispered to their friends, snide giggles erupting here and there; a few reared quickly away, nostrils flaring as if they smelled something distasteful. Surprisingly, a few afforded her shallow curtseys and barely perceptible bows.

"There, you see," Lynette whispered gently, "they welcome you back with open hearts."

Jeanne almost guffawed out loud. "If these are open hearts, then I am King Louis."

As if the mention of his name summoned him, the crowd parted and the great sovereign strutted into the center of the circle.

There are men others will instinctively follow, for whom they will act with blind obedience. Louis XIV was such a man. Some called him the handsomest man in France. Jeanne thought it was his persona, his courtesy, reticence, and an almost inhuman tranquility, which made him appear larger than life. In reality, Dieudonné de Bourbon the man was only five-five, just an inch taller than Jeanne herself. His vast selection of wigs, worn in lieu of his own hair for the last ten years, added inches to his stature. His deep-set, heavy-lidded, dark eyes carried the secrets of the universe within their depths. The full-lipped mouth topped with the tightly manicured, curving moustache showed the devilishly playful side of the Sun King.

Louis had changed little in the seven years since Jeanne last saw him; while slightly rounder at the middle, he still projected the bearing of greatness, perhaps more than ever in the midst of his magnificent palace. The long, dark curls of Louis' periwig flowed over his coat of dove-gray silk boasting thick, silver-embroidered buttonholes running all the way down the full skirt of his jacket. Inches and inches of Venetian lace flowed from cuffs and collar. Scarlet, tightly fitting trunk hose matched the deep red heels of his diamond-buckled leather shoes and the deep red of the many plumes of his dove-gray felt hat.

Standing on the outskirts of the entourage, Jeanne was grateful Louis had not noticed her. The moment when she must face him would come, but she did not wish it to be today. The King knew her well; as a small child she had spent many hours playing in the royal nursery with the Dauphin, the King's son and heir. But it was the child Louis would remember; Jeanne knew not what he would think of her, the woman, and despite herself, she cared deeply of his opinion.

The bevy of people began to rustle, anxious to be off on one of the King's walks; they jostled and pushed in their eagerness. Off to one side of the King stood a ravishing blond woman, resplendent in violet satin and lace.

"Pray, Lynette, who is that woman?" Jeanne used her gaze to point.

Lynette rose up on tiptoes to see around the piled-high hair and towering hats obstructing her view. A distinctive light sparked in her soft blue eyes.

"Why, my dear, that is Athénaïs herself."

Jeanne's mouth formed a small but perfect circle, surprised and delighted to finally see the woman. Athénaïs, the Marquise de Montespan, was the King's powerful, titular mistress, famous for her beauty and sophistication. In the full sun of midmorning, Athénaïs glowed. Her radiant and abundant blond hair, the shimmering cerulean eyes, and the perfect pink mouth, like the opening of a rose, sat supremely above the slim but curvaceous figure.

"She looks so young," Jeanne whispered for her friends' ears only. At forty-one, the marquise was only three years younger than the king.

"Evil never ages." Olympe smiled, staring at Athénaïs.

"Evil?" Jeanne's brows rose high on her forehead, creasing the soft, pliable skin.

"Not now," Lynette hissed to her friends, moving to stand between them like a mother separating her wayward children.

Françoise-Athénaïs Rochechouart de Mortemart was not the first mistress to warm the King's bed. The French people had long come to accept the King's behavior; he had married for the political health of their country. He deserved to find satisfaction wherever he could. His subjects could not begrudge him whatever joy he might find, even if it was in the arms of a mistress or two.

The path to be the most favored had been difficult for Athénaïs, a married woman. For the King to cuckold another man was a scandalous affair—though conversely, the more women the King conquered, the greater his power grew. After years of Athénaïs's beauty and glamour infecting the court, the people had come to grips with her married status. Even the church acknowledged the King's right to a titular mistress and recognized Athénaïs, giving her the same power as the Queen, just as the courtiers and commoners did.

"Where is Louise?" Jeanne asked, referring to the previous favorite, Louise de La Vallière.

"Usurped and dismissed," Olympe eagerly responded. "Years ago."

"Where?" Jeanne asked, though Lynette fiercely pinched the soft skin of her wrist.

"The Carmelite convent." Olympe slapped Lynette's hands away from Jeanne's, getting a tight-lipped scowl in response. "Sister Louise de La Miséricorde."

"*Non?*" Jeanne's eyes popped wide.

"*Oui.*" Olympe beamed.

Jeanne smiled back at her friend, as much at Olympe's obvious delight in gossiping as in the gossip itself.

"And who, pray, is that?" Jeanne tilted her head at the austere, darkly garbed, full-figured woman standing near to Athénaïs.

"Ah," moaned Olympe with the delight of the obese man as he sits down to a feast. "That is Madame Françoise Scarron, the governess to Louis and Athénaïs's children. Now, *she* is making things quite interesting. They say—"

"Mesdames, mademoiselles, messieurs." The King's deep vibrato captured everyone's attention. "Let us walk."

With many a "Yes, Your Highness" and "*Certainement,* Your Majesty," the procession began. They followed obediently behind the King as he strutted off on his red leather-covered cork-heeled shoes. Olympe leaned toward Jeanne, whispering a conspiratorial "later" as she winked one dark eye. Jeanne winked back delightedly, turning her attention to the head of the procession and the King.

"Ah, *chère duchesse,* it is such a pleasure to have you with us this fine day. It is such a joy to show my home to someone who has never seen it before."

Jeanne studied the King's guest. Her brows knit at the gaudiness of the duchess's *accoutrements.*

"She must be a supremely strong woman," Jeanne said to Olympe over Lynette's head.

"How so?" Olympe asked.

"To be able to hold oneself upright under the weight of all those jewels must take mammoth strength." The duchess had served as the mistress to many. As each affair ended and she was dismissed by an apologetic but completely satiated married man, she had been given another magnificent piece of gemmed adornment.

"She wears them like medals she has earned in a war," Olympe whispered.

"Has she not?" Jeanne's lips curled in a cynical smile, her gaze hard and cold.

With such a reverent audience, Louis lauded the splendor of Versailles in great detail.

"The bricks were formed by hand, one by one. Do they not match perfectly those of the original building?" His question was rhetorical; his enjoyment was in the sound of his own voice and the greatness of his home.

Versailles, located on the main road between Normandy and Paris, was situated on the vast private property of the Bourbon family.

"So close, we are, so close," Louis continued, pointing to the north and south wings, those allocated to the Secretaries of State, where the work still progressed.

Scaffolds stood like the building's external skeleton while thousands of workers flitted to and fro, like ants on a farm, scurrying to the notions of the King. Twenty years ago, when the renovation work had begun in earnest, there had been close to thirty thousand laborers on the grounds.

"My château is almost finished."

"Château? He still calls it a château?" Jeanne hissed with a harsh whisper. "*Mon dieu*, it is the size of a small village."

"Shush!" Lynette remonstrated, eyes narrowed in warning.

Jeanne looked back over her shoulder. From this vantage point, far into the garden, she could see almost all of Versailles in one glance. The group of buildings forming the entire palace stood on a slight rise overlooking the village. The huge additions and front gate pilasters echoed the original exterior of warm russet brick and creamy stone with a roof of blue-gray slate. The front faced east and emphasized a hospitable aspect by enclosing three sides of a black-and-white marble quadrangle courtyard, the breathtaking *Cour de Marbre*.

"How can France and Louis afford such lavishness?" Jeanne continued, heedless of her friend's warning.

"He is obsessed. The cost is trivial," Olympe murmured, gaze narrowing at Lynette as she gave her friend a warning of her own.

"Now on, on to my water gardens." The King continued his narration, turning now and then to include the rest of the party, his voice loud and resounding. The courtiers hung on every word though they had all heard them many times before, following in a precise procession, like a herd of cattle trailing after their leader.

"I've spent hours and hours, days and days designing the magnificence you see here." Louis spread his arms wide as if to embrace the entire estate.

"I am sure Le Nôtre, Caysevax, and Le Vau will be delighted to hear that." Jeanne snipped the names of the real designers in her friends' ears.

Without a turn of her head, Lynette poked her elbow hard into Jeanne's stomach.

"Oof." The air rushed from Jeanne's lungs. She gave Lynette a small, sheepish smile but said nothing more.

"I will take you through my favorite route." Louis turned the group to their left and immediately the delightful fragrances of exotic flowers and orange blossoms assaulted the senses.

"Do you know the King is writing a book about these gardens?" Olympe asked.

"*Oui*," Lynette chimed in, a look of relief at the appropriate conversation quite evident on her pale features. "It is said the treatise will give, in detail, the correct path to take through the grounds."

From the *Parterre d'Eau* they walked to the Orangery and then onto the Ballroom Grove. Within the massive, asymmetrically designed landscape, sunken garden rooms existed between box hedges, blossoming archways, and delicate trellis work. Each area was spectacularly furnished with stone and marble chairs, benches and tables, and hung with silken drapes and tapestries.

A pond, one that symbolized each season, was centered by bronzed tritons and nymphs and stood as a reminder that the Sun King controlled not only the days but also the year. As the King strode forward, the water park came to life. Louis approached one of the fountains, and its sleeping mechanisms sprang into action, spurting water in a torrent of tender teardrops, spraying in a circular pattern, sending gentle, cooling sprinkles on the whole entourage, each drop glistening like a tiny jewel in the bright sunlight.

The courtiers dutifully oohed and ahhed. Jeanne, unfamiliar

with the spectacle, stopped with mouth agape and eyes wide like a child on Christmas morn. Lynette and Olympe smiled fondly at Jeanne, the adoring, watchful parents. Jeanne turned with a giddy grin to her friends, then back to the exhibits. Once the King passed the first fountain, its geyser ceased to flow, and the cessation of sound and movement left a silent, empty void. Jeanne jumped as the adjacent fountain spurted into action, jets of water gushing out with a roar just as the King passed. A colorful, almost mythical, rainbow formed in the mist, capturing the King in the zenith of its arch.

"Is it magic?" Jeanne turned her face to the sun, and the soothing droplets of water flowing over her features stuck to her skin like gems, sending her face into a sparkling reality.

Olympe came and, with a condescending grin, took her friend by the arm, pulling her away from the water.

"Silly woman," Olympe chided. "See those men?"

Jeanne turned to where Olympe pointed and spied the inconspicuous guards stationed at each fountain. Dressed in dark green velvet tunics, pants, and hose, the slim cavaliers blended into their environment.

"Their sole purpose is to make certain these waters flow for the King," Olympe continued, seeing the look of confusion on Jeanne's face. "They whistle, dear, when the King approaches, each with a different note. It alerts those manned at the switches when and which water to turn on."

Jeanne glanced round, seeing the other men sitting below the line of trees, dressed in the same camouflaging outfit, hands posed on metal levers. She smiled in bemused appreciation.

"Brilliant," she said in genuine awe.

"Ah, *oui*," Olympe agreed, pulling Jeanne's hand, stepping quickly with her to catch up with Lynette and the rest of the group.

Jeanne listened with rapt attention as the King prattled on for another half hour and they passed sculptures and fountains and ponds and basins until the tour ended its almost circular path at the back entrance to the palace only a few feet away.

A few of the older courtiers took their leave of the group with graceful bows and curtseys, no doubt in need of rest after the long walk. Others hung about, pretending to be deep in conversation while in truth watching the King closely. With a bow to Athénaïs and Madame Scarron, Louis allowed himself to be led away by the duchess.

"No doubt she is petitioning the King on behalf of a paying customer," Olympe jeered toward the elaborately plumed woman. "Everyone knows it's the only way she can continue to dress and gamble as she does."

Jeanne watched the retreating back of the woman, the corners of her wide mouth lowering perceptibly.

"Come, dearest Jeanne," Lynette broke her friend's sad reverie, "my *maman* would be so delighted to see you."

"*Oui*, Lynette, it would do me much good to see her as well," Jeanne replied, shaking off her despondency.

"Olympe? Olympe?" The call came from behind them, and the three friends turned to see two young women and a cavalier walking briskly toward them. The small, auburn-haired girl in the lead waved her hand frantically at them.

"*Bonjour*, Mademoiselle de Chouard," Olympe said, looking down her long, straight nose at the women before her.

"Is it true, what we have heard? Are you to wed Monsieur de Loisseau?"

"Oh, dearest Daphne, is he one of those who wishes my hand?" Olympe looked around. "There are so many, I cannot keep track."

Jeanne blanched at her friend's egotistical rejoinder and was astounded when the group laughed in response.

"With such a wit it is no wonder they are lining up at your door," the young man said, taking Olympe's hand and brushing his lips across her translucent skin.

Olympe bowed. "Monsieur La Porte, Mademoiselle La Vienne,

Mademoiselle de Chouard, pray say hello to Lynette, whom you all know, and to Jeanne, whom I should hope you remember."

Jeanne recognized Daphne de Chouard from chapel, having seen her pray with great vehemence on more than one occasion.

"Ah, Mademoiselle La Marechal, a pleasure as always to see you," Daphne greeted Lynette; her companions nodded their enthusiastic agreement. "We were just speaking to your father. What a wonderful, kind man."

"Many thanks, mademoiselle." Lynette offered them a small curtsey, giving Jeanne a gentle push forward.

The courtiers' eyes stabbed at Jeanne for a brief moment. Then the trio turned away.

"Keep us informed, Olympe," Daphne called over her shoulder. "We wish to be the first to know of your betrothal."

Olympe waved a limp hand at them, turning back to Jeanne. She watched with Lynette as anger and embarrassment colored their friend's face.

"Do not bother with them." Olympe twisted Jeanne away. "They are no one to be concerned with. You must learn to know the court. The plotting is constant on a grand scale, and *whom* to plot against is of most importance. From the Queen to the King's many paramours, the ministers and the courtiers, they are all in it."

Jeanne froze, aghast at Olympe's words. Lynette twined her arm through Jeanne's, pulling her forward toward the château.

"You must learn not to let the machinations of the courtiers affect you so, *ma chère*." Lynette spoke softly, stroking her friend's arm.

Jeanne smiled sadly, nodding her head.

"I know, I know, yet I have little tolerance for their hypocrisy. There is truth to the fashion of courtiers wearing masks, for some are indeed two-faced. They profess profound piety, yet their behavior speaks of anything but. They judge and belittle others they perceive as beneath them and hate any they deem as competition."

Jeanne stopped, turning to her friends.

"I ask you, is this how God intends for his most righteous followers to behave?"

She held her heavy-heeled shoes in her hand as she tiptoed on stockinged feet down the long, empty corridor. On the floor above her rooms, Jeanne stealthily made her way to the farthest chamber. The oppressive heat of midafternoon pressed thick around her, and the sweat slid down her brow and between her breasts. She'd told Lynette and Olympe that she needed a nap, but instead she'd headed for this classroom, her refuge, as it had been almost every afternoon since her return.

Jeanne smiled gratefully as she reached the portal, thrilled to see it open, no doubt those within hoping for a stray breeze or two. She slipped into the room, gracefully dropping to her knees, sliding the rest of the way into a small cubbyhole as she did. From here she could hear everything taking place in the room and, when she dared peek out, could see those within as well. For the most part she kept herself utterly still, not wishing to expose her position, for to reveal herself would be to incur expulsion and more disgrace.

In her mind's eye she pictured the room and all its details: a dozen or so young boys, aged from six to sixteen, wearing flamboyant clothing and bored expressions, lanky limbs draped across the scarred wooden chairs as they pretended to pay attention to the tutor. Bright light from the one wide-open window cast strange shadows across their faces, throwing their high cheekbones and long, straight noses into stark relief.

"The Romans believed in many gods, some of whom our own King pledges allegiance to, such as Apollo." The tall young man perched on a chair at the front of the room spoke with elegance. His clothes showed signs of wear and overuse; the son of a lowborn baron, as were most tutors, the instructor was rich in knowledge but little else. Jeanne thrilled at his voice as well as the subject matter.

The study of history was one of Jeanne's favorite subjects and one intentionally omitted from her own formal education. History was considered recreational study, and there was nothing recreational allowed at the convent. She'd received instruction in only the basics: reading, writing, arithmetic, and diction. She had gleaned her love of history at the convent, but not from the nuns.

Had she been twelve or perhaps thirteen? Jeanne couldn't remember. She'd been assigned to clean the convent library; a library the priests from the adjacent monastery accessed as well. Dusting the shelves with a dirty, ragged cloth, she'd picked up *Julius Caesar*, by William Shakespeare. When she dropped the old tome on the floor, the pages had fallen open, revealing, like the freshly burst flower reveals its stamen, all of the magnificent secrets hidden within. By the second page, Jeanne was enraptured. The gladiators, the Senate, the law. Her mind whirled as the words spun her back through the ages.

Sister Marguerite allowed Jeanne to clean the library for many weeks, until the young girl was discovered sprawled beneath a heavy oak table, sound asleep, Chaucer's *Canterbury Tales* as her pillow. Jeanne was forbidden to ever clean the library again, but the damage had been done: her love of history, books, and learning had become as much a part of her as her own soul.

"The intrigue among the senators was a many-layered briar patch." The sarcasm lay heavy in Monsieur de Postel's voice, the similarity of the times he spoke of to the present day apparent to him and Jeanne, if not to his pupils.

Jeanne smiled, silently congratulating this man for his insight. She admired teachers, thought teaching a noble profession, one she'd considered for herself, but only for a moment. A woman could only teach as an instructress at a convent, and the thought of ever again entering one of those dismal, depressing places was abhorrent.

He has accepted his position well, she thought, hearing no dissatis-faction, only enthusiasm, in his voice. His father had been a member of the lower cabinet, a much more esteemed position than the tutor held. But M. de Postel was a Huguenot.

Louis' grandfather had passed the Edict of Nantes eighty-four years ago, giving Protestants protection to practice their faith in freedom. During the last few years, the relations between the Catholics and the Huguenots had once again grown strained, and the King had slowly, and as inconspicuously as possible, begun weeding the Protestants out of positions of authority at court. Once a lawmaker, Baron de Postel was now one of the many tutors situated at court charged with the early education of the nobility's children.

Jeanne leaned in and risked a quick glance at the man pontificating with such exuberance. His long, bony arm stretched outward, an imagined sword held firmly in his hand.

Why can I not be as accepting of my fate as he? Jeanne wondered. Pulling herself back into her hiding place, she closed her eyes to the brimming tears and her mind to all such errant thoughts, allowing only the words of the past to enter.

From *The Secret of the Glass*

The scalding heat rose up before her, reaching deep inside her like a selfish lover grasping for her soul. The fiery vapors scorched her fragile facial skin; yellow-orange flames seared their impression upon her retinas. When she pulled away, when she finally turned her gaze from the fire, her vision in the dim light of the stone-walled factory would be nothing more than the ghostly specters of the flames' flickering tendrils.

Sophia Fiolario performed the next step in the glassmaking process in an instant of time, her instincts and years of practice leading the way, from the feel of the *borcèlla* in her hand, from the change in the odor and color of the molten material as it began to solidify. This was the most crucial moment, like the second of conception, when the glass was barely still a liquid, yet on the precipice of becoming a solid. Then, and only then, would she use her special tongs to conceive its ever-lasting form. If she didn't perform perfectly, if her ministrations were inelegant or slow in the tiny void in time, she would have to start again, reheating the glass and returning it to a shapeless blob.

The layers of clothing encasing her body trapped the energy

thrown by the furnace. With a stab of envy, Sophia pictured the men of Murano who worked the glass clad in no more than thin linen shirts and lightweight breeches. As a woman, forbidden to work the furnaces, particularly during these prohibited hours following the evening vigil's bells, she had no choice but to stand before the radiating heat clad in petticoat, chemise, and gown. The sweat pooled beneath her full breasts and trickled down the small of her back. Within minutes of stepping into the circle of sweltering air thrown by the furnace, a heat in excess of two thousand degrees, she became drenched in a cloying layer of her body's fluid. Her own pungent odor vied for dominance over the caustic scent of the melting minerals and burning wood.

Sophia pulled the long, heavy metal blowpipe out of the rectangular door, the ball of volcanic material retreating last. With a mother's kiss, she put her lips to the tapered end of the *canna da soffio* and blew. The excitement lit deep within her as the ball of material expanded and changed, a thrill unlike any other she had ever known elsewhere in all of her nineteen years.

Now was the time; this was the moment. The glass came alive by her skill and her breath. The malleable substance glowed with an internal energy, the once-clear material now a fiery amber, having absorbed the heat of the flames as well as its color. It waited for, longed for, her touch as the yearning lover awaits the final throes of passion. Quickly she spun to her *scagno*, the table designed uniquely for glassmaking. She sat on the hard bench in the U-shaped space created by the two slim metal arms running perpendicular to the bench on either side of her. Placing the long *ferro sbuso* across the braces, her left palm pushed and pulled against it, always spinning, always keeping gravity's pull on the fluid material equal. With her right hand, Sophia grabbed the *borcèlla* and reached for the still-pliable mass. For a quick moment, she closed her eyes, envisioning the graceful, distinctive shape she imagined for this piece. When she looked up, it was there on the end of her rod. She could see it, therefore she could make it, and she set to her work.

When the man moved out of the corner's shadows, Sophia flinched. He had been quiet for so long, she had forgotten him. As he stood to stoke the *crugioli*, she remembered his presence and was glad for it. Uncountable were the nights they had worked together like this. From her youngest days, he had indulged her unlawful interest in the glassmaking, teaching and encouraging her, until her skills matched those of his—Zeno Fiolario, one of Venice's glassmaking *maestri*, her papà.

Zeno moved from furnace to furnace, adding the alder wood wherever needed, checking the water in the plethora of buckets scattered throughout the factory. The glow of the flames rose and spread to the darkest corners of the stone *fabbrica*. The pervasive, sweet scent of burning alder tree permeated the warm air. For his daughter, Zeno often fulfilled the duties of the *stizzador*—the man whose sole function was to keep the fires of the furnaces blazing—and his old frayed work shirt, nearly worn out in spots, bore the small umber burn marks of the sparks that so frequently leapt out of the crucibles.

His steps were slower than in years gone by, his shoulders permanently hunched from so many years over the glass, yet he jigged from chore to chore with surprising agility. As he passed Sophia, Zeno brushed a long lock of her deep chestnut hair away from her face, thick and work-roughened fingers wrapping it behind her ear with graceful gentleness. The touch was a succor to her soul and a jolt to her muse. Her wide mouth curved in a soft smile but her large, slanted blue eyes remained staunchly focused upon the work before her.

"It was the Greeks you know . . . uh, no," her father began, faltered, tilting his head to the side to think as he often did of late.

Sophia felt the urge to roll her eyes heavenward as young people are wont to do when their elders launched into an oft-repeated tale, but she stifled the impulse. She could have finished the sentence for him. She had heard this story so many times she knew it by heart, but she let him tell it at his own pace. She would work,

he would talk, and though he feigned unconcern for her method-
ology, his narrow, pale eyes, fringed with thick gray lashes, followed each flick of her wrist, each squeeze of the pinchers. Her
smile remained, undampened by the least twinge of impatience;
she had learned too much, been loved too well by this man to begrudge him his rapt study of her work.

"The Phoenicians, that's it." Zeno's voice rang out in triumph.
"They had been merchants, traders of nitrum, taking refuge on
the shore for the night. They could find no rocks to put in their
fires, to hold their pots while they cooked, so they pilfered a few
pieces of their own goods. You can imagine their surprise when the
lumps began to glow. This was years and years before the birth of
our Lord and these were simple, uneducated people. When the
clumps liquefied and mixed with the sand, the beach flowed with
tiny trickles of transparent fluid. They thought they were seeing a
miracle, but they were seeing glass . . . the first glass."

Her father's voice became a cadence, like the lapping of the la-
goon waves upon the shore that surrounded them; its rhythmic vibrato paced her work. Her left hand twisted the *ferro sbuso* while
the right manipulated the tongs, pinching here, shaping there.

"Our family has always made the glass. Since Pietro Fiolario's
time four hundred years ago, we have guarded the secret."

Sophia stole a quick glance up; the young eyes found the old
and embraced in understanding. This secret had been the family's
blessing and its curse. It had brought them world renown and an
abundance of fortune greater than many a Venetian noble family.
And yet it had made them prisoners in their own homeland, and
Sophia, a woman who knew the secret, doubly condemned.

Time was running short; the glass was getting harder and harder
to contort with gentle guidance. Already its form was a visual
masterpiece, the delicate base, the long, fragile flute, the bowl a
perfect symmetrical shape. Her hands flew, creating the waves on
the rim, capturing the essence of fluidity to the rapidly solidifying
form.

With a deep sigh, an exhalation of pure satisfaction, Sophia straightened her curled shoulders, bending her head from side to side to stretch the tense neck muscles, tight from so long in one position. She studied the piece before her, daring to peek at her father. In his glowing eyes, his shining pride, she saw confirmation of what she herself felt, already this was a remarkable piece . . . but it was not done yet.

"Now you will add our special touch, *sì?*" her father asked as he retrieved the special, smaller pinchers from another *scagno*.

Sophia smiled with indulgence. Keeping alive the delusion for her father was yet another small price to pay him. The technique she would do next, the *a morise*, to lay miniscule strands of colored glass in a pattern on this base piece, had made their *fabbrica* famous. Since its release to the public, her father had reveled in the accolades he received over its genius and beauty. Her father had never, *could* never, reveal that the invention had been Sophia's.

"*Sì*, Papà." Sophia lay down the larger tongs, flexing the tight muscles of her hands. She gathered the long abundance of brunette hair flowing without restraint around her shoulders, unbound from its usual pulled-back style, and laid it neatly against her back and out of her way. Taking the more delicate pinchers from her father's hand, she rolled her shoulders once more and set to work.

Zeno hovered by her shoulder, leaning forward to watch as her long, slim hands worked their magic, as she wielded the pinchers to apply the threads of magenta glass, smaller than the size of a buttercup's stem, in perfect straight lines. Dipping the tip of the tweezer-like device into the bucket of water by her side, releasing the hiss and smoke into the air, Sophia secured each strand with a miniscule drop of cool moisture.

"A little more this way," Zeno whispered, as if to speak too loudly would be to disturb the fragile material.

"Yes, Father," Sophia answered reflexively, like a much-said prayer's response.

"It's patience, having the patience to let the glass develop at its will, to cool and heat, cool and heat naturally." Zeno chanted close to her ear, his voice and words guiding her as they had done since she was young. His muted voice small in the cavernous chamber; their presence enveloped by the creative energy. "As the grape slowly ripens on the vine, the sand and silica and nitre become glass on the rod. Ah, you're getting it now—*bellissimo*."

"*Grazie*, Papà."

"Next you're going to—"

The bang, bang, bang of a fist upon wood shattered the quiet like glass crashing upon the stone; the heavy wooden door at the top of the winding stair jangled and rocked. Someone tried to enter, yet the bolted portal stymied the attempts. It was locked, as always when father and daughter shared these moments.

Zeno and Sophia stiffened in fright, bulging eyes locked.

"Are we discovered?" Sophia's whisper cracked, strangled with fear. She shoved the rod into her father's hands, dropping the slender metal pinchers on the hard stone floor below, wincing at the raucous clang that permeated the stillness.

"Cannot be." Zeno shook his head. "It can n—"

"Zeno, Zeno!" The urgent, distraught male voice slithered through the cracks of the door's wooden planks. "Let me in."

Parent and child recognized the timbre; Giacomo Mazzoni had worked at the Fiolario family's glassworks since he was a young man, his relationship evolving into that of a dear and familiar friend. The terror in his recognizable voice sounded undeniable; the strangeness of his presence at such a late hour was nothing short of disturbing.

With an odd calmness, Zeno pointed toward the door. "Let him in, Phie."

The dour intent upon her father's wrinkled countenance told her he would brook no argument. Gathering the front of her old, soiled gown, she sprinted up the winding stairs, glancing back at the wizened man who stood stock still, rod and cooling piece still in hand.

Sophia pushed aside the bolt with a ragged, wrenching screech. The door gave way the instant it was free. Giacomo rushed through the portal, pushing past Sophia where she stood on the small platform by the door. Clad in his nightshirt, a pair of loosely tied knee breeches flapping around his legs, he looked a fright with his short hair sticking out at all angles, and his black eyes afire with burning intensity. Flying down the stairs, he ran to his friend and mentor, grabbing him by the shoulders.

"They're dead, Zeno, dead."

Befuddled, Zeno stared at his friend, pale eyes squinting beneath his furrowed brow. "Who, Giacomo? Who is dead?"

"Clairomonti, Quirini, Giustinian, those who tried to get to France."

"Dio Santo." The words slipped from Zeno's mouth through the lips of his falling jaw. His legs quivered. With a shaking hand he reached into empty air, groping for a stool. Rushing to his side, Sophia grabbed the wooden seat, yanking it forward and guiding her father into it by the arm.

Zeno looked to his beloved daughter's face. Once more, their frightened gaze locked.

"They've killed them."

They entered through the bell tower entrance, their footfalls echoing upon the marble floor to rise up into the tall confined space of Santo Stefano's brick *campanile*. Dawn's pale light touched the land and the peal of the bells summoning all to work reverberated in the new morn's fresh air; the powerful warmth of the late spring day had not yet crept in to muffle the mesmerizing sound.

Men of all ages, shapes, and sizes filed in, their wondrous diversity as varied as their styles; some dressed in the grand fashion of the Spanish, with embroidered doublets, sword and dagger hanging from their waist. Long hair flowed past their shoulders and thin mustaches or goatees adorned their faces. The less-ostentatious wore simple linen or silk shirts and breeches, with plain but elegant waistcoats. From the chins of the older, mostly bald, gentlemen hung long, dignified beards, while the younger, still pretty men preferred clean faces and closely cropped caps of hair. They converged from almost every glassworks on the island, the owners and their sons, concern and fear tempering any joy to be had in their assembly.

The sun hovered at the horizon, its rays imprisoned by the

close-set buildings, and the gloomy shadows clung to the parish church's interior. In the muted light, the solemn procession soon filled the church pew's wooden benches. These men were the *Arte dei Vetrai*, the members of the glassworkers' guild. In their bonds of craft and dedication, this league of *artigiani* united in self-protection, to provide aid for the sick and aged of their profession, and to the widows and children of their lost loved ones.

Deep, solemn whispers rumbled through the air, permeated with incense, pungent pockets of aroma hiding in the small statue-filled alcoves and candlelit transepts of the church, remainders from the dawn's devotions. In Murano, as in other parishes of Venice, there were as many churches as there were winding curves of the canals. The *Arti* had chosen Santo Stefano as their home decades ago, selected for its simple grace and its centralized location on the Rio de Vetrai, the main canal through the glass-making district. Legend held that it had been built by the Camaldolese hermits at the time of the millennium, and had been restored and renovated many times since. The cloister of the old monastery flourished with beautiful gardens and within the vestry hung a painting by Jacopo Robusti, the Venetian master the world knew as Tintoretto. The *Arti* gathered their inspiration and strength here, their power and determination from the imposing sepulchral monument to Bartolomeo D'Alviano, a *condottiero* of great renown, perhaps one of the land's greatest soldiers.

The rapping of a gavel upon the podium broke the reverential discourse as Domenico Cittadini, owner of the Leone d'Oro glass-works, and steward of the *Arti*, called the meeting to order.

"It is with great sadness that we come here today to discuss the deaths of our compatriots, Hieronimo Quirini, Norberto Clairo-monti, and Fabrizio Giustinian."

"*Parodia!*"

"*Terribile!*"

"*Orribile!*"

Cries of protest and outrage rang out like cracks of thunder. They volleyed and ricocheted against the stone walls of the church, lofting to its high, vaulted ceiling and out the windows where the women of the town stood and listened, huddled together with heads straining as close to the partially opened windows as they could.

"*Silenzio!*" Cittadini countered with a return volley. The veins on his forehead bulged upon his skull in stark relief, his olive skin splotched with color, and his dark eyes bulged under thick salt-and-pepper brows. "The *Capitularis de Fiolarus* is clear."

He threw a thick wad of string-bound vellum on the floor with a violent release. The men in the front pews flinched from the resounding slap. The statutes imposed upon the glassworkers by the Venetian government were a long, imposing list.

"I am as ravaged by their demise as any of you, but our lost brethren knew what could happen when they left for France, when they allowed the foreign devils to entice them away with promises of riches and fame."

His words hung heavy in the oppressive silence; almost two hundred men stifled any immediate countering protests that lingered distastefully upon their tongues, attention focused firmly upon their leader. Cittadini had thus far served a scant two months of his one-year, elected term of stewardship, but he had shouldered his duties with utmost dedication, already meriting the men's early respect.

From the back, wood creaked as a slight, elderly man rose up, unfurling his curved and bent body as he slid a blue silk cap from his balding pate. Every head swiveled at the sound. Every ear strained to hear the words of Arturo Barovier, descendant of one of the greatest glassmaking families in the history of Murano.

"For over two hundred years they've kept us prisoner and now they've killed." His warbled voice vibrated through the congregation like warbling birdsong. "We must tolerate this no longer."

Impassioned, angry diatribes erupted, scarlet-faced men pointed fingers at one another as they punctuated their arguments, any semblance of order dispersed like smoke on the breeze of discontent. The debate fell not upon the existence of the restrictive control of their government, but whether or not it was warranted. Under the guise of protection for the workers, *La Serenissima*, the government of the Most Serene Republic of Venice, had begun its meticulous ascendancy over the glass-working industry nearly four centuries ago. A fanatical Republic, one that took complex and convoluted steps to keep absolute power from falling into any one hand, it was ruled by perversely tyrannical patriots, motivated by a deep and profound love of their country; there was no action too egregious if it would benefit the state.

Their control spread, as did the renown of Venetian glass. They spoke of fear for the growing population living in mostly wooden structures and the risk of fires posed by the glassmaking furnaces. The decree restricting all *vetreria* to the island of Murano came late in the thirteenth century, and the virtual imprisonment of the glassmaking families began. The regime's sophistry was an ill-fitting disguise and it was not long before the true intention of their actions became clear. It was not safety at the crux of the regime's concern, but the secret of the glass.

They meant to isolate the glassworkers, to inhibit any contact with the outside world, curtailing any opportunities for the industry's intricacies to be revealed to foreigners. As time passed, the pretense of the edict dissipated as clear and outright threats of bodily harm were made to any defecting glassworkers and their families. The seclusion was to protect the secret, and nothing else, for the exquisite *vetro* of Venice brought the state world fame and filled the government's coffers with overflowing fortune.

The statutes of the *Capitularis* swelled to include the *Mariegole*, a statement of duty for all glassworkers. It told them who was allowed to work and when, when the factories could close for vacation and for how long, going so far as to dictate how many *bocche* a furnace must have, as if the government knew better than the workers the best number of windows a crucible needed. In these infant days of the seventeenth century, their malevolent control had surpassed all acts that had come before; their hand of power had turned into a fist and would pummel anyone who publicly defied them.

Sophia stood as close to the brick-trimmed apertures of the church as her height would allow, nodding her head in silent yet fervent agreement with Signore Barovier's sentiment. As a woman, she could only make the glass, indulge in her one true passion, in secret, another of the *Serenissima*'s dictates; she was no supporter of their fanatical controls.

"Sshh," she hissed at the murmuring women around her, a pointed finger tapping against her pursed lips, surprising everyone—herself included—with her boldness, straining to hear the discussion continuing within the dim confines of the church. She was too desperate to hear to remain hidden in her usual timidity.

Vincenzo Bonetti stood up, long face and long nose bowed, one of the youngest men there but still the *padrone* of the Pigna glassworks.

"I would like to hear what signore Fiolario has to say."

Wood groaned and fabric rustled, all eyes looked to Zeno, quiet so far, amidst the disparate discussions boiling around him.

The men often looked to Zeno for his counsel. Though he had not been the steward of the *Arti* for almost ten years, some considered him the best there had ever been and many sought his wisdom like the child seeks approval from the parent. Like the others before him, Zeno stood, twisting his thin body to face the assemblage.

The morning sun's first rays found the stained glass of the long, arched altar window and a burst of colorful streaks illuminated Zeno's angular features with hues of shimmering moss and indigo. He appeared like a colorful specter, prismatic yet surreal.

"We are like precious works of art, cloistered in locked museums, trotted out for show when visiting royalty appears, but kept behind bars otherwise."

"*Sì, sì,*" incensed cries of agreement rang out. Heads waggled with accord, hands flew up in the air as if to beseech God to hear their entreaties.

Time after time, the *Serenissima* flaunted the talent and wealth of Venice in the faces of sojourning royalty, using the artisans of Murano for audacious displays. Not so very long ago King Henry III of France had been the most exalted guest of the Republic. Many prestigious members of the *Arte dei Vetrai* had been ceremonial attendants, including a younger Zeno just achieving the apex of his artistry, participating in exhibitions for the delight of the visiting monarch.

At the sound of her father's voice, Sophia had stood on tiptoes to see in the high windows. She waited now in rapt attention, as did they all as calm descended once more, for Zeno's next sagacious dictum.

Zeno stared at the expectant faces. His lips floundered, but no words formed. His head tilted to the side and his gaze grew vacant. He looked down at the empty space on the pew beneath him, and without further statement, sat down.

Sophia released her straining toes and flexed calf muscles and leaned her back against the warm russet bricks of the church. Her young features scrunched unbecomingly; she didn't understand why her father had not said more. He had appeared as if about to speak but the words or their sentiments had been lost on the journey from brain to lips.

Within the church, the same confusion cloaked the congregation; men shared silent, questioning glances, their faces changing in the shifting shadows as the rising sun began to stream in through the windows.

Cittadini took advantage of the appeasement. Stepping out from the podium, he crossed the altar, and stood in line with the first of the many rows of blond oak pews, at the intersection of forward and sideward paths.

"Tell me, de Varisco." The steward addressed a middle-aged man sitting close to the front, Manfredo de Varisco, owner of the

San Giancinto glassworks. "You are not a nobleman, yet you live in a virtual *palazzo*. You own your own gondola. *Sì?*"

De Varisco nodded his head, dirty blond curls bouncing, with an almost shameful shrug.

"And you, Brunuro, you are always wearing your bejeweled sword and dagger."

Cittadini strode down the aisle, approaching a handsome man, black-haired and ruddy, sitting a third of the way down. Baldessera Brunuro, with his brother Zuan, ran both the Tre Corone and the Due Serafini.

"Would you enjoy such privileges, such luxuries, if you weren't glassworkers?"

No one spoke, though many shook their heads, for the answer was most assuredly no; other Venetian members of the industrial class did not—could not—relish such refinements as did the glassmakers.

Jerking to his right, the robust and rotund Cittadini raised an accusing finger, pointing to another middle-aged man, one with finely sculpted features, the owner of Tre Croci d'Oro.

"You above all, signore Serena, your daughter is to marry a noble. Your grandchildren will be nobles. For the love of God, your male heirs may sit on the Grand Council, may one day become Doge, *Il Serenissimo*, the ruler of all Venice!"

Cittadini punctuated his impassioned plea, throwing his hands up and wide with dramatic finality.

Serena's brown eyes held Cittadini's, beacons shining from out of puffy, wrinkle-rimmed sockets. He struggled to stand, his long white beard quivering from his chin onto his chest with each strain of exertion. For a few more seconds he held the steward's rapt attention in the preternatural quiet of the packed church. The women outside became captives, their noses pressed to the sills, their fussing and fluttering ceasing once and for all.

"None of us wants to give these things up, these glories that make our lives so rich, so abundant." Serena spoke of their splendors, yet the sadness in his face, his furrowed brow, his frowning mouth, told another tale. "But at what price? It is naught more than extortion. We should be, we must be, able to live as we please, go where we please. We have earned the right."

Cittadini didn't answer. He studied the familiar face of his friend. He turned, impotent, to the righteous faces all around and curled his broad shoulders up to his ears. "Then . . . what do we do?"

Within this house of God, amidst the aura of his benevolence, no one had an answer.